W9-BAB-677

THE
LITTLE GREEN BOOK
OF
CHAIRMAN RAHMA

Other Books
By Brian Herbert and Jan Herbert

Ocean

By Brian Herbert and Kevin J. Anderson

Dune: House Atreides
Dune: House Harkonnen
Dune: House Corrino

Dune: The Butlerian Jihad
Dune: The Machine Crusade
Dune: The Battle of Corrin

Hunters of Dune
Sandworms of Dune

Paul of Dune
The Winds of Dune

Sisterhood of Dune
Mentats of Dune

Hellhole
Hellhole: Awakening
Hellhole: Inferno*

By Frank Herbert, Brian Herbert, and Kevin J. Anderson

The Road to Dune
(includes the original short novel *Spice Planet*)

By Brian Herbert

Dreamer of Dune
(biography of Frank Herbert)

*forthcoming

THE
LITTLE GREEN BOOK
OF
CHAIRMAN RAHMA

Brian Herbert

TOR®

A TOM DOHERTY ASSOCIATES BOOK

NEW YORK

This is a work of fiction. All of the characters, organizations, and events portrayed in this novel are either products of the author's imagination or are used fictitiously.

THE LITTLE GREEN BOOK OF CHAIRMAN RAHMA

Copyright © 2014 by DreamStar, Inc.

All rights reserved.

A Tor Book
Published by Tom Doherty Associates, LLC
175 Fifth Avenue
New York, NY 10010

www.tor-forge.com

Tor® is a registered trademark of Tom Doherty Associates, LLC.

The Library of Congress Cataloging-in-Publication Data is available upon request.

ISBN 978-0-7653-3254-7 (hardcover)
ISBN 978-1-4668-5605-9 (e-book)

Tor books may be purchased for educational, business, or promotional use. For information on bulk purchases, please contact Macmillan Corporate and Premium Sales Department at 1-800-221-7945, extension 5442, or write specialmarkets@macmillan.com.

First Edition: July 2014

Printed in the United States of America

0 9 8 7 6 5 4 3 2 1

This book is for Jan,
the wise and beautiful woman who is the love of my life.

Acknowledgments

I OWE A tremendous debt of gratitude to my agent, John Silbersack, and to my editor, Pat LoBrutto, for the enthusiastic support they provided for this project. I also wish to thank my father, Frank Herbert, my good friend Bruce Taylor, and my wife, Jan Herbert, for steering me toward critically important environmental causes.

In the Corporate War of 2041–2043, the multinational corporations lost every major battle in North and South America, and were vanquished by the counterculture AOE, the Army of the Environment. In full disarray, the few surviving Corporate elements in the Americas went into hiding, and a new, all-encompassing government was established by the victorious radicals to rule what had previously been multiple nations on the two continents. Led by Chairman Rahma Popal, the environmental activists renamed their domain the Green States of America. Their stated goal: a Golden Age in which all citizens and companies live in harmony with the environment, so that the bulk of the land can be completely transformed, returning it to nature.

—*Green Shock* (a history of the Corporate War)

SciOs! Collectively, the power of the Science Overseers is roughly equivalent to that of Chairman Rahma himself, because they are responsible for providing critical scientific technology to the Green States of America. Under the GSA Charter, they are able to keep their scientific secrets while maintaining a monopoly on such technology, providing equipment to the government that contains fail-safe devices to prevent tampering. Most of all, the SciOs closely guard the secrets of their Janus Machines.

—a children's ecology primer

SciOs! They are the most sophisticated and devious of all green profiteers. There are even suspicions that they have sold military technology to the sworn enemies of the Green States of America. The SciOs are a nation within a nation, with autonomy stemming from their crucial contribution to the victory of the Army of the Environment against unscrupulous Corporate interests.

—*The Green Profiteers* (Anarchist Press, banned)

THE
LITTLE GREEN BOOK
OF
CHAIRMAN RAHMA

1

For the environmental health of the American continents, all inhabitants who survived the Corporate War will be relocated onto densely populated human reservations, with the remaining land slated for either collective farms or comprehensive green-forming, returning it to the pristine beauty of nature. As part of his historic Edict 101, our beloved Chairman Rahma Popal has announced, "Anyone who resists will be dealt with severely. He will be recycled."

—government news flash, March 17, 2043

THE NUCLEAR-POWERED TRUCK flexed its long body around highway turns without slowing, its air whistle keening to ward off wild animals. Inside the passenger dome sat a man and a woman in complementary uniforms—his forest green and hers black, with peace symbols on the lapels. They held hands and gazed out at the sun-mottled trees of autumn, bearing leaves that were a spectacular array of golden-brown hues. This was an old road, bumpy from decay and debris, having fallen into disuse because of the mass exodus of population in the last two decades. It was the year 2063 in the New England Conservancy, and soon there would be no more need for this route.

Ahead of the vehicle and behind it, police cars created a security zone, their strobe lights flashing and fender-mounted weapons glow-ready, while a Greenpol aircraft flew low overhead. For years there had been attacks by disaffected Corporate elements against GSA assets, and the Chairman had ordered extra precautions to secure his valuable equipment and personnel. Greenpol was the special police force he had created, with divisions to stop eco-criminals, prosecute other crimes, and bodyguard his person.

Presently the big armored truck slowed and turned onto the rough, weed-encrusted surface of an abandoned parking lot, where it screeched to a stop. Outriggers shot into position and adjusted for the uneven surface, leveling the great machine mounted on the chassis. The two passengers, both eco-techs, exited the dome and stepped onto a wide turret platform on the vehicle. They secured their stylized, owl-design helmets and dark goggles, then grabbed hold of safety bars. Other crew members rushed to their stations, to operate the complex equipment and monitor the results. They wore black trousers, jackboots, green jackets, and shiny green helmets.

The platform rose to the proper height, and the twin, opposing barrels of the Janus Machine telescoped out to their full extensions, pointing in opposite directions. The barrels— one bright green and the other deep black—began to glow intensely. While the man waited, the woman climbed into a bucket seat at the rear of the long black barrel and tapped keys on an instrument console. The turret swung around, so that the barrel was pointed at the center of the industrial plant.

"It's Black Thunder time!" she shouted, as she began the three-minute countdown.

Joss Stuart smiled as he watched her admirable efficiency. Kupi Landau, tall, light-skinned, and willowy, was his lover as well as co-worker. In her mid-forties, she was his senior by a decade and a half, but he still found her attractive and exciting. Her waist-length hair was close to its natural auburn now, though she sometimes dyed it a bright color, which was not uncommon in the Green States of America. Her face was oval, with large brown eyes.

With a stubble of brown beard on his face, Joss had long hair, secured by a silver ring at the back. He was muscular and around her height, a mixture of races that gave his skin a smooth, light brown hue. Barely thirty, he was commander of the seven-person crew, having been transferred to this division from Greenpol, where he'd been a decorated eco-cop, busting wetlands violators, polluters, murderers of endangered species, and other heinous environmental criminals.

He nodded to her, then scanned the jobsite arrayed before them, a cluster of shabby, deteriorating metal buildings and smokestacks, sitting dull and lackluster in the light of midday. Years before, this had been a major military products factory, belching pollutants into the atmosphere and draining contaminants into the nearby river system, as the greedy Corporate owners lined their pockets at the expense of the environment. It was one of many polluting industrial sites in the old days, before Chairman Rahma set society on the correct course and began the widespread greenification of the Americas.

Patting his uniform jacket, Joss felt the reassuring presence of his copy of *The Little Green Book,* a slender forest-green volume containing the favorite sayings of the Chairman, along with his sagacious, environmental-oriented poetry. Often during the day, Joss liked to bring out the volume and find some piece of useful wisdom to inspire him, and guide him in his decisions.

He felt good about the contributions he and Kupi Landau were making to the grand ecological dream. Today Joss was leading the crew of Janus Machine No. 129 on a run through the conservancy, hitting sites that had not yet been reverted when nearby cities and towns were emptied of people, leveled, and returned to nature. In only a few moments Kupi would complete her portion of the task, and Joss's turn would follow.

More than two decades ago, she'd been a member of the legendary Berkeley Eight revolutionary committee that spearheaded the struggle against the Corporates and their lackeys, fighting for the inspirational Chairman and his anti-war, anti-establishment army. Kupi's anarchistic, violent talents had been useful then, and were useful now in the aftermath of the conflict.

In a designated safety zone on the pavement, behind a clearplex blast shield, a handful of government officials had gathered to watch alongside black-suited anarchists and bearded, middle-aged men in green uniforms, all veterans of the Corporate War who now called themselves J-Watchers. The bearded vets were well organized, and liked to follow the routes of Janus Machine teams and cheer them on.

Joss noticed that three men wore patches indicating they had been Weather Warriors, a radical group that bombed Corporate and U.S. government facilities during the revolution, including dams and power stations. He also saw a man wearing the round patch of the Green Planet Brigade, whose followers had burned sport-utility vehicles in the old United States, and torched homes that were not constructed according to green building standards. In those days, these men (and others like them) were called domestic terrorists, but now they were decorated heroes.

Half a dozen young women in flower-design dresses and beads joined the J-Watchers and began dancing in a circle. In another protected area, feral dogs and cats had been rounded up, and specialists were using sonic devices to roust out rodents, raccoons, and any other critters that might be inside the buildings and on the grounds, saving as many of them as possible.

The observers, in a festive mood, were among a small, elite class of citizens who were granted permits to leave their reservations for specific purposes—in this case to bolster the morale of J-Mac crews. Behind the protective barrier, they clapped and cheered, and exchanged stories from the revolution. Everyone was pleased that the good work of Chairman Rahma Popal was proceeding methodically, covering the Green States of America with magnificent trees and other flora, so that animals could thrive in their natural habitats.

The dancers began chanting, louder and louder: "Rahm-m-m-m-a . . . Rahm-m-m-m-a . . . Rahm-m-m-m-a . . ."

Kupi's countdown went through its final seconds in a beeping of electronics. Preparing himself, Joss secured the noise-protective system of his helmet. He heard a low, gathering roar, and saw the big black barrel spew waves of stygian particles at the factory structures and split them all asunder, separating the components on a molecular level and then transforming them into a gooey gray amalgam of basic elements. For artistic effect, she left three of the smokestacks for last, then blasted their bases out from under them one at a time, sending the tall structures thundering down in a dramatic display of flying debris and vanishing shapes, as if they were ghostly creatures of the past, dying from the inside out. Never again would such ugliness reign over the American landscape. The onlookers clapped and cheered for her showmanship, making muffled sounds in Joss's headset.

"Black Thunder has spoken," Kupi Landau said to the crew, over the comm-radio. She was referring to what the SciOs called the black barrel of every Janus Machine, more commonly referred to as a Splitter or a Splitter Cannon. Janus Machine technology was secret and closely guarded; only the SciOs could build new units, and if anyone tampered with the machines, the units would self-destruct.

Kupi was particularly well suited for her job, still able to vent her simmering anger against the foul remnants of Corporate civilization. Splitting was an anarchist specialty, one of the few GSA-authorized professions that the government haters actually seemed to enjoy. It was a union job, of course, like every profession in the Green States of America. Even soldiers in the Army of the Environment were unionized.

Now it was Joss's turn. The bright green barrel had a SciO name as well: The Seed Cannon. Most people called it a greenformer, though, and the process was known as greenforming. He sat at another instrument panel behind that barrel, tapped the opening sequence to make the turret spin around slowly. He made subtle, last-minute adjustments to the seed mixture, tailoring it to this locale more than he'd already done in the setup, further eliminating any elements of vegetation that, even though native, he had now decided were not appropriate for the site. Like the work Kupi did, this was an art form, though one that religious radicals liked to call, derisively, "playing God." He didn't pay attention to such comments. They came from scofflaws, fugitives who were on the run from Greenpol.

Over Joss's headset, pre-war rock music surged on, the hard-driving beat of an old Grateful Dead song, harking back to a time of fantastic idealism in the prior century, when the seeds of rebellion were sowed, and ultimately cultivated. His job gave him a good feeling that he was doing something significant, something important. Brave Greenies had died in order to provide him with this opportunity. He held a privileged, high-level job, and appreciated having it.

He had the turret in position now and ran the test circuits through their course, causing an array of colored lights to dance across the top of the instrument panel. Using a view-screen, Joss sighted along the top of the long, glistening green barrel and aimed carefully at the center of the gooey amalgam of elements that Kupi had left for him. Taking a deep breath, he held down a button at the center of the panel, then felt a percussive thump as cartridges spewed into the air and detonated over the landscape like a green fireworks display in the sunlight, scattering micro-organisms, infinitesimally tiny seeds that would grow quickly, replacing the factory eyesore with beautiful vegetation.

He fired twice more to fill in bare spots, using smaller bursts. Finally, his task completed, he rose and tilted back his owl helmet in satisfaction. The music went off, and he heard the applause of the onlookers. On one side of the turret, Kupi stood at the rail gazing out on the landscape, as if imagining she could already see the new plants sprouting. Joss chuckled. He had used a fast-grow recipe, but it was not *that* fast. In a matter of weeks, maple and oak trees would be half a meter high, and soon the animals, insects, and birds of the forest would reoccupy their habitat. It was only justice, he thought, returning the land to its rightful inhabitants, after humans had carelessly abused it for so long. . . .

LATER THAT AFTERNOON, the Janus Machine crew was on its way to the next site. Inside the dome, Kupi sat on a cushioned bench with Joss. She took a long drag on a juana stick, exhaled the smoke, and said, "This rig has only been on fifty-seven missions, and it's already getting long in the tooth. I felt more than the normal vibration when I fired the cannon. Did you notice it, too?"

Joss shook his head. "No, not when you fired, nor when I did, either."

"Well, I sure noticed it. Damn thing shook my chair, hurt my teeth, and made my bones feel like they were turning into jelly."

"Part of the mystery of Dark Energy?" he asked, referring to the term for the destructive splitting technology, a power that reportedly was not fully understood by the SciOs who had discovered and harnessed it. The stuff was like a wild bronco, he'd been told, but on an exponentially higher level. The strange technology was rooted in the days of the revolution, when it enabled Chairman Rahma and his ragtag army to defeat Corporate armies—using the black cannons of early-model Janus Machines as weapons.

Kupi scowled and said, "Damned SciOs build these rigs so that they have to be replaced frequently. Just like the old Corporate crooks and their diabolical theory of 'planned obsolescence.'"

"I wouldn't go that far," Joss said. "Our cannons have unknown key components. Maybe the SciOs don't have any other way to build them."

"Yeah, yeah. True Green Joss, accepting everything you're told to think. You'd better wake up, sweetie. Our lives could be at risk running these machines, and do you think the SciOs give a rat's ass what happens to us? Do you think Chairman Rahma does?"

Joss fell silent, knowing he didn't accept everything blindly at all, though she seemed to think he did. Even so, he didn't want to argue with her. He gazed forward as the truck sped south, with peace symbols and stylized tree designs sparkling on the hood, and triangular green GSA banners fluttering on the front fenders. He liked Kupi personally, as a lover and as a friend, but when she started talking politics, she invariably made comments that made him uncomfortable.

Politics often put her into a bad mood, and he saw no point

in debating with her. At times like this, his lover needed to be left alone.

He wished Kupi would watch her tongue. It could get her into a lot of trouble—and by association, him, too.

2

Animals are not lower life-forms than humans.
They are in fact superior to us.
Count the ways.
—Chairman Rahma, *The Little Green Book*

THE MAN CROUCHED low as he peered over a snowbank at the bleak white landscape sloping up to the ridgeline. A cold gray fog was beginning to settle over the mountain, though some patches of sunlight remained. Moments earlier, he'd seen movement at a higher elevation by the body of a freshly killed ibex, a blur of motion. Now, nothing. Looking in that direction through binoculars, the gray-bearded man didn't even see prints in the snow where the cat had been, feeding on its prey. The creature seemed to float over the surface, moving entirely in another realm.

There were countless legends about the magical powers of snow leopards, but legends were one thing and reality quite another. Because of the animals' reclusive, solitary nature, attacks on humans were rare. Even so, the man's heart beat rapidly. These rare animals were powerful and fast—and if this one decided to turn on him at any moment instead of avoiding him, he might not have a chance. So far the creature was keeping its distance, while remaining close enough to watch over the bloody body of the horned ibex, preventing other predators from taking it away.

With a start the man remembered he was in EVR—enhanced virtual reality—and wasn't actually on that faraway slope, except as a three-dimensional, projected avatar. Such magnificent technology, and so realistic that if persons really in that remote mountain region saw his projection they would think he was actually there, too. In addition, if his avatar was near any other people there, he could see them, hear them, and speak to them, and they could do the same with him. Animals could see and hear avatars as well, and had even been known to go after them, though they usually relied on scent, and that was one thing the Chairman's EVR figure did not have. Now he reimmersed himself into the action on the snowy mountain—a speck on the white snowfield watching the predator and its ibex.

A snow leopard was not able to consume a kill of this size in one feeding. For that reason it often lingered nearby for days, going back repeatedly and eating from the carcass, while watching warily in all directions.

It was the Achilles' heel of their species, a weakness that a hunter could use to advantage—and he'd seen evidence of hunters in the area. But Chairman Rahma Popal was not like other human beings around there. Snow leopards were an endangered species, with only a small number of them known to exist on Earth. He needed to capture this one alive, which he could do even in EVR, with the aid of two men and a woman collaborating with him on the ground—GSA operatives who had taken great physical risks to slip into the enemy state of Panasia, far across the globe from the GSA. Rahma had sent operatives into enemy territory before on such ventures, as well as on spying missions, and he'd gone there as an avatar, too—aided by clever technology that the SciOs had surreptitiously inserted into one of the Panasian satellites, secretly compromising the orbiter so that some of their transmissions were put to GSA use.

The three others were arrayed on the slope near him, in their sealed survival suits. For these brave citizens, this special assignment was much more dangerous than any threat from bad weather or from a predatory animal. Because of the hostile nature of the Panasian government and its cavalier attitude toward animal protection, the rescue squad had to get in and out as quickly as possible.

Anger filled the Chairman now. The Panasians—ruling over Asia, Australia, and most of the Pacific islands—allowed their people to hunt and kill these beautiful animals for organs and other body parts, using them for traditional medicine, talismans, and trophies. How could anyone be so ignorant and short-sighted? What did they intend to do when there were no more snow leopards left to harvest?

Eco-criminals on a huge scale, the Panasian government did not care a whit about the welfare of endangered species, and their polluting industries were the worst in the world, no matter the propaganda they issued to the contrary. The Eurikans weren't much better, ruling over the continents of Europe and Africa. They just put on a better public persona, posturing and acting as if they were environmentalists, when in fact they were not. To a large extent the Eurikan leaders were blue-blooded aristocrats, tracing their roots to noble lineages and old money, and taking political and economic steps to protect their own interests.

Breathing hard in the simulated atmosphere of his EVR survival suit, the Chairman glanced at a holo-screen that hovered in the air by him, showing a satellite zoom of the snow leopard. It was a barely discernible mound of fur perhaps a couple of hundred meters above him on the slope, a tight ball of gold, black, and white. He saw the other team members, and himself, on the satellite image as well, and knew that the cat could close the distance to the nearest operative in a matter of seconds.

Since the fall of the Corporates, there had been increasing tensions between the Panasians and the Green States. The two governments had been sponsoring terrorist attacks against each other, using surrogates that could not be traced easily to either side. Rahma knew he had a technological advantage over his enemies—his alliance with the SciOs. But it was a tenuous advantage, because of the secrets that the arrogant SciO leader Arch Ondex and his cronies kept to themselves. The Chairman sometimes suspected—but could not prove—that Ondex was playing both sides. And yet no matter how much he disliked the patrician man, he didn't want to believe that could possibly be true.

Rahma scanned his instruments. The outside air temperature was dropping quickly as the fog continued to settle. Visibility was worsening, and his people would need to get off the mountain sooner than anticipated.

The avatar stepped onto an air platform near him and powered it up, a virtual-reality craft. A control bar rose in front of him, and he gripped it in simulation. The three other team members did the same for real, on separate craft.

The four of them rose into the air on triangular wedges of technology. A slight wind from the valley floor below buffeted the craft, but the units compensated and sped smoothly toward the snow leopard. From his remote position of safety the Chairman watched the altimeter reading on his control bar. Over 4,300 meters now, more than 14,000 feet. He felt the simulated oxygen level increase inside his suit.

The animal held its ground for several seconds, then bolted away upslope. This time the Chairman saw the tracks it made in the snow, confirming that the creature was not anything supernatural. Quickly, the cat moved out of deep snow onto rocky surfaces, leaping great distances from one ledge to the next, rising ever upward in elevation, heading for a jagged line of ice caves.

The pursuers had anticipated this; the satellite report had told them the path the snow leopard would probably take, toward one of those icy habitats where it lived. But they needed to divert the animal, keeping it from reaching the safety of an area that might be honeycombed with escape routes.

Pressing a lever on the control bar to accelerate, Rahma Popal caused the platform to surge past the animal. He then turned in the air and headed back toward the snow leopard, diverting the cat and causing it to take a lateral course along a ridgeline, with the two male team members flying close behind. They were too close, and the Chairman signaled for them to fall back a little. They needed to be careful. The leopard appeared to be panicking, and he didn't want to kill it.

He motioned for the female operative, Agent Trumbull, to come alongside his craft. At his further command, she touched a button on a transmitter, firing a shaft of emerald light at the snow leopard, a lasso beam that slowed it down. For a moment the animal became the color of the light, a running, struggling blur. Trumbull fired a ray of bright red light now, a powerful sedative. The leopard went limp, only a short distance from the edge of a precipice, where it might have gone off.

Accompanied by his team, the Chairman hovered over the leopard, a few meters above it. He watched as Trumbull unsnapped the transmitter from the handlebar and made it a hand-held unit. Then, leaning down and using the electronic lasso to lift the animal into a cradle that tightened on contact, she made it snug against the undercarriage of the air platform. A screen on his own control bar showed Rahma the vital signs of the sedated animal, a male. The readings were good, but he did not breath a sigh of relief yet. He still needed to get the large cat out of the country.

Now Rahma fell in behind the others, flying downslope, speeding toward a wooded area where a stealth transport craft awaited them. Presently, when the rescued animal was loaded aboard, along with the passengers and equipment, the Chairman switched off the EVR transmission and found himself back in the welcome, green reality of his own game reserve in the Rocky Mountain Territory.

He slipped out of his survival suit, tossed it to one of his many administrative assistants, a robot who stood nearby, anticipating his master's "return." Zeebik stood as tall as a man, with a flat-screen face that bore the image of a stern human officer with narrow little eyes and dark, overhanging brows, a countenance Rahma had chosen from historical military archives. The image was locked in place; once the selection was made, he could not alter it.

"Holo-net report just came in," Zeebik said, in a resonant voice the Chairman had also chosen from historical records. "The Black Shirts recycled four hundred twenty-seven eco-criminals this morning—polluters, tree cutters, animal poachers—the usual." The robot was referring to black-uniformed anarchists by a common term they liked to use in describing themselves, harking back to the legendary days of the revolution when the violent Black Shirts were an important part of the victory. Following the defeat of the Corporates, these anarchists were formally organized into an army division known as the Revolutionary Guard—front-line defenders of the revolution.

For a couple of minutes, Rahma scanned little holo-images of the executions, death sentences that were primarily carried out by anarchists with Splitter rifles, turning the victims into macabre heaps of goo. Two of the criminals received a special brand of punishment, befitting the severity of their crimes. A husband and wife, they had been trusted members of the government who had forsaken their vows and turned over state secrets to the Panasians. (Even that was considered an "eco-crime" under one definition, because it threatened the Green States of America.) He watched as black-uniformed anarchists strapped them to posts in the middle of a beautiful, flower-covered field, and then opened wounds on their bodies, so that they bled profusely. The victims writhed and tried to shout, but their mouths were gagged.

Moments later, the pair was swarmed by powerful carrion birds—vultures, owls, and eagles that had been trained for this purpose. A vulture ripped the gag loose from the female, and Rahma heard her high-pitched screams of terror. Sharp talons and beaks gouged out her eyes, and she slumped at the post, bleeding from the orifices. Beside her, the traitorous husband's face was already gone, a bloody pulp of torn flesh, and soon hers was as well. The birds kept attacking, tearing at flesh and feeding, finally leaving the ripped-apart bodies and flying off, their bellies full.

The Chairman rubbed his gray beard, nodded somberly. He had ordered the mass executions before going on the EVR rescue mission, and the decision had made his heart heavy. But it had been necessary, one of many he'd made—for the sake of the planet, he could not afford to be lenient. He hated having to kill people, but it was either that or let them kill the planet, which he could not allow.

His gaze lingered on the gory scene, and he reminded himself of what his followers often said about him, that he was a good and kind man. However, no matter the justification, he didn't feel that way at the moment.

Sadly, he switched off the viewer.

3

The Green States of America is protected by the NDS, the Non-human Defense System. Operated entirely by robots that analyze data and make judgments, the network has control over an array of small but powerful defensive and offensive missiles. Our revered Chairman Rahma Popal, may he live in eternal greenness, does not trust human beings with this critical assignment, fearing they might make pre-emptive strikes for emotional, illogical reasons—strikes that could result in retaliatory measures that would destroy much of the important environmental work he has done.

—Ticker History, a continuous data feed to schools

FOR MOST OF a week, the crew of Janus Machine No. 129 reverted industrial sites in the New England Conservancy, working sixteen-hour days. It was a grueling schedule, but Joss Stuart knew that he and his companions were taking the necessary steps to correct a terrible historical wrong, the grievous wounding of the planet by polluting Corporate interests.

As a human being it was his duty, his sworn responsibility, to rectify what people had done. And beyond that, Joss was a dedicated eco-tech, more zealous than anyone he knew. He considered his work equivalent to blazing new green pathways into the heart and soul of the Earth, removing blighted areas from human control and returning them to the domain of Mother Nature, who had her own timeless priorities and goals, her own sacred sentience.

Like other assignments he had been on, these past days had involved a seemingly endless series of work shifts at site after site, splitting and greenforming so many factory scars in succession that everything began to run together in his fatigued brain.

It was sunset when the long armored truck pulled into a military base on the outskirts of the Bostoner Reservation for Humans, with the tall, gleaming buildings of the densely populated urban center visible beyond a red-glowing security perimeter. This reservation was one of ninety-seven that Chairman Rahma Popal had set up on both continents of the green nation so far—confining more than a billion people to set-aside areas and prohibiting the vast majority of them from ever going outside. Joss's team would spend the night in Bostoner and depart by maglev train the following morning, bound for their homes on the west coast.

Despite the rigors and demands of his career, Joss was proud to be one of the people allowed to go off reservation and embrace the beauty of nature, while actually doing something to enhance it. Truly, he was a fortunate citizen of the Green States of America! To some extent his privilege had to do with his Uncle Trig Stuart, who had fought valiantly in the Corporate War, and had been awarded a chest full of medals by the Army of the Environment. That legacy of his uncle (who raised Joss) had opened the door for the young man, but he had kept it open himself; he had earned his own success.

The truck squeaked to a stop at a security station, and in the red glow the driver stepped out to complete the necessary documents. Inside the passenger dome of the vehicle, Kupi grumbled and paced around. "I need a juana stick," she said, "but I'm all out. You sure you don't have any on you?"

Joss shook his head. "Sorry, but you know I don't toke while I'm on duty."

"We're off duty now."

"Not quite, not until we get clearance to step off the rig. But I still didn't bring any with me."

"Not smoking weed is anti-patriotic," she said with a scowl.

"I smoke."

"Not nearly enough."

Joss glared at her, then looked away, toward the reconstituted forest lands they had just driven through. He was too tired to argue with his lover now, but she smoked too many of the powerful cigarettes, and was always moody when she ran out of them. Her assertion about patriotism was true, but she didn't understand the concept of moderation. Just because marijuana and virtually all other recreational drugs were legal did not mean they should be abused.

Kupi waved a hand, sending a signal from her ring that caused the dome to darken, so that no one could see in from outside. She sent a second command, and Joss heard the hatch click, locking it. He knew what was next; they often made love in here during breaks. But now—at a guard station—did not seem like an appropriate opportunity to him.

She went to his side, nuzzled against his neck and nibbled at his earlobe. "I think we should make up," she said.

Joss pushed her away.

As she sputtered in protest, Joss heard a loud explosion, followed by a second one, even louder. He lightened the dome, enabling him to see a brilliant flash of light in the sky to the west, then heard another explosion. Sirens went off, followed by three black aircraft speeding overhead, looking like great birds of prey. The attack craft were very fast and maneuverable, their guns blazing. A rocket shot from the undercarriage of one of them, exploding into a barracks building and setting it afire.

"What the hell?" Kupi shouted. "The security perimeter has been breached!"

She snapped on her black owl helmet, grabbed an automatic rifle, and ran out onto the turret platform with Joss right behind her, carrying his own weapon, pressing buttons on it to prepare the energy chamber. Because of the danger of attack from disgruntled Corporate elements, every Janus Machine crew had trained for defensive operations. The Splitter barrel could even be used as a cannon, a newer and more powerful version of weapons that had been employed by the Army of the Environment during the war.

Red lights flickered on and off around them, suggesting something was wrong with the security perimeter. In the distance, Joss saw the three aircraft circling around, coming back. Ground artillery guns opened fire on them, but the wide-wing craft released electronic flak beneath them, deflecting any shots. In order to penetrate the shield, the forces on the ground needed to scan that flak and find the right combination of electronics.

Kupi jumped into the bucket seat of Black Thunder, tapped keys on the instrument panel. The platform rose to its highest level as she telescoped the barrel out. Joss crouched by her, ready to operate the machine if she was injured. She aimed the long black barrel and waited for just the right moment. . . .

Joss gripped the handle of his energy rifle tighter, took a deep breath as precious seconds ticked by. The fast-approaching aircraft were studded with advanced weapon systems, proof that the disaffected Corporates had substantial resources. The Janus Machine was armored, and its crew had activated its own electronic veiling system, but had the enemy already seen them? The aircraft were getting closer, but did not seem to be flying on a direct line toward the machine. Still protected by their flak screens, the attackers opened fire on the center of the military compound, and Joss saw heavy equipment go up in flames. Moments later, defenders managed to penetrate the electronic veils of two of the aircraft, detonating them and sending them plunging into the nearby woods. Alone now, the third craft banked overhead.

This time it sped directly toward the Janus Machine, and Joss heard the gathering roar of power from the heart of the SciO unit. Kupi opened up by shooting waves of black particles that hit the aircraft's flak system and melted it. Moments later her Splitter waves hit the craft itself, causing it to blacken into an unidentifiable, shapeless amalgam, which tumbled out of the sky and thudded onto a grassy expanse at the center of the compound. The J-Mac crew cheered.

"A longer-range Splitter would be nice to have," Kupi said.

"You did great with this one," Joss said.

Still keeping a wary eye on the sky, she shrugged and said, "Guess I'll have to notch my cannon barrel now."

Joss heard the sirens of emergency equipment and watched black-uniformed anarchist soldiers running toward the three crash sites. In the distance he saw something large and tube-shaped on the ground, but for only a few moments before it exploded and burst into flames.

BECAUSE OF THE commotion, with Revolutionary Guardsmen running around and sirens continuing to wail, the security clearance for Joss's truck was being delayed. From the platform he saw two anarchist soldiers below him talking with the driver, and heard them order the man to keep his rig parked until the base commander gave security clearance.

"My crew is dead tired," the ruddy-faced driver protested,

"and we've just shot down an enemy aircraft. Isn't that clearance enough for us to proceed?"

One of the soldiers shook his head. "We're concerned about your safety as you proceed into the reservation, so we need to perform security checks on all entry roads. That's an expensive machine you're driving, and you've got at least one hero onboard." He nodded toward Kupi, who stood at the railing of the platform, looking down at him. "I know you're all tired, but we want to ensure that you make it to your beds tonight."

The driver grumbled, and looked up at Joss, the commander, for instructions. Joss shrugged and spread his palms in acknowledgment that nothing else could be done, so the driver sat on a running board to wait.

In the distance, Joss heard more explosions, and saw fireballs and smoke rising into the sky. The better part of an hour passed. Finally a procession of military trucks rumbled into the center of the base, filled with boisterous anarchist troops who waved energy rifles in the air and fired off celebratory bursts in various colors. The trucks screeched to a stop and the soldiers dragged out the charred bodies of enemy fighters—perhaps thirty in all from the first two aircraft, though certainly not from the one that Kupi had split into raw elements. They piled the dead on the grass, poured fuel on them, and lit them on fire.

In another truck, Joss saw more Revolutionary Guard fighters with a pair of live prisoners, undoubtedly taking them somewhere for interrogation. He didn't recognize the enemy uniforms, which appeared to have only common green-and-brown camouflage designs on them and no easily identifiable markings.

The wind was blowing toward Joss, filling his nostrils with the sickening odor of burning human flesh. Yet he knew this unpleasantry could not be avoided. It was just one of many examples in which anarchists were permitted to vent their anger against Corporate interests. There had been so many years of frustration when the anarchists could do little except protest against the old United States government, and now the Chairman was channeling their raw aggression into useful purposes, permitting them to employ unfettered carnage against enemies of the state, be they Corporate remnants, common eco-criminals, or any other opposition groups.

There were many stories of anarchists going too far, killing animals and damaging ecosystems during violent attacks against people, and he'd heard that the Chairman sometimes admonished the black-uniformed men and women for their lack of discretion. A rumor held that Rahma worried about what would happen if the Black Shirts ever ran out of Corporate guerrillas to kill and turned their rage against the GSA—because anarchists had a long history of opposing governmental authority, and might only be cooperating as long as it served their interests to do so. Because of this, Rahma Popal had reportedly set up systems to monitor and control these fighters.

Joss and Kupi raised their arms in victory, and fired their own rifle shots in the air, as did the rest of their dedicated crew.

4

___

Chairman Rahma constructed the myth structure around himself carefully, beginning with a powerful, compelling concept and enhancing it with symbolism, a pantheon of political and pseudo-religious leaders, and a highly organized bureaucracy.

—*The Book of Forbidden Thoughts*
(Anarchist Press, banned)

A STOCKY MAN with a narrow face and dark, probing eyes, Dylan Bane stood on a platform high over the subterranean cavern, looking down on his builders and engineers as they prepared immense voleers—military cargo haulers that were built according to his precise specifications. He was inside the main cavern of his base camp, deep beneath the mountains of Michoacán in central Mexico. It was an ideal location for launching attacks north and south, against both continents of the Green States of America.

Long and tubular in shape, each armored voleer had Splitter tubes on the front to break open underground passageways, through which the machine would flow through soil and rock, compressing the debris and passing it to the rear, where built-in earthformers closed the tunnels behind. Vanishing tunnels, he called them, or VTs, giving him the advantage of surprise that enabled him to make guerrilla attacks and then disappear back into the ground.

With his short-cropped hair, clean-shaven face, and suit-and-tie uniform bearing medals and braids of rank, the self-proclaimed general looked like the antithesis of his enemies. He loathed the long-hairs with every breath he took, and had laid careful plans to annihilate them. Bane called them "Tree Nazis" and any other insult that came to mind. He was always thinking of ways to bring them down, and not without reason. Despite acting as if they loved peace, they were actually homicidal hippies, operating under a pack mentality that caused them to run roughshod over anyone who dared to disagree with their radical environmental views. For the Chairman's minions, there were no shades of interpretation or meaning. People were expected to accept his green doctrines one hundred percent, without questioning the slightest thing. In the alternative, nonbelievers were recycled.

That had been the fate of most of Bane's family, including his parents, siblings, and half of his cousins—all split into goo and dumped on the earth as if they were nothing but garbage. Because of his own high-level connections he'd escaped their fate, and had even taken a loyalty oath to Chairman Rahma that he didn't actually believe. To keep up appearances, he'd worn a beard for a time and appeared to be a contributor to the new reality, while actually waiting for his chance to get even with the GSA government and its powerful supporters.

He wasn't proud of his self-serving actions, but they'd enabled him to stay alive, so that he could fight another day. Rahma had created the deadly laws under which people were recycled for the slightest perceived infraction, even based on the word of others who simply disliked them. Survival under such conditions often required ingenuity and cunning, in a society that seemed like a brutal experiment in social Darwinism, fostered by a madman.

The path to Dylan Bane's personal survival niche had been difficult for him, one in which he had been forced to compromise his most closely held principles. Now his old self no longer existed. It, like much of his family, had been murdered.

For all of that, Bane would never forgive the Chairman, or anyone associated with him.

UNDER NORMAL CIRCUMSTANCES, the voleer-construction activities would have been quite loud in this immense underground chamber, but at the moment he had electronic noise suppressers and diverters in place, making it unnecessary for anyone to wear ear protection equipment. It was just one of several technological advantages Bane had, all of which were working in concert to get him to his goal. In addition, he had placed the facility beneath the central Mexican plateau of the Green States of America, where there were no densely populated reservations for humans and hardly any government-run facilities at all—just a few remote game reserves and eco-study outposts.

He nodded to a female officer who stood at attention nearby, waiting for him. Young, prim, and proper in appearance, the shapely brunette wore a silver uniform that bore the image of a white shirt and a patterned blue tie on the front, except with lesser designations of rank than the General wore. A former mercenary solder who knew martial arts and how to use virtually any weapon, Marissa Chase was as tough and smart as she was gorgeous. And, though he hesitated to fully trust her because of her history, the two of them seemed to have reached an understanding. It was quite simple, really, and amusingly classic in comparison with many male-female relationships throughout history: If she slept with him and he enjoyed it, she got perks—in this case, faster promotions. She was a Blue Looey now, a Blue Lieutenant who had risen through the ranks of non-com officers while under his command.

At his signal she approached stiffly and pointed a glowing ring on her finger at a more ornate ring that her superior wore. As the spheres completed their electronic connection, Bane focused on receiving a message in his brain, one he could have listened to had he desired to do so. Instead, he closed his eyes and read it like a printed letter in the ether, dark purple lettering against a white background.

There were numerous pages and he flipped through them mentally, skimming the words. It was a summary report, providing information his clandestine agents had obtained about GSA troop movements and other military matters that could affect his own tactics and strategy. One item caught his attention, an attack on the GSA military base outside the Bostoner Reservation for Humans.

"You read all of this?" he asked Marissa, opening his eyes to look at her.

She nodded, after making an electronic connection that enabled her to see what he was reading. "Do you think it was Zachary?" she asked.

Bane looked over the report, wishing he could find evidence that the Bostoner attack had been committed by other opposition fighters hiding around the GSA, groups without any central command structure or coordination.

"I'm afraid so." He shook his head sadly.

From descriptions of the aircraft involved in the attack

and of a tube-shaped transport vehicle that had emerged from the ground just before the assault, he was certain it was committed by a breakaway element from his own forces, led by a hotheaded young officer named Reed Zachary—a Red Major with great talent, but little patience. Refusing to wait any longer for Bane's tunneling machines to be constructed and fully tested, Zachary had wanted to employ immediate guerrilla methods against the widely dispersed GSA forces. After arguing vehemently with Bane over this, he left without permission, using a ruse to take a voleer and three aircraft with him, along with their crews and soldiers, both human and robotic.

The equipment he took was from a construction shed, and not yet fitted with all weaponry and accessories. Somehow Zachary had jury-rigged various operating systems, but apparently not the Splitter cannons on the aircraft—or the GSA reports would say something about that. Bane was confident that the subterranean transporter, the aircraft, and the robotic soldiers all had self-destruct mechanisms to prevent their secrets from falling into enemy hands—systems that Zachary could not possibly have disabled.

Bane's group was undoubtedly the largest among the disaffected, and had drawn officers, fighters, engineers, and war matériel from a number of groups—Corporate and otherwise—that benefited his interests and accepted him as their commander. Now he had hundreds of military aircraft, two thousand armored vehicles, and three old-style nuclear-missile submarines. But all of that, and the seventy thousand fighters in his force, would never be enough to defeat the Chairman and his powerful armies by conventional means. Only guerrilla attacks had any possibility of success; on that he and Zachary had agreed—though not about the timing or other details of attack.

Despite their difficult relationship, Bane felt no happiness at the possibility—the *probability*, actually—of the officer's death.

"That will be all," he said to Marissa. Then, with a crooked smile he added, "For now."

"You realize that you're a sexist bastard, don't you, sir?"

Dylan Bane nodded, and watched the wiggle of her figure in the uniform as she walked away. He imagined going after her right now and pulling off her clothes. No one would say anything if he forced himself on her, certainly not her. But he didn't want to risk a loss of decorum in the ranks, a diminishment of respect for him. He would wait for a few more hours, until their preappointed time and place.

He looked back down at the cavern floor and the work that was progressing there. For most of the two decades since the fall of the American Corporates, he had been supervising the construction and testing of VT-machine prototypes, and now he was preparing a nasty surprise for the Greenies who had taken power. Bane's hidden forces would rise from the ground like demons from hell and strike wherever he pleased.

And the element of surprise was not all he had.

With special access to technology, he possessed small and large weapons to match the Splitters of the SciOs. He understood the primal secrets of Dark Energy, and the easier-to-comprehend (though no less natural) technology of greenforming. He even knew that the SciOs had secret, quasi-religious rituals involving these two opposing forces, and believed they needed to be in constant interplay in order to balance nature—an infinite process of destruction and regeneration.

Bane had a vast fortune with which to fund his operations, accumulated from the assets of wealthy people who continued to join his forces, from high-level politicians who didn't join, and from coordinated raids that his specialists made all over the world, using two-man mini-voleers to steal gold, precious jewels, artwork, and other valuables.

His financial and political contacts were very high-level.

5

Despite the oft-expressed opinions of our anarchist brothers and sisters who are contributing mightily to our green cause, we are not against all technology; we do not propose reverting to the woods, or to the Age of Agriculture, or to the Stone Age. The problem with technology is not technology itself. Rather, it is the *misuse* of it by Corporate and allied interests, who find ways of detaching themselves from the concerns of average citizens, hiding behind armor plates of machines, and reaping huge financial rewards.

—joint statement of the Berkeley Eight,
just before their stunning military victory

JOSS SAT AT a window table as his train sped along a maglev rail that had been cut through the wilderness, with evergreen trees towering on either side that made it look as if he were going through a narrow green defile. He hadn't eaten most of the lunch in front of him, and pushed it aside. He and Kupi were bound for their next gig, in the Quebec Territory, having completed their important transformative work in New England. Their subsequent assignment did not involve Janus Machine duties, not the usual sort, anyway. Instead, they were scheduled to attend a gala event in Quebec with high-level progressives to talk about environmental issues, and to provide a demonstration of splitting and greenforming work.

He heard the smooth hum of machinery around him, along with the voices of passengers and the tinkle of silverware on plates. The pungent, ever-present odor of juana sticks lingered in the air, casting a brown haze throughout the car. There were a number of J-Mac crews riding inside the string of passenger cars, and huge flatcars brought up the rear of the train, with environmental restoration machines strapped to them.

Thinking back, Joss wondered who the attackers had been near Bostoner, an onslaught that undoubtedly led to the rigid security inspection the train and its passengers had been forced to undergo before departure. When the train finally pulled away he'd seen flatbed trucks carrying pieces of charred, unidentifiable debris from the battle. Presumably they were from the destroyed aircraft and the tube-shaped vessel he'd seen before it exploded—a vessel that reportedly had emerged from the ground and launched the aircraft. Undoubtedly the mission was carried out by one of the small resistance groups that kept cropping up. Nothing of real concern to the Chairman or his followers.

Kupi sat across the aisle in one of four seats facing another table, smoking a joint and chatting with an anarchist like herself, a slender man who wore the signature black garb of their ilk—except Kupi had a golden peace-symbol medal on her lapel, awarded to her by the GSA government for her bravery and quick thinking with the Splitter Cannon. Her companion's preference was red wine, not juana, and he was drinking straight from a large bottle.

Occasionally Joss saw the remnants of cities, towns, and industrial sites whiz by outside, locations where the linked processes of splitting and greenforming had been incomplete, for any number of reasons. Sometimes in the rush to map and chart all details and set priorities for J-Mac work crews, mistakes were committed that other crews needed to correct later. If a Splitter Cannon was not calibrated and aimed properly, for instance, it could result in the incomplete melting of buildings, infrastructure, and other man-made objects. He had also heard of some greenformers not loading the proper genetic materials into their Seed Cannons, thus resulting in plants not surviving in particular localized environments, or in the introduction of invasive species or parasitic organisms that required additional eco-tech work.

Knowledgeable in plant pathology, Joss was proud of his own careful attention to detail and meticulous work ethic. He looked down on others who were inattentive to their duties. As a team, he and Kupi Landau were highly rated for their skills, which put them in demand for the most challenging assignments, where their superiors didn't want mistakes to be made.

Joss worried as he thought of Kupi and her tendency to be independent, no matter the consequences. On the job she always performed her assignments with technical proficiency and thoroughness, never leaving any target standing after firing her black cannon, thus setting the stage for Joss to follow and scatter the seeds of his profession. But she was by no means an example of the perfect J-Mac employee. Her attitude and sharp tongue often got her negative attention, and if any other person ever said the things she did, that person would be summarily dismissed, or worse. Kupi kept getting away with more than others could, because of the important connections she'd made in the Corporate War and her significant contributions to what the Chairman called "our great and glorious green victory."

So far she had eluded serious trouble but there had to be a limit, and Joss remained wary. He genuinely cared about the older woman and wanted to protect her, but didn't want to lose his own career by his personal involvement with her.

He feared that one day she would step so far over the line with her comments that no one would be able to save her, not even Chairman Rahma Popal, Kupi's former lover during the war.

Now Kupi was telling stories from the legendary early days of the Army of the Environment again, when the Chairman's closest friend Glanno Artindale had been a hero of the revolution. He was killed in Atlanta in February 2041, when a U.S. Army battalion opened fire on a crowd of peaceful demonstrators that the Chairman was leading. Glanno Artindale died in Rahma Popal's arms, a scene that was immortalized in an iconic photograph used as a recruiting poster for the rebellion. The incident on Peachtree Street made him a martyr, and the words "Remember Glanno!" became a rallying cry for the ragtag army of environmentalists, anarchists, hippies, animal-rights activists, draft-card burners, and the homeless that ultimately overthrew the powerful Corporates and their entrenched allies.

Joss heard Kupi talking about her affair with Popal now, describing how they met more than twenty years ago when both of them were members of the radical revolutionary council in California that became known as the Berkeley Eight. They were the ones who first conceptualized the Army of the Environment, with its expressed goal of throwing out the greedy Corporates and their puppet United States government, and replacing them with a new and altruistic form of green governance. In one celebrated brainstorming session, where the participants consumed heroin-laced marijuana, LSD, and other powerful hallucinogens, Kupi had helped come up with the words of the GSA Loyalty Oath, in which citizens pledged fidelity to "one nation under green, and the greenocracy on which it was founded."

"Rahma swept me out of my sandals," Kupi said to her

tablemate now. Then, with a girlish giggle, she added, "And out of the rest of my clothing!"

Having heard her say this before, Joss exchanged smiles with her across the aisle. Though she and Joss were lovers these days, she'd been quite open with him about her sensational past. The tall, willowy woman had been the Chairman's number one girlfriend for more than two years. She'd also been a key strategic adviser in the fledgling army that ultimately overthrew the entrenched power brokers and their cronies.

That was heady stuff. *Really* heady stuff.

"Of course, I wasn't Rahma's only girlfriend," Kupi said, looking back at her fellow anarchist as she sipped a cup of tea thoughtfully. "He had many, and I never questioned him for his sexual proclivities." She laughed. "At least he wasn't interested in little boys."

Joss gazed outside again, remembered how he and Kupi had met almost five years ago at a ceremony where he'd received a national award for his achievements as an eco-cop, after busting a ring of notorious environmental criminals and killing three of them in a shoot-out, a group that was secretly cutting old-growth trees in wilderness areas and shipping wood products overseas. He'd found the older woman attractive and seductively mysterious, with her enigmatic personality, black clothing, and exotic beauty, and they'd hit it off immediately. Later that evening there had been an explosion of sex between them, and in the ensuing days it had not abated.

During one intimate moment with her, he'd expressed his desire to retire from Greenpol, admitting that killing eco-criminals—as necessary as that had been at the time—had not been something he could stomach again. It was not something he'd wanted to reveal to his supervisors on the force, because of the harm it could do to any career he chose, since "good citizens" should be happy to kill as many eco-criminals as they could. In fact, according to *The Little Green Book*, "Murder in defense of the planet is not murder," and Joss believed that wholeheartedly, but he'd exterminated more than his share of bad guys—nineteen in his career—and he could bear no more.

At his request, Kupi had kept his feelings secret, and in a matter of weeks she'd used her influence to get him transferred to the Greenforming Division of the government and a position on her Janus Machine crew, where he learned how to operate and maintain the equipment. He'd shown almost immediate skill as a greenformer, and in three years he was promoted to command the small crew, with the suggestion from his Berkeley managers that he could eventually rise much higher.

His sudden status above Kupi had not been a problem at all; she had encouraged his promotion and had not wanted to run the crew anyway. "I don't ever want to be the boss," she'd quipped. "I just want to complain about them."

Joss felt a slight jolt as the train switched from one electromagnetic track to another, and then accelerated. Off in the distance, beyond a cleared area, he got a glimpse of one of the latest relocation reservations for humans that was under construction, with cranes towering overhead. He looked back as the site vanished from view, uncertain of the name of that one. Joss thought it was a good idea to keep people on such reservations and prevent them from going out of bounds and harming the environment. There had been too many millennia of rampant ecological abuses committed by human beings, with their filthy industries, endless wars, and outright neglect of anything beyond their small circles of self-interest.

The fellow anarchist at Kupi's table said something to her in a low tone that Joss couldn't make out. He was a soft-spoken, effeminate man.

"I'll always care about Rahma," she replied, "but I could never live with him again. He has so many . . . eccentricities!"

Joss shook his head, hoped she didn't finally say something that would be the proverbial last straw. He knew she had been forced out of a leadership position shortly after the AOE defeated the Corporates, because of her outspoken criticisms of powerful progressive leaders surrounding the Chairman. A number of her shocking comments from years ago were still remembered, including her accusation that many of the GSA leaders were "living for the wrong kind of green—the money kind."

So far she had never questioned the honesty or integrity of the Chairman himself, and that must have been her saving grace, because he continued to watch out for her welfare. And as for those she had spoken against, some had tumbled from power under the withering, disapproving eye of Rahma Popal and Greenpol. But others remained, and new green profiteers kept cropping up, like noxious weeds.

Across the aisle, the anarchist rose and staggered away, unsteady on his feet. He'd consumed a lot of wine at this sitting, and Joss had seen him drinking earlier as well.

"You're unusually quiet today," Kupi said to Joss, scooting into a place across the table from him and stubbing out her juana stick in an ashtray. "You're not jealous of me talking to another man, are you?"

He watched the man go through a door between cars, said, "With a gay guy? Hardly. But I am jealous of you. You're a better person than I'll ever be, Kupi, the most honest person I've ever met, unafraid of the consequences of truth." He smiled gently. "Unlike me, you have the full courage of your convictions."

"Or I have the stupidity of them." Her brown eyes glistened with fire. "Sometimes I don't know what you see in me. I'm a lot older than you are, more than fifteen years."

"I never noticed." He leaned across the table, kissed her tenderly.

"Shall we find a private place?" she asked.

"We should wait," he said. "We're almost to Quebec Territory."

Even without a sleeping compartment, there were still places on the train for them to make love; they'd done it before. But he pulled away and looked at her, knowing that the two of them cared about each other, but he was coming to realize that the physical side of their relationship was most of it—and without that, they would have little in common. She was mysterious, which he would normally find intriguing, but she kept too many secrets to herself for his liking, saying he wouldn't want to hear them anyway. It had become a barrier between them.

Joss had slept with a number of other women in his adulthood, to see what it was like before settling down. Now he longed to be with one person, and though he was only thirty he felt a mounting urgency to find her. By any measure, his relationship with Kupi Landau was unusual; she was one of a kind, and that was interesting to him, even alluring. But he couldn't feel really close to her.

Whenever Kupi made love to Joss it was a raw, primal thing, from a deep-seated anarchist violence in her that both excited and terrified him. She was like a wild thing from the deep woods—a creature that could never really be civilized and did not belong here. She only tolerated civilization, only tolerated *him*, and would ultimately break free.

"What is it?" she asked.

"I was just thinking about you," he said, with a gentle smile.

6

Is it possible to go too far for a good cause? If Chairman Rahma's radical environmental policies are allowed to continue, couldn't it result in the total extinction of the human race? Is that what he really wants?

     —Unanswered Questions for Chairman Rahma,
             a banned book

IT WAS INDEED a day of celebration, with long-haired, braless women and bearded men dancing in circles on the grassy area by the yurts, in the midst of blaring Rolling Stones music and juana smoke drifting in the air. Though only mid-morning it was already warm, and Rahma Popal felt perspiration forming on his brow. The distinguished, gray-bearded man wore a lightweight, long green robe, with yellow ribbing on the collar and sleeves, and a golden peace symbol pendant around his neck. In his late fifties, he prided himself on remaining physically fit.

He smiled as he looked out on the people, many of whom had obtained passes to visit him at the Montana Valley Game Reserve, where he maintained his austere home and government headquarters. A number of them carried copies of *The Little Green Book*, and some had the volumes open, reading the sayings and poems of the Chairman.

Others were women who lived with him on the set-aside land, including one who kept watching his every move, Dori

Longet. After being with him for more than a decade, the small, curvy blonde had become his favorite, but he'd been noticing irritating traits about her, jealousies that annoyed him. She claimed to understand his need to have sex with numerous women, but often she attempted to act as a go-between for him and his various liaisons. At times he found this especially irritating and unnecessary, like a layer of bureaucracy that other women had to go through to get to him.

And yet he'd grown increasingly reliant on her intelligence, to the degree that he had her arranging his daily schedule— keeping track of the appointments he had with government and business officials, as well as with other visitors, and taking care of many of his personal matters. Dori was usually well organized and businesslike, and he appreciated her for that. At times, though, she expressed her displeasure at his wide-ranging sexual interests, especially if she thought a particular woman was manipulative and deceitful, and didn't really care about him, as she did. Truly, Dori was a remarkable woman. He had to admit that.

The newcomers among the dancers were from a select list of invitees, having passed stringent security and progressive loyalty tests. The festivities would extend far into the night, an orgy of sex and drugs. He enjoyed such activities himself, but whenever he partook of them he invariably felt guilty afterward, that he had succumbed to yet another human weakness. But these were private thoughts, which he shared with no one. After completing his work today, he would join the party, enjoying the various delights anyway. Despite his lofty goals, he was only human after all, and these pursuits were not harming the planet. In fact, he rationalized, they provided a sense of camaraderie between himself and his avid followers, and he used every opportunity—sometimes even while making love—to espouse the gospel of green.

He lifted his arms in the air, and the dancers began to chant to him lovingly, "Rahm-m-m-m-a . . . Rahm-m-m-m-a . . . Rahm-m-m-m-a . . ."

Around the perimeter he saw scores of yellow-uniformed hubots looking on attentively, human-looking robots who attended to security details and other matters for Rahma Popal, sometimes working with special Greenpol police who had been assigned to guard him. Constructed of synthetics that simulated human beings in their appearance and motions, each of them contained a small amount of functioning biological components—organs and other body parts that had been salvaged from dead people, often heroes of the Green Revolution. This was one of the Chairman's ways of honoring their memories. The hubots also had simulated human emotions, as well as humanlike odors and other characteristics that made them hard to discern from the real thing.

It was to this game reserve in the Rocky Mountain Territory that Rahma initially brought the snow leopard and other endangered species that were rescued, either from missions in which he participated personally or those that were conducted under his orders. The reserve, which he used as his base of government operations, was in a verdant river valley surrounded by slopes of evergreen trees and mountains, north of the Missoula Reservation for Humans.

A number of yurts encircled a central expanse of grass, buildings that were used for administrative, medical, and other purposes and as barracks for hundreds of his own children who lived on the compound with him, along with some of their mothers, but not all of them. Several had run off; others had been assigned to jobs around the GSA, and two were recycled for criminal activity—one for murdering a rival for the Chairman's affections, and the other for an egregious environmental crime.

Rahma always had a stream of new women coming to live with him on the compound, and there were invariably competitions among them, sometimes involving naked exhibitionism to gain his attention. He liked attractive women around him; the more the better. He called those on the compound his "wives," though there were never any marriage ceremonies involving them.

Gradually the chanting died down, though the dancing and music continued. One of the hubots stepped forward to hand the Chairman a sheet of recycled paper. His name was Artie. Like others of his kind, except for a slight translucence to his skin that was visible up close, he was almost indistinguishable from a human in appearance. For this reason, hubots were required to wear wide armbands that bore the silver, stylized image of a machine mechanism on it.

"Dori asked me to give you your daily schedule," the hubot announced, in a male voice.

"Oh?"

"I fear she's a bit perturbed with you today, Master."

"Did she say why?" Looking over at her, Rahma caught her hostile gaze.

"She did not."

Sometimes the Chairman didn't understand why she was upset with him, or what he might have done wrong in her eyes. No matter, it would pass. Her moods always did, and the two of them would resume their relationship as if nothing had happened. "Thank you," he said.

Around the same height as the Chairman, the hubot gazed at him with dark blue eyes that had been salvaged from a dead human and bio-fused into a droid robot. The eyes were reused in this fashion after having been salvaged twenty-two years ago from the body of Glanno Artindale, the iconic hero of the revolution who died after a Corporate attack on peaceful demonstrators. Now Artie was not only a top aide; he was very special to the Chairman, because Glanno had been his closest, most loyal friend. Sometimes when Rahma looked into the eyes of the hubot he saw his fallen comrade again, all the way to his soul. It was like that now, giving him pause. With programming that Rahma had specified, Artie even had mannerisms and expressions that mimicked those of the dead man. The hubot even knew many of their old stories, of times Rahma and Glanno had shared.

Artie even liked some of the same jokes as Glanno, such as the one about a redneck and a green-neck, and how they differed because the redneck drove a pickup truck with a gun rack, while the green-neck drove an electric car with a bicycle rack. Rahma could still hear Glanno's great, boisterous laugh resonating whenever he told a funny story, or heard one.

Glanno had been more than a comrade, and more than a friend. During an extended marijuana binge the two men had even become intimate, but that had ended when Glanno sobered up and realized that Rahma would never give up his numerous female lovers, not even for him, not even because of the closeness of their relationship. After their brief affair they continued to be friends, but it was never the same between them, and Rahma always felt a certain tension that never seemed to go away.

Then Glanno died, on that awful day in Atlanta.

Now, after a moment to regain his composure, Rahma Popal scanned his schedule. Later this morning he would meet with his children, to give them lectures on ecology and on treating animals properly. And before that, he had a meeting with a government official, a little over an hour from now.

Through hazel eyes he gazed thoughtfully toward the slopes

of the tree-covered foothills, and up to the snowy mountains beyond, where the male Panasian snow leopard had been released, after fitting it with an electronic tracking device. The beautiful animal would require special attention; there were not many of them left on the planet, and Rahma had only three others up there with him, one of which was female. He sighed as sadness enveloped him. Ultimately it might not be possible to save this remarkable species, but he would make every effort.

Beneath his feet there were underground GSA offices and data banks, laboratories, genetic libraries, and artificial habitats where other endangered animals were bred in captivity, for eventual release into the wild. The snow leopard was not sent down there, however, because it needed to roam in cold climes and develop its territory, or it would have a markedly higher likelihood of dying. In the subterranean labs, sick or injured animals were also treated, and viruses were carefully segregated to prevent them from spreading.

There were other animals kept underground as well, a small menagerie of previously extinct creatures that had been brought back to life—strange animals from long ago, kept inside habitat enclosures that were under the direction of Artie. There were dodo birds down there, as well as great auks, various other birds, thylacines, wolves, foxes, and rodents, all resurrected through a process of computerized genetic reconstruction that Glanno Artindale developed, and which Artie now understood better than anyone. One day Rahma and Artie hoped to release the creatures into the wild, but first a great deal of research and experimentation was needed, in order to make certain they could survive on their own, and to avoid setting off chain reactions of detrimental ecological consequences.

It deeply saddened Rahma Popal that more than 99 percent

of the animal species that had ever lived on the Earth were now extinct, and a quarter of the living species were endangered. Some of the die-offs had occurred as a result of natural disasters, but too often the disasters were unnatural and man-made—owing to industrialization, sprawling human settlements, and clear-cutting of trees that destroyed wildlife habitats, along with millennia of endless, terrible wars. The ecological blights caused by man and his greedy, selfish ways seemed endless. Most human beings had not been living in harmony with their environment since the Age of Agriculture ended long ago, when man embarked hell-bent on a course of wreaking havoc on the Earth for the sake of his own selfish creature comforts.

As just two examples, the dodo bird and the thylacine had been decimated by humans who hunted them: the dodos for food on the island of Mauritius in the Indian Ocean, and the thylacines on Tasmania because they were preying on ranchers' sheep. In his heart, Rahma liked Glanno Artindale's "Resurrection Plan," but he worried over how practical it really was. So much had changed since the legendary days when the exotic, romanticized creatures thrived on the planet. . . .

Just behind the Chairman was his residential yurt, round and made of renewed-growth cedar, with a single, high-ceilinged room and a retractable roof that enabled him to lie on his cot and gaze up at the stars on clear nights. Out in the vastness of space—so far away that he could hardly imagine the distances involved—there had to be pristine regions untrammeled by mankind, worlds and star systems where ecosystems had not been destroyed. He couldn't imagine any place worse than Earth, and even with all the restoration work he had ordered on the northern and southern American continents, a great deal remained to be done before the planet was healed.

The regions that were now under Rahma's green government, with their varying ecosystems, were like wounded animals that needed to be brought back to health, and he considered himself a steward of nature, the chief steward of nature. Unlike the Panasians and other nations that ignored the environment, and even bragged about doing so.

He remembered the old pre-revolution days when environmental activists worked with the regulatory departments of towns, cities, and states to obtain wetland designations, conservation agreements, fish habitats, parks, bicycle lanes, and the like. On numerous occasions they had also attempted ambitious national improvements as well, such as clean air and water regulations, laws for the restoration of the ozone layer, for the combating of global warming, and for the preservation of forests, as well as endangered species designations. There were even international efforts to encourage the cooperation of industrialized nations with one another.

But corporations and other entrenched interests pushed back extremely hard on the bigger issues, employing legions of lobbyists and lawyers to make clever but disingenuous arguments that got the laws watered down, enabling the tycoons to keep generating huge incomes for themselves. The whole process of trying to make meaningful changes was so slow and frustrating that Rahma decided to do something much larger than anyone had imagined before. He and his comrades elevated the epic struggle to protect the planet, speeding up the process by carrying their critical messages into the streets. They did so with great determination. And powerful weapons.

Now the Chairman realized he had come a long way, and

deserved to be proud of his accomplishments. But he couldn't rest on his laurels, and didn't want his followers to do that, either—because complacency left the openings that the enemies of environmentalism looked for, the openings they would plunge through if given the opportunity.

7

There are certain controls necessary to maintain our green economy and its allied political underpinnings, to keep the Green States of America from being undermined. Among the most important: absolute sovereignty over the holo-net communication system, restricting it to our nation and monitoring every user. This electronic surveillance and control program was initiated by pro-green hackers who once specialized in eavesdropping on Corporate and U.S. government interests, and were instrumental in disrupting their use of the Internet during the revolution. After the formation of the GSA, the hackers used their talents to protect the radical new government. Thus, in a supreme historical irony, they focused on accomplishing the exact opposite of what they did before. They became part of the new establishment.

—Advisory Committee to the Chairman,
among its key findings

SETTING ASIDE HIS worries for the moment, Rahma Popal joined one of the circles of dancers for a few spins to a modern version of "Strawberry Fields Forever." He held hands with a buxom redhead on one side and a tall, long-haired man on the other. The woman, in her early twenties, had pretty, dark green eyes that sparkled mischievously. Her hair was waist-length and straight, except for one braided section.

She smiled at him and squeezed his hand hard, holding on

momentarily when he decided to pull away and leave the circle. In another group of dancers, he saw Dori Longet watching him again.

"Your Eminence," the redhead said, with a smile, when she finally let go. "I'm Jade Ridell. You'd like to spend time with me this evening?" He recognized the code words; they were not difficult to interpret.

"Of course." So many girls called themselves Jade, Olivia, Emeralda, Ivy, Fern, or some other variation of (or suggestion of) green, sometimes forsaking their birth names. This pleased him very much, but their compliance also amused him. When it came to women who he liked to spend extended periods of time with, he preferred the ones who were able to think more for themselves. Dori was like that, and so was Valerie Tatanka (a Native American doctor who ran the medical clinic on the game reserve), but both of them had their share of irksome traits. As he left Jade, he saw Dori walking toward her purposefully.

The Chairman smiled at Jade, then watched as his hubot assistant, Artie, crossed the grass to the administration building, a much larger yurt with seven floors and upper-level patios for viewing antelope, bison, moose, white-tailed deer, grizzlies, wapiti, and other wildlife.

But Artie was not going upstairs. He had other matters to attend to in the underground levels, matters in the Extinct Animals Laboratory that the Chairman considered of doubtful utility. And yet it was something his long-lost friend Glanno Artindale had wanted, so out of respect for the dead man's wishes, Rahma had allowed the program to continue.

It certainly was altruistic, tending to dodo birds and other resurrected, formerly extinct species, but of what use were such animals in modern habitats, and what potential harm could "the newcomers" inflict as invasive species? It all seemed—well, he hated to use the phrase—but it all seemed as if the program should be as dead as the proverbial dodo bird.

SOUTH OF THE game reserve, in the Missoula Reservation for Humans, a man stood in line in a large room, waiting to speak with a clerk. This was the JAO, the Job Assignment Office of the government, and he was reporting as ordered for reassignment. The walls were adorned with murals of trees, mountains, and rivers, except for one wall that featured a towering artist's rendition of Chairman Rahma Popal, surrounded by martyrs of the revolution—those who had given their lives so valiantly in the formation of the green nation. It was warm in the room, with the faint odors of juana smoke and body odors in the air. Doug Ridell hardly noticed such smells at all, since they were so commonplace.

With all of the automation available to the GSA, he didn't understand why his job reassignment couldn't be handled in some more efficient manner, so that he didn't have to appear in person. It seemed like a waste of time and energy. Still, he would say nothing of this, for fear of being considered a social nonconformist, which could result in having him put under observation by the authorities—or worse.

Taller than most of the people around him, Ridell had a neatly trimmed brown beard and wore his best green-and-orange paisley suit (with bell-bottom trousers), along with a patterned tie and sandals with dark socks. Other men were similarly attired, so he knew he didn't stand out from them; but then again, he didn't want to be different, at least not in any bad way. Still, he did hope for a good assignment.

While in line he thought about his wife, Hana, who worked for the reservation's parks department on one of the numerous gardening crews. He wished the two of them had better jobs, and that they had a larger apartment, and more privileges. At breakfast that morning their eleven-year-old daughter, Willow, had asked what her older sister, Jade, was doing in her job for Chairman Rahma. No one had given the child details before this, though they were well known to the parents. Jade was a member of the great man's harem now, selected for her beauty and intelligence to join him on the game reserve where he lived.

"Something to do with caring for the animals," Hana had replied, as she exchanged a knowing glance with her husband.

A *human animal*, Doug had thought, and he'd said, "We don't know what her job assignment is yet."

Ridell hoped his beautiful older daughter did well. It was important to the entire family. . . .

When his turn came he handed the female clerk a small electronic device called a précis, which contained a summary of his life, including details of his education and family, where he had worked, and (in a code that he could not read) information on his personality—whether he took orders well, learned quickly, and the like. The hand-held device had an illuminated amber screen. She touched one of the control pads on it.

"I was a machine-repair technician before," he said, "in a factory on the outskirts of the reservation."

She said something, in a low tone that he could not hear. The woman had short black hair that glistened with a gel that made it stand out in little spikes.

"Excuse me, but what did you say?" he asked.

Her dark eyes flashed. "I can see where you worked." She pointed at the screen on the hand-held device. "It's all right here." The précis screen, which previously had been amber, now glowed pale orange.

"Of course, I'm sorry. My previous job was noisy, and I have some hearing loss from it."

"I see." She asked him a number of questions, details of his experience. Repeatedly he had to ask her to speak louder, which she did.

The woman made entries in the hand-held device, then connected it to a computer at her desk, which took a moment to process the new data. Finally the screen on the connected précis turned pale green. She removed it and handed it back to him.

"This is your new assignment," she said. "Report tomorrow at seven a.m."

The screen showed that he was going to be working for one of the government's robotics servicing units. An address was provided on the south side of the reservation, and the name of a contact person.

Out on the street Ridell passed a greengrocer, a drug-injection booth, and a family guidance center (an abortion clinic), then waited for bicyclists to pass before crossing the wide street. On the other side he stepped onto a sidewalk that had sensors embedded in the surface, to collect the energy of his footsteps. The buildings on this side of the street had terraced vegetable gardens running up their outside walls, and he knew the accumulated energy of the sidewalks was used to pump water up to the gardens.

He turned onto a street that sloped upward gradually, toward the apartment building where he lived with his family. Ahead in the street, he saw a produce truck slowing for bicyclists going uphill ahead of it, who showed no inclination to get out of the way. They were even swarming over the oncoming lane, going in the wrong direction, so that the driver could not pass them. Since bicycles always had the right of way against motorized vehicles, he waited patiently, going slowly behind the pack.

Seeing something out of the corner of his eye, Ridell turned to his left, just as another bicyclist raced past him, went around the car, and approached the rear of the group of bicyclists.

A pedestrian, an elderly woman near Ridell, shouted, "He has a gun!"

He saw her pointing at the bicyclist, but couldn't see any weapon. The rider caught up with the group, and now Ridell heard him shouting, and saw him waving a handgun, causing the other bicyclists to scatter. To Ridell's horror he fired at a woman several times, causing her to crash and fall to the pavement.

The attacker darted down a side alley and disappeared from view. The woman didn't move; blood pooled around her head. Hesitantly, a man and a woman approached her, in an apparent attempt to give aid. To Ridell, however, she looked dead. Maybe it was a lover's crime of passion, a relationship that had gone terribly wrong.

Police sirens were already whining.

To avoid getting involved, Ridell turned and hurried down another street, taking an alternate route home. Surveillance cameras would identify and track the killer as he fled. Undoubtedly the man was already being monitored—and he must have known he would be caught quickly by the efficient, high-tech methods of the police. But his hatred of the victim must have run so deep that he didn't care. There would be no trial. The cops would kill him on the spot, the moment he was apprehended.

Reaching another street, with the siren noise a couple of blocks away, Doug Ridell thought he might like his new job better than the old one. The factory noise had been driving him crazy, and he was happy to get away from it. Still, he was eager for Jade to advance in her own career, so that she and the entire Ridell family could move up to a higher social rung, with a larger apartment and all of the perks that went with it.

He wondered if his daughter was having sex with Chairman Rahma at that very moment. . . .

ARTIE WENT THROUGH an open doorway and took an elevator to one of the lower levels, where he boarded a slidewalk that transported him through a long tunnel. After rounding a corner, the hubot sent an electronic signal from his AI core, causing thick double doors to slide open ahead of him, doors that were carved with raised images of extinct animals. Disembarking from the slidewalk, he walked inside, where he felt a slight change in air pressure.

There were separate forest, arid bush, jungle, and other environments here, with vegetation stretching far into the distance. It was a network of complex subterranean habitats, with sunlight passing through the techplex ceiling overhead to warm the irrigated, nutrient-fed interiors. In the sky visible through the ceiling, he saw the sun peeking around puffy clouds.

At the front of the enclosure, he paused to examine an array of settings on a control panel, specifying the humidity for various zones of the underground facility, zones that were separated by electronic barriers that flickered and waved slightly from delicate disturbances in the air.

Two robot technicians worked the controls, part of a larger team of automatons that were linked electronically to Artie and transmitted a constant stream of valuable data to him.

The hubot saw a red gazelle run by, darting through the

bush section and vanishing into the distance, then heard the warbling call of a thrush—both among the once-extinct creatures that had been resurrected with a combination of cellular material, historical information from observers, habitat information, and other data, forming what the inventor of the system, Glanno Artindale, called "genetic blueprints."

Many animal species went extinct in the past five hundred years because they were hunted by humans, or because they were killed by predators such as rats, snakes, monkeys, or owls that were brought in by humans who had no understanding of the consequences of their actions. Often the habitats were destroyed by humans or by other related conditions—and to a very large extent the unfortunate creatures went extinct on islands, where their numbers were limited and where conditions changed enough to wipe them out. On those islands, they were sometimes visited by the crews of sailing ships, careless men who had no concern for what they were doing to endangered species.

In order to resurrect a particular species, the laboratory technicians entered all of the known data into the Artindale Computer System, including descriptions of the creatures made by centuries-past sailors (often Portuguese and Dutch) and other observers, along with the data from scientific papers and even the wildest of conjectural writings. This included genetic, hair, and other cellular information that had been assembled, as well as known facts about the habitats in which these creatures lived, including what they probably ate as well as data on other creatures that competed with them for resources or preyed on them—and which creatures the extinct species might have, in turn, preyed upon themselves. The tiniest, seemingly most innocuous observations were included, and the computer system then filtered out the most improbable data, focusing instead on characteristics that the creature most likely had.

Artindale also came up with a variety of chemical solutions in which to nourish and grow the cells, and developed charts of various ingredients to add or subtract, depending upon cellular reactions. In some cases there were inadequate cellular samples with which to begin the process, so Artindale developed what he called "educated assumptions," which were used to generate artificial cellular materials, and to build creatures that he said would "closely approximate" extinct life-forms, matching all but an infinitesimal percentage of characteristics and traits. This was something Artie knew, having gleaned it from the technical electronic files left by his mentor, but it was not anything Rahma would be pleased to know—because it suggested a certain lack of genetic authenticity and purity.

All of the thirty-seven resurrected species, some involving adult pairs with offspring, and some individual adults, were comparatively recent extinctions from a historical standpoint, having come to the terminus of their genetic lineage between 1582 and 2036. He had decided to focus on this time period because, as a general rule, there was more data on comparatively recent species that had gone extinct. Glanno Artindale, and in turn Artie, could have gone back further if they wished, but the more recent species they'd brought back were more than enough to keep Artie and his team busy. On occasion, the hubot found evidence of likely candidates for resurrection that were much more ancient (but only if a wealth of intriguing information was available), yet he always set them aside for future research teams to work on.

This time Artie tinkered in the laboratory for around half an hour, supervising the assistants, answering their questions, making his own settings on the controls. He was about to enter the complex of habitats and walk around inside when he heard a familiar voice behind him.

"Oh, there you are," Rahma said, as he came up beside the hubot. "Are you about finished here? I have important things for you to do."

"Somehow that doesn't surprise me," Artie said, with a smile.

Just then, a large gray-and-white bird emerged from the jungle section and strutted slowly around the mango and papaya trees, pausing to eat fruit that had fallen to the ground.

"The dodo bird!" Rahma exclaimed.

"Our one and only," Artie said. "The legendary flightless pigeon." It was far and away the most popular of the creatures in his menagerie.

The legendary bird's wings were quite small in relation to the size of its body, preventing it from flying. Rahma knew this was one of the reasons it had gone extinct on the island in the Indian Ocean where it lived, because over generations it became accustomed to a comfortable existence foraging on the ground, where food was plentiful. Until the arrival of humans and other predators (brought by humans) that hunted the dodo birds down with ease, and made them extinct.

The fat male bird stared at them for several long moments, showing no fear or aggression. It made a clucking sound, then waddled back into the thick undergrowth.

"We're growing a girlfriend for him in the laboratory," Artie said, "and hopefully they'll like each other."

"You have more than thirty species here, right?" Rahma said, "but only two have successfully bred with their own kind so far? The Labrador ducks and a species of mouse?"

"That's still the case, sir. The two species you mentioned are doing well; others are not, and I'm afraid they can only be grown in the laboratory. For those that have not bred yet, we've been adjusting breeding conditions, and in a few cases we're growing more of them in the lab in the hope that they will eventually breed."

"And if they won't?"

"Then they're doomed to eventual extinction." He paused. "They'll go extinct for a second time."

"How sad," Rahma said.

"It is that, sir. As you know, this is a potentially huge-scale project, and very time-consuming, so I've backed off on generating new species in order to keep the operation small enough to manage."

"Wise decision. I was wondering if you were going to blow out of this habitat, and start asking for funds to expand."

"My department can always use additional funds, Chairman. Oh, remember a few weeks ago when I mentioned a new species?"

"Yes, you said you had a small marsupial, a juvenile."

"That's right," Artie said. "It is growing faster than anticipated, and is already half of what we think its adult size will be." He walked to a window and pointed into an enclosure that was physically walled off from the other habitat sections, with clearplex partition walls.

Rahma moved to his side, looked in. His eyes widened. "What the hell is *that*?"

Artie took several moments before replying. The enclosure was forested with kentia pines, palms, a variety of eucalyptus, and a dense undergrowth of shrubs and ferns. On the lower branch of a eucalyptus tree, the marsupial lay on its nest of twigs and leaves. Around the size of a small dog, it stared at Rahma with pale yellow eyes, its batlike wings folded over its body like a tent. The snout was long and pointed, and the thin lips separated slightly, showing large, razor-sharp incisors and canine teeth. The animal had reddish brown fur and a white streak down the center of its face.

"A marsupial wolf," Artie said. "A female."

"It can fly? It sure looks like it."

"It's more of a glider. After scampering up trees she launches herself from high points like a flying squirrel or fox. She can also catch currents of wind and lift off from the ground. I call her a glidewolf."

"She's also a marsupial, with a pouch?'

"That she is. You're looking at a rather complex creature that went extinct around the year 1700 on Lord Howe Island, a crescent-shaped volcanic isle halfway between Australia and New Zealand—at least that's where the skeletal remains were found, buried under lava. The trouble is, since the creature glides, it could have come from a different island, or even from the Australian mainland. It's small now but is still growing, so in its adult form it might glide for great distances, riding air currents and perhaps even setting down on the water until the wind picks up again, then taking off by lifting its wings to the wind. It's semi-nocturnal, doing most of its feeding at night. But it doesn't sleep all day, like fully nocturnal creatures. Instead, it has a great deal of sustained energy, and is often quite active during daylight hours."

Artie watched as the Chairman considered this information. The hubot had omitted certain details in describing the production of this creature to him, such as the amount of educated guesswork he'd had to do to produce it—conjecture that amounted to a quarter of one percent of the genetic mix—information that would trouble Rahma, and which he didn't need to know. Even Artie's assistants didn't know about this genetic impurity (despite their electronic linkage with him), because he had the ability to conceal information from them, connecting with them only when he wanted to do so, and then transmitting only limited data.

"Do the wings flap?" Rahma asked.

"Only a little, which seem more like adjustments for gliding. When the creature is airborne and its wings are extended, the tail lifts and becomes a rudder for steering. It's quite an interesting life-form, very unique."

Obviously intrigued, Rahma asked, "Can I go inside for a closer look? It's not dangerous, is it?"

Opening the door, Artie said, "The glidewolf is not carnivorous, that we know for certain. But we're experimenting with her diet, putting various plants inside for her to eat. She seems to have a preference for the leaves, bark, and branches of eucalyptus trees, rather than anything from palms or other plants that are native to Lord Howe Island. Perhaps eucalyptus trees once grew there in abundance and then died off from a blight of some sort, and the creature lost the food it preferred. One thing in its favor, though—this one doesn't seem to be a fussy eater, a trait that has led to the demise of other species. The glidewolf seems to be highly adaptable, which bodes well for its survival."

"But it still went extinct."

"That it did." Artie led the way inside, walking over a groundcover littered with leaves and sticks, crunching the debris underfoot. Rahma followed. When they reached the branch on which the marsupial lay, the creature hardly moved. It stared at the hubot, an inquisitive gleam in its pale eyes. Artie heard a low hum coming from the animal, and a series of barely audible clicks. His lab assistants had been studying the intriguing vocalizations, but had not yet established clear patterns.

The marsupial's wings were thin and tentlike, with lines of thick cartilage where they folded. In recent days Artie had been noticing that the creature shifted its wings around depending not only upon when it intended to glide, but upon its moods. Now the glidewolf was doing something it had done with him previously—leaning toward Rahma and extending a wing over him, using the appendage to draw the Chairman closer.

"She likes you," Artie said, watching as Rahma nuzzled nervously and uncomfortably against the breast of the glidewolf, and the outside of its marsupial pouch.

"It does seem that way. I . . . I think I feel its heartbeat. Yes, I'm certain I do." Finally the Chairman pulled free and stood a distance away, looking at the animal with a bemused expression on his bearded face.

"Master, I'd like your permission to release her into the wild for experiments, to see what else she might want to eat. She's not carnivorous, so there'd be no danger to other animal species—and I'm confident she could elude any predators out there, or match them in a fight. Look at those claws and teeth."

"You want to release her onto the game reserve?"

The hubot nodded. "With an electronic tracker attached, of course, and a videocam to record everything she does."

"And if she causes trouble with the ecosystem?"

"One creature? How could she? If we see anything we don't like, we just follow the tracking device, sedate the animal, and bring her back."

"You make it sound so simple."

"We need to do scientific research, and I get the feeling that the glidewolf requires a larger territory than we can provide down here."

"I didn't notice any eucalyptus trees growing out there."

"Such trees prefer lower elevations, and coastal regions. But the creature seems to be adaptable, as I said. Maybe she will find something else to eat."

"All right. In the name of science." The Chairman moved toward the doorway. "Now, in case it slipped your mind, we have a visitor due in a few minutes."

"I didn't forget," Artie said. "I have an internal clock, remember?"

"Right. You're all machine, except for your eyes and your simulated programs."

AT THE MAIN level of the administration building, Rahma and the hubot strode up a spiral ramp to the third floor. Women in long flower-print dresses and peace-symbol necklaces greeted the Chairman as he made his way past the cubicles and bamboo desks of the outer offices.

In the waiting area outside Rahma's office, a tall man in an elegant white robe rose from a chair and bowed slightly. "Your Eminence," he said. His bushy lamb-chop sideburns made his face look wider than it really was.

Chairman Rahma glanced at him coolly, then strode toward the office without saying anything.

Arch Ondex, the Director of Science for the Green States of America, was second in command behind the Chairman, but by some measures he held the most power of the two men, because he led the SciOs and controlled their secret, essential technology. A member of the Berkeley Eight revolutionary committee, Ondex's scientific contributions had been crucial in defeating the powerful Corporate armies, while Rahma Popal had been the inspirational leader, the one who envisioned the best path to follow and led the raging mobs to victory.

The Chairman entered his office, with Ondex right behind him. Pompous and overbearing, the Director came from a wealthy Bay Area family that had been allowed to keep its fortune after the Corporate War because of its longtime record of endowments for the environment and for poor people. Unfortunately, Ondex and the Chairman only tolerated each other, and just barely, sometimes seeming to come close to blows. They had an uneasy alliance of common interests, knowing that one of them could not exist without the other.

As Artie remained outside and closed the office door, Ondex slipped into a deep-cushion visitor's chair, beneath a sign on the wall that read "All for Green and Green for All."

Intentionally ignoring the man for the moment, Rahma Popal walked to a large window of his office and gazed out on the remarkable, calming beauty of the greensward, with its arrangement of wetlands and irrigated grazing lands. In the foreground he saw wranglers working with small, energetic dogs to keep a herd of elk away from the unfenced compound of buildings. In the distance buffalo grazed on the grass, a timeless scene of pastoral serenity. Above them a platform floated low in the air without touching the fragile habitats or disturbing the birds or animals, with a crew onboard collecting information on the wildlife.

"You think to drive me a little mad, eh?" Ondex said, "with your attitude and outright disrespect?"

"My contempt for you does not go beyond this office," said the Chairman, still keeping his back to him.

"It's too bad you feel that way toward me, because I've never felt that way about you, Rahma. Perhaps it is my manner that irritates you more than anything else? But I can't help how I speak or carry myself. Woe is me, I was born into great wealth, and these things were ingrained in me from an early age."

Rahma turned to face him. "Is that an apology for your rude, condescending demeanor?"

Ondex smiled tightly. "Only an explanation. Might I suggest that we set aside our personal discomforts for the good of the nation, for the critical matters that we must handle with efficiency?"

The Chairman nodded somberly and exchanged the sign of the sacred tree with him—each man saluting with spread, bent fingers that represented tree roots. (It was an exchange that the Berkeley Eight had developed during the Green Revolution.) Then Rahma asked, "Well, what is it this time?"

"You heard about the most recent guerrilla attack, just outside the Bostoner Preserve? The Corporates are at it again."

"Yes, yes, most of the attackers were killed, and of the two that were captured, one died in interrogation and the other slipped into a coma from his injuries, both without revealing anything. AOE special agents are doing what they can to find out what happened."

"But how do you plan to prevent future attacks?"

"I don't have the intelligence reports back yet, but you SciOs provide science to the government, including some military technology. Why don't you put your researchers on the task?"

"We are a scientific organization, not a military one. This is a national defense matter."

"Then why are you here?"

Ondex bristled. "You are supposed to be the inspirational and strategic leader of the GSA. In contrast, I lead a group of scientists, nerdy technicians who provide environmental and law-enforcement technology. It is your responsibility to use the J-Macs to improve the environment, and to protect our nation with conventional and nuclear military forces. And need I remind you, the GSA Charter lays out our lines of authority quite clearly."

"But I have one hand tied behind my back because of your paranoid secrecy and the self-destruct, non-tamper mechanisms on SciO equipment. You have secret information that you won't share with me. Maybe your laboratories could find evidence of who's behind the guerrilla attacks and prevent them from doing it again."

Ondex shook his head. "National security is *your* responsibility. Don't try to twist things and make it mine."

"You SciOs are so very clever. Surely, some device in your bag of tricks can ferret out these bad guys, these terrorists."

"Our bag of tricks, as you call it, saved you and your hippie army from annihilation, when we used Splitter Cannons to tear through enemy forces."

"That was only part of the reason we won. Your Splitter Cannons were only short-range, and we didn't have nuclear weapons then, while the Corporates and their captive governments did. But we had numbers on our side, tens of millions of common people hitting the streets in mob armies on two continents, bolstered by many more who left the Corporate militias and government forces and joined us. It was a grassroots movement, a groundswell that would not have been possible without my leadership."

"And the rest of us on the revolutionary council, we did nothing?"

"I didn't say that. It was a team effort, I'll admit that. But don't try to overstate your contribution."

"That goes both ways, Comrade Chairman. Now we have nuclear weapons to defend our nation, but they are of no use against the Corporate guerrillas. You understand, don't you, that the guerrilla attacks are probes designed to test our defenses and responses?"

"That is but one option. There are others. Intelligence reports indicate that there are different Corporate groups operating in the GSA without strong overseas sponsors. They are not one cohesive unit, and have no unified plan."

"But environmental sabotages seem to go hand in hand with military attacks, the way our enemies also spread eco-cancers through the areas we have greenformed—nasty blights and viruses that cause plants and animals to die, not to mention the forest fires they keep setting."

"Only minor inconveniences. We can greenform faster than they can sabotage. There are countermeasures to eco-cancers, and ways to put out the forest fires quickly. Besides," the Chairman added with a smile, "those problems keep our people working, and keep us unified against the terrorists."

"Just as long as the opposition forces don't get too strong."

"You worry too much. Since you insist on secrecy, you must leave the countermeasures to me. You take care of your area of responsibility under the Charter, and I'll handle the rest."

"Somehow, I don't feel assured," Ondex said. He stood abruptly, and left.

8

Greenforming is like terraforming, making things grow and thrive in human-damaged and otherwise desolate lands, turning barren landscapes into wombs of life.

—a children's ecology primer

"AS YOU CAN see," Kupi said, "the Quebec Reservation for Humans is different from most others. This one has a pre-war nucleus of old buildings in the French quarter that were not torn down." She sat beside him in the rear of an antique, elegant town car with a landau roof, driven by a chauffeur wearing a crisp uniform and cap. He was separated from them by a closed partition window. The whisper-quiet car, like others, had been converted to operate with a non-polluting engine, from a variety of technologies that were allowed by the government—technologies that did not use fossil fuels.

"Just look at this fancy rig," she said, taking a puff on a juana stick. It was one of the stronger-smelling types she used on occasion, with the scent of basil in the smoke. She waved a hand gracefully. "Posh posh. And this is just the beginning. Wait until you see the ultra-exclusive private club. It dates back to 1735."

They wore dress versions of their working uniforms, his green and hers black, both of which included gold epaulets and piping with tree and root designs worked into them. He'd lit a juana stick himself on the train, but had stubbed it out after only a few drags. His stubble of brown beard was trimmed to the length he liked it, giving him a rugged look.

The long car drove past government-run drug injection booths fronting the street, and Joss hardly gave them a thought. Though he was not much of a recreational drug user himself, many people were, and it was perfectly legal, as long as consumption didn't interfere with the operation of priorities in the green-oriented society. Every reservation had facilities that provided the citizens with marijuana, cocaine, LSD, alcohol, and a host of other legal drugs.

The driver took them through an area of aged, stylish buildings overlooking the St. Lawrence Seaway. Behind them, a bright orange sunset splashed across the sky, casting colors over the water. Lights began to flicker on along the shores. "It really is quite beautiful here," Joss said.

"For an inhabited region, you mean," she noted, with a small smile.

"Of course."

In the distance, he saw what looked like two large elm seeds floating gracefully on air currents, dropping slowly to the ground. They were SciO Recharge Facilities, more commonly known as ReFacs. Portable buildings filled with SciO technology, ReFacs were heavily guarded by the secrecy-obsessed organization, and used for the recharging of Janus Machine cannons. The existence of ReFacs here meant that there were still industrial sites in the area that needed to be split and greenformed.

The car pulled into an elegant porte-cochere, where tall doormen in red jackets and tails waited beneath a sign that read TREETOP CLUB. After the car stopped, the men opened doors on both sides.

"I don't know what the original name of this place was," Kupi said as she stepped out of the elegant vehicle, "but it was once reserved for the robber barons of industrial and Corporate society, a meeting place where they made plans to pillage resources from undeveloped nations and take advantage of poor, uneducated people. For them and their imperialist, colonialist predecessors, everything was a resource to be exploited. Now it's the favored social establishment of a different sort of elite, one that's risen on the crest of the Green Revolution. And make no mistake about it; they're robber barons too, but of a different sort, camouflaging themselves behind liberal causes." She grinned as she fell into step beside him, going through ornate gold-emblem doors that were held open for them. "Meet the new bigwigs; they're exactly like the old bigwigs."

Joss felt uneasy at her conversation, noted that one of the doormen had overheard her and was looking at her strangely. Joss took a deep breath, resisted the urge to say anything. She had a playful, bemused expression on her face, and sometimes she did this sort of thing to get a rise out of him, to see how he would react. He presumed she was doing it again.

Just inside the entrance, a man in a red uniform and tails bowed and said, "Greetings, *madame et monsieur*. I am the maître d', and I will show you to the dining hall." He motioned toward a grand staircase, where the waitstaff and chefs were lined up on either side of the steps. Men in black or white tuxedoes and women in ball gowns were going up the stairs between the rows of servants, along with a number of high-ranking SciOs in white robes. A number of the people were pink-cheeked and quite portly.

Kupi excused herself and slipped into the ladies' room. When she emerged a few minutes later, she smiled prettily at Joss and slipped her arm through his. "Shall we?" she asked. He presumed that she had swallowed a purple peace pill in there, or some other calming drug from the pharmacopoeia she carried in a pouch on her person. Her brown eyes looked more relaxed as a result, which could be good or bad—it might make her less agitated, but she could still slip and say the wrong things.

The maître d' led the way up the grand staircase to the next level, where a long dining table had been set with fine linens, silver, and crystal goblets, while men in red tuxedoes and top hats were helping guests into their chairs and placing white lace napkins on their laps. The walls and high ceiling of the great hall were covered with electronic murals from bygone eras, depicting old sailing ships, timber mills, frontier forts, and battlefields with opposing soldiers in red or blue uniforms, with natives on both sides, dressed as warriors. Three crystal chandeliers hung over the table, illuminated with soft lights that cast interesting, multicolored prism patterns around the room.

Two chairs were at one end of the table, side by side. "For our guests of honor," the maître d' said, as he seated Joss and Kupi. The man looked at Kupi, added, "We have heard of your exploits."

"Uh-oh," she said with a smile, as men in top hats made them comfortable.

"I mean, the way you fought off attackers with your Splitter Cannon, madame. Very brave, everyone is saying."

"Well, perhaps that will make up for some of the other stories about me," she said.

He bowed stiffly and backed up to take his leave.

For half an hour, the two of them sipped fine sauterne wine from crystal goblets. When all of the dignitaries were seated, murals on one wall faded away, revealing an expanse of clearplex that featured the seaway, the harbor, and the early evening lights of ships glimmering on the water. Joss had never been on a waterborne vessel himself, because that was something reserved for SP3 cargo seamen and other specialists, or for military purposes. In contrast with the old buildings of the French quarter of the Quebec reservation, the ships on the seaway were quite modern, with blinking electronics on their superstructures and speedbarges secured alongside for loading and unloading purposes.

At the far end of the long table, bright green lights sparkled like a small display of fireworks, and as the brightness diminished, Joss saw Chairman Rahma Popal appear there in an enhanced virtual reality projection, sitting and gazing beatifically out on the assemblage. He wore an emerald green robe, with an oversized golden peace-symbol pendant around his neck. His gray beard looked freshly trimmed.

"Welcome everyone, welcome," the Chairman said. "I wish I could be here in person instead of by EVR, but my schedule is so incredibly busy nowadays. Nonetheless, I am pleased to welcome my old comrade from the revolutionary council, Kupi Landau, and her talented young J-Mac commander, Joss Stuart."

Rahma Popal made the sign of the sacred tree and said, "'May green blessings rain upon you like water from the sky.'" It was one of the Chairman's favorite sayings from *The Little Green Book* he'd written, a copy of which every citizen possessed. Joss had his own copy of the slender volume with him, as did Kupi. There were always government functionaries checking, making certain that citizens carried it.

The GSA leader looked down the long table, as if he were actually there. "It seems my old friend Kupi has been using her talents in unexpected ways. Congratulations on your heroic actions in shooting down an enemy aircraft."

Rising to her feet, Kupi said, "Thank you, Your Eminence. I only did my duty."

"But extraordinarily well. Undoubtedly you saved the Janus Machine and your entire crew." He waved his hands in such a way that passed the floor to her.

Just then a muffled explosion sounded, and several people pointed toward the window wall. On the other shore of the seaway, a ball of flame rose into the night sky. More explosions followed, and more fireballs.

"CanAm Field!" a man shouted, running to the window. Joss and other diners joined him.

Another man said it was a military base, which Joss already knew. He could see that aircraft had exploded on the ground over there, counted half a dozen fireballs. Two vertical-lift planes took off from the airfield, GSA craft that went straight up in the air and then circled the base. Moments later, a flurry of GSA fighter planes took off on parallel runways, and Joss saw that whatever was happening seemed to be confined to the six destroyed aircraft that were still burning. Alarm sirens wailed over there, and spotlights illuminated the airfield and the sky.

Within minutes, the air was full of GSA aircraft, including police copters. Some aircraft circled the field, while others buzzed low over it, their weapons systems glowing.

"The situation is under control," Chairman Rahma said. "I just received a report that we already have the saboteurs in custody. They will be questioned and executed in due course. Now, let us return to tonight's festivities. My time is valuable, and I must stay on schedule."

Feeling unease, Joss returned to his seat.

When everyone was in their place, Kupi began her presentation. With impressive clarity, she spoke at length about what their typical day was like on a Janus Machine crew, splitting and greenforming, traveling from one blighted site to another, reversing the ravages of industrialization and human selfishness.

She spoke as well about her recent battle exploits, and of an attempt that was made to destroy their J-Mac several weeks before, using a flying, radio-controlled bomb—a device that was detected and disabled by an alert Greenpol patrol.

Then, just as she was about to sit back down and turn the discussion over to Joss, she straightened and said, "Oh, did I mention? My commander and I are lovers now, because His Green Eminence, our venerated Chairman Rahma Popal, will not have me any longer."

On the other end of the table, a loud guffaw arose from the EVR projection, and his face lit up in mirth. "Is that so? As I recall, it was the other way around. Oh well, no matter, we have both moved on with our lives."

"Perhaps," Kupi said, "but sometimes the human heart has a longing apart from the intellect, and distinct from reality."

"You are far too kind, dear lady," he said.

The servers began bringing in miniature bowls of seafood chowder, spicy carrot soup, and artistically crafted hors d'oeuvres from the adjacent kitchen, and even placed portions in front of the Chairman's simulation, before he waved his hands impatiently and called attention to their error. Flustered, a server removed the items from his place and hurried away.

The dinner guests chatted and ate generous portions. Joss noted that a number of them sat quite far from the table, because of their girth. Each course had a different wine served with it, building up from interesting whites to richer, more complex reds. There were two centerpieces to the meal—one a vegan casserole and the other a meat dish, which the elite of society and deserving J-Mac crews were permitted to eat on occasion. As Joss looked down the table at the EVR of the Chairman, he thought the man—who always touted animal rights—looked uncomfortable with the menu, though he said nothing of it.

The meat tray was, in fact, grotesquely large, carried by four waiters and containing racks of lamb Provençal, which the chef announced had been prepared in the old country way with lots of garlic and subtle spices, as his granmère from the ancient Eurikan village of St. Paul de Vence had taught him. The lamb was to Joss's and Kupi's liking, because they'd had their fill of protein substitutes while on duty.

When the sumptuous meal was almost over, including a delicate mango flambé and a complementary aperitif, Joss rose to his feet and prepared to speak. Most of the diners did not seem to notice him standing there, because they continued to drink and chatter.

He felt a flush of warmth in his cheeks, from alcohol and from the revelation about his personal relationship with Kupi Landau. He didn't like others knowing details of his private life, though he imagined that his association with the Black Shirt woman must have already been common knowledge. Even so, the bluntness of her revelation had taken him by surprise, and during the entire meal he'd been wondering how to respond to it. It didn't anger him against her; he still cared for her, but it was one more thing that told him how different they were, and how a long-term relationship between them would be nigh impossible. As he stood there, he felt his ties to her stretching thinner, and knew they would sever entirely one day.

Once, long ago, it seemed to him, Joss had been truly in love. It had been in his late teens, with a girl he'd met at one of the most prestigious environmental academies in the GSA. In terms of years, that had not been so far in the past (a bit over a decade), and the time he'd spent with Onaka Hito had been sweet, though entirely too short. Of Japanese descent, she had taught him many things about her people in Panasia, their ancient traditions and arts. The two of them had clicked from the moment they locked gazes on each other; it had been a thing known without the necessity of words.

They'd shared a room and the most intimate of moments, physical, spiritual, emotional, and even intellectual, as they were both members of the Earth Rescue Force, an idealistic environmental group that published an anti-corporate newsletter and was involved in fund-raising efforts for progressive causes.

After knowing Onaka for a few weeks, she'd confided to him that her father's business interests in the old country were on the decline because he'd fallen out of favor with the Panasian government, and was not getting the lucrative military manufacturing contracts that had once been almost a birthright to him—going back for generations in his family, as they took advantage of the spheres of power and influence.

One evening when he came home after school, Joss found Onaka sitting on the edge of their bed, weeping softly. "Something is terribly wrong," she said. "I have not heard from my family for nearly a week, and that cannot be good."

He'd tried to reassure her that she was mistaken, that they were just busy, but she would not hear any of it. The very next morning, a holo-net message arrived from her elder brother. Her hands had been shaking as she retrieved it. Then, as she read it, tears welled up in her eyes and she fell to her knees, sobbing uncontrollably. Her father, having lost the entire family fortune, had stabbed Onaka's mother to death and had then committed ritual suicide by disemboweling himself with a samurai sword—a weapon that had been passed on in his family for eight centuries, since the days of the earliest shoguns in the twelfth century. The murder and suicide were devastating to the girl, who had been close to both of her parents, and especially to her mother.

Despondent and inconsolable, Onaka had made arrangements to return home for the funeral services. Days and weeks passed after she left, and then months. At first her letters had contained financial and other excuses for not coming back to the Green States. Then, gradually, her correspondence had stopped entirely, and he'd lost touch with her. He hoped she was happy, that she'd found a way to continue her life, and even that she'd found someone to love. But losing her had been a crushing blow to Joss, and he'd been a long time recovering. He wasn't sure if he ever would, not entirely. She'd been the love of his life. . . .

In the back of his mind, Joss heard one of the dinner guests talking, and Kupi's voice, describing an aspect of her daily work schedule, and the important environmental restoration work she and her fellow crew members were doing.

Kupi said something to Joss, and he nodded, coming out of his somber, drifting thoughts. The diners had grown quiet, and were looking at him.

"I am indeed fortunate to manage my particular J-Mac team," he said to his table companions. "As a boy, before this marvelous technology was known, I had no idea I would ever hold such an important position." He dipped his head in reverence to Rahma Popal. "It is my goal to never disappoint my Chairman or my country."

"Don't worry about that," said one of the wealthy men at the table, "just don't disappoint Kupi in bed."

Joss found the comment irritating, but Kupi raised a wineglass beside him and said, "That can never happen. Trust me, it can't."

"That is not what we are here to discuss," Joss said, scowling for a moment. "And, though Kupi's descriptions of our daily duties are eloquent, she has often told me that nothing can take the place of actually being there." He looked at the maître d', asked, "Our Janus Machine is ready?"

"It is, sir."

Joss and Kupi led the way outside and down a lamppost-illuminated walkway that led to the bank of the seaway. A barge was tied there in the dark water, with their own Janus Machine No. 129 secured to its deck. The two of them stepped aboard and donned their owl-design helmets, then put on their goggles and climbed up to the wide turret platform. Other members of the crew were already at their stations.

"We're like circus performers for these progressive dandies," she said to Joss, out of their earshot. "But instead of animals doing the tricks, it's us."

Joss nodded. Her choice of words was often harsh, but he had to agree with her this time.

Almost everyone from dinner had followed them down, even some of the serving staff and the lifelike virtual image of Chairman Rahma Popal. Members of the J-Mac crew moved a clearplex barrier into place to protect the observers, and specialists cleared raccoons, deer, and other animals from the grounds with sonic devices.

A short distance downshore, the target had been marked with orange paint—a series of old cabins on the riverbank where the staff of the club used to live. Kupi fired up the Splitter, causing the black barrel to glow along with a low, mounting roar—and then she cut loose with waves of black energy particles, splitting and melting the structures into gray, gummy masses on the shore. Moments later, Joss swung the platform around and let fly with his greenforming Seed Cannon, spewing cartridges into the air and detonating them with sparkles of green in the night, scattering seeds that would soon begin growing a native ground cover.

Behind the observation barrier, the dignitaries clapped and cheered.

As Joss finished, he joined Kupi on the turret platform and they waved to everyone, while the applause continued. "These are a bunch of limousine liberals," she said to him, "unscrupulous people who have used the Green Revolution to line their pockets with cash. Rahma only accepts the new elite grudgingly for the sake of green manufacturing and services, and I know he's tried to rein in the excesses. But he's changed since the revolution, lost some of the idealism I remember in him."

"That's understandable," Joss said. "He's getting old."

"Maybe we should split and greenform this whole stinking group," Kupi said, "to remove bad elements from the human gene pool. Our Chairman is always talking about creating a more perfect, unselfish human being. Well, we can give him a boost in the right direction, and greenform the pile of slime that's left over."

"That would *not* be a good idea," Joss said.

The auburn-haired woman looked at him, her eyes feral and sensual, in a way that he recognized. "All right," she said, "I have a better idea anyway."

9

Eco-crimes are worse than any others, bar none. Compare them with the rape of a person, for example, or murder—or any number of other traditional crimes. But all of them pale in comparison with the rape and murder of a planet—and that is what eco-crimes are, causing the destruction of a beautiful, sacred thing. This is the worst sort of crime, ravishing the Earth Mother who gave birth to human life. What can possibly be more contemptible, and what penalty must mankind pay for this?

—Commentaries, Charter of the Green States of America, March 17, 2043

DYLAN BANE STOOD at the center of the command bridge of the great machine, watching the bright purple webwork of light around the hull as it bored through the mantle of the earth at more than seven hundred kilometers per hour, passing through all types of rock and soil as if they were not obstacles at all, and then closing the tunnels behind. He heard the faint, high-pitched keening of the process.

Around him, silver-uniformed officers and crew members worked the controls of the subterranean craft, using powerful ground-penetrating radar to guide the way—making course corrections based on this, while taking into account the ground-mapping data they had accumulated from prior journeys. This voleer machine could pass through earth, rock, underground springs, and even magma, though the pilots made efforts to avoid the latter because high ambient temperatures expended more fuel in the cooling process.

Bane had eighteen of these great machines now, all of them a clever adaptation of the secret splitting and greenforming technologies that the SciOs guarded so closely, and upon which they based their power structure. Like a huge underground submarine with no conning tower, the voleer was a tube as long as ten soccer fields and as high as a three-story building. From his vantage on the forward slope of the hull, he not only had a view outward, but inward as well, through clearplex decking to the huge, mostly empty cargo hold.

He smiled to himself, certain that he would eventually bring the loathsome SciOs crashing down, along with Chairman Rahma Popal, using secret machines like this one to transport troops and war equipment. But he had to implement his guerrilla plan precisely, based on exquisite planning. There was no room for mistakes, such as those made by others in the attacks on Bostoner and Quebec. Those were small-time military assaults, no more than bee stings on the corpus of the Green government that were soon healed. When Bane finally made his move, it would be much, much bigger.

As soon as an additional twenty-seven voleers were completed and fully tested, he would have forty-five great machines back at his base camp in central Mexico, filled with armaments and fighters—enough to attack and retreat in numerous places, disappearing into the ground at will. It would drive enemy commanders crazy trying to figure out a way to retaliate, and before they could respond, all of their forces would crumble into dust, along with the vile hippie government.

And none of them would understand how it had happened. Though he had been raised in a well-to-do Corporate family, in his youth he had refused to follow in his father's footsteps with Bane Enterprises, a company that manufactured plastic bottles. He'd loved his parents, but had seen the environmental damage caused by plastic, and didn't want to earn money from that source. As a result, he'd pursued his own interests and developed his own talents, going to work for a laboratory in California and earning his way as a research scientist.

For years Dylan Bane had gone to work every day, staying with the laboratory when it was taken over by the post-revolution SciOs, and ultimately becoming one of their most trusted researchers. This résumé had served him well later when his family came under attack for their activities. He alone had survived among them.

Now he glanced over at Marissa Chase as the young officer approached him. "Within three hundred kilometers of the Buenos Aires Reservation for Humans," she reported, with a crisp salute. "Making our final course correction to Delta Fifty-seven."

Bane grunted, looked away. He had no time for his customary thoughts about the attractive woman. Moments later, the ship came to a grinding stop inside a large underground cavern that was quite deep and high, considerably larger than the voleer.

As hatches slid open he heard a buzzing over the rumble of the idling voleer engines, and saw the inside of the Delta 57 cavern, an expanse that was full of shipping containers that hovered in the air like giant bricks, each of them remote-controlled and self-propelled. In the midst of these containers flew tiny, black, bumblebee-shaped guideships, each with a human operator inside, for the purpose of air-traffic control and loading efficiency in the confined airspace.

Looking at the black chrono embedded in the skin of his wrist—a mechanism that had the appearance of a tattoo with the numerals in motion—Dylan Bane set the timer on the multifunction device for eighteen minutes, which sent a transmission throughout the ship and cavern, synchronizing the loading operations. He needed to get loaded and be on his way quickly. This was not just a practice maneuver, though that was part of the reason for the trip to the Argentine Territory of the Green States of America. He had another purpose in mind as well, one of equal importance. His operatives in this region had been accumulating essential materials, soldiers, and military equipment.

On missions such as this one over the past several months, using a number of voleer tunneling machines, he'd been making clandestine trips to obtain assets that he needed for the war effort—taking military personnel and matériel back to Michoacán. His far-flung martial operations were completely underground and electronically veiled, in multiple locations linked by vanishing tunnels, bases that could be reached quickly by machines that regenerated rock and earth behind them, leaving no apparent tunnels in their wake.

Around the sides of the immense vessel and on top of it, cargo hatches slid open and containers sped aboard, stacking and interlocking themselves in the holds, sometimes adjusted by the pilots of the tiny guideships. A number of the self-propelled containers held soldiers who had passed through Bane's stringent security-screening procedures and selective memory wipes—and these troops were loaded into a separate cargo hold, where they could leave the boxes and move into more comfortable quarters. But first, they had to be loaded aboard quickly and efficiently.

It had not been difficult to obtain conscripts from disaffected people who had been forced into adverse conditions by the radical GSA government and its severe environmental and human-relocation policies. The trick was to get the right people under the right circumstances, and put them to the best possible use. Though Bane had his own harsh methods, at least he valued *people* and what they could contribute—unlike the fascist Chairman and his animal-loving, tree-hugging legions.

He watched the minutes and seconds pass, then saw yellow lights flash in the cavern, indicating that they had only two minutes for all outside personnel and equipment to get clear of the vessel before it relaunched. A mad scramble of guide-ships and unloaded containers ensued—bumping into one another as they tried to pull back to the perimeter of the cavern, not nearly as smoothly as Bane had seen in other secret caverns he had in the Americas.

At precisely the eighteen-minute mark, the immense voleer closed all exterior hatches and surged ahead, leaving the cavern behind and intact, except for those guideship and container occupants who didn't get clear in time.

For those who survived, he would order more drills.

10

For reasons of patriotism, children are encouraged to report their parents, relatives, and friends for violations of the law. Throughout history certain governments have understood this, and so shall we, when it comes to dealing with criminals. Children, hear me! The state is your family, and I am your true father.

—Chairman Rahma Popal, remarks to the
First Assembly of the GSA on Earth Day 2043

AS JOSS CROSSED the continent by train from the Quebec Territory, he scanned a holo-net card from his Uncle Trig asking him how he was doing, and when they might get together—a message that had been delivered to him by an automated system that lowered it from the ceiling. Uncle Trig Stuart lived alone on the Salt Lake City Reservation, his wife, Gertie, having died the year before. Joss spoke in a low tone to the card that hovered in front of him, watched his own words appear in the reply section. Just a few comments about where he'd been and how he didn't expect to be in Salt Lake City for several more months. He didn't say so, but it could be even longer than that; his important job was keeping him very busy, and he didn't want to interrupt his career by asking for too much time off.

After completing the message, he watched it seem to melt into the ceiling, for transmission back to his uncle. It was after dinner, and daylight was waning, fading like a ghost into the approaching darkness.

He tuned out the conversations around him, watched the scenery whir by outside. Joss couldn't recall ever having seen so many pristine mountains, lakes, wetlands, and evergreen trees as there were on this route. Truly, it was stimulating for him, and gave him some hope for the future of what the Chairman called "the wounded planet."

It seemed odd to Joss that he and Kupi had witnessed two attacks against GSA military installations in the last few days, first in Bostoner and then in Quebec. He'd commented on this to her, but she'd said it was just happenstance. There were always attacks around the country, caused by Corporate interests, criminals living in the wilderness, and other groups that didn't like Rahma's new form of government, one that was unlike any in the history of human civilization.

At one time, this northern region of the Green States of America had been part of Canada. Even before the massive, ragtag revolution against the Corporates, it had been one of the nations that showed concern for the environment, and took steps to protect it. Most of that impetus, however, came from the common people, and less so from the government, and only grudgingly from Canadian and multinational Corporate interests that had operations in the country. When the Chairman's regime took over, this region still needed considerable cleaning up, but not nearly on the scale of the blighted regions to the south.

The maglev train in which Joss rode could have completed the four-thousand-kilometer journey in less than a day, but it made stops along the way to drop off some of the Janus Machine crews and their machinery at work sites. He and his crew had not been among those with assignments, owing to the demanding schedule of splitting and greenforming they'd already endured in the east. As a reward for their hard work they were bound for their homes in the Seattle Reservation and a brief vacation. Within the hour, they had just returned from a sumptuous dinner in the dining car, and Joss still felt the warmth of roast pork and a fine Pomerol wine in his belly.

At the moment, Kupi sat across from him at a passenger compartment table, dealing samba cards to him as well as to two other male members of their crew, the tall, jocular J-Mac driver Bim Hendrix and an aging mechanic for the non-proprietary vehicle systems, Sabe McCarthy. The deck of cards had photos of filthy, smoke-belching industrial sites on the backs, each with a red line across it; other decks depicted notorious Corporate tycoons, eco-criminals, and Army of the Environment military victories.

"Doesn't it ever strike you as curious that we get to eat meat," Kupi asked, "while hundreds of millions of other people are told to eat protein substitutes?"

"Not at all," McCarthy said. "We work our butts off for the state, and deserve the few perks we get. We put in longer hours than other folks, get more important work done."

"Right," Hendrix said, picking up his cards and sorting his hand quickly. "Kind of makes you wonder, though, doesn't it? What if we got fired and had to eat regular food?"

"Pray to Green that never happens," Kupi said.

"The sarcasm of Kupi Landau," McCarthy said, scowling as he studied his cards.

"Be careful," Kupi said with a tight smile, "I do have a talent for violence."

"And for dealing bad cards," McCarthy said.

Annoyed, Kupi narrowed her gaze and stared hard at him.

"Enough of that," Joss said. "Let's save our hostilities for industrial sites, OK?" He didn't like the way the conversation was going. His crew had been on the road for nearly a month, and with the accumulated fatigue, emotions had a tendency to get raw.

Grunts of affirmation passed around the table, and the samba game proceeded. Fortunately for Kupi's state of mind, she made a number of good draws and captured the pot, which enabled her to meld cards on the table. As her simulated wealth accumulated she began to smirk at McCarthy, but he didn't react.

The train slowed down on its maglev rail. Joss heard two bells over the public address system, followed by a woman's voice. "The signaler is routing us onto a siding, ladies and gentlemen, to wait for a relocation train to pass."

"It has the right of way," Hendrix said.

Everyone at the table knew that. Relocation trains were full of people who were being moved from their previous homes in polluted areas onto new reservations for humans that were being constructed as massive public works projects, with much of the labor performed by convicts. Due to the rushed construction schedules there had been many safety-related deaths—but to justify that, the Chairman said the program was a priority even higher than the work of Janus Machine crews, since dense population centers harmed the environment much less than sprawled developments and their infrastructures. Because of high demand for reservation space as they continued to be built, however, many people were confined to their previous towns and cities, or placed in rudimentary containment camps under armed guard—until something opened up for them.

Looking at a viewing screen on one end of the passenger car, Joss saw images of a long train approaching from the rear, speeding around a curve of tracks. Guided by maglev engineers, hundreds of shabby, green, windowless boxcars thundered by, causing Joss's train to shake and shudder. Out the window, he saw the train disappear into the distance. Thousands and thousands of people were crammed inside those cars. He'd seen relocation trains before and didn't like to think about conditions inside them—except he assumed the high-speed maglev trips were short.

A government information video appeared on the passenger car's wallscreen, showing the various methods of relocation, including trains like the one ahead of them and huge transport aircraft that carried thousands of people at a time. The planes looked pregnant with their big bellies full of people.

The image switched to a utopian reservation for humans, showing crowds of people going about their daily business with saccharine smiles on their faces. "Historically these northern territories have been sparsely populated," a female announcer said, "and now hundreds of millions of people are being relocated here. 'Relocation is good. Relocation is green.'" It was one of the mantras.

DOUG RIDELL HAD a full schedule, going to apartments in the more prestigious districts of the Missoula Reservation, maintaining and repairing the robots of privileged citizens who were above his own station. He wore a pale green work coverall and a backpack filled with tools.

He considered his new job something of a promotion, though there had been no talk of a pay increase or providing his family with more benefits, and he could only wait to be notified about such things. But for the most part he had been enjoying the reassignment, despite having no previous experience dealing with the public, with their varying personalities and moods.

On the forty-second floor of a gleaming, glass-walled apartment building, Ridell placed his hand-held précis against a scanner on a tenant's door. After confirming his identity, a fashionable woman let him in; he knew her name from the assignment log: Mrs. Kristine Longet. An attractive blonde with a figure that filled her expensive clothing nicely, she was perhaps forty-five or fifty, with cold blue eyes and an icy expression that exuded superiority.

"I thought you would be here an hour ago," she said.

"Sorry, ma'am, I have a real busy schedule today." He smelled expensive incense, a subtle fragrance that was much more sophisticated than the common variety.

She arched her eyebrows in displeasure. "Our cleaning bot has been down for more than three days, causing us all sorts of discomforts. We have allergies to dust, you know."

"I'm sorry to hear that, ma'am, but we'll have the little guy up and working in short order."

"Either that or I want a new one."

As the stylish woman led him through a corridor and then into a comfortable living room, Ridell looked around in envy at all the things her family had. The apartment was at least twice as big as his own, with expensive gem-beads hanging in the doorways that made a gentle tinkling sound as they passed through them. The living room was filled with leisure technology, and one wall featured images of drum circle percussionists, playing repeated patterns. The furniture was all post-revolution and high-end, with ornately stitched patriotic slogans on the tan cushions of the couch, fancy dispersion lamps that used hardly any energy, and a long decorator table on one wall, containing a very realistic-looking model of a Janus Machine, complete with crew.

"Over there," she said, pointing to the non-functioning household robot in one corner. A metal mound with soft bumpers around the perimeter, the unit had a golden sensor array encircling its body and a standard panel box on top, with a remote-control unit in a slot. The machine's undercarriage was low to the floor.

"Does your robot have a name?" he asked, kneeling and looking inside the panel box. He removed his backpack, brought out a test bundle, and connected it to the circuitry.

"A name? Whatever do you mean?"

"Some families name their robots, sort of an affectionate thing to do." Ridell watched the small screen on the test bundle as the device ran through its program, looking for the problem. While waiting for the results, he checked the unit's remote transmitter.

"It's just a machine," she said. "Name a robot?" She paused, and seemed to soften a little. "I suppose I *have* heard of people doing that, but it makes no sense to me. I just want what the machine does for me, the product of its work; I don't want to imagine it's a family member, a little friend, or anything like that."

"I see."

The woman was a bit haughty, knowing that she occupied a social station well above his own mid-green status. But she seemed to be making an effort to be pleasant. As he worked, she mentioned that she was also having trouble with her food preparation machine, and asked if he could fix it, too.

Even though he could probably repair that unit, it was not in his job description, and there were strict union rules against performing tasks that were the domain of other union shops. He didn't explain all of that to her, though, and just said, "Sorry, I only know how to service cleaning bots. You'll need to turn in another work request."

"Oh, very well."

The test bundle reported a problem with the servo-motor synchronization, causing the bot to shut down to prevent damage. He made adjustments inside the panel, then flipped the unit over and checked the undercarriage wheels, sensors, and suction devices. Then, removing the remote-control unit from its slot, he dispatched the robot to clean the room. Whirring smoothly, it ran over the carpets and synthetic wood floors, then up the wide legs of a table and, perching on top, it used extension arms and blowers to dust carefully around a replica Ming vase and an electronic image in a picture frame.

The framed image was locked in place, and caught Ridell's eye. It showed a pretty young redhead standing with a green-robed Chairman Rahma, suggesting that this family had high connections.

Noticing the direction of his gaze, Mrs. Longet said proudly, "My daughter Dori is a close adviser to our beloved Chairman Rahma. That picture was taken earlier this year."

"At the Montana Valley Game Reserve?" he asked.

"Of course. That is his home and headquarters, and Dori works for him there."

"Well, what a coincidence! My daughter Jade is with our beloved Chairman at the game reserve, too—recently joined him." Then, feeling a sudden camaraderie with the woman, he extended a hand to her and added, "It's nice to meet another parent."

Dori's mother froze up, looked askance at the hand as if it were dirty, and did not shake. "Mr. Ridell, you get whatever Chairman Rahma says you get, so don't try to curry favor with me! Just complete your work here and be on your way."

Red-faced, he completed the task of checking the robot, while wishing he knew how to program the machine to strangle this arrogant, condescending woman. In a matter of minutes he was out the door and into the hallway, his thoughts punctuated by the sound of the door closing securely behind him, and the clicking of the security locks.

He hurried away, hoping he never had to see her again.

JOSS'S TRAIN GOT under way again, and accelerated to a high rate of speed.

A short while later, it came to another stop, and this time Joss could see why without being told. The relocation train had turned onto a sidetrack, but many of its boxcars at the rear were still on the main track, blocking it. To the right of the long train, he saw a huge containment camp, a fenced area where people were kept until reservation space could be found for them.

Doors on most of the green rail cars opened, and people streamed out of them, carrying their meager possessions. There were adults with children, and children carrying their little brothers or sisters. Joss recoiled in surprise and revulsion at the conditions he saw in the camp where they were being herded—a sprawl of improvised shacks and tents, with open sewage ditches running between them and children playing in the squalor. Couldn't the GSA government provide better facilities for its citizens? He'd never seen anything like this, hadn't imagined it could possibly be this bad.

"Kind of makes that dinner turn over in your stomach, doesn't it?" Sabe McCarthy said.

Joss felt like saying something too, but just stared out the window, disgusted and transfixed. He heard shouting that sounded like it was coming from inside his own train, from one of the forward cars. Just then the doors thumped open at the front of his car and a man in ragged clothing ran through, chased by two black-uniformed soldiers. One of the anarchists drew and fired, dropping the man in the aisle by Joss. The man wasn't dead and didn't appear to bleed, so they must have used a stunner on him. He looked groggy as they dragged him away and out of the coach. Joss saw a growing number of Revolutionary Guardsmen outside along the track, all wearing shiny black helmets with green tree emblems, and gleaming black jackboots.

"It's a wild, rough country out here," Bim Hendrix said.

Now several more boxcars at the rear of the relocation train opened up, and Joss saw people pour and tumble out, shackled adults in prison garb. A few resisted and shouted protests, but to no avail. The others looked numb and stumbled along, doing as they were told. All were herded by the anarchists onto a barren, raised clearing.

A squadron of anarchists appeared, marching in formation from the front of the relocation train. They carried Splitter rifles.

"Uh-oh," Sabe McCarthy said. "I've seen this before." He slapped his cards down on the table, rose to his feet. His face went ashen. "I'm going to my cabin."

Joss didn't move, felt so paralyzed that he was unable to even toss his hand of cards on the table. He suspected what was going to happen next, but had only heard rumors about it before. So it was true! He hated to think of it.

The prisoners stood on a surface that looked like it had been split previously, leaving a hardened gray amalgam that had not been greenformed, an apparent killing field of bodily remains. In the background, he heard the government announcer describe nonchalantly how roving bands of scofflaws were pursued and rounded up in the wilds, and how most of them could "never be rehabilitated."

A shudder ran down Joss's back. They were going to be recycled.

Outside, the anarchist squad pointed their Splitter guns at the prisoners and fired little bursts of black death. For a lingering moment the hapless prisoners were outlined in black like a macabre art piece. Then they disintegrated and crumbled into a horrific, gooey conglomeration on the ground.

Sickened, Joss looked away, into the face of Kupi across the table.

She did not appear to be pleased by what they'd just seen, yet she nodded toward the killing field and said, "Some things are unavoidable for the greater good."

Joss nodded, but inwardly he could not agree. Later he would think back on this moment many times, and would identify it as one of the turning points in his life.

11

It was so easy to discover bad things about large corporations, and so difficult to find anything good. As just one example of their transgressions, the major corporations provided only a tiny percentage of the employment in the United States, but were plundering a much higher percentage of human and planetary resources. The bottom line was, they contributed the minimum and took the maximum.

—Chairman Rahma Popal, Commentaries

CHAIRMAN RAHMA STOOD at the balcony railing outside his third-floor office, feeling the warmth of afternoon sunlight on his gray-bearded face. The greensward stretched into the distance, with its wetlands and grazing pastures for buffalo, elk, and other animals—a pastoral view that was edged by evergreen forests extending from the valley up to the mountains. Several hundred meters to the left, he saw the net- and fabric-covered aviaries and the adjacent clearplex-and-alloy greenhouses, a network of connected structures that were filled with endangered species of birds and plants.

In the other direction stood the Shrine of Martyrs, a black marble mausoleum where ten of Rahma's fallen comrades from the revolution were entombed. Their electronic images adorned the interior walls, and there were reliquaries for each hero containing some of their personal things—a piece of uniform fabric, a ring, a watch, a pair of eyeglasses, a little book of haiku, a lock of hair, and the like. Rahma used the shrine as a private sanctuary, where he could visit with his dead comrades and honor them. There were hundreds of facsimiles of the shrine around the GSA (all built to scale), for the use of the public.

He had just finished a sparse vegan lunch and midday tryst with Jade Ridell, a young redhead he had invited to become one of the women living in his personal compound. She was pretty and had a cheerful personality, as well as considerable intelligence, though he didn't think she could ever be a threat to his favorite for the past two years, Dori Longet, or to Valerie Tatanka, the doctor at the clinic who was also his lover.

At his desk inside, he'd just read several reports, one on the Quebec attack that took place two days ago. Half a dozen Army warplanes had been destroyed there by a small rebel group, one that didn't seem to have any Corporate financing. The saboteurs had been questioned and summarily executed.

Another report concerned the much more troubling Bostoner attack that took place four days ago. A pair of enemy combatants who survived had been interrogated. One had refused to answer questions and had died during the grilling process; the other had received a serious head wound in the battle, and had lapsed into a coma. Yesterday, however, the man began slipping in and out of consciousness, mumbling incomplete sentences with unintelligible words, such as "voleer," and references to something that sounded like "VT digging technology," which Rahma's investigators and engineers suspected had something to do with the craft burrowing underground.

Thus far, no one understood how the mysterious burrowing machine worked, because it had been detonated by a self-destruct mechanism. There had been evidence of a place where the machine emerged from the ground, but further investigation of the site had revealed nothing more. Had it been hidden there and dug its way out for the sneak attack, like a desert fighter hiding in sand and leaping out to strike? That sounded like the most plausible explanation, but if the attackers had buried the sizable machine there, how had they eluded detection from satellites? Weather patterns were being analyzed in detail now, to see if there had been extended periods in which visibility from orbital space might have been impaired. With no more answers yet, Chairman Rahma tried to think of something else.

As he gazed out on the broad expanse of greenery and the snowcapped mountains, he could almost envision an entire planet like his cherished game reserve, much the way it had been millions of years ago. How marvelous that would be! In his mind's eye he imagined vast forestlands as well as mountains, rivers, lakes, and seas, all undamaged by mankind in his self-seeking, relentless drive to hold domain over every aspect of Earth and its resources.

In his boyhood Rahma had imagined becoming a dedicated environmentalist one day, working to preserve nature habitats for future generations of humankind to enjoy. By the time he reached his teens he came to realize, however, that his goals were too small and that his focus on humanity was wrong, that his thoughts were being filtered by a worldview that had proven harmful to the Earth. He became politically active, after deciding that he had to think on a much larger scale, and that he wanted to reverse the historical course of ecological ruination by man, in whatever way he could. In the process he developed a more mature worldview, in which people mattered only to the extent that they could protect and enhance nature. He often reminded himself that his own life no longer mattered, except to advance the restoration of the planet.

His involvement with the street revolution and the Berkeley

Eight revolutionary council had been momentous in his life, enabling him to disseminate his ideas to a wide audience. The subsequent work he had performed as Chairman of the Green States of America had been a stepping-stone in a larger plan in which he hoped to expand greenification to other regions around the world. But entrenched Corporate and other political interests held foreign lands in such vise grips that he had grown to think that it might be impossible to ever expand beyond the Americas, and that he would have his hands full maintaining what he had accomplished here. Every day he received reports of guerrilla tactics being employed against GSA interests—hit-and-run attacks that often did not result in the perpetrators being killed, caught, or even identified.

He regretted the human deaths that resulted from forcing more than a billion people to relocate, but the tens of millions who died were either weak or resisted. Their ongoing deaths were not his fault, and he felt very little personal guilt over them.

This planet comes first, he thought.

Going back inside his office, the Chairman saw a red light flashing on his bamboo desk, in a code that indicated he had a visitor waiting for him. He voice-activated the door to his outer office, and it slid open with almost no sound. The trusted hubot Artie stood in the open doorway, looking in with the eyes of the Chairman's dead friend Glanno Artindale. "You have a visitor," the hybrid said, in a throaty voice that approximated that of Glanno.

"I have no appointments scheduled this afternoon."

"We thought you would want to see this one, Eminence. It is Director Ondex and one of his subordinates."

"Ondex again? What does he want this time?"

"He would not tell me, only said it was a matter that he could discuss only with you."

Rahma Popal's shoulders sagged. "Very well. Send the bastard in."

Moments later, the tall, patrician man marched in, followed by a female assistant in a white gown and two Greenpol officers carrying their helmets. The assistant had a large volume under one arm.

The Chairman exchanged signs of the sacred tree with Ondex, then sat at his desk. The visitors remained standing.

"You have not yet submitted your identification package for the genetic database," Ondex said.

Rahma smiled. "A joke? A bit of amusement? Why are you really here?"

The Director of Science scowled. "No joke, Eminence. It is required."

"Don't be absurd! I do not need to submit an identification package! I am the Chairman of the Green States of America!"

Ondex snapped his fingers, and the assistant handed the thick volume to him. Rahma noticed that it was a federal law book.

Opening it to a marked page, Ondex read, "'For the good of the GSA, every citizen must comply with identification procedures.'"

"You SciOs don't run the ID database," Rahma said. "Greenpol does, and need I remind you? *I* control the police." He nodded to the officers, but they were looking at the floor, not at him.

Ondex smiled. "But under the GSA Charter, every branch of government—including mine—has access to the police database."

"You're going over the line now, you nitpicking SOB. You tend to your duties, and I'll tend to mine."

"Since you helped draft the law, you should understand it better than anyone. Aren't you a citizen of the GSA?"

"Of course, but—"

"Then you must submit cell samples to the DNA bank, along with details of other identifying features of your body. This should have been done years ago."

The Chairman shook his head, but more out of dismay than anything else. The genetic database had been his own idea, so that his Greenpol forensic pathologists could study the brains and cellular material of eco-criminals and other miscreants, to come up with medical treatments that would prevent the living from repeating their crimes—drugs, brain wipes, genetic reprogramming. But his researchers were having trouble coming up with useful patterns or treatments, and Rahma had been considering abandoning the program.

"All right," he said, in exasperation. "If the bureaucracy must be fed, let's get it over with."

Ondex closed the volume, and snapped his fingers crisply.

The Greenpol officers stepped past the Director of Science and stood on either side of Rahma Popal. One took cell scrapings from the skin on his arm and neck, along with fingerprints, and snippets of gray hair from the back of his head. The other officer performed retina scans and caliper readings of Rahma's ears and nose and took a series of photographs of his face from several angles. Then both of them performed thermal imaging of his brain, using scanners that cast varying colors of light on different portions of his cranium. After that, they ran another scanner over his clothing, picking up all the details of his body.

"I feel like I'm being arrested by my own police," the Chairman said, as he watched the officers accumulate the information and mark off a checklist on an electronic clip pad.

"In view of your high position, Eminence, no one would

object if you supplement this with updated information from your doctor each time you have a physical examination," Ondex said.

"Well, don't you think of everything!"

Director Ondex narrowed his eyes and said, "Perhaps your information should be analyzed to form the basis of the perfect human being that you seek—one that reveres the planet Earth and takes every possible action to enhance nature."

"Ah," Rahma said, "but I'm not perfect and I've never claimed to be."

"Oh, but you are! At least, we've been led to believe that. You represent the ideal of goodness and selflessness, the ultimate and faultless human that you would like to create among your followers." His mouth twisted in a cruel smile. "Think of it—an entire race of Rahma Popals. I could put some of my own SciO researchers on it right away."

"Greenpol analyzes my ID package, not you."

Ondex bowed, but his eyes flashed in a way that made Rahma realize that he would do it anyway.

"It's a pity you can't read my thoughts from cell samples," Rahma said, "or you'd learn what I really think of you."

"I think you've made that abundantly clear," the SciO leader said. He moved toward the door, with his assistant close behind him. The two Greenpol officers hesitated, now awaiting instructions from the Chairman.

He nodded, said, "Go ahead and add my information to the database."

They bowed, and hurried off.

In a short time the data would be assembled and organized onto computer files, then loaded into the GSA genetic library system for distribution across the network. Every department in the government would have quick access to the identification package via terminals.

How ironic, Rahma thought, that a program of his own design had found a way to annoy him. And he wondered what, if anything, the researchers would discover when they analyzed his file. Under the Charter he had no way of stopping the process, or of reining it in.

The question was, what would the SciOs do with the information? Find some way to compare Rahma Popal with known eco-criminals? Was this part of a coup attempt?

He didn't want to believe that.

FOLLOWING THE MEETING, the Chairman and Artie took an elevator down to the lowest subterranean level beneath the game reserve, to a bunker that could not be blasted open by ground-penetrating bombs of any kind—not Splitter, nor conventional, nor nuclear. They strode past banks of computers inside clearplex, temperature-controlled chambers, with hubots, robots, and human technicians operating the controls. These terminals accessed databases of human genetic material, as well as Greenpol files on criminal activity throughout the nation's two continents.

The crime files were supposed to be complete copies of everything that Greenpol had in its files, updated moment by moment as new information was obtained and modified as a result of their forensic studies and other scientific investigations. Rahma saw the blinking lights and shifting tallies, the graphs that flashed across viewing screens as more surveillance and criminal information on GSA citizens was added constantly, and the files of the deceased were moved to other sections—more than a billion names of the living and dead, with more being added each moment. He was certain his own information was not in the system yet.

Continuing on, they passed the International Section,

which contained additional data on humankind that was collected by other police agencies around the world—much of the information Eurikan, and only a little of it Panasian—all shared with the GSA.

Greenpol officers and hubots assigned to the large bunker worked at the machines, bustling back and forth inside the clearplex enclosures and in the corridors as Rahma and Artie walked by.

The Chairman paused at a wide viewing window, where Greenpol officers busily tended to monitors that displayed reports on different types of criminals—Ecological, Corporate, Monetary, Violent, and others. There were overlaps among the categories, with some names appearing on more than one, but this was accounted for in statistical summaries.

"Give me the Most Wanted lists," Rahma said.

Touching his robotic hand to an interface on the wall, Artie used AI thought commands to bring up the required data, and display it on half a dozen screens that the Chairman could see. For each category of criminal behavior there were lists of names, and the faces of the most-wanted fugitives.

For a moment Rahma looked over the rogue's gallery of Corporate criminals, noting that some had no faces shown, because the perpetrators had been clever in covering their tracks. "Look at all of these files on criminals, with their devious, sneaky minds," he said. "If only more humans were like you, Artie, without guile or selfish cleverness. Truly, all of the worst is represented here in these files."

"Yes, Master, many of these are immoral minds. But data on great humans is archived here as well, and soon your own personal information will be included in the records, adding to the weight of good."

"Mmmm. Yes, Artie. Nice of you to say that."

"Would you like me to access thermal images of human

brains, to compare the cerebral cortexes of criminals with those of great people?"

"Not today, Artie."

"Master, if I may say so, I'm looking forward to seeing the information on your brain in the data system. There is much to be learned from you, in all respects."

"I am not without fault. I've admitted this many times before, to many people."

"But Master, if green were a full-blown religion, you would be a saint. Actually, a god."

Rahma chuckled, but said, "Environmentalism is not a real religion. It only has elements of similarity."

"Shall I list the similarities, Master?"

A long pause. Then: "No. My zealots accept the green mantra without questioning it, and many people refer to me as a green guru, or a minister preaching the gospel of green. There are other religious parallels as well, but I hope they are only temporary, until we can restore natural balance to the planet."

"You are right, Master. Might I recommend one exception to your 'temporary' comment, sir—the sacred tree? That is a very nice concept, an enduring symbol of ecology, and I think we should keep it."

"We'll find a way to do that, Artie."

"Very good, Master. I have already added our discussion to my data banks. Someday it will undoubtedly prove useful."

"It must be interesting for you to have access to so much information, Artie, so much more than you can possibly tell me, or reveal in the highlights you provide."

"I am interested in whatever I am programmed to be interested in."

"Of course you are." He patted the loyal hubot on his humanlike shoulder, marveled at how real he looked. He'd even seen women on the compound flirting with him, until they realized their mistake.

The Chairman then focused on another list, one that included the white-bearded, pockmarked image of Mord Pelley, one of the most notorious at-large eco-criminals. A former rancher in Texas, he lost his property to eminent domain and killed three government agents who tried to serve papers on him. Afterward he went renegade, and from hiding he charged that the government was a spoils system for revolutionaries who were misusing their authority, and profiting unfairly from it. Others (such as Rahma's ex-lover Kupi) had made similar remarks, but not nearly so vociferously or with as much vitriol.

Privately, Rahma thought that Pelley had been right about some of his criticisms, but he had not said so at the time and never would, because of the egregious crimes that the man had committed. Reportedly he was living in one of the North American wilderness regions, leading hundreds of followers in despoiling greeneries instead of remaining legally on one of the reservations for humans. Pelley was also an avowed Christian, a follower of one of the banned religions. There were no legal religions at all in the Green States of America. It was a one-hundred-percent secular state, with no exceptions, no loopholes.

Chairman Rahma sighed. He didn't have time to think too much about the reasons that people rebelled against his rules. He would rather retrain people who ran afoul of the law, but that was a lot of trouble. For some time now, he'd been thinking it would be easier to just have 99.9 percent of the GSA population recycled and be done with them—despite his regrets about killing people.

He moved on, leading Artie down the corridor.

His government had many failings. In order to form the Green States of America, Rahma had made concessions out of necessity, especially to the SciOs in gratitude for their contributions to the victory over the Corporates. But at times he wondered if the new system was really better than the old. As one of the adverse side effects of his greenocracy, he'd been noticing the emergence of power structures around him that mimicked decadent old systems that the Corporates and their predecessors had developed. Oligarchic systems that were intolerable to him, but he had not yet come up with a way of eliminating them without causing problems in relationships that were important to him.

It seemed to him that these familiar power structures were exceedingly human in their makeup, and that he could never prevent the worst aspects of human nature from constantly reasserting themselves.

To some extent he isolated himself from the nastiness of politics and vying personal interests by living on this game reserve and spending as much time as he could with the animals he loved so much. But he couldn't bury his head in the sand like the proverbial ostrich. He had to keep track of what was going on in his government.

The two of them walked past laboratories in which sick and injured animals were being treated, and a bank of separate elevator systems for the animals—to take them up to the surface when they were well enough to be released onto the preserve or taken to another site with more suitable environmental conditions.

Presently they paused in front of another genetic bank that the Chairman maintained separately from the one operated by Greenpol. This system, networked to other game reserves that were under GSA control, contained information on all of the animal species on earth, with the exception of humans, whom Chairman Rahma considered to be the most dangerous animal of all.

They spoke for a long while, and again Rahma expressed something that was always on his mind, either at the top of his awareness or near the top—his ongoing disappointment in mankind.

Considering this for a moment, Artie said, "Perhaps I am fortunate that only my eyes are human, Master."

12

The Corporates used an insidious form of social engineering on masses of people, enticing them to live in widespread suburbs and drive personal vehicles across vast networks of roadways. Our valiant leaders reversed that process on the American continents and eliminated the sprawling infrastructure, as well as internal-combustion engines. They also made great strides in changing the mentality of people who craved such things.

—a children's history primer

THOUGH JOSS AND Kupi had discussed living together during the past year, they maintained separate apartments in the Seattle Reservation for Humans, a few blocks apart. Each of them had government-assigned roommates to share their compact living units, though that could be altered if they completed a series of electronic reassignment applications and went through the approval process.

A year ago Kupi had mentioned the possibility that she could be in love with Joss, though he said he was not so certain of his own feelings. And besides that, Joss told her he wasn't sure how an anarchist could feel love for someone who didn't share her extreme belief system. In response, Kupi had insisted that her feelings for him were deep and "transcended" anything else. Thereafter, even without his commitment to her, she frequently said she loved him, and it had been making him uncomfortable.

His separate living arrangements from her were for the best, Joss had decided, because he'd been trying to find a way to tell her that the two of them were hopelessly different, and he didn't see how their personal relationship could continue. Finally, after she asked him repeatedly what his feelings for her were, and not getting a response that pleased her, Joss sensed that Kupi might be getting resentful. The last time they'd made love, before boarding the train for the final leg to Seattle, the experience had been awkward, without the usual ease and wild passion they had shared so many times before. But it was more than that, he believed strongly. They thought differently about so many issues that he'd lost count.

Above all, Kupi could never possibly replace the lost love of his life, Onaka Hito, who had loved him so briefly, with such grace and beauty, and then had vanished back to her distant home in Panasia.

Joss intended to discuss the situation with Kupi the following day, when they went on an eco-tourism trip that was being given to them as a bonus for their hard work on the Janus Machine crew. Other members of the crew had selected different bonuses, so they would not be with them. It would be a semi-automated flight with no pilot or other passengers, so Joss and Kupi would have time to talk while they exercised on machines that generated power for the craft.

The Seattle reservation where they lived was a dense concentration of high-rise buildings between the snow-capped Cascade and Olympic mountain ranges, and home to more than twenty-eight million people. Before the Green Revolution this had been a center of Corporate and military-industrial power, with the head offices and plants of many of the leading companies, whose shares were traded on the corrupt, risky stock exchanges that were manipulated by Corporate interests for their own excessive profits.

To make way for the new reservation, Chairman Rahma had ordered the destruction of facilities that had once been owned by well-known corporations that used to be based in the region—all of which he considered decadent, because they were so large and exerted so much influence in the governmental corridors of power. He also flattened the sprawling suburbs, knocked down bridges, and contracted the footprint of Seattle and the surrounding cities, so that greenforming could take place around the new reservation. Today the Seattle reservation utilized a minimal amount of land for residential and business purposes—and it was a center for green industries manufacturing solar panels, electric-powered vehicles, wind and wave turbines, rooftop hydroponics systems, bicycles, ornithopters, and other ecology-oriented products.

During the current break from his busy work schedule, Joss had been home for two days, sleeping more than usual and staying inside for the most part. It was nearly dinnertime now, and he stood at a control panel in the kitchen of his fourth-floor apartment, punching buttons to order two automated stir-fry meals containing spicy tofu and soy protein—one for himself and one for his always-punctual roommate, Andruw Twitty, who was due to arrive at any minute. Joss made his own meal even spicier, adding a three-star measure of red chili sauce.

Here on the reservation he did not have the option of ordering meat dishes. Ordinarily those were only for the road, and for what the esteemed Chairman called the "favored few" who contributed the most to his greenocracy. Joss had never understood the morality or logic of who could or could not eat meat, and when. Conceivably, he would have thought that the vegan Chairman and his government would mandate that everyone give up eating the flesh of dead animals, but that was not the case. Maybe the inspirational leader was just being realistic. In any event, it was not something that Joss talked about much, for fear that he could lose his dining privileges, and possibly cause others on his Janus Machine crew to do so.

He heard a soft whir as his automated kitchen processed ingredients to prepare the food, finally heating it with stored energy from solar panels and wind turbines far up on the roof of the ninety-story apartment building. It didn't take long before two meals dropped onto a tray beneath a glowing orange light. Joss glanced at the watch embedded in the skin of his wrist, smiled at the pinpoint timing as he heard the front door open and click shut. Presently his roommate strode into the kitchen.

A Greenpol eco-cop, Andruw was short and square-jawed, with a narrow blond mustache. In his mid-twenties, he removed his polished green helmet and hung it on a hook by the door, then removed his holstered handgun and set it on a bench. His face glistened with perspiration, and his uniform was uncharacteristically wrinkled and soiled. He had a strange gleam in his pale blue eyes.

"Looks like you've had a tough day," Joss said. He had been an eco-cop detective himself, before the transfer to a Janus Machine crew that Kupi had arranged for him.

"You heard about the four escapees from the reservation?" Andruw asked.

Joss nodded. Every news board had been carrying their descriptions. "Our meals are ready." He placed the two trays on the small dining table, along with wrapped packages of napkins and serving utensils.

Andruw pulled up a chair and sat down, his expression suddenly smug. "We got 'em good today. The perps were living in the woods, killing deer and birds, cooking meat on open fires. In clear violation of environmental laws."

"No doubt about that." Joss brought two glasses of beer

from a dispenser. He took a sip from his own as he sat down, savored the hoppy, slightly bitter flavor that he had specified.

Andruw quaffed his own glassful, then said, "I recycled two of the bastards this afternoon, in the name of Chairman Rahma. They tried to get away, but I hit 'em between their shoulder blades with energy beams." He grinned. "I've been practicing on the range, and I'm a pretty good shot now."

"Sorry that had to happen." Feeling a twinge in his stomach, Joss knew this was the first time that Andruw had killed anyone, and he thought of the many times he'd had to use lethal force against perpetrators himself—especially the last occasion, when he killed three and found a way to change careers afterward. For him it had never been easy, but Andruw was taking it differently, as if he enjoyed it. The man's eyes gleamed with a wild ferocity that made Joss uncomfortable.

"People like that don't appreciate the wonderful utopia that Chairman Rahma established for the benefit of all life in the Green States of America," Andruw said.

Joss swallowed a mouthful of stir-fry with its seasoned tofu. "You couldn't have used a stunner setting and captured the fugitives instead of killing them?"

He wrinkled his blocky face in displeasure. "That's an odd comment for you to make. I'll try to forget you said it, though perhaps I shouldn't be surprised, considering your close relationship with Kupi Landau."

Joss bristled. As an eco-cop, his roommate could submit authoritative testimony about what he had just said. Andruw had earlier shown an interest in what he called the "disloyal" comments of Kupi, but her occasional faux pas were widely known and tolerated at high levels of the government. So far, at least.

Staring across the table at his roommate, Joss felt anger

and mounting concern, which he attempted to conceal. His own record was outstanding and he was Kupi's boss, but he didn't want to step over any lines. Any citizen could turn in another one for making disloyal remarks or activities, as long as they could provide proof to the authorities. He'd heard of evidence being accepted that seemed less than convincing. But evidence from an eco-cop carried weight, and besides that, Andruw was from an influential family. Both of his parents were high-level GSA bureaucrats, having been appointed to their positions by Chairman Rahma, rewarding them for their contributions to the victory against the Corporates.

Joss was ambitious himself, but in a different way. As a child, he had dreamed of doing something important with his life, but he had always planned to advance through legitimate good work, not like this Andruw and his nefarious ways.

With Andruw, his ambition seemed increasingly twisted and creepy. He wanted to advance his career so much that he would take any opportunity to do so, and would even distort information, putting a spin on it to make whatever point he was trying to assert. More and more, Joss had noticed him twisting facts in everyday conversation and in his dealings with other people, and he had no doubt that he would use similar tactics against Kupi and Joss as well, if he saw the opportunity and felt it was personally safe to do so. This roommate was no friend, and Joss was looking for an opportunity to break off the relationship, but in a way that would not make it look like he was trying to hide something from an eco-cop.

"There was nothing wrong with my question," Joss said, holding his gaze with the younger man. "The Chairman likes to put on public trials of criminals as examples for others, as preventative measures. When I had your job I was taught to use deadly force only as a last resort."

That got him! Joss thought, seeing a flash of worry on An-druw's face. *Now* I'm *on the offensive.* Joss pressed forward. "You considered the alternatives, I presume?"

"It's all in my report," Andruw said, his pale gaze darting around. "By the way, how's your relationship going with that middle-aged anarchist? You still playing doctor with her?"

"My . . . relationship . . . with Kupi is none of your con-cern."

"Is she still complaining about worn, overused Janus Ma-chines?" Andruw was trying to use something to his advantage that Joss had told him in casual, unguarded conversation.

Leaning forward on the table, Joss raised his voice, for con-trolled effect. "Need I remind you, Andruw, that Kupi Landau is still a trusted comrade of Chairman Rahma? I would sug-gest that you consider not only your actions today, but what *you've* been saying to me! You seem to be out of balance." He paused for effect. "Perhaps I should report you?"

Andruw looked as if he had been spanked. He turned to his meal, but his lower jaw moved oddly as he chewed, and his eyes showed fright and frustration. Fumbling in his pocket, he brought out a juana stick and lit it, then took several drags to calm his nerves, finally stubbing it out in an ashtray, but not completely. A thread of gray smoke rose from the remnant as the men ate their meals in uneasy silence.

Looking out the window, Joss had a nice view of one of the larger parks in the reservation. His lower-floor unit was among the advantages of his position running a Janus Machine crew, though he'd never thought it was fair how Andruw—the holder of a substantially lesser position—had pulled strings to become his roommate. The young man was crafty, and seemed to have a way of advancing his career by saying the right things to the right people in government.

Down in the commons, Joss saw a large section of fenced

pea patches, bathed in sunlight, and men and women working the crops, along with schoolchildren and their teachers. He smiled, liked the thought of children learning where food came from, and how to grow it. Some of the kids were also pulling weeds as their classroom assignment, because insecticides were not permitted anywhere in the Green States of America. Other youngsters were tending to the composting piles.

The children had all been born after the formation of the GSA. While still in their mothers' wombs, they'd heard the soothing sounds of the ocean and the wind played for them by their parents, and when they were babies these sounds were piped into their basinets. When they were old enough to understand language, they wore headsets for an hour a day, over which they heard various natural sounds of the earth, along with subliminal messages about the need to care for the planet. In a sense it was brainwashing, Joss realized as he thought about it, but it was for a fabulous cause.

Outside the fenced areas, red foxes, raccoons, and a variety of other wild animals ran loose. Greenpol cops strutted along paths on their normal inspection rounds, ticketing or arresting anyone who violated the eco-rules or damaged the park environment in the slightest way. These police were eco-vice beat cops and had a zero-tolerance policy, with humans permitted only in certain areas on defined pathways, and not allowed to litter, damage any plants, or even to step on a bug or swat a fly.

At least not in public view. Inside residences and offices it was a different matter, and people found ways to eradicate pests. Both Joss and Andruw had killed insects and laid illegal traps for mice, with hardly a comment exchanged between them about it. Such violations were minor and technical, and everyone except the most avid animal rights zealots ignored them—fanatics who didn't mind if animals or birds defecated in their homes, or if cockroaches contaminated their food.

He also noticed a white-robed Science Overseer strutting about the park, with people on the path getting out of his way. The SciO stopped and spoke with a green-uniformed police officer, and pointed to a man walking ahead of them. Though the SciOs and Greenpol were different government agencies, they sometimes worked in concert with each other on crimes. The Greenpol officer hurried after the man, for some infraction.

Joss preferred to watch from here, instead of putting himself in a position where he might receive an infraction. His apartment building had a nice health club with a swimming pool and jogging track on the seventy-eighth floor, and he intended to go up there this afternoon for some exercise.

Looking across the table, he said to Andruw, "Maybe you should have a couple of drinks and try to wind down. Whether you realize it or not, you've been through a difficult event."

Andruw's eyes flashed, but he nodded.

Joss finished eating and rose from the table, carrying his biodegradable foodware items to a garbage chute, where he tossed them in.

13

Chairman Rahma sometimes defies security measures that are in place to protect him; he likes to mingle with crowds while his hubot guard force scrambles to keep up. This is an obvious weak point that could be exploited, should we ever wish to assassinate him. But that would make him a martyr, and potentially more dangerous in death than in life. Better to exploit his other known weaknesses, and bring him down militarily. He and his progressive followers don't like to fight. Despite the mob violence they demonstrated in the Corporate War, they are essentially apologists, appeasers, and peaceniks—not hardened for battle like us. But do not underestimate them, especially the violent anarchists in their midst. The Greenies have their own will to survive, and access to powerful SciO technology.

—Dylan Bane, in a speech to his military officers

DYLAN BANE DID not like the secrets harbored by other people, but he very much liked his own. At the moment, he was riding in one of them, burrowing through the Earth at a high rate of speed, listening to the faint keening sound and watching the play of lights around the hull as the voleer cut through rock and earth, then closed each tunnel behind it, as if it had never been there.

He stood on the command bridge inside the twenty-sixth craft of this type that he'd ordered built, taking a test ride with the pilots. The voleer was beneath the Yucatán Peninsula in the Southern Mexico Territory, heading in a northerly direction.

"The problems with this ship are minor, sir, and easily fixed," said a man in a smudged gray work suit. One of the design technicians, Brad Powell, activated a wall screen, showing close-up details of the elaborate cross-beams of light that were caused by friction around the hull as it cut through the crust of the Earth and plunged forward.

"Look there," he said, using an electronic pointer to identify an illuminated strand in a webwork of light on the forward section. "See how the color of that section is faintly purple?"

Bane grunted.

"As you know, it should be brighter purple, reflecting a higher rate of burrowing speed. We just need to calibrate the cutters and angles when we get back to the shop. Not much delay at all, sir, you can still make your schedule."

"Very good. Take care of it."

"I will, sir." The man moved away, went about his duties.

For several moments, Bane watched the hypnotic dance of lights, the intricate play of webbing that seemed to stretch and bend around the ship, as if the beams of light were shoring the tunnel to keep it open, preventing it from collapsing. He knew it was far more complicated than that, because once he had been a SciO researcher and engineer himself.

Shortly after the formation of the Green States of America in 2043, the SciO leadership had assigned Dylan Bane to be in charge of a top-secret SciO research team, investigating all possible uses of splitting and greenforming technology. At that point it was only known to have environmental and offensive military applications, but Arch Ondex and other SciO leaders suspected that there might be others.

In a little less than three years, Bane's team thought they had found something significant, something he called "vanishing tunnel technology." In initial tests it worked on a small scale, but would not scale up to the proportions needed to make the tunnels useful from the military standpoint that he knew Ondex wanted, proportions large enough for war machines and soldiers to pass through them.

Then one evening, working alone in the laboratory, Bane performed a complex series of high-order calculations and executed drawings that solved the problem. As he stared at the pages in detail, he knew without a doubt that the vanishing tunnel technology *would* work on a large scale.

By that time, the GSA government had wiped out the rest of the Bane family for their involvement in Corporate affairs, first taking their assets and then their lives. Dylan Bane, laboring in a secluded laboratory, had been overlooked; ostensibly he had been a contributor to the new reality, something he secretly called the "new unreality."

So he'd decided to keep the scientific discovery to himself, and had laid the groundwork for this by making certain that all information about the project went through him to higherups, and by entering falsified technical information about the project into the SciO computer system.

For some time, Bane had seen enormous profit potential in the vanishing tunnel technology, and he began to rationalize about keeping the entire benefit for himself, because he had contributed more to the discovery than the rest of his team combined, and most of his family had been murdered—a family that he'd loved despite their failings. He'd never liked being a SciO lab technician, having to follow their unending rules, the reasons for which were never explained to him in any way that made sense.

Three weeks after coming up with the vanishing tunnel solution, Bane had put to death his entire research team with an acidic poison gas, sprayed in their faces. He then faked their suicides by leaving computer notes ostensibly written by them, asserting they killed themselves because they couldn't complete the project and didn't want to live with the shame. He'd even left a facially mutilated body that was supposed to be his own, but in reality was brought in from the outside and wasn't even a team member. To falsify the identity of that body, Bane had salted it with a fake skin overlay—an undetectable spray that he'd prepared from his own DNA, making it appear to be his body if anyone took a skin scraping.

Before making good his escape, Bane destroyed his calculations and drawings, along with all lab records, prototypes, molds, blueprints, and backup files—leaving behind counterfeit technical information to lead the SciOs astray when they attempted to resurrect the experiments.

The rest had been comparatively easy. After building his first small voleer machine, he'd been able to travel underground and pop up wherever he pleased, stealing whatever he needed—food, money, raw materials, even priceless artworks and other valuables.

He recalled one of the raids he'd made a couple of years ago. After boring through the planetary crust beneath the Atlantic Ocean, he'd navigated the subterranean craft so skillfully that he'd emerged inside the grounds of a chateau in the Loire Valley, where a retired French industrialist was supposed to have lived. The man was a collector of paintings by Monet, Matisse, Cézanne, Gauguin, Van Gogh, and Renoir—and reportedly he had billions of dollars' worth of artwork in this one location.

In possession of advance information on the security system, Bane was prepared to shut it down with electronic signals, then go in and remove the best paintings from their frames, roll them up, and cart them off. But when he surfaced on the northern perimeter of the estate, he saw scaffolding all around the chateau, and work crews operating around the clock—affording him no opportunity to get past so many people.

Bane had departed, perplexed, only to learn that the chateau had been purchased by an American businessman in exile, a former Corporate mogul who was turning the elegant old building and the grounds into a tacky amusement park with a Louis XVI–Marie Antoinette theme, including a large gift store to sell reproductions of clothing, jewelry, and furniture from the period. Through further investigation, Bane learned that similar amusement parks and casinos were being constructed throughout Europe, usually with some fairy-tale or cartoon theme. To Bane, it seemed the height of foolish decadence, but he saw humor in it. When the Corporates were driven out of the Americas, they took some of their bad taste with them.

But he and his subordinates made other raids, highly lucrative ones. In the process Bane raised enough money to construct additional small voleers, scores of them, followed by larger and larger machines, until he set forth on the present military strategy with the largest machines of all, and tens of thousands of human and robot soldiers—along with elaborate security precautions to protect his compact but powerful army.

For what he had in mind, he wouldn't even need the three nuclear submarines that were in his arsenal. He preferred to use his own Splitter Cannons (transported by voleers), employing Dark Energy technologies that made even the most advanced nuclear missiles look totally out of date. He visualized the voleers surfacing and disgorging troops, assault vehicles, and high-speed aircraft to strike the targets, and strike them *hard*.

Dylan Bane felt certain that his magnificent plan would work. He intended to bring down all of his arrogant enemies, and they would not know what hit them.

14

_____

The greatest leaders have woven a mythos around themselves,
an embroidery of legends and half-truths that make them seem
larger than life. But embroideries are destructible, and so are
the men and women they protect.

—Chairman Rahma Popal, private notes

ARTIE HAD BEEN monitoring the progress of the unusual creatures in the Extinct Animals Laboratory, looking in on them
whenever he could get a few moments away from the ongoing
demands made on him by Chairman Rahma.

The glidewolf had been growing quickly, having nearly
doubled in size in the past couple of weeks. It was around the
size of a full-grown wolf now, but with reddish brown fur, a
marsupial pouch, and batlike wings. The creature had been
fitted with an electronic tracking device and a camera, in a
combination unit mounted on top of its head in such a way
that it did not irritate the animal, and so that it could not remove it.

Now the hubot stood in the creature's subterranean eucalyptus forest habitat, gazing upward as the glidewolf climbed
a trellis to reach the ingress and egress hatch high up in the
techplex ceiling, a hatch that had been made large enough to
allow for the creature to grow even more, or for other, larger
creatures to get in and out, should they be permitted to do so.
The wolf went through, and disappeared from view.

On an internal receiver, Artie watched topside videos of the glidewolf loping across the oval-shaped techplex toward the nearby evergreen forest, where it scampered up tall cedar and fir trees and then launched itself into the air, gliding for great distances over the grasslands and wetlands of the game reserve. The marsupial's head-top camera showed views straight ahead of it as the creature soared on thermals, with its long feathery tail raised high to form a rudder, and its wings extended to each side—a wingspan of almost three meters.

The robotic laboratory technicians were reporting single glides of more than two kilometers. In one series the wolf climbed seven trees, with an equal number of glides that carried it almost twenty kilometers before it turned around and performed additional tree-launched glides, finally returning to the ceiling hatch and descending to the floor of the forest habitat.

Though the glidewolf nibbled on fir and cedar needles, bark, leaves, and other edibles out in the evergreen forest and surrounding areas, it always returned to the habitat to consume the eucalyptus diet it preferred. Artie had mixed feelings about this, liking the fact that the animal came back, but worried that it would not be able to adapt to the environment in this region. Perhaps, the lab technicians suggested, it should be relocated to a climate where its favorite trees grew in abundance—but this did not seem practical under the circumstances. For the foreseeable future, with all of the other pressing issues requiring the attention of Artie on behalf of the Chairman, the hubot didn't have the staff, time, or resources to perform his extinct animal studies anyplace but here.

Now Artie had another thought. Perhaps they could force adaptation, by cutting back on what the creature ate in its habitat. He would give that more consideration.

On the way out to the slidewalk that would transport him

to the elevator bank, he stepped to one side to allow half a dozen robots to enter, followed by carts filled with broad-leafed plants that were being added to the dodo bird habitat.

As he watched them work, he realized he had not been thinking much about the other animals in the habitat for several weeks. Each time he came, he went straight to the glidewolf habitat and focused on how she was doing. On a regular basis the robots reported to him by electronic streaming, but he really needed to see what was going on firsthand.

He wondered if he should respond to a question that had come up about growing another marsupial wolf in the laboratory, a male to keep the female company. His robotic assistants had asked him about this the day before, and Artie had not replied, though he knew it was a logical next step to take.

Now he went off to one side and sat down. Taking a moment, he accessed his internal data banks, where he stored complete records of all extinct animal projects in the laboratory—with some of the information under deep encryption, such as the quarter of one percent he had secretly added to the genetic mix of the glidewolf, after making educated guesses and assumptions. With his computerized mind, it seemed to Artie that he should have perfect access to every one of the steps he'd taken to grow the glidewolf in the laboratory, just like the records he had for the genetically pure dodo birds, Labrador ducks, and a number of other formerly extinct species that he and his robotic assistants had brought back to life. But when he tried to access the information on the glidewolf, he was able to retrieve everything except for the deep encryption on what he had added to the mix.

Surprised, he tried different ways of retrieving the data, without success. Then, confounding him even more, when he attempted to access separate backup files where he'd stored all data, he discovered that the same deep encryption was also gone—evidence of some sort of contamination in the information. Everything else was there in both his internal and backup files, but not the quarter of one percent on the glide-wolf. Not even the robots connected to him electronically had the data or knew he was trying to access it now, because he had the superior capability of releasing only the information that he wanted them to know.

As he stood up, a stark realization came over him: The animal he'd created was one of a kind, and seemed fated to never have a companion like it. This creature was not genetically identical to anything that had ever lived on the planet, and could never be replicated.

He would just tell his assistants no, without explanation.

15

To keep us together as a society, it is best to have an enemy. We are the in-group, and they are the out-group. No matter how you look at it, even from the opposite point of reference—theirs—the leadership of each side consolidates its power because of a threat from the other. Why, then, would either of us want to annihilate our sworn enemy? On a certain level it makes no sense, does it? We thrive because they thrive, and vice versa. It is a form of détente, in which we define each other's existence. This presumes, however, that each side is sane.

—Chairman Rahma Popal, private observations

THE AUTHORIZED ECO-TOURISM flight was physically demanding, but Joss had anticipated that. After long days on the road and two weeks of recovery at home, he needed the exercise, and Kupi had said that she looked forward to it as well. Now she seemed less certain, as she wheezed and panted at the power station next to his, struggling to keep up with his level of exertion.

For both of them this was like a gym in the sky, with their legs turning high-gear-ratio bicycle cranks and their arms moving forward and back in a rowing motion. Their coordinated physical exertion caused the ornithopter's articulated wings to flap and the craft to fly over treetops and lakes south of the Seattle Reservation for Humans.

On a sunny autumn morning they crossed over a small

town, on the outskirts of which sat a structure that looked like a huge elm-tree seed, the characteristic architecture of a SciO Recharge Facility, or ReFac. This suggested that there were one or more Janus Machines nearby as well.

As Joss and Kupi flew over the broad Columbia River gorge, featuring spectacular canyon views, he realized that in one sense the two of them were utilizing a primitive means of propulsion. In another, though, it was a reasonably advanced example of low-carbon-footprint green technology, with ergonomic fittings and efficient gear ratios that transmitted energy equally to the wings and flapped them with the natural motions of a large, graceful bird, propelling the craft smoothly and rapidly through the sky, without the need for a polluting engine.

The pair didn't have to operate flight controls; that part was automated, based on settings they made before taking off. Now they just needed to pedal and row long enough to get them where they wanted to go. Instruments in front of Joss showed the distance traveled, the speed, and where they were.

For several moments the two of them stopped exerting themselves at all, leaving the aircraft to glide on warm air currents, floating aimlessly over the chiseled landscape, maintaining elevation with backup systems. Joss looked at a navigation screen that named the mountains and other features in the region, but he glossed over them in his mind. Out here, names did not matter. The pair could slack off for twenty minutes at a time, relaxing and talking while the onboard systems kept the wings flapping, utilizing stored power generated by their efforts. Any longer than that, and the ornithopter's automated systems would give them the option of resuming their efforts immediately, or flying them back to their home reservation on solar-reserve battery power.

Joss considered how to bring up the subject he'd wanted to

discuss with Kupi, their increasingly awkward relationship. He couldn't quite frame the words.

"It's so quiet and peaceful up here," Kupi said, interrupting his thoughts. "Don't you ever wish you could get away from the J-Mac crew and just live in the wilderness?"

"You mean like those renegade forest people we've heard about?"

"Yes, it has a romantic sound, doesn't it, a free and easy life? Logically, people shouldn't be able to elude detection by the GSA government, because the authorities have such sophisticated scanning and search devices. But between you and me, Joss, there are renegades living in the woods anyway, using electronic scramblers and other methods to keep from being discovered. I have friends in touch with me by various means, so I know this is true."

"Anarchists, presumably?"

"Some are, but others have been persecuted for their religious beliefs, because they follow Christianity, Judaism, Islam, and other banned religions. In the wilderness, they are free to worship as they please."

"People are out there living the high life, eating berries, leaves, grub worms, and red ants?"

She made a face. "If I lived in the woods I'd rather fish and hunt. Just think of it, Joss, we could eat meat whenever we feel like it."

"Yeah, as long as we can knock it off the hoof."

Kupi stared out a side window. "No rules except one: survive. I like the sound of it."

"You would, Kupi, being an anarchist. You say there are people out in the woods, hiding and living off the land. But what if there were so many anarchists out there that they needed to form rules in order to keep from bumping into each other and having problems? What if the anarchists found they needed—I hate to say it—some form of government, or just a police force?"

She smiled. "You seek to trap me with your logic, but you're extrapolating too far, setting up a preposterous scenario. Yes, there are anarchists living in the woods at this very moment, beyond GSA control, but there are not so many that they would consider forming governmental or quasi-governmental entities. True anarchists would rather die first."

"And are you a true anarchist?"

She reddened. "Perhaps not, but if I am not pure I am not alone in having flaws. There are, admittedly, certain attractive elements to the lives that you and I lead. I must admit that I get a major rush whenever I fire Black Thunder!"

"And when we run out of areas to split and greenform? What will you do then?"

"What any good anarchist would do. I'll just fade to black."

"Meaning?"

"I haven't thought it through completely."

"How about our relationship? Have you thought that through completely?"

Kupi swung out of her power station and leaned over Joss, kissing him on the neck and moving around to his mouth. "What's to think about?" she asked.

"A lot," he said. "Sometimes I think we're too different to last."

"Then live for today, my love." She kissed him passionately.

He pulled away and looked at her, feeling his mounting desire, but trying to suppress it. "What about tomorrow?"

"We're back to work tomorrow, Joss. You know that. We're taking a train to the Berkeley Reservation, the glorious capital of Rahma's counterculture revolution."

"You know I'm talking about more than that; I'm talking about all of the tomorrows in our lives."

"How romantic, and poetic. So, you want to talk about our relationship, eh? I thought that men were terrified of the 'r' word, but here you are bringing it up."

"I just want to know where we stand."

She smiled, and it struck him how much younger than forty-five she looked. In her early thirties like him, he thought, as she nuzzled against him and breathed hot air on his ear.

Trying to resist her advances, Joss said, "If you don't want to talk, think about this. In seventeen minutes, the ship's computer will demand that we resume our power output, or it will fly us back to the reservation."

"It took us an hour to get here," she said, unbuttoning her blouse and revealing her bra. As always, her underclothes were black.

"That was with us propelling the plane. Without us, the return speed could be faster."

"Then we'd better hurry up," she said, loosening his belt and pulling off his trousers and shoes.

He felt too weak to resist her, at least physically. Moment by moment, Joss found her animal nature consuming him, taking him over completely. And without another word, they tumbled onto the deck. Their lovemaking was better than ever before, feral and spontaneous.

Joss had not been able to find the right words, didn't want to hurt her. But afterward, looking into her brown eyes and seeing the pain and sadness there, he realized that she understood what he'd been trying to say anyway. Their passion was only delaying the inevitable.

16

Corporate religious fanatics have called us amoral, but that is not correct. It's just that we have a different moral compass from theirs, and the two do not point in the same direction. Our goals are selfless; theirs are self-serving.

—Chairman Rahma, *The Little Green Book*

IT WAS A chilly, damp morning on the game reserve, with lacy mists lingering over the ground and the grazing animals. Rahma Popal had been up since dawn three hours ago, when he and Dori Longet had made love and watched the play of colors across the hills to the east. Afterward she had gone over his daily schedule with him, preparing him for the business of the day. Then she went to breakfast with her parents, who were allowed to visit her on occasion. He'd seen them walking toward the communal dining area.

As the Chairman strode to the central meeting yurt he wore one of his simpler robes, a plain brown garment with a white peace symbol on the lapel. His advisers didn't like him to dress in this manner, without the trappings of high office or impressive government sigils, but he didn't care what they said. The Green States of America was really a separate entity from him, and it had its own energy, its own momentum. To keep himself sane and free of hubris, and to avoid being consumed by the GSA, the Chairman had developed a habit of dipping in and out of its various structures and formalities.

In doing this he sometimes thought of his former girlfriend from the revolutionary days, Kupi Landau, the fiery anarchist who used to dream of separating herself entirely from the cruel societal games that humans liked to play, and all of the attendant configurations, whether petty or significant. Since their amicable breakup almost twenty years ago, he'd been monitoring her progress with various reports that came in on her, and often he worried over her well-being. She was so outspoken! Even so, despite all, he still cared about her, albeit in his own way. Rahma cared about all of his women, whether they were still living with him or not.

In the past year he'd received numerous reports about Kupi's personal behavior, with some of the most interesting specifics coming from Andruw Twitty, the roommate of her present boyfriend. Chairman Rahma had never met Twitty personally, only by avatar projection whenever the young man passed along secondhand information, things that Kupi's boyfriend had purportedly said about her. But Rahma knew Twitty's parents, and remembered their valuable contributions to the victory over the Corporates, when they firebombed a key enemy military building. They held administrative positions now with the GSA's important Quality Control Division, responsible for ensuring that products were manufactured according to strict green guidelines.

Twitty was one of the informants scheduled to report to Rahma this morning, with the topic being the activities of anarchists who worked for the GSA government. Though all Black Shirts had promised loyalty to the government and its philosophical underpinnings, they still needed constant monitoring, because of the naturally rebellious nature of their kind.

Strolling across the grass to the meeting yurt, Rahma saw Artie out in front, talking with yellow-uniformed hubots on the security force as they ran electronics over the building and around the grounds, constantly looking for breaches. It was just routine, one of the periodic checks that they performed in cooperation with the special Greenpol police who had been assigned to guard him. The hubots were very good about details.

"No problems, Master," Artie said.

"Very good." The Chairman swept by him and entered the yurt, where he sat cross-legged on the wooden floor at the center of a large room. Waving his hands in readiness, he began to see the avatars of men and women appear out of the ether and take seats in a half circle facing him. He counted eight realistic apparitions.

This morning he would take their reports in the alphabetical order of their surnames, a diversion he'd decided upon at the last moment. All informants were not given the honor of being in his presence in this manner. There were thousands of them who sent in information on a regular basis, but through a culling process handled by his subordinates, these were the ones he would see today, on a particular topic. Some, if their information proved useful, would receive monetary rewards or other perks.

And, though he could see their projected faces and they could see him whenever he addressed them separately, the EVR system had been set up so that none of the informants could see the others, and they could not hear one another's words, or the Chairman speaking to the others. For Rahma's convenience, the eight of them seemed to be sitting together as simultaneous visitors, but in reality he carried on compartmentalized, private conversations with each of them. It was enhanced virtual reality, customized for the Chairman's purposes.

IN THE DINING yurt, Dori and her parents selected from the buffet of organic vegan foods. She noticed that her father avoided the fresh cherry tomatoes, as he always did, opting instead for a synthetic Montana omelet and a large glass of papaya juice. Pierre Longet was a successful businessman, selling small, highly efficient solar collectors that were exported to rural areas of Eurika, for the use of farmers and villagers who did not have access to centralized power grids.

A small, stout man with a high forehead and thin white hair, he was always quiet, and allowed his wife to dominate conversations. This often frustrated Dori, because she enjoyed being with him, and often had to go out of her way to draw him out. He had a wealth of interesting stories that had been told to him by his old-country French grandparents, and he had a way of bringing old events back to life with words—if Dori could only squeeze them out of him.

Now she listened while her mother went on a complaining binge, as she sometimes did, especially when she didn't get a good night's sleep—which was the case with her now because she'd had to rise early to catch the maglev train from the Missoula Reservation. Out of earshot of any other diners she'd been criticizing the buffet selection, the cool temperature in the yurt, and even the slight wilting of wildflowers in vases on the tables.

They selected a corner table, well away from others in the large room, where they could talk privately. Kristine Longet removed her heavy coat and laid it over an extra chair. Simulated gold bracelets encircled her wrists. As she sat down she looked across the table at Dori and said, "An awful, impertinent serviceman came to our apartment the other day to work on our cleaning bot. He actually had the temerity to try to shake my hand. And do you know why?"

Dori took a sip of the strong coffee. "No, Mother."

"Because his daughter is here on the game reserve." She lowered her voice even more. "He says she's one of the Chairman's women."

Dori smiled. "Well, he does have quite a number of ladies around him all the time. He's always liked the companionship of the opposite sex."

"I've never understood how you could be so relaxed about that," the older woman said. She nibbled on a small vegan patty, one of several on her plate, of varying colors and flavors.

"Maybe it's because I'm his favorite."

"Well, you'd better watch yourself. Her name is Jade Ridell, and her father seems overly ambitious."

"That's her over there," Dori said, nodding toward a table across the room. "The pretty redhead reading an e-book."

Kristine Longet stared long and hard, wrinkling her face into a scowl.

"She seems nice enough, Mother."

"Don't ever trust her. Women can be very manipulative."

"Oh, don't worry, Mother, I've always had lots of competition around here, and I manage to fend them off."

"You are getting older, dear. Don't forget that."

"I'm only thirty-one!"

"You can't hold on to your beauty forever."

"You seem to be managing well for yourself," Dori responded, while catching a bemused glance from her father.

This pleased her mother. "Thank you for that."

"Besides, the Chairman depends on me to keep track of important business matters for him." The pretty blonde paused, thinking of the liaisons with other women she sometimes coordinated as well. "And certain personal matters."

AS SHE SAT across the dining hall, Jade Ridell was reading an interesting electronic book, *Mega-Corporations: The New Colonialists*. It described a time before the Green Revolution when the largest international corporations were like colonial nations, except instead of plundering third-world nations of their resources, the gluttonous, amoral corporations plundered average consumers of their hard-earned assets. This occurred in the United States, in Europe, and in every region where people could afford discretionary spending. The big corporations sucked up their money like huge vacuum cleaners.

Jade happened to be looking up from the book when she noticed the evil glare from Dori's mother. On one level she didn't understand how the woman could be that way, but on another—on a very *female* level—she understood completely. The mother wanted her own daughter to retain her primacy among Rahma's women.

Although her own family (and especially her father) had pressed Jade to do well, to advance in this haremlike realm, she was not consciously trying to harm anyone else in the process, or hurt their chances. Whenever she was with Rahma (and they would be together after his meeting), she just tried to be herself, showing her natural strength of personality while generally deferring to what he wanted. In every dealing they had, be it sexual or just going someplace together on the game reserve, she let him know the obvious—that he was the boss—but she didn't wilt to his every whim. She showed considerable backbone, but not too much, not so much that it irritated him. He seemed to like this about her.

She wanted so much to please the great man. And in that respect she felt very good about herself, because she genuinely liked him. Not just because he was so powerful, or physically attractive for his age, but because of who he was in his heart, because of the far-reaching, unselfish dreams he held for this planet and its life-forms. She had never met anyone who resembled him in the smallest degree; he was, truly, one of a kind.

Above all, Chairman Rahma wanted the Earth to thrive, and as much as she could, Jade intended to keep him happy so that he could complete his important work, and do it well. If that meant she spent more time with him than Dori or the others did, so be it. Jade was just being herself, after all. She was just caring for Rahma, thinking of what he needed. In this manner, she felt she was doing her own small part for the sake of the environment.

AN HOUR PASSED in the meeting yurt, as the Chairman continued to sit cross-legged on the floor, listening while the avatars of two men and five women spoke of the activities of several anarchists whose activities warranted scrutiny. One of the anarchists, an elderly man named Onas Eedle, was said to be in ill health but was still causing some problems, asserting that the government surveillance of his activities was a violation of his privacy. The charge was, of course, patently absurd. Individuals had no rights under the Charter of the Green States of America; individuals were allowed to exist only if they continued to serve the cause of the greater good. Later today, Rahma would tell his military agents to have the miscreant recycled discreetly, while giving out the story that he had died suddenly of natural causes.

In another matter, a Black Shirt from the days of the revolutionary council, Abby Miroc, was now Mayor of the New Orleans Reservation, having set aside his anti-establishment beliefs enough to become one of the GSA leaders. A week ago, he had filled out an application requesting permission to take a trip to Eurika, where he said he wanted to meet with opposition political leaders. On the surface, that might be all right, because Rahma had often criticized the Eurikan government for only giving lip service to environmental issues. But the female informant this morning provided testimony that such meetings were only a front for something else, and Miroc was actually a Eurikan spy.

This was a very serious charge, and gave Rahma considerable pause. It was not a good sign for anyone to be trying to leave the country like that; the Chairman had a policy in force to deny virtually all such requests, based on the theory that the government should nominate who would travel and who would not—instead of waiting to be approached by interested parties.

Rahma pondered this particular situation for a moment, trying to decide how best to handle it. Perhaps a trap could be laid to catch the Mayor (just in case he really was up to no good), or to catch the informant, if she had her own reasons for lying about him. Human beings could be so devious, requiring extra measures to unearth their true motives and intentions. The matter would take some thought, but he would remove it from his own plate by delegating the decision to one of his top aides in the New Orleans Reservation.

Finally, the avatar of only one informant remained, with the others having faded back to their sources. The short Andruw Twitty avatar rose to his feet, dressed in a spit-and-polish Greenpol uniform with shiny green jackboots; he held his helmet in his hands to show the proper respect. "It is good to see you again, Comrade Chairman."

Rahma didn't respond, watched the avatar's blond mustache twitch nervously and the pale eyes dart around. This had never seemed to be a stable personality to the Chairman, but perhaps it was because he was nervous in the presence of the GSA leader. Twitty's superiors in Greenpol reported that he was a rising star in the organization, and one day could even become Chief of the Eco-Crimes Division. They said he had an observant eye, and a way of getting useful information out of suspects. Recently, he had killed two fugitives outside the Seattle reservation, evidence of his intensity. But despite all that, he wouldn't even be here if he didn't have high-level connections in the government, as a result of his parents.

"First, sir, just a few brief comments about Joss Stuart. While he is a very talented greenformer, one who reportedly never makes professional mistakes, he is not always forthcoming when it comes to reporting anti-government comments made by a member of the J-Mac team, Kupi Landau. In Stuart's defense, many of her comments are well known anyway, such as her occasional remarks that Janus Machines should be replaced more frequently, before they get 'long in the tooth.' "

"Yes, I know she's said such things."

"Perhaps Stuart feels that others will report what she says, and he does not have to. In taking this approach, however, he is technically in violation of the law, which as you know requires the reporting of all infractions, whether they are activities or remarks. Since Stuart is my roommate, he knows that I am a Greenpol agent and that I am duty-bound to report all I know about him, and about Ms. Landau. Even so, I have noticed a reticence on his part to reveal certain things to me about her. He has been, uh, clamming up lately when it comes to her."

"Well, she is his girlfriend. Perhaps he feels that you are prying unnecessarily."

"Hmm, perhaps. But you've said yourself that no one in the GSA has an inalienable right to privacy, and you should know that on his personal time Stuart does not smoke very many juana sticks, or partake in other legal drugs much at all. Some people would view such behavior as unpatriotic, as anti-GSA."

Rahma scowled. "Maybe drugs disagree with him physically. Did that ever occur to you?"

"He's never said so to me."

"And the two of you are close personal friends?"

"Actually, no. I think we tried to be at first, but now we only tolerate one another as roommates. We are quite different, actually, and at times I think he finds me irritating."

"I wonder why."

The sarcasm went right over Twitty's head. Instead, he took the words literally. "It must be because I'm so serious about my duties, sir, always trying to do my job as a cop, ferreting out the bad guys no matter where they are, or who they are."

"Yes, Twitty, that must be it." *Along with your other irritating personality traits,* Rahma thought, *you derrière-kissing sycophant.*

"Stuart isn't a bad citizen, sir, I don't mean to imply that. But the government does not want him to be negatively influenced by Kupi Landau's . . . colorful . . . attitude, so that must be constantly watched. She has an excellent record of service herself, of course, but some of the things she says sound unpatriotic. Sorry if I'm overstepping my bounds here."

Rahma narrowed his gaze, didn't respond in words. He was growing impatient and sensed that Twitty didn't have much more to say. The man was babbling, filling the air with useless comments and wasting time. Undoubtedly he had used his family connections to get the ear of Rahma's guardian-screeners, and then exaggerated the importance of the information he had to provide.

"Of course, Kupi Landau's past relationship with Your Eminence is widely known. In view of that, her laudatory service on the Berkeley Eight revolutionary council, and her recent heroics, perhaps Stuart feels that you will give her a pass no matter what she says."

"Leave the psychological analyses to trained professionals, Twitty."

"Yes, sir."

"Is that all you have for me today?"

"Sir, yes, it is. I'm sorry if my information seems minimal, but I just thought you should receive everything I know right away so that you can catch potential problems early and take any necessary actions before things get out of hand."

The Chairman nodded and waved his hand dismissively, causing the avatar to vanish in a puff of air.

FROM HIS MANSION in the eucalyptus-covered hills, Director Arch Ondex had a view of the gleaming high-rises of the Berkeley Reservation for Humans and the blue waters of San Francisco Bay. On the other side of the bay, he saw the forested San Francisco peninsula. Once an important city had been over there, a cosmopolitan center of international Corporate interests. Now it was just another portion of the vast woodlands and nature preserves that covered most of the Green States of America.

A holo-screen beside him provided another, more interesting view for him, a secret satellite view of the Rocky Mountain Territory and the Montana Valley Game Reserve that had become the headquarters of Rahma Popal.

Yes, Ondex thought, *Rahma Popal. He is just a man, not really the godlike figure he's made himself into, the green savior of our planet.*

For some time now, Chairman Rahma and the Panasian Premiere, Woo Hashimoto, had been exchanging personal insults, increasing the rhetoric between them to the point where the two nations could very well engage in a nuclear war.

The latest insult from overseas accused Rahma of being the dictator of a fascist green regime—a police state. Rahma responded that he found the thought preposterous, and a huge distortion. "Fascists are always right wing," Rahma had asserted in a government-to-government transmittal, "not left wing! What an exaggeration!"

He'd gone on to cite a host of reasons why Hashimoto was actually the proverbial pot calling the kettle black. The Panasian leader had murdered tens of millions of his own people for no good reason, Rahma pointed out, except to protect the oligarchy that ruled the nation through repression and an elaborate system of political favors, much of it favoring the Japanese, Chinese, and Korean members of his own large family.

Rahma understood the need for political favors (and he gave them out), but he did not practice any form of nepotism. When his own brother came up on a relocation list, and later on a list of people to be recycled for criminal behavior, Rahma did not intervene on either occasion. Most of the people who had to be put to death in his nation, the Chairman insisted, died for a good cause—the environment—not like the situation in Panasia where severe actions were taken against the populace with one object in mind, ensuring the power of the ruler and his cronies, and lining their pockets with cash.

Ondex didn't want to think about the similarities between the two governmental systems, though they were certainly obvious to him, no matter how much Chairman Rahma tried to deny them because of his own altruistic motives. Ondex shook his head in dismay. The battle of name-calling seemed juvenile to him, and a waste of energy. If the Green States and Panasia ever got into a nuclear war, much of the fault would lie with these two quarreling leaders.

Rahma could be a difficult man to get along with (as Ondex knew only too well), but the Director still held a degree of affection for the aging guru, because of the man's idealism and his relentless desire to protect the planet. You could argue with Rahma's methods, which were harsh, but not with the results. As a result of his work, air quality was much better in the Americas, with greenhouse gas emissions and other pollutants down dramatically. People were breathing fresh air, and the Earth was breathing more easily too, with decillions of additional trees planted under Rahma's stewardship.

Ondex's holo-screen view was from a SciO satellite connection concealed inside what was supposed to be a GSA communications satellite. But that particular orbital platform had something else onboard as well, something known only to SciO leadership—a Janus Machine that was more powerful than any ground cannon used for splitting and greenforming, or for firing bursts of Dark Energy at Corporate forces . . . and even more powerful than any nuclear weapons ever built, or any combination of them.

SJM—the Satellite Janus Machine.

With one blast from its massive Splitter barrel, it could wipe out everything in the Panasian nation, and a secondary blast from the orbital Seed Cannon would greenform it all, making the land look like it did millions of years ago. Everything on the orbital platform had been cleverly concealed from view with telescoping and modular units. The apparatus was like a Chinese puzzle box, with hidden mechanisms that the SciOs could activate to put the weapon online in a matter of seconds.

He didn't think that Chairman Rahma, even with the animosity he held toward Hashimoto and the Panasians, would want anything like that, anything that insane. And neither did Ondex. But the weapon was necessary, given the state of tensions in the world.

A copy of *The Little Green Book* sat on a table. In a burst of impetuosity, he grabbed the slender volume and hurled it into the fireplace. At his thought command, the gas in the fireplace flickered on, and flames consumed the book. It was a small, albeit secret, commentary on his part.

Others had their games, but Ondex knew how to play, too, by his own rules. He took a deep breath in an effort to calm himself.

For his own protection, and the protection of key SciO personnel, the organization had installed its own bunkers deep in the crust of the planet, hundreds of meters down, with so many layers of protection that anyone—or anything—inside them would not be harmed.

Activating the Satellite Janus Machine would be madness, casting a horrific swath of death across huge areas of land. He didn't want that on his conscience. But as a businessman he did want leverage, and this had the potential of giving him exactly that, in a big way. It was a bargaining chip, to be played against Rahma or Hashimoto (or both of them) at the right moment. He didn't want to forget the Eurikan Prime Minister, Grange Arthur, either. The man always seemed to be lying in the weeds, awaiting an opportunity to advance his interests.

Ondex switched to a clandestine satellite view of London, a live transmission that showed Prime Minister Arthur acting like a pompous king, riding through London at night in an ornate open carriage, drawn by prancing Arabian stallions. His attractive brunette wife, Karin, sat beside him, smiling and waving to throngs of people along the way, as they went to the opera. The famous couple's clothing was overdone, more like the extravagant costumes of an actor and an actress than those of a head of state and his lady.

His wife was with child, expected to deliver her baby in a matter of weeks. The citizens especially adored Karin, because of her charming personality and all the time she spent raising money for the poor. Despite the cold night air, the onlookers stood shoulder to shoulder along the carriage route, cheering and clapping.

Other live views from Eurika showed a soccer match, an African village that had been turned into an amusement park, and an outdoor street party that was a masked ball. The Eurikans worked fewer hours than others around the world and had a more relaxed view toward life and maximizing their pleasure. They vacationed longer, ate more, drank more, and had more sex. Unlike the Panasians, the Eurikans did not make overt displays of their weapons in parades or military-equipment shows. The Prime Minister's guards (as well as the police and soldiers) carried traditional sidearms and rifles, and not always the latest technology.

Like the Green States and the Panasians, the Eurikans had nuclear weapons and a large air force, army, and navy—but they did not saber-rattle. They also were not the overt eco-criminals that the Panasians were, and were instead more guilty of neglect of the environment than direct assaults on it. The Eurikans even had a number of programs to reduce carbon emissions and energy usage, and excellent recycling systems. Still, they were not the GSA; much of their population was spread out into small towns, instead of concentrating them more efficiently in densely populated reservations for humans.

For some time now, the GSA had been a cash cow for Ondex and the rest of the privileged SciO leadership. Popal's obsession with greening the planet, and with the related businesses he and his cronies controlled, had been a great opportunity for the SciOs to capitalize on their ground-based Janus Machines, and on other technology they had invented for the GSA. All of it was highly profitable for the SciOs.

But that was *not* the extent of J-Mac power. Far from it.

Ondex had other concerns about this dual-sided power that could destroy and create. Years ago he had nearly lost control of a form of the technology, when he didn't monitor a research team closely enough. All of them ended up killing themselves and taking the secret of vanishing tunnels with them. As a result, a new team had been assigned to the clandestine project, and they started essentially from scratch, with only a few clues left behind by their predecessors.

It was but one of numerous top-secret research programs that the SciOs had under development. All of that cutting-edge science, and nuances of it. He controlled the most powerful organization in history.

But Arch Ondex did not view himself as the only true God on the planet, though he might have done so. Rather, he was a sane man, an eminently practical one, and his Corporate father had—irony of ironies!—imbued a sense of morality in him, a sense of giving something substantial back to the people, a share of the profits. As a result, Ondex would use the new power for good, and would not abuse it.

The talented scientists on his staff had also come up with significant advancements in the fields of medicine and other technologies to improve the quality of life for mankind, things that were widely used, but not widely publicized.

In one regard, he thought that he and Chairman Rahma shared common ground, a desire to do good works on a very large scale. They were both idealistic men. Yet a major dividing line between them had to do with Rahma's misguided insistence on punishing humankind for past transgressions and on denying them material comforts, even refusing such things for himself. In contrast, Ondex believed people should not be herded around and controlled in every aspect of their lives, placed into densely populated, velvet-lined prisons for the protection of the environment.

As but one man, albeit an important one, Ondex intended to live a luxurious life himself, for as long as he could. He felt he had earned the right to do so, whether Rahma liked it or not.

17

"Rahm-m-m-m-a ... Rahm-m-m-m-a ... Rahm-m-m-m-a ..."
When chanted, his name has a sound reminiscent of eastern religion, and he has been called a guru. Though he denies the existence of a green religion, his choice of the name Rahma is not accidental, for the Chairman was not born with it. The man we see today is a carefully constructed individual, composed of components designed to please his followers. Much of his biography, at least that portion preceding his involvement in the revolution, has been fabricated.

—Artie, encrypted data file

JOSS HAD BEEN on the maglev train for more than an hour with the six other members of his Janus Machine crew, speeding south from the Seattle Reservation. On the way, he and Kupi had reviewed details of their next job assignment, occasionally looking outside at the spectacular tree, mountain, and water views. Sitting separately now, they were crossing a bridge over the northern reaches of San Francisco Bay, with the gleaming high-rise buildings of the Berkeley Reservation dominating the view ahead. It was late morning, an overcast, drizzly day.

Considered the flagship of all reservations for humans, Berkeley was a dense population center of seventy-three million people that extended inland—east, south, and north of the old, much smaller city site, thus consuming the former decadent metropolises of Oakland and San Jose, as well as many of the sprawling suburbs. The original university district of Berkeley, called Old Town now, had been largely preserved and was considered a revered and legendary site, the secular equivalent of hallowed ground. This was where Chairman Rahma and the revolutionary council had fomented the populist rebellion in 2041 that spread across millions of square kilometers and brought down the avaricious corporations of North and South America, along with their lackey governments.

West of the bay, the San Francisco peninsula had been split and greenformed into woodlands, lakes, and waterways, including sanctuaries and habitats for important bird, animal, and plant species, now known as the Golden Gate Conservancy. Ponds, lakes, and streams had been generated to mimic what might have been there thousands of years ago. Stands of fast-growing trees covered the hills where rich and powerful tycoons and their ladies had once cavorted, and the ugly, pollution-engendering scars of bridges and highways had all been destroyed. People didn't belong in such beautiful places and had been moved out of the way, so that the natural processes of the Earth could resume.

The train slowed way down as it entered the Berkeley Reservation, heading for the station in Old Town. Through the window, Joss saw balcony and rooftop gardens on many buildings, as well as signs that read "Safe Injection Booths" and "Needle Exchange," and he watched drug patrons going in and out of the old buildings that housed these facilities.

OUTSIDE THE TRAIN, a ragged-looking man was shouting at a bearded gentleman who wore one of the new suit designs, adorned with a stylized tree. The well-dressed man turned and tried to walk away, but the ragamuffin leaped on his back-side, knocking him down, and began pummeling him with fists. A railroad security officer ran toward the scene, his gun drawn and shouting commands.

The aggressor paid no attention and kept hitting the fallen man, drawing blood from his face.

The cop fired a projectile, apparently something to just stun the attacker, because when it hit him there was no blood, but he stiffened and stopped moving. The officer then put a restraining device on the man's wrists and hauled him to his feet, while the victim struggled to recover and answered questions from the officer.

"Crime is everywhere," Kupi said, "even here in Berkeley, the showplace of the GSA."

It was one of the cynical comments that were so typical of Kupi, who at times seemed contemptuous of the Green States, and said exactly what others would like to say, but didn't dare.

The train rolled on, leaving the crime scene behind.

IN THE KITCHEN of their small apartment, Doug Ridell and his wife prepared the evening meal. Several times a week they preferred to make fresh salads, soups, and stews with vegetables and fruits from the street vendors, instead of processed food from their own automated kitchen.

Doug was not in a good mood, because that afternoon he'd learned that Kristine Longet had filed a formal complaint against him alleging that he had not repaired her robot properly, and because of his "incompetence," she wanted someone else to work on it. Doug had tried to tell his supervisor what the real reason was, but the man wouldn't listen, and from the look on his face, it would be a blemish in Doug's personnel file. The despicable, arrogant woman had probably sabotaged the robot, just to make him look bad.

He finished cutting carrots, cauliflower, and onions, then used his knife to scrape scraps into the garbage processor. The machinery whirred as the pieces dropped into the refuse chute, without grinding them. Periodically, garbage technicians inspected the bins in the basement (a separate, marked bin for each apartment), to make certain they did not contain unauthorized materials, such as plastics, polluting chemicals, and other contraband substances that were in violation of the basic tenets on which the GSA was founded.

Other government technicians monitored energy use through smart meters on appliances, and audited the interiors of apartments (by surprise inspection) to make certain that all facets of a citizen's home life were within the sustainable standards laid out in the Charter of the Green States of America. The government had numerous other behavior-monitoring programs as well, designed to reduce the carbon footprint of each person, thus reducing global warming and other ecological harm to the planet.

Doug slammed the knife down on the counter, removed his apron, and hung it on a wall hook. "You finish up, Hana. I don't feel like eating anything."

"You don't want any dinner?"

"No, I just want Jade to work harder, so we don't have to put up with this life anymore."

Head down, he passed his other daughter in the hallway, without saying anything to her.

Just before retreating into the wretched little bedroom he shared with his wife, he heard Willow ask, "What's the matter with Daddy?"

THROUGH THE WINDOW of the train, Joss saw banners on walls proclaiming the benefits of injection booths and needle exchanges, asserting that they reduced drug overdoses, hepatitis C, and HIV-AIDS infections. On his last visit here, Joss and Kupi had been given a tour of the reservation, including the old and new sections, and shown where citizens injected cocaine, crystal meth, heroine, and other popular legal drugs. There were drug-consumption facilities in every GSA population center, but the process seemed to flow more smoothly in Berkeley than anywhere else, perhaps from a tradition here that predated the Corporate War, going all the way back to the 1950s, when so many of the countercultural ideas began to foment.

And, though Joss did not consume recreational drugs on anywhere near the scale of the average citizen, he still understood the need for providing government services in this manner. He couldn't help feeling a patriotic surge of excitement every time he came here. So many famous radicals had been in Berkeley, and so many legendary events had occurred in this place. He felt the presence of their ghosts, could almost hear their stirring speeches at rallies on the old campus of the University of California, which was now a park and environmental learning center, the buildings having been converted to GSA uses.

Kupi Landau had been part of it, one of the Black Shirts who spearheaded many of the attacks. Now, smoking a juana stick, she came over and sat by him. The smoke smelled faintly of cinnamon.

"Thinking about the glory days here?" he asked, as the train passed a large section of pea patches, where schoolchildren were working.

"Perhaps." She smiled, offered him a hit on the stick.

He took a small toke, passed the stick back to her. "Thanks," he said, feeling a burn in his throat. It was strong, special-order stuff.

"I never cease to be amazed when I remember the old days," she said, "the way Rahma used to lead demonstrations and juggle beautiful girls on what he called his 'bedroom dance card.'"

"He hasn't slowed down, from what I hear."

She nodded, lit another stick of marijuana, and offered it to him.

"No, thanks," he said. "That one was enough. Besides, I'm getting high just sitting next to you and inhaling your smoke."

On impulse, he leaned over and kissed her on the cheek, a gentle peck. "You know how different we are," he said. "Sometimes I wonder if we can stay together, or even if we should stay together."

She looked at him with a hurt expression, didn't say anything.

"Even if we don't stay together—as a couple, I mean—I want us to remain friends. Good friends."

"My, aren't you the harbinger of happy tidings."

"This has been building up for some time now. Don't tell me you haven't noticed."

"I've noticed."

Sadness lingered in the air between them, like smoke from a burned-out juana stick. The train pulled into the station, and they hurried off, pulling small luggage cases behind them.

JOSS AND HIS crew checked into rooms at the Hotel Mario Savio, named in honor of the mythical leader of the 1960s Free Speech Movement, more than seven decades before the

Corporate War. The crew lunched in a sidewalk café on Dwight Way, then made their way a few blocks to the old campus of the University of California, which was now cordoned off by green-uniformed police because of an environmental problem that had occurred there over the weekend. This was the new jobsite for Joss and Kupi, one so sensitive that it required their expertise. They'd been told to use a local Janus Machine instead of their regular rig. He had not seen the machine they would be using yet, but did see the seedlike shape of a SciO Recharge Facility, for the servicing of J-Mac cannons. . . .

Almost a century ago, the students of Cal Berkeley (and radical infiltrators) took over this campus for a short time, including the student union center and the administration building, where they staged sit-ins. They even commandeered police cars, and stood on their roofs shouting "Kill the Pigs" about the cops, while demanding free speech and a voice in the affairs of the university. The protesters burned bras and draft cards, set up tables covered with Marxist literature, and flooded the campus and the streets with demonstrators carrying anti-war and free-speech signs.

Eventually the left-wing radicals retreated against the onslaught of police thugs and soldiers, but additional grassroots movements arose in the following century, including the biggest of all, led by Rahma Popal's revolutionary council. Popal had learned lessons from the experiences of Mario Savio, Abbie Hoffman, Jerry Rubin, and other twentieth-century counterculture radicals, and had been able to go much, much further than they had, riding the crest of environmental and anti-Corporate waves. In the face of great adversity, the idealistic Popal had refused to retreat, and through courage and ingenuity he had won the ultimate victory.

On the Shattuck Street side of the old campus, Joss and his

crew were stopped at a checkpoint by green-uniformed police officers. The crew showed their identification cards, then proceeded across the main square, passing the large fountain and the Campanile tower, and going through two more checkpoints. Joss noted scaffolding on several buildings, and workers busily repairing damage from a recent earthquake. Old bricks, stone blocks, and chunks of concrete were piled on the ground in several areas, for reuse by construction crews or for eco-friendly disposal.

At the far side of the square, Joss saw a high, opaque fence and gate, blocking any view of the worksite beyond. A Janus Machine was parked in front of the gate, with white-robed SciO technicians aboard it, checking the systems out. Both cannons were glowing, and the group was firing unloaded test capsules. The machine was an older model, with an ornate railing around the turret platform. It appeared to still have its original paint job, with a number of small dents, and showed signs of weathering.

"Looks like one of the Battle for Berkeley relics from two decades ago," Kupi groused. "They must have pulled it out of a museum and refitted it. Look at that worn numeral on the side; it's old Number Two. And it has an old-style atomic reactor on the back."

"It looks kind of beat, but I assume the operating systems are still good."

"I hope the thing is safe," Kupi said.

"I'm sure it is. We're in Berkeley, after all, the heartbeat of the Green States of America."

Joss had already reviewed the assignment with Kupi, and now he took time to brief the rest of the crew. They gathered around him in their green-and-black uniforms, a short distance from the weathered old Janus Machine.

"This is a highly sensitive cleanup site," Joss said. "Somehow the Corporate bastards tunneled underneath the old campus and buried industrial waste down there, barrels of really nasty, highly toxic stuff. The site was so well hidden, even from scanners, that our government didn't know it was there."

"Until an earthquake ruptured the land open," Kupi said, "bringing down walls and causing dangerous chemicals to leak out of the barrels, contaminating the ground and water."

"The Corporates went to a lot of trouble and expense to build a tunnel and storage area," one of the crewmen said, a man who passed his own helmet back and forth in his hands as he stood there. "Why would they do that?"

"Several reasons," Kupi said. "First, they were under assault from environmentalists to deal with toxic wastes safely, and not to create them in the first place. Even before the Corporate War there were political victories against industrialists, forcing them to go to great expense to clean up their crap. It's all about money, isn't it? Obviously the bad guys found it was cheaper to tunnel under Cal Berkeley and hide the bad stuff where the environmentalists wouldn't think to look."

"It was like thumbing their noses at the Greenies," Joss said. "Maybe the Corporates even hoped an earthquake would eventually open things up and contaminate the area. Greenpol has been over the site with a fine-tooth comb, and they can't tell for certain where the stuff came from. The criminals covered their tracks well."

"And now it's our job to clean up the mess," Kupi said, "or should I say, it's my job. I need to aim straight, because there are historic buildings all around."

"That's right," Joss said, "and then I greenform a new park area. One more thing. All of us are sworn to secrecy about this job. The discovery of a toxic waste dump is an embarrassment to the administration, and they just want it fixed, with no fanfare. This is Ground Zero for the Green Revolution. They plan a cover story about the new park, saying it will be a new GSA rescue center for trumpeter swans, California condors, and other birds that need special protection."

Joss led the way to the Janus Machine, where the SciO technicians were finishing up. He talked with the white-bearded foreman, who informed him that everything was in readiness with the exception of specialized cartridges of microorganisms for the Seed Cannon, which were being prepared now at the Recharge Facility.

"Toxic wastes are leaching into the soil," the foreman said, "so it's advisable for you to split the area as soon as possible. Then you can take the machine over to ReFac and get your seed cartridges loaded."

"Right," Joss said.

The SciOs departed, and he ordered his own crew to board the unit. Moments later, as Joss and Kupi stood on the turret platform, the gates opened, revealing a large, irregular area littered with building debris and toxic waste barrels, some of which were broken open. At least two historic buildings had been destroyed in the quake.

The Janus Machine rumbled over a short bridge that crossed a trench. Joss had already explained to his crew that the entire affected area was surrounded by new protective trenches, and he saw red flags fluttering around the perimeter, just inside the fencing. The gates closed behind them, to keep out prying eyes.

He and Kupi secured their owl-design helmets and dark goggles. She swung up onto the chair behind the black cannon barrel, and ran through test sequences on the control panel.

"Let's get this over with," she said, shaking her head in dismay. "It's one of the most raggedy-looking J-Macs I've seen, but we have to assume the SciOs have checked it out." She glanced back at him. "Any concerns, Commander?"

"Your sequences all check out?"

"They do. A little slow, but it's older technology. I think it's all right."

"Get on with it, then," Joss said.

He ordered the other crewmen to their stations, then stood behind Kupi while she tapped keys on the instrument console. The turret swung around noisily, so that the glistening black barrel was pointing at the farthest perimeter of the toxic waste site, where inspectors had placed a line of red flags. All of the on-site personnel hurried to safety zones behind clearplex blast barriers, and animals were cleared away with sonic devices. Then a special warning siren sounded to clear the area of human beings.

Joss and Kupi had discussed the tactics for this project, and agreed that she would seal that edge of the site with focal Splitter blasts to prevent further damage to the old campus beyond it, and then she would hit the site itself with a more powerful blast, preparing it for the infinitesimally tiny, customized greenforming micro-organisms that were being prepared now in ReFac.

"Black Thunder time," Kupi said, over the comm-radio.

Joss secured the noise-dampening system inside his helmet, but still heard a low, gathering roar. Seconds ticked by, more than customary with the newer machines. Finally the black barrel spewed forth with waves of black particles, a fine pelting around the far edge of the site. Kupi turned the turret and did the same around all of the other edges. Then she fired larger blasts into the center, digging down and disintegrating all of the toxins and melting away every bit of debris, preparing the site for Joss.

"My turn next," Joss said, across the communication system. He waited while the crew prepared to move the machine to the Recharge Facility. . . .

18

For humankind, hope often seems like a flickering, dying ember.

—Chairman Rahma, before the strange
transformation of Joss Stuart

WHILE SCIO SECRECY was essentially impenetrable, there were small concessions, unnoticed by some people but important to others. Reportedly, Chairman Rahma had negotiated a number of compromises with the Director of Science, Arch Ondex, during the push and pull in the formative days of the Green States of America. One was a procedure that enabled GSA eco-techs such as Joss and Kupi to inspect the loading of new seeding and splitting cartridges in their cannons at SciO-operated Recharge Facilities, if the techs wished to do so. In the alternative, Science Overseers would load the cartridges without them. Other Janus Machine crew members were excluded.

Being very conscientious and particular about his work, Joss always accepted this option. Kupi, on the other hand, did what she usually did, and took a pot break with the rest of the crew.

Joss stood alone on the turret platform, holding on to a railing while the twin barrels of the machine retracted. He nodded down to his crew, who stood nearby, smoking their juana sticks and watching while the big rig went into remote-control mode and rolled toward the seed-shaped ReFac building.

SciOs inside the structure were operating the J-Mac by remote control now; as Joss neared the facility, he saw the armorplex windows of the control room in the bulbous section on top, and white-robed men inside. He'd always thought these buildings were quite pleasing in appearance, with their aerodynamic elm-seed shapes that enabled them to soar upon the wind when they were being transported. He always found the beauty of nature stunning, and respected the fact that SciOs had been inspired by this when they designed their Recharge Facilities.

A huge door on the front of the ReFac building irised open, and the Janus Machine rolled inside, with the door closing behind it. In a sense, Joss felt as if he were inside an alien world now (despite the natural-looking exterior), or in an exotic barn for animals other than horses. His machine rolled forward noisily, slowly passing between windows on either side where white-robed Science Overseers worked in laboratories, formulating different types of cartridges.

Another Janus Machine was already inside the building on the other end, a newer model that was having its black Splitter barrel loaded by men with a long black hose, who used sealed fittings. Joss noticed a very fine dust floating in the air between the machines, more than usual, and he sneezed. No telling what sorts of pollens might be floating around in here.

He'd seen dusty facilities before, and had asked his managers about the integrity of the seed cartridges that were assembled in such places and the safety of loading explosive projectiles into Splitter barrels there. In response, he was always assured that cartridges and projectiles were prepared and sealed under strictly controlled conditions, and that any dust out on the floor of the loading areas was brought in from outside by Janus Machines. There was nothing to worry about, he'd always been told.

The old J-Mac truck came to a stop, and as Joss stood on the turret platform he felt it turn, so that the glistening, retracted barrel of the Seed Cannon was facing a metal deck beneath one of the side windows. Two SciOs stood on that deck, operating a mechanical arm with a large metal hand on it that held four new seed cartridges. Joss had seen this done many times before.

"Swing the cartridges over here so I can take a look," he shouted to them. This was part of the concession that Chairman Rahma had obtained, enabling an eco-tech to examine each cartridge before it was loaded. For greenformers such as himself, it was a matter of making certain the ingredients were correct and suitable for particular environments. For Splitters like Kupi, it was more a matter of safety. If anything went wrong with her cartridges, it could blow up the Janus Machine in the field and kill the crew. As her superior, knowledgeable in all aspects of J-Mac operation, Joss always inspected her cartridges as well as his own.

"Okay," one of the SciOs shouted back, "but you know the rules. Don't touch." This man had a long bald spot running down the center of black, shaggy hair. His robe was smeared with green and brown.

Joss nodded, and held on to the railing as the mechanical arm swung over to him, and the metal hand opened to display the cartridges on its palm. He checked code numbers on the cartridges and compared them with his own notes, confirming that these were the mixtures he had specified for the eco-tech assignment at hand.

"Now run spectrals," Joss said, "to be extra sure these have been filled correctly."

"We've already done that," the SciO said.

"I want you to do it again. I'm within my rights as a G-One eco-tech to demand this."

"Well, aren't you the fussy one!"

Grumbling to himself, the SciO brought the seed cartridges back to himself, and ran a spectrometer over each of them. Joss heard four beeps, saw green lights on the device as the mixtures were confirmed. He was not permitted to see the actual readings, had to presume they were accurate.

"All right," Joss said. "Go ahead and load."

With a tight smile, the SciO said, "Well, thank you very much."

While still holding all four cartridges, the mechanical hand loaded one at a time, waiting for each to snick into place in the Seed Cannon's holding chamber.

When they were finished and the onboard greenforming equipment was properly sealed, the operators performed a ritual on the deck that always seemed quasi-religious to Joss, though the scientists were said to be secular—like every other citizen in good standing. Facing the Janus Machine, they knelt and raised their hands in the air, with the fingers splayed. A long moment passed as they murmured something that sounded like an incantation, as if they were performing sorcery, not science.

Then they stood and operated hand-held electronic devices to swing the turret platform around to the other side, where two other SciOs were prepared to load the Splitter barrel. These men held a thick black hose containing the explosive projectiles that were fired by Splitters.

"That's not necessary," Joss said to them. "We already did the splitting portion of the job, and I'm only here to get the special seed preparations, because they weren't ready when we arrived. Just send me back out now, without any delay. This is a sensitive environmental cleanup site."

"Aren't they all," one of the SciOs said. He was stocky,

with a scruffy red beard. "You oughta know, buddy, we're not supposed to send out half-loaded J-Macs."

"Well, you did earlier," Joss said, "because when I got here the machine only had the Splitter barrel ready to go."

"We didn't prepare this machine that way," the man said. "Must have been an earlier crew. No matter, they made a mistake, shouldn't have sent the rig out like that. Don't expect us to do the same thing. We have regulations to follow, you know."

"Oh, for—" Joss caught a curse in his throat. "All right, but I want to inspect everything before it's loaded."

Joss ran through the inspection process, checking each black cartridge that they planned to load, noting the seals, the quality-control codes, and other details.

"Everything OK?" the red-bearded SciO asked, as Joss checked his notes, and added to them.

"Right," Joss said. "Go ahead."

"It will only take a few minutes." Then the man shouted back to another SciO, "Hey, Tokko, get me another adapter for this thing. It's one of the old rigs."

Joss shook his head in dismay, watched while they fitted another adapter onto the end of the hose, and then connected it to the rear of the Janus Machine's black barrel. Moments passed as both SciOs held the hose in place. This looked peculiar, because it was supposed to fit and hold on its own, but maybe this was the way they did it on the old machines. He heard a suction noise as the equipment made a connection and began loading the sealed explosive charges. Like everything else on Janus Machines, they were designed to detonate if anyone tampered with them. To further protect their monopoly, the SciOs also had surveillance cameras mounted on the J-Mac trucks, with live relays, to make doubly certain that no one tried to steal any of their technology and attempt to duplicate it.

As Joss waited he felt increasingly uneasy, and finally reached back to an instrument console, where he called up readings about the truck's functions. A screen showed that two splitting projectiles had been successfully loaded, with two more to go.

He took a deep breath, watched the technicians at the other Janus Machine. They appeared to be finishing up, preparing to send the rig on its way. Yes, he was certain of it, because the SciOs were going through another quasi-religious ritual, standing reverently on the decks at each side of the machine, with their hands raised in the air to signify that the unit was fully loaded, sealed, and ready to go.

The exit door on that end of the ReFac building was still closed. Joss noticed a lot more dust between the two machines than he'd seen before, swirling high in the air now, and he heard something hissing—an unfamiliar sound that caused his pulse to race. He smelled fumes, a peculiar odor of strange gas.

Something is not right! he thought.

The hissing was coming from the fitting on the black barrel of his own machine, he realized, and the smell must be coming from there as well. Some kind of leak in the fitting? That couldn't be good.

The SciOs were trying to adjust the connection. Someone shouted to shut off the loader. But it was too late.

Joss was consumed by a blinding flash, and a deafening noise. Moments passed, in which time and reality seemed to stand on end. He felt as if he were an outside observer, watching as waves of pulsing blackness assailed him, disintegrating his cells, tissues, and organs into their most basic elements. For a moment it all hovered in the air in the shape of a human being, a ghostlike apparition. Then green-and-black parti-cles sprinkled over the form like a warm, gentle rain from the heavens, and he saw an aura remaining where his body had been, an empty, glowing husk.

Whether it was a dream, a nightmare, or a burst of con-sciousness at the finish of his life, he couldn't tell—but the abnormal experience continued over the course of what may have only been milliseconds, though it seemed like much lon-ger. He heard a faint susurration, a whispering and murmur-ing as the empty husk of his body was filled with the cellular DNA, chloroplast, amino acids, and proteins of green plants, along with a flow of reconstituted elements and cellular mate-rial from his human body . . . and something more, from the stygian, primal violence that the SciOs had harnessed for their Splitter technology.

Dark Energy, he realized.

The result was an amalgamation, a humanoid creature re-sembling Joss but with a light carbon cast to his skin, and for-est green, keloid scars (or veins) that wound around his arms, legs, and torso like vines. He felt imbued with strange powers, and saw himself standing outside the ReFac building, lifting his arms in triumph as the structure exploded behind him.

But it must have been a dying dream, requiring only an in-stant to occur. Abruptly, everything blacked out around him.

19

Unknowns are a fact of life. A person has but to consider this for a few moments to realize the universality of the concept. That field of grass and flowers, for example, holds secrets, and so does the person standing in the meadow. Now look in all directions as far as the eye can see, and you will be astonished at what you do not know. Look at the countless mysteries of our planet and the infinite details of space, beyond anything you can even begin to imagine.

—Joss Stuart, remembered thoughts from his boyhood

CHAIRMAN RAHMA POPAL felt like a schoolboy as he walked through the aviaries with Jade, holding her hand while exotic, endangered birds flew overhead and cried out to one another in their cacophony of sounds. Afternoon sunlight filtered through the net-and-fabric ceiling, splaying across the colorful bodies and wings of the birds and brightening the green leaves of the trees and plants. It was moist in here, and a little humid because of the connected greenhouses and the retractable, atmospheric-control roofs over the aviaries that were closed now.

Only twenty-three, Jade made him feel young again, but even more than that, he genuinely liked her. She had her failings, her little immaturities, but she was innately intelligent and knowledgeable for her age. The young woman was always trying to improve herself, always trying to please him, and he liked that. She was also outspoken, and had interesting things to say, insightful observations about people and the animals of the game reserve. Now she had her pretty red hair clasped in a wood hair band, because he'd told her once that he liked it that way.

Oftentimes Rahma felt as if he was getting old. He would be sixty on his next birthday, reaching one of those decade markers that reminded him so cruelly and unavoidably of his mortality. In his lowest moments he felt the inexorable decline seeping in around his life, the unseen, insidious malady that decayed his physical and mental capabilities; eventually he would wind down entirely, return to the soil of the planet in a process of entropy, and be recycled naturally. It was part of the great circle of life and death, but he was far from ready to be taken away from his conscious relationship with this earth that he loved so much. He still had important work to do.

He thought he might be losing his virility, because he had not fathered a child in more than four years, though he was as active sexually as ever. Maybe Jade would bear a child for him; they had not been using any birth control methods or other protection. He wouldn't mind if she did join the long list of women who had given birth to his children, and if she did, he thought he might keep this one around and take part in raising it—unlike most of the others, who were scattered all across the GSA, and perhaps the world, for all he knew. Still, Jade had said nothing to him about being pregnant, and she certainly didn't look it.

She smiled when he looked at her.

Just then, a rare blue-and-gold finch landed on her head, and with the bird perched in her hair and her eyes trying to look up at it, she looked so comical that he couldn't help laughing.

"Take a picture of me," she urged, her voice even softer than usual. He could tell she was trying not to disturb the tiny creature.

Mentally, he activated the neuro-optic connection of his implanted camera, which worked through his own eyes, and he gave the silent command to capture the image. He took several, and then said, "Those are great. We'll transfer them to the backup system later and I'll print you copies."

The energetic little bird landed on her open hand, then hopped over to Rahma's hand. He recognized the signs of a budding relationship. He and Jade were building memories together.

IN THE PAST two weeks, the marsupial wolf had unexpectedly grown quite large, to the point where its body was the size of a small horse, but to Artie it looked even bigger than that, because of the batlike wings it flexed and extended frequently, even when not flying. The rate of growth this creature had exhibited was astonishing to Artie and his robotic assistants, and he wondered to himself if it had something to do with the educated guesses and assumptions he'd made when growing the animal in the laboratory. The quarter of one percent he had secretly added to the genetic mix.

The skeletal remains of its extinct ancestor that had been found on Lord Howe Island near Australia were considerably smaller, leading to unanswered questions. So far, the hubot had fended them off by saying that one individual skeleton might not fairly represent the species. He was controlling the dissemination of information, and certain details didn't make it into the reports that he passed on to Chairman Rahma.

The glidewolf's appetite for eucalyptus seemed insatiable,

and many of the trees in the habitat showed evidence of this, with stripped leaves and bark and bare, scarred branches, as well as missing branches that the creature had ripped apart and chewed into pulp that it could swallow. The sharpness of the creatures' claws and teeth gave Artie considerable pause, not out of concern for his own safety (because he was a hubot), but out of concern for humans that could be injured by them, or worse. Still, the animal was supposed to be herbivorous, not carnivorous.

It was evening, and Artie stood near the tree where the creature nested on a large lower branch. He watched her as she watched him, her pale yellow eyes glinting in the low light of the habitat. "You're not a meat eater, are you?" Artie said aloud.

As if in response, the glidewolf stirred from her nest and descended the trunk of the tree headfirst, keeping her wings folded over her body. Reaching the ground, she walked toward Artie on all fours. Her actions seemed peculiar to him, indeed, because she had never done this before, but Artie held his ground, unafraid. Except for his eyes, he only had artificial skin that could be repaired or replaced, so if necessary he would put his body on the line for the sake of science. He looked human, even had human scents, mannerisms, and other characteristics built into his body, so whatever happened next could be an indication of what the glidewolf might do to a real person.

Reaching Artie, the glidewolf rose up on her haunches, so that she stood more than a head taller than the hubot, in an apparent fighting posture with her forepaws and sharp claws up. She looked down at him with those pale, eerie eyes. It concerned him that the eyes were cold and alien, suggesting a lack of empathy. Her teeth and claws could rip him apart. He reminded himself that he wasn't human for the most part, and he could be repaired if necessary. Even his human eyes could be made to function again if they were damaged, with modern medical techniques.

Fur on the glidewolf's chest pouch rippled a little, and the pouch opened at the top, which was at Artie's face level. The hubot leaned forward to look inside, but saw only darkness.

The pouch opened a bit more, as if in invitation. Artie looked up at the glidewolf's face, seeing the long snout, the mysterious eyes, and the sharp teeth, and feeling very small and powerless himself. Yet Artie had been programmed with the emotions and mannerisms of Glanno Artindale, along with elements of the hero's bravery and his intelligent, scientific curiosity.

Tentatively, the hubot touched the top edge of the pouch and felt it give way and loosen with only a slight amount of pressure from him, as if he and the wolf were of one mind, with the same goal. Now the animal leaned forward slightly to make it easier for Artie, and he climbed inside feetfirst, with his head sticking out of the pouch and his hands holding on to the rough edge. The pouch tightened comfortably around him.

Abruptly the glidewolf turned and scampered up the tree, with Artie holding on. As the hubot watched in amazement, this time as a participant instead of viewing it through a camera feed, the marsupial leaped from a high point and extended her wings, gliding to the top of another eucalyptus tree. Again it leaped, and again it glided, circling around the dimly lit airspace between the treetops and the techplex ceiling of the habitat and then using her clawed feet to grab hold of the vertical trellis that led up to the ingress and egress hatch.

Quickly the wolf scampered up the trellis, nudged open the

hatch, and exited the enclosure into the night. Then, without even climbing a tree, she lifted her wings and picked up a strong breeze that enabled the creature and her humanoid passenger to soar upward into the night sky, over the game reserve.

With his simulated senses, Artie felt the coolness of the night air against his face, and with his programmed emotions he also felt exhilaration. To the west he saw the buildings of Chairman Rahma's headquarters compound, as well as the Shrine of Martyrs, the aviaries, and the vaulted greenhouses—all dimly lit—and also the large, oval-shaped rooftop of the subterranean network of extinct animal habitats, glittering with illumination as if it were a decorative pond.

Upward the glidewolf soared into the starlit darkness, finding one air current and then shifting to another, gliding expertly this way and that, as if cavorting in the night sky. Then, gradually, she circled and returned to the ground near the ingress-egress hatch. There in the illumination she hesitated for a moment, looking down at Artie with eyes that had become noticeably larger during the flight, evidence of the nocturnal side of the creature, an aspect that seemed to come and go, because she was so often energetic in the daytime as well as the nighttime.

The marsupial opened the hatch with one sharp claw, climbed inside, and descended the trellis headfirst, facing vertically downward. For a moment, Artie thought he would fall out of the pouch, but it tightened comfortably around him during the descent, so he hardly had to hold on (though he did anyway).

When it was over and Artie found himself back in his laboratory office, he reviewed the information he had just accumulated in his data banks. It was fascinating! Then on a screen he watched the glidewolf on a tree branch, scraping bark free and chewing it. The creature had a voracious appetite, and seemed to grow visibly larger as it fed. He wondered how much bigger it would get.

20

Though most of us deny being religious, the GSA contains a pantheon of progressivism, a group of gods or saints, or whatever you choose to call them. In our eyes, they can do no wrong. We call them the Berkeley Eight, and they are an integral part of the myth structure that Chairman Rahma Popal created in order to sustain his government. Did he do this for altruistic reasons, to benefit the planet, or with another motivation in mind? That is another question, isn't it?

—Unanswered Questions for Chairman Rahma,
a banned book

KUPI AND JOSS'S crew stood at a hospital viewing window, peering into the room where he lay in a coma, breathing slowly and regularly. For nine days he had not moved, with the exception of the slight and regular motion of his chest as he breathed, and the intermittent fluttering of his lips as air passed across them. He was on his back with his head propped up slightly by a pillow, and intravenous lines connected.

It was early evening. Kupi Landau and her companions had just arrived by high-speed train from the Southwest Territory, where they had been assigned to work temporarily with another greenformer until Joss recovered. Kupi and her coworkers had been here three times since the explosion, and this was the first occasion they'd seen Joss's cop roommate, Andruw Twitty, in the viewing area. He wore street clothes.

188 • BRIAN HERBERT

Two doctors were in the room now, using instruments to run tests on the patient. Kupi pressed against the clearplex to see better. Joss had only an uncle still living in his family, so his friends had been given permission to visit him—but they could get no closer than this. As everyone could see from the light carbon color of Joss's skin and the forest green, vinelike scars that wound around his body, he was no ordinary patient.

The hospital room was soundproof, so Kupi could not hear what the doctors were saying to each other, but they looked perplexed. One of them shrugged, while the other typed notes on a data pad.

Just a few minutes ago, a nurse had entered the viewing area and told Kupi that Joss had no internal bleeding and no apparent hemorrhage in the brain. Miraculously, he was healing rapidly from what seemed to be superficial injuries, but the doctors could not explain his appearance or bring him out of the coma. They'd been trying different things, and performing a battery of tests.

The nurse had struggled for words. "I don't want to speak out of turn, but I've been informed that all of you are close to him, so I'll tell you what I can. Joss's cellular and chemical makeup have . . . changed dramatically. You can see his skin, and it isn't just the appearance. Tests reveal that he's a hybrid—part human, part plant, and part something else."

Alarmed, Kupi had asked, "What do you mean?"

"In the explosion he was infused with the DNA and cellular structures of trees and other plants that are native to the Berkeley area, along with something else that we can't identify."

"Why does his skin look like that?" Twitty had asked. Kupi had noticed a flatness in his tone, more coldness than usual. He seemed unconcerned, but curious. In contrast, Joss's crew was worried about whether or not he would survive, and whether he would ever return to consciousness.

"We don't know." The nurse had seemed to dislike Twitty, and she'd left soon afterward without saying much more.

Now Kupi glanced dispassionately at the young eco-cop, and caught his nervous gaze before it flitted away. No one on the crew was saying much to him at all, leaving him off to one side by himself.

He appeared ill at ease, said, "I can tell that none of you like me, and I want you to know that I don't care."

"We don't care that you don't care," said the stout, aging mechanic, Sabe McCarthy. He was the shortest of the crew, and glared over at Twitty. They were about the same height.

In recent months Joss had complained to her about his roommate, saying he suspected he was collecting information to report to higher-ups, and not only about Joss but about Kupi as well. Having met Twitty before, she had no doubt of that. He had a peculiar, sneaky way of behaving around her, of sliding around the edges of a room and trying to look at her when he didn't think she was looking.

He was doing that now, darting gazes toward her and then looking away quickly.

Kupi didn't want to be around him anymore, and needed a break from the whole sad situation. She glanced at the black chrono implanted in her wrist, then whirled and left, with the rest of the crew close behind her.

21

What do we perceive, or think we know?
By these measures we make our way through life,
probing for pathways.
But where do they lead us?
—Chairman Rahma Popal, private files

AT FIRST HE felt a sensual awareness coursing through his veins, like sweet rainwater passing through capillaries in the trunk of a great tree, nurturing even the topmost portions of the plant and enabling it to stretch toward the heavens. He moved the fingers of one hand, and oddly they seemed like little branches with leaves on them, moving ever so slightly to absorb more of the nutrients of the sun, like a process of photosynthesis that was necessary to generate chemical reactions and drive the green engine of a plant.

His thoughts seemed frighteningly alien to him, and he had a dawning impression that much of his corporeal structure was nothing familiar, nothing he'd ever imagined could be possible. And yet he retained links to things he knew, things he had learned and experienced.

I have fingers. More than three words, this was a thought, accompanied by visual memories.

He felt warmth on those fingers. From sunlight? It was a certain kind of warmth, seemingly natural.

And eyes. I have eyes. As the fingers warmed, he opened his eyes and struggled to look in that direction. But his vision was fogged.

More awareness seeped into his mind. In memory he envisioned an entire human body, remembered moving about in one, spending a lifetime with it. But details were indistinct and disjointed, didn't have significance to him.

Other senses penetrated his consciousness, guided it. He realized now that he was lying on something soft, like feathers piled on the duff of a forest floor. But it did not smell like a forest (had a faint antiseptic scent instead), and when he touched the surface with his fingers, it didn't feel like decaying organic materials. He heard distant sounds, couldn't determine what they were, but got the distinct impression that they represented something intrusive and dangerous.

Animals. They intend to harm me!

With a great effort he moved his entire body, and suddenly he felt himself falling, tumbling, finally landing with a hard thud that sent a shudder coursing through his body, along with a dull awareness of pain. Awkwardly, he found a way to rise and stand, and had the distinct sensation that he was something quite different from other life-forms, alone and separated from any known type of organism.

He squinted in bright light, felt like a newborn, but with a twist. *I am the first of my kind, the only one of my kind.*

The creature felt confined by his remaining, hybridized humanness, the musculature assembly that fought his efforts to direct it. But to survive he needed to coordinate the cells, the connective tissue of that body, that form with all of its corporal limitations. He needed to move within its confines, and understand what lay beyond.

I must protect myself against animals . . . human *animals.*

His eyes became more accustomed to the light, and through a haze he saw a room, and a bed he must be lying upon. A hospital room, he decided, noting intravenous lines that he had torn loose, and which dangled from a stand. He felt where they had been connected to his arms, slight, prickling sensations of pain on rough skin surfaces, and noticed that he wore a thin gown, open at the back.

Menacing human shapes became apparent through the haze. People were watching him, speaking about him in urgent tones. The creature knew that he should understand their words, but he could not, no matter how hard he tried. There were significant gaps preventing comprehension, gaps that stretched across an abyss from his human past to whatever he was now.

He became aware of clearplex windows on one perimeter of the room, and of sunlight streaming in, splashing warmth over him and making him feel just a little better. There were interior viewing windows as well, where a man stood looking at him, observing, collecting information.

The creature began to understand some of the words spoken by others. They were uttered by nurses and doctors, but not by the man behind the viewing window, who seemed apart from them, and a quiet threat.

Abruptly his own name came back, floating on currents of memory: *I am Joss Stuart. I am a greenformer and commander of a J-Mac crew; I live in the Seattle Reservation for Humans.*

These memories and realizations were links to a past that he knew could never exist for him again. Everything was changed now.

Shapes moved toward Joss, doctors and nurses with instruments to sedate him and get him under their control. He could not allow that, and backed away from them, knocking over a rolling table. His ears detected a faint roar, as from far away. It grew louder by the moment.

Their voices were urgent, and strong fingers gripped Joss's arm. "I've got him!" a man shouted. "Get over here and help me!"

Joss pulled free and kicked the man with a bare foot, causing him to tumble over a chair and shout curses.

"Grab his arms!" a woman shouted.

But Joss whirled away and kicked out several times, surprisingly powerful thrusts that prevented anyone from capturing him. The people in the room were shadow shapes now, like figures from a nightmare.

Looking down, Joss realized that he stood on his bare feet and was in a slight crouch, with his hands stiff and the fingers pointed straight ahead, like a martial arts pose—training he'd never had, but the menacing posture was keeping them at bay. He wasn't sure how he had accomplished that posture. The skin on his hands looked odd and veiny, and his fingers were darker than the rest of his skin, and seemed to glow a little. A trick of light?

Interrupting his thoughts, Joss saw movement on his right behind the viewing window. Involuntarily he spun on his bare feet, so that his fingers were now pointed at whoever was on the other side of that clearplex—as if to protect himself against a threat there. A name came to Joss's awareness as he recognized the person: Andruw Twitty, his roommate from the Seattle Reservation.

He felt a surge of anger, didn't want him there, looking in and intruding.

The five fingers of Joss's left hand became even darker, then black, and he saw them glow more, as if they were little Splitter barrels about to fire. Suddenly streaks of black light shot from the fingers, breaking the plex of the viewing room, exploding it into fragments and melting it into a gooey mass that dripped onto the floor.

He heard Twitty scream out in pain. It was an alarming sound, and Joss hoped he had not seriously injured the young man, despite his irritating, self-serving ways. Looking at the melted plex, Joss wondered if he had tapped into some sort of Splitter power. He shuddered, fearing that something terrible had found its way into his body, and that he didn't know how to control it. He lowered his hands, tried to calm himself.

In his moment of hesitation, he felt strong arms around him, holding his arms and legs, tearing his gown and wrestling him to the ground—and the pricking of needles into his body. He didn't resist, though he sensed that he could escape if he wanted to.

But Joss wasn't sure if he wanted to get away. He wasn't at all certain what form of life he had become, and worried about the harm he might cause away from this hospital, the havoc he might wreak on the outside world if allowed to roam free. He didn't want to hurt anyone.

I am the first of my kind, he thought again, *the only one of my kind.*

22

Dark Energy and Green Vigor are opposite sides of the same reality.

—from a secret SciO rite

KUPI HAD AN uneasy feeling when she entered the Greenpol station and walked down the long corridor. In her pocket, she carried a small slip of recycled paper that simply read "SUMMONS," along with a brief description of the location where she was supposed to report in the Berkeley Reservation, and the deadline for doing so.

The legal document contained no information about what the authorities wanted. It was something bad; that much she could figure out, or it wouldn't involve the cops. Had the GSA government finally run out of patience with her? Had she said something that tipped the balance and put her in trouble? She tried to tell herself it was not that, because if she'd done anything really serious they would have already arrested her. If it involved a complaint against her, it might just be a warning. She'd received those before.

No telling what these green fanatics were up to. She loathed these eco-cops, with their officious ways, the little power games and mind fornications they played on average citizens, always justifying their actions by claiming they were protecting the environment or the eco-friendly government. It was all a convenient rationalization, one that could not easily be assailed. The cops in Berkeley were pigs, green pigs.

The summons had been served on her while she was on a greenforming jobsite in the Southwest Territory, more than nine hundred kilometers away. She had considered refusing to report and going AWOL, just vanishing into a forest and ridding herself of the bureaucratic controls that so often irritated her. But something had told her not to do that. They wanted her to report to Berkeley. Joss was still there, and she'd been worrying about him. Hopefully he was OK.

It was early afternoon now. Two hours ago, with a little time to spare before her Greenpol appointment, she'd tried to get into the hospital to see Joss, but without success. The nurses would give her no information on him, just said they would take her name and someone would contact her later. Standing at the counter, she'd wondered if he had died. Her pulse had raced, and desperately, she'd hoped that was not the case. . . .

Now she entered a Greenpol waiting room where a man at the front desk had directed her, and she dropped her summons into a tray, as she'd been told to do. Perhaps twenty other people sat in chairs, looking nervously in the direction of a closed door. Kupi sat with them, and soon found herself looking toward the door as well, because green-uniformed officers would appear there periodically, call out a name, and take that person inside.

Several citizens were summoned by officers, and Kupi noticed that some of the people, but not all of them, were later released through the same door. What happened to the others, she didn't know, but it was a grave concern. The Berkeley cops were said to be among the worst and most aggressive, undoubtedly because this was supposed to be the GSA's model

reservation for humans, and the pigs wanted to keep everything in order.

The door opened, and she was alarmed to see Andruw Twitty
just inside, talking with a uniformed female captain. Though
Twitty was a Greenpol officer he wasn't wearing his uniform,
perhaps because he didn't work in this locale. Curiously, he had
a bandage over his forehead, and there were scratches and
bruises on his face, as well as on his arms and hands.

Joss's young roommate saluted the captain with the sign
of the sacred tree, then strode out into the waiting room. He
spotted Kupi right away, paused near her, and said, "Your little friend did this to me after you left. I'll bet that makes you
happy."

"My little friend?"

"Joss." He pointed toward the door. "They want *you* now."

Perplexed, Kupi rose to her feet and made her way to the
officer. The woman had Kupi's summons in her hand, and led
the way to an inner office, where two officers in starched uniforms awaited her, sitting at a table. Their perfectly polished
green helmets sat on the table, next to a small video screen
that was dark.

Both officers were middle-aged men, one heavyset with
thick-lens eyeglasses and loose jowls; he had a deep voice,
which he used to command her to sit across from them. His
companion was Asian, with dark, probing eyes that seemed to
absorb their surroundings like a sponge.

She sat in the only place available, on a hard wooden chair
that wobbled. At first she tried to steady the chair beneath
her; then she noticed that one of its legs was not quite in contact with the floor. She suspected it had been done intentionally, to keep people off balance.

Kupi attempted to hold the chair steady, with some difficulty.

Reminding herself to be calm, she placed her right hand on a copy of *The Little Green Book* that was thrust in front of her and swore to tell the truth, the whole truth, and nothing but the truth. Then she clasped her hands and put them on top of the table.

"You serve on a J-Mac crew with Joss Stuart?" the first officer said. He wore a nameplate identifying him as G. Edrok, and she noticed now that his companion was W. Yama.

"Is he all right?" she asked.

"Answer the question," Edrok said.

"He's our crew leader on Number 129 and other rigs. Don't I have a right to know if he's OK?"

"Your sharp tongue precedes you, Ms. Landau," he said. "*We* intend to control this interrogation."

"I'm sure you have a dossier on me, and that doesn't matter, because I've done nothing wrong."

"That may or may not be true, but we are not here to inquire about that. It seems that Joss Stuart caused a bit of trouble at the hospital, so we must ask certain questions. Just as we asked his roommate."

"I would strongly suggest that you double-check everything Andruw Twitty said, because he has it in for Joss, and for me. The pathetic little man will say anything to advance his own career."

Edrok smiled a little, then stiffened. His Asian companion, stone-faced, switched on the machine on the table, showing an audiovisual recording of Joss's room, with him lying on the bed, being attended to by nurses. The screen fast-forwarded, then slowed to normal speed. Kupi watched in amazement as Joss came out of his coma and tore the room apart, finally shattering the clearplex of the viewing area where Andruw had been standing. So that was how he got his injuries.

"What's wrong with Stuart?" Edrok asked. "How did he do that? It looked like he fired Splitter rays out of his body."

"Out of his fingers, to be precise," said Officer Yama. He turned off the screen.

"His roommate says that Joss has been acting suspiciously for some time now," Edrok said.

"Suspiciously? What did he say?"

"Have you noticed unusual behavior, too?"

"Certainly not! What did that little worm say about Joss?"

The officers just stared at her in response.

"Where is Joss now?" she demanded.

"Under close guard," Officer Edrok said. "You saw the video. It's obvious why."

"So he's been moved from the hospital, and put into police custody?"

"My, but you ask a lot of questions," Yama said, with a hard smile. "Would you like to apply to be an officer?"

"No, thanks." She grimaced, couldn't picture herself dressed as a green storm trooper, strutting around officiously.

They asked Kupi a few more questions, seemed to be on a fishing expedition. She continued to press them for information on where Joss was, and when she could see him, but they deferred the matter to higher-ups, saying that was not for them to comment on. That much, at least, sounded true to her.

Kupi left feeling unsettled, even more than when she arrived. She didn't like what she saw on the video or the way Twitty was here, obviously trying to elevate himself at the expense of Joss. She didn't worry about herself and what the . . . she smiled to herself . . . what the little *twit* tried to do to her. But she did care about Joss, and wanted to do whatever she could to protect him. She'd done that in the interview, though it had not been much.

As she walked the few blocks to her hotel, she caught a glimpse of a man following her—undoubtedly a Greenpol plainclothesman.

I'm one of the Berkeley Eight! she thought, feeling indignant anger, an emotion that had not surfaced during the interrogation session. She considered whirling and confronting the police tail, but reconsidered. That could only make matters worse, by making it look as if she were trying to hide something.

But it was also a perplexing tactic for Greenpol to use. They had satellite tracking devices and computer chips implanted in the cerebral cortexes of GSA citizens, so they could determine exactly where people were all the time anyway—assuming a person didn't avoid getting a chip implanted, or find a way to disable it. She was too well known to try anything like that, but she had friends who had safely gotten rid of the devices.

With the police surveillance technology, why were they physically following her? It was strange and irritating. As she considered this, she realized it must be their intent to annoy her and see if she would do anything impulsive and disloyal. Her words had not been enough to get her into trouble, but actions could.

She felt as if they were out to get Joss, and her.

Greenpol, she thought, with contempt. The organization that cultivated the wormlike, conniving Andruw Twitty. Undoubtedly it had others like him.

CHAIRMAN RAHMA NEEDED to spend some quiet time with his departed comrades, to commune with them. In particular, the body of Glanno Artindale—one of the greatest heroes of the revolution—lay in the Shrine of Martyrs ahead of him, growing nearer as he strode across the grass toward the domed building. Rahma had seen the hubot Artie a couple of hours ago, had looked into Glanno's salvaged eyes and thought of his long-lost friend.

The GSA leader was not a religious man, but in the shrine he always felt the presence of his comrades, their *spiritual* presence. It had nothing to do with any belief in God, because in Rahma's view there was no God. Rather, it had everything to do with the paranormal realm of heroes that the fallen fighters occupied now, a region that had no relationship with any conception of heaven or hell.

Dori Longet walked at his side, carrying an electronic clipboard in place of the VR heads-up display she usually preferred. Having already gone over his daily schedule with him, she said, "We should have more on Joss Stuart later today. Greenpol is interviewing people who are close to him, collecting information on his background, and on what he did in that hospital room."

They had both seen the video recording of Stuart's strange outburst, his frightening display of violence. It had been stunning, and they had watched it over and over, in disbelief.

Rahma cleared his throat. "Under any other circumstance, I might think that SciO lab explosion was an act of sabotage, ordered by Corporate elements who want to avenge SciO's involvement in their defeat. But with the effect of the explosion on Stuart, that tosses out sabotage as a possibility."

"It does seem to do that," she agreed.

They parted, and he went alone into the shrine, through the wooden entry door. Inside the lobby, he stood beneath a silvery dome that provided solar-generated illumination to the interior. Crypts were visible through heavy glass in the floor, all tightly arranged and side by side, as if the dead soldiers were ready to rise from the dead and surge into battle.

He was about to walk toward a marble bench across the lobby when he stopped suddenly, shocked at the sight of a bloody lump on it. Had an injured animal gotten in here and died? But as he neared it, he saw to his horror that it was a bloody human fetus, with a printed note next to it.

Almost gagging, he leaned down to examine the note, saw it was addressed to him. Without touching it, he read:

"Chairman Rahma, this fetus, ripped from a mother's womb in one of your 'family guidance centers,' is a true martyr of the revolution. Because I honor life, I will not harm you physically, except to ask how you can consider yourself a man of peace when you kill your own people in so many ways. You have stolen all human dignity; you have turned the American dream into a nightmare."

Rahma felt a surge of rage. This sacred place had been violated by a right-wing lunatic, whose narrow-mindedness dripped from the words on the page! Aborting unwanted children was not only a woman's right; it was good for the planet, preventing overpopulation. But whoever wrote those words would never understand that, would never have the brain power (or the compassion for the Earth) to understand.

He looked around. How had the wacko gotten in? Was it an outsider, or someone who worked with him on the game reserve? The latter seemed possible, perhaps even likely, because he—or she—had slipped through layers of security to bring the fetus from a guidance center. Or was that part a lie? Had one of his own women aborted the child and left it here?

He would order a full investigation, including fingerprints, DNA tests, everything—and an immediate increase in security.

THE LAB REPORT arrived just as Rahma was getting ready for bed. It appeared in the form of a high-priority holo-net transmission that beeped and then floated in the air by him, a signal that homed in on the Chairman via the identity chip implanted in his body. The report's audio feature was off, so the information was in visual mode, red letters against a white background.

He read quickly, then switched it off in disgust. No fingerprints or other evidence to identify the perpetrator. Even the fetus, which did provide DNA, was of no help, because the genetic information was not in the national database—meaning the fetus had not come from one of his family guidance centers. Whoever did this had to be off the grid, perhaps among the fugitives living in the forests of the Green States of America. Or a foreign agent.

He slipped into bed, and felt very alone in his thoughts and troubles. And very vulnerable.

23

After Europeans arrived in the Americas and stole the land by murdering and enslaving the native inhabitants, the two continents were held for centuries through the expert application of violence—and more than anyone else in modern times, corporate moguls were the beneficiaries of this dark heritage. Against such ruthless oligarchs, we had only one way to take the land from them and begin to restore the Earth. We needed to kill as many of them as possible, and drive the rest out.

—Chairman Rahma Popal, remarks
to a biographer, October 19, 2052

JOSS WAS NO longer in a hospital room, though medical personnel came and went in the thick-walled security cell, taking skin and blood samples from him and performing an array of scans on his body—all the while using video recorders and other devices to keep a detailed log of everything they did, and every movement their patient made, every word he uttered. . . .

To get him there they'd injected him with sedatives and strapped him to a gurney, then transported him across the Berkeley Reservation by ambulance. He'd been conscious all the way, had just lain there watching the doctors and medical research assistants assigned to him, two of each. When they saw that his eyes remained open and his pulse actually *accelerated* with additional sedative injections, they'd become alarmed and whispered among themselves.

"I don't know why the drugs have an opposite effect on me," Joss had said to them, "but you don't need to worry. I don't intend to resist; I want to know what's happening to me as much as you do." His words were very rapid, as if linked to his amped-up pulse.

One of the assistants had moved closer to him in the ambulance, and she'd smiled at him. "That's good," she'd said, "because we only want to help you."

Joss had smiled at her in return, and nodded. He'd considered asking her to remove the restraint straps, but knew she wouldn't do that, because they'd think it was a trick on his part. Maybe he could remove them himself anyway, but he hadn't wanted to try because he feared injuring or killing someone, or upsetting people even more.

The raw violence he'd displayed in the hospital room suggested that he had some variation of SciO Splitter power, and he might employ it to get free. But first he needed to understand more about controlling the power, if that was possible, and more about his altered body. So, for the rest of the ambulance ride he'd fallen silent and tried to calm himself, taking deep and regular breaths. After a few minutes he'd heard the research assistant saying that his pulse was slowing, returning to normal.

They'd wheeled him into another building, this one gray and bleak, and down to what appeared to be a series of windowless, bombproof bunkers. They passed white-robed men and women in the corridors and rooms, along with heavily armed SciO security officers in white uniforms. The obvious SciO presence gave Joss a sinking sensation, and a realization that the mysterious organization was undoubtedly more concerned about the leakage of its secrets than it was about him.

As he'd thought about this, he'd realized that maybe it didn't matter so much who had taken him into custody. Whatever happened in the ReFac explosion needed to be figured out, and who was more qualified to do that than the SciOs? After all, Chairman Rahma trusted them, and Joss revered the man. Yes, Joss decided, he would cooperate because his beloved Chairman would want him to. . . .

After getting him into the security cell, the original doctors and medical assistants had not reappeared; instead, the patient had been handed off to another set of medical personnel who wore SciO robes.

Then, tending to him for an hour, taking their samples and such, the new group left and a tall man entered the room, wearing a white robe with gilded trim. He had glittering blue eyes. "I am Dr. Mora," he said, "Chief of the Dark Energy research division." He leaned over the gurney and spoke in a low tone. "You know what Dark Energy is?"

Joss felt his pulse quicken, and his words came quickly, as if linked: "Only in general. I've heard that's the SciO term for it, and I've seen Kupi Landau use it on jobsites."

"Ah yes, well, we seem to have an interesting situation here. We've analyzed the audiovisual records of your . . . *event* in the hospital, shall we call it? Yes, your event. It seems, Mr. Stuart, that you have captured some small amount of Dark Energy in your own body. To be honest with you, we aren't certain how that could happen. You'd like to know yourself, wouldn't you?"

"Very much. I don't want to cause harm with it." His heart pounded inside his chest.

"And we appreciate that. You are known to be a loyal subject of the Green States of America, so if something like this had to happen to anyone, we're pleased that you're the one involved, and not someone who could cause trouble."

"I don't want to cause trouble." As before, Joss tried to calm himself by controlling his breathing, and this time he felt his pulse slow in a matter of only a few seconds.

I'm getting better at this, he thought.

Dr. Mora placed a hand on the straps that held Joss to the gurney, and said, "I'm going to loosen these, so that you can move around more freely in this chamber. Even with the Dark Energy that you seem to possess, it is not strong enough to break out of here, so don't even think about trying. The most powerful atomic bomb could be set off right on top of us, and it wouldn't break through."

That sounded impossible to Joss, but the SciOs had amazing technological abilities. He nodded, watched as the doctor released the straps and then helped him off the gurney and onto his feet. Joss wore a torn hospital gown that did not cover him very well.

"There," Dr. Mora said. "Isn't that better? You'll find that this chamber is connected to two others that have been provided for your use, one of which is a private sitting and entertainment chamber, and the other your own dining area and automated kitchen alcove. You also have access to a private bathroom that has a soaking tub and a shower—both with recycled water, of course."

"Thank you. I'd like to start out by getting cleaned up. Do I have to wear gowns like this?"

"No. We'll bring fresh clothes for you. Consider this your own suite of rooms. One more thing. Gradually, as soon as we figure out how best to accomplish it, we'd like to conduct a series of controlled experiments with your power . . . assuming you still have it, that is."

"Would you like me to find out right now?"

"Ah no, not just yet."

OUT OF AN abundance of caution and patriotism, Joss had accepted the arrangement at first. But as days passed, and the medical personnel came and went, he began to feel as if he had no privacy, not even in the adjoining, completely enclosed bathroom. Though he saw no obvious detection devices in there, he presumed that someone was collecting his urine and stool samples, and even the saliva from brushing his teeth. He suspected they had cameras somewhere in the bathroom as well, to watch his every activity and see just how alien he had become.

Alien.

He'd heard the medical staff using that word several times, including Dr. Mora. And, though Joss had not objected, it didn't seem to correctly describe him—at least not in the extraterrestrial sense. Not even if he *had* become the hybrid that two of the doctors had mentioned in his presence, because he was a composite of human and plant cellular material from Earth, and of the Splitter power that the SciOs developed on Earth as well—the Dark Energy component. Presumably the SciOs had not gone off-planet for such technology, because the Green States of America had scrapped the space program as "wasteful spending," but with the SciOs one could never be certain. They might even have their own secret space program, for all Joss knew.

Alien? Perhaps it is true. . . .

Still, the Chairman trusted them, and Joss tried to keep that in mind, despite being treated like a prisoner, reminiscent of the way animals used to be treated when it was legal to confine and use them for medical purposes.

Joss couldn't help but notice the changes in his own body, and not just in the light black color of his skin, and the vinelike green scars that traversed the epidermal surfaces, wrapping around his arms, legs, and torso. (One even crossed his forehead and ran down the side of his face to his neck.) Whenever he didn't pay attention, his pulse seemed to quicken on its own, and he would find himself walking around the bunker very rapidly, eating quickly, talking fast, doing everything at a heightened pace. He had to keep slowing himself down consciously. It was this way when he went to bed as well, as he found his mind racing while he lay there, and his heart pounding inside his chest, until he focused and put himself to sleep by sheer willpower.

One morning while Joss was shaving with a straight razor, taking great care to move slowly and not cut himself, he suddenly put down the razor and went into the entertainment chamber, where he knew his handlers had installed surveillance cameras, because he could see them high in every corner.

He placed a videobook on the floor. Then, gradually and cautiously, he raised his left hand and pointed the fingers at the book. It was a particularly dull story anyway, one that was of no interest to him, and he'd set it aside, intending to ask for it to be removed. Perhaps he could take care of that little chore himself. The fingers darkened and glowed. He felt his metabolism rising and heard a gathering roar in his ears, like the mounting power of the Splitter on Janus Machine No. 129.

Joss heard a man's voice on the speaker system: "Don't do that!" But it was too late.

He took a deep breath to slow his pulse a little, and focused a small degree of animosity on the videobook. To his amazement, thin streaks of black light darted from his fingertips, but did not reach their target. Instead, like threads floating in the air, they hovered right over it. He sensed that they were under his control—or that they could be, if he handled this right.

Now Joss intensified his feigned animosity toward the book, which raised his pulse again. He saw the black threads thicken and cover the target, melting it into a small heap of yellow gunk. The remaining strands of Dark Energy crackled in the air and vanished.

Interesting, Joss thought, ignoring the SciOs who gathered around him and protested. Previously, streaks of black light had shot out of his fingers involuntarily and caused damage, like the waves from hand-held Splitter guns, which were small versions of the waves that resulted whenever Kupi Landau fired the powerful Splitter on the Janus Machine. It was a matter of scale, and he seemed to have a minuscule version of the remarkable energy in his body.

And he *could* control it. But what degree of dominion did he have over it, and why had it occurred without his volition the first time, in the hospital room?

Why too, did the power seem to come only from his left hand? (He was right-handed, after all.) Then, as he wondered this, the fingers of his right hand began to darken, as if sending him a message. Moments later they returned to normal coloration.

"There," Joss said, looking around and meeting the disapproving gaze of Dr. Mora. "Our first controlled experiment. I'd call it a success, wouldn't you?"

"Perhaps," Mora said, nodding.

"Let me experiment a little on my own," Joss said. "My mind is directly linked to the Dark Energy, and I think I can fire it whenever I want to, if I decide to do so." He moved one hand around in the air slowly, causing black threads of light to appear and linger, before vanishing.

The SciOs moved back a ways, but everyone in the room

seemed to know that there might be no safe distance from Joss, if he ever became upset and turned his rage against them.

"I'm able to control it by focusing on my emotions," Joss said, "playing them up and down."

"Ah yes, that's interesting," Dr. Mora said.

"Without volition, I do tend to make sudden movements," Joss said, "so everyone near me should bear that in mind. If I'm not completely focused on what I want to do, if I don't plan every movement, something really bad could happen."

Dr. Mora pursed his lips. "Shall we all sign forms agreeing not to pursue legal action against you?"

Joss smiled. Then, motioning the SciOs back, he sat on the floor, raised both of his hands in the air, and moved them around to create circles and ovals of black thread, then caused them to dart this way and that. Now the threads thickened in the air, and were visible for considerably longer before fading slowly when he let go, like the contrails of a jet. After practicing for a while, he found that he was able to adjust the thickness of the strands at will, by alternately increasing and diminishing the output of energy. . . .

That night Joss awoke from a peculiar dream, one that suggested variations on what he'd already discovered about his own body and the strange power it contained. He rose from his bed and flipped on a light.

Could those new variations be possible, more than just a dream?

This time, instead of using his hands, he waved both feet in the air, trying to generate power from his toes, as the dream had suggested he could do. Nothing happened. He felt a surge of anger at his own naiveté, thinking a dream could foreshadow or mirror reality. What utter foolishness!

He turned toward the bed, when suddenly the fingers of both hands glowed black and stiffened—little Splitter barrels.

Focusing on his fingers and adjusting his emotions like a control panel—moderating anger with serenity to find balance points—he formed strands of energy around his hands, hovering in the air. Then, with a mental command, he made them coalesce and used them like a black laser to slice a small hole in one thick wall, all the way through to the corridor. Next he tried another experiment, using more mental intensity to create a larger hole.

It worked both times. The dream had not been at all accurate, but the startling nature of it had caused him to awaken, and to discover something new he could do.

Finally, leaving the two holes in place, he withdrew, turned off the light, and returned to bed. This time, when he tried to calm himself to go to sleep, he had much more difficulty, before finally succeeding.

So many thoughts insisted on racing through his mind, so many astounding possibilities. . . .

24

There is an undercurrent of suspicion spanning both continents of the Green States of America, a rumor that the SciOs are only fair-weather allies of this nation and could betray us all. But evidence is lacking.

—a confidential Greenpol report

THREE MORE DAYS passed in confinement, and Joss was feeling less and less cooperative. Though he was patriotic and dedicated to the ideals of the revolution, it was beginning to look as if he had exchanged his privileged, interesting career as a greenformer for something far worse. He was living in a velvet-lined cage as a glorified lab rat. Yes, a lab rat. He longed for a return to his old life—to his friends, family, and co-workers. It all seemed far away and long gone, irretrievable.

Messages had come in from many people, but he only knew the names, not details of what they said or what they wanted. Each day Dr. Mora let him know who they were, but said every one of them would have to wait until the experiments were completed. Joss was suspicious of how the doctor was handling this, suspected he was using those people as leverage, trying to get him to cooperate faster. The previous afternoon there had been three visitors turned away, among them his roommate, Andruw Twitty. A positive note, after all.

"Tell Andruw not to come around anymore," Joss had said.

"Warn him he could be in danger, based on what I did to him in the hospital room. The power contained in my body could just cut loose and kill him, without my intent. Tell him to have all of my things packed up and sent here, and to avoid me entirely. For his own safety."

Joss had watched Mora's eyes narrow, and the man had responded, "Are you threatening *me* as well? Anyone who displeases you, in the slightest degree?"

"I never said Andruw displeases me."

"But he does, doesn't he? We have his reports, so we know how you were not always forthright with him when he asked you questions."

"He was supposed to be my roommate, but he had a habit of acting as if I were an eco-criminal being interrogated. It wore on me."

"Just as I do?"

"Are you trying to provoke me, Doctor? Isn't that a bit dangerous under the circumstances?"

Mora had shaken his head. "No, just trying to understand you."

"Well, don't believe everything Andruw says. He's ambitious and self-centered, doesn't care who he has to run over to advance himself."

"Sometimes words mean very little, don't they?" Mora had said. It had been an interesting comment, perhaps designed to engage Joss in conversation, to let his guard down and draw him in. But instead he had retreated inward, without responding. . . .

Today, galvanized by Joss's impromptu discoveries, Dr. Mora had been conducting additional experiments in the confinement area, getting Joss to target various types of objects that were made of different materials, from a soft pear to bars of steel and titanium. Joss had disintegrated every object and transformed it into runny goo, discovering in the process that he had quite a good aim, which gave the handlers some degree of relief. Using the fingers of one hand or the other (or even both hands at once) to originate the blasts didn't seem to matter; in any of these ways Joss could perform the trick, but they were going to conduct further tests on intensity.

Next, Dr. Mora and two assistants brought in a cart that contained a variety of electronic instruments, some of which he said would check the discharge strength every time Joss fired the beams of energy. In a form of target practice, they'd lined up bottles on a ledge, from a rubber bottle to a dark gray one made of an alloy so dense and heavy that it required a particularly large, strong man to carry in the object and put it in place.

They then asked Joss to aim carefully at the bottles, one at a time, while not damaging the ledge, if he could. This proved to be no problem, and he amused himself a little by bringing forth either hand at a time, or both at once, for his weapon source, and then firing as quickly as he could. With his heightened metabolism, that proved to be quite fast, and he heard gasps of astonishment behind him as black threads of energy coalesced into beams and struck the bottles hard, melting them, one after another.

It didn't surprise Joss to learn that it required more power to disintegrate and transform the alloy than the rubber. That seemed like common sense. The level of variation, however, was not very much. When an assistant reported this to Dr. Mora, Joss noticed concern in the doctor's face, and saw him take the assistant aside to discuss it further with him in private.

Finally the doctor came forward and said, "I'd like you to repeat what we saw you do on surveillance the other night—cut two holes in the wall." He looked at the wall that Joss had damaged, and marks where the damage had been repaired.

"All right." As before, Joss pointed the fingers of one hand, shooting streaks of black to cut two new holes. As before, the second one was larger than the first.

One of the assistants reported the power readings, technical jargon that Joss didn't understand. A young man with round spectacles, he read from a screen on his instrument cart.

"Only a little more power than for the alloy," Dr. Mora said.

"You reinforced the wall on the other side," Joss said. "I noticed a difference. What did you use?"

Dr. Mora shrugged. "Who knows what they come up with in SciO laboratories? Even if I knew, I couldn't tell you. But honestly, I don't know. One more thing of note. The power readings are the same from either of your hands, and do not increase at all when you use both hands at once."

His gaze narrowed as he added, "Look, I'll be frank with you. I'm wondering if you can generate more power than we have seen here. This may be too confined an area to check, and I don't want you to do so now, but do you feel like you could do more than you have so far—I mean, melting or cutting larger or denser objects?"

Joss scowled. He found himself glaring at the instrument cart and all of its intrusive technology. "Even if I know, perhaps I shouldn't tell you."

The doctor smiled stiffly. "You're joking, aren't you? Aren't we trying to figure this out together?'

"Maybe I'm just tired of it for today. Please, go away and leave me to watch some movies or listen to music, OK?"

"If you wish, but—"

"Do you think it's easy being a lab rat? I'm a human being, remember, and I'm getting sick of watching you collect data on—" Joss caught himself, as he wondered how *human* he still was. He had cellular remnants of that, certainly, judging from the shape of his body and his speech patterns, and—he thought—the way his mind worked. But he was especially troubled by that green keloid scarring on his skin that resembled vines, and he was fatigued from trying to control the very disturbing power inside his body, the intrusion of SciO technology.

"But *are* you still human? Isn't that what you were just wondering?"

"So far, my private thoughts remain my own," Joss said. "Now go, please. Just go. We'll talk again tomorrow."

With only a few conciliatory words in response, Dr. Mora turned and led his assistants out of the chambers, taking their rolling cart and all of its instruments with him.

Exasperated, Joss sat on the couch in his private entertainment area, but he had no interest in a movie or music. For several moments he stared at a projection on one wall that showed a view of the sun-drenched Berkeley skyline, and fleecy clouds in a blue sky. He longed to be free, to actually be *out* there. He didn't even have a real window, so the images he saw by projection could be entirely false. His handlers were worried about him escaping.

The more he thought about it, the more he realized that there might never be an end to the probing and testing, the endless questions and demands from unrelenting, ever-curious scientists. He envisioned the ordeal of moving from one stage of analysis to another, with each thing he did leading to more questions, and additional experiments that no one had yet imagined.

He heard buzzing noises, and looking up he noticed flies darting around the ceiling of the chamber. Lots of flies. Where were they coming from? He noticed a pattern, that they seemed to be coming from the dining chamber—and they were descending, buzzing around him.

Damned things! They must have been released intentionally by the SciOs.

Joss stared dumbly at his hands, focused on the fingertips. Suddenly, without his apparent volition, he felt an awakening in his body, the now-familiar gathering roar of power in his ears that he thought might be blood surging in his veins, like a river of white water roaring through tubes.

He hadn't commanded the energy to reemerge, but it was doing so just the same, and this time he didn't think he objected. Maybe he would use it against the pesky little insects! Then he realized he'd been upset with them just before the surge in power, the emotional factor again. It also seemed to him that he needed to be careful if he ever became upset with a person. Would he still be able to control the discharge of Dark Energy?

A shimmering black thread—a single, thin strand—shot from his left forefinger and zapped a fly, turning the creature into goo and dropping it to the floor. With a casual, involuntary wave of Joss's hands, additional focal threads came out, killing more flies. Now he interjected his own conscious thoughts, and found that he could fire from one finger at a time, or from two, or from all of them at once if he wished— and this time the threads of energy didn't coalesce; they remained separate, each of them with striking power. He killed one fly after another, and even ten simultaneously with a set of micro-blasts from both hands.

Then, looking into the adjacent dining chamber, he saw more flies flitting around. This time he found that he could fire the threads longer distances, and every time he saw one of the creatures fall he understood a little more.

Thought to action. Nearly instantaneous. *Zap, zap, zap!*

It was almost fun, but it also frightened him. Operating as

it did from his fingers, the power seemed to almost be a super-charged form of kinesthesia—muscle energy and muscle memory, resulting in death. . . .

He worried that he might not be able to control the invasive energy in his body. Because of this, Joss didn't want to go to the next stage quite yet, if there was one. So he decided to withdraw the strands and reassess the situation. He sent that mental command.

But against his will, the threads remained stubbornly in the air, near his fingertips. He became conscious of his pulse racing, and as he realized this, it slowed immediately.

Experimenting, he wove an energy field in the air between the fingers of both hands, creating additional black threads with casual gestures, and hardly any mental impetus. Just a little was all that was required.

Even more flies appeared from the dining chamber, flitting about, racing from one point to another without alighting. Not learning from their predecessors, they circled Joss's head, diving this way and that. He counted four, five, then eight. This time he didn't zap them. Something else seemed possible.

With practice he found that he could weave the threads of the energy field around his body, keeping them there, and sure enough, the remaining flies moved away from him, repelled by the field. As moments passed, the field weakened, and the flies drew nearer, but not too close, as if sensing danger.

This was intriguing to Joss, and he was gratified that he was able to exert some control over the discharges and the patterns they formed in the air. Maybe with practice the threads of energy would go away. He made several more attempts, generating new energy fields and leaving different black contrail patterns in the air around him. The airborne shapes he created didn't seem to matter much, because each time he recharged the system the flies flew farther away. With practice, he found that the fields lasted longer and longer—up to several minutes.

Curiously, he detected flashes of color around the edges: blues, reds, greens, and yellows . . . Then, as if his earlier mental command had finally taken hold, the fields dissipated.

25

The Green States of America contains its own seeds of destruction, and eventually the nation will rot away like organic forest matter and vanish into the Earth on its own. Just the same, we have chosen to add a catalyst, in order to hasten the process.

—General Dylan Bane, in an address to his allies

SELECTING THE PLACES to strike had been like picking from a tray of glittering jewels. There were so many enticing targets in the Green States of America—two continents of government offices, military installations, and reservations for humans. In the end, he narrowed the list down to nine military bases of the Army of the Environment—Berkeley, San Diego, Seattle, Bostoner, Baltimore, Miami, Panama City, Rio de Janeiro, and Valparaiso. All were ports where the GSA had naval bases, including submarines armed with the most advanced nuclear missiles. At each location, he had plans to disable any subs that were docked, or commandeer them. He had intelligence reports that only fifteen percent of their underwater warships were out to sea—a defensive lapse—so he might just catch the enemy napping.

The powerful entities that gave Bane money trusted him to make his own decisions, because their interests aligned with his, at least to a degree. But he had ways of maintaining control over all of his dealings, secrets his allies did not know, and never would. It was that way in all of his affairs; no one ever learned *everything* of importance about him, or what he was thinking.

Dylan Bane didn't care one way or another about any loss of life in the military assaults. He thought only about inflicting maximum physical and psychological impact on the enemy, on causing panic in their ranks and sending the survivors scurrying for cover like rats from a storm. There would be no hiding places for some of these green rats, and especially not for his own former superior, Arch Ondex, or for the hypocritical guru Rahma and the rest of the GSA hierarchy. He had planned horrendous deaths for that bunch.

But now, just as he was about to launch forty-five voleers in attack squadrons from his subterranean Michoacán base, he felt a trembling around him, and saw most of the master control panel lights arrayed before him flicker off.

"Earthquake, sir!" one of the young male officers reported. His voice wavered. "It's centered a hundred and twelve kilometers southwest of here, and it's put eight of our squadrons offline, forty voleers. They're working on getting them online again."

"Any damage to our ships?"

"Not known yet, sir; we do have some small cave-ins that can be cleared. Most serious seems to be the problem of fleet electronics. Hopefully the techs can solve it quickly."

"Well, I'm not waiting!" Bane exclaimed. He tapped the sequence of three buttons to launch his remaining attack squadron of five ships, led by his own vessel. Their destination: San Diego. It was one of the most powerful GSA bases, with nuclear submarines, stealth bombers, mechanized land units, and a host of other military equipment. . . .

MINUTES LATER, THE self-proclaimed General stood on the command bridge of Voleer One as the armored transport craft burrowed its way through the crust of the planet with four other voleers behind it, all carrying his specially designed weapons of mass destruction and six thousand soldiers. This would be the opening salvo, and as soon as the problems were solved with the other squadrons there would be more afterward, coming out of nowhere. He planned to play a violent game of hit-and-run, until the enemy threat was ended.

Bane intended to put his enemy completely out of business.

Now his fleet of voleers was crossing beneath the deserts of northern Mexico, heading in a northwesterly direction, tunneling through the earth hundreds of meters underground. On a wall screen he saw that the navigators had recommended final course adjustments, and the pilots were setting the proper coordinates.

His voleers carried military vehicles and attack aircraft, brimming with Splitter technology to inflict the maximum possible non-nuclear damage on the target. Bane had old-style nuclear weapons back in his Michoacán arsenal (and still accessible), but he had not brought them with him, seeing no need for them at this time. There was more downside than upside potential if nukes were used and triggered the destruction of the entire planet. An atomic war was madness, and he would take measures to avoid using such weapons at all.

He glanced at the master control panel, but knew he was out of range of any underground signals from the other eight squadrons in his fleet. He hoped they had all launched, and were speeding toward their various targets. For the moment, he focused on San Diego.

In annihilating that military base he could not avoid destroying much of the adjacent reservation for humans, undoubtedly killing hundreds of thousands or even millions of people.

It was unavoidable. The same held true for every other target, as soon as they were hit.

The GSA had to fall, and the nine attacks should make them capitulate. If not, he would call for additional strikes against hundreds of additional targets.

He thought about the hotheaded Red Major—Reed Zachary—who had stolen three aircraft and made his own ill-fated attack. It was too bad the young officer had not waited. He'd been impatient to hit the enemy, had refused to wait and had paid the price for it with his life, along with the lives of the crews and soldiers who had accompanied him. It had all been a waste, a loss of talent and equipment. Bane hated to lose good, highly trained people, and he particularly missed Zachary, whose argumentative personality had been stimulating, and had caused Bane to think about a number of things he might not have otherwise considered.

Looking around the command bridge, Bane saw Marissa Chase, the pretty young officer with whom he'd been sleeping. Arguments with her were often stimulating, when they had arousing sexual overtones.

It occurred to him now that in his zeal he was acting precipitously, just as Zachary had done before him, going off with an inadequate force, overeager to do battle. Maybe this was a mistake, if the techs couldn't launch the other voleers. He shouldn't attack only one base, if the other strikes were not also being made. An attack on San Diego by one squadron, even with a series of attacks on other bases by the same squadron afterward, would alert the enemy and cause him to stiffen his defenses. The SciOs would be called into action with exotic weapons, and the GSA already had many Janus Machines that could be used as powerful cannons.

Simultaneous surprise attacks would be much better.

Abruptly, General Bane altered the command coordinates,

and a short while later his five voleers surfaced in the darkness, but with nothing to attack. They were in the arid Painted Desert of the Arizona Territory. The ships had electronic veiling so that they could not be detected by satellites or other surveillance technology, but now he could communicate with the rest of his fleet and his base back at Michoacán. He sent a coded transmission across his encrypted, clandestine system, to the voleers and the base.

The message was not received there, but went instead to an unmanned outpost he maintained on the Pacific coast of the Mexican territory, west of the Michoacán base. This concerned him a great deal.

An AI response came back to him, reporting the bare facts in a smooth, asexual machine voice: "A second temblor hit Michoacán after you left, caving in the base on forty voleers. Suggest you call off your mission and return to aid in rescue and salvage operations."

Bane cursed into the chill of the desert night. He didn't see how this could have happened! Taking into account the history of quakes in the region, his engineers had designed seismic reinforcements into the construction of the base. Central Mexico had the advantage of location from a military standpoint, enabling him to attack both continents, north and south. He was likely to lose that advantage now, and perhaps a great deal more.

Burrowing underground again, leading his single squadron back to the disaster site, he worried about the logistical and technological problems of getting the other vessels out of the cave-in (if they were even salvageable) and how to avoid detection by the enemy.

After so much preparation in recent months, he had been eager to make the opening salvos of a powerful guerrilla war. Instead, he had suffered a huge reversal before firing even a single shot, a setback that would require him to go back and rework his entire plan. If he could save more of the high-tech voleers (and that was a big "if"), he would set up a new subterranean base in a more stable area from a seismic standpoint. In any event, he would need more money from his allies, and they would not be pleased about that.

He ordered the squadron to top subsurface speed.

26

Does the end ever justify the means employed to achieve it? When considering the welfare of the Earth and its inhabitants, is it even a question of morality, or is it more about the survival of the planet, about setting priorities that boil down to this: Which species deserve to survive and which do not?

—one of Artie's encrypted data files

WEARING HIS GREEN cop uniform and shiny helmet, Andruw Twitty stood at the barricaded main entrance of the Montana Valley Game Reserve. It was early morning on a crisp, overcast day. Leaving a Greenpol squad car nearby, he had just announced his presence to one of the guards, a petite woman whose uniform seemed too large for her. She was a hubot, he determined from her machine-design armband and the slight translucence of her skin, so she had some human biological component in her body. The Chairman was known to keep hundreds of the humanoids around here.

Twitty couldn't tell what this one might have in her body to qualify her as one of the hybrids. Perhaps she had a human internal organ—a heart, a lung, or a kidney; there were often interesting stories about where the body parts came from. Some had been salvaged from the bodies of Corporate War heroes, people that Chairman Rahma wanted to glorify for his own propaganda purposes, always enhancing the mythology of the revolution. There was even a rumor that a hubot had run amok in one of the relocation camps, murdering people because it had received a demented brain, like a robotic version of Frankenstein's monster. Twitty had always doubted that story; it sounded apocryphal to him.

To get to the Rocky Mountain Territory by maglev train, Twitty had used his police credentials, which not only enabled him to leave the Seattle Reservation but to travel a good distance from it. Then, around a hundred and fifty kilometers from the game reserve, he'd obtained the use of the Greenpol car.

In the past, he had reported to the Chairman by EVR transmission, but his attempts to get through in that manner this time had been thwarted, with stiff responses that the GSA leader was "unavailable." The responses sounded canned to Twitty, and he was convinced that Rahma did not even know he was trying to get through to him.

Perhaps he would have more luck by showing up in person and asking for an audience. Confidential Greenpol reports indicated that the Chairman was in fact at home. Twitty was convinced that what he had to say merited a personal audience with the great man, and that he would be grateful once he heard the additional information about Joss Stuart and Kupi Landau. Damaging information.

Momentarily, the guard returned and shook her head. "The Chairman is unavailable," she said. It was the same irritating message that had been transmitted to him at the Seattle Reservation, after he returned home and submitted his report to Greenpol authorities there.

Annoyed, Twitty said, "You know I am a police officer who has previously reported directly to Chairman Rahma, and I assure you that what I have to say is of the utmost importance."

The guard shook her head adamantly.

A shadow crossed the ground, and Twitty noticed a large creature in flight overhead, with immense, batlike wings that extended outward from a doglike—no, *wolflike*—body. He shuddered as the animal flew closer, and seemed to be looking directly at him with eerie, pale yellow eyes. It was much, much bigger than a wolf.

"What the hell is *that*?" Twitty asked.

The guard looked up, but seemed unconcerned and just shrugged.

With a scowl, Twitty wondered what manner of creature this was. Some endangered species, no doubt, that Rahma had rescued from overseas. Odd, though. He had not heard any publicity about this one. He wished he had brought along his sidearm.

"Hear me out for a minute," Twitty said, keeping a wary eye upward. "This morning, a government broadcast said there is no evidence to blame Joss Stuart for the destruction of the ReFac building in Berkeley. They're saying that all indications point to the explosion being an accident—one that has given Stuart 'cute little talents' that he can use at party games to impress women. Listen, the son of a bitch is my roommate, so I know him personally, and I assure you he has more than 'cute little talents.' Stuart is quite dangerous, and has threatened to harm me if I . . ."

Again she shook her head, and interrupted to say, "Send your report through normal channels. The Chairman doesn't have time to listen to everyone who wants to break into his busy schedule." The guard smiled. "Please understand, I hear some *very* creative stories here." She waved a hand dismissively. "Now go, or I'll have to put you on report."

Twitty reddened, but he turned and left. As he drove toward the nearest maglev terminal, he saw the airborne wolf tracking him, flying low, swooping this way and that across his path, making sure he saw it. The thing gave him the creeps.

Finally, the creature turned and flew back toward the game reserve.

IN HIS OFFICE, the Chairman had refused to even speak with the guard over the security system, which had the effect of sending the pesky eco-cop on his way. Rahma had been following the ongoing reports on Joss Stuart and his strange powers, and under other circumstances he might have allowed Twitty a few minutes of his time. But nothing involving Joss Stuart came close to another matter that had come up.

A much more important matter.

Just before Twitty's arrival, the Chairman and Jade Ridell had been making love on the couch in his office, but had been interrupted by a high-priority holo-net transmission that beeped and appeared in the air by them.

Now Chairman Rahma sat naked on the edge of the couch, staring at the confidential holo-report that floated in front of him, an update from the Army of the Environment on the troubling attack that occurred near the Bostoner Reservation. His old girlfriend Kupi Landau had destroyed one of the aircraft, saving her Janus Machine and its crew. He had already lauded her heroic actions when she was in Quebec afterward, and he'd arranged for her to receive a medal. But he had something else in mind for whoever organized that attack, if they were still alive. Public executions to show he would not tolerate opposition.

He scanned the report quickly. To his dismay, it didn't have any additional information on the attackers, and especially not on how they might have used that tube-shaped transporter to get to the site. The large machine had emerged from underground just before the attack, that much was certain, but how had it gotten there? He scowled, recalling that the vessel had been detonated by a self-destruct mechanism, and not by weapons fire from his defenders.

The report went into some conjecture about who might have been responsible for the attack, from the Panasians to the Eurikans to renegade Corporate elements, without drawing any definitive conclusions. Essentially, the communication was a waste of time to even read.

Jade slipped back into her clothes. "Try to think of the good side of this," she said, having seen part of the electronic document over his shoulder. "At least the attackers didn't damage much. I mean, it was a small-scale operation, and it failed."

He glared at her, and shouted, "You naïve girl, don't you understand that I need to know who was behind this?" Rising to his feet, he considered striking her but resisted, because he abhorred violence and used it only when necessary to maintain the order of the state. "There is nothing good about this situation, no matter how you try to spin it. Now get out!"

Jade had quickly become one of his favorite female companions, having advanced past everyone except Dori Longet and Valerie Tatanka. He might even be having sex with Jade more now than the other two, but he didn't enjoy conversations with her as much. Despite her intelligence, Jade's inexperience and outspokenness got on his nerves at times, irritating him to the core. This was one of those times.

Now the buxom redhead blanched. "I was just trying to cheer you up, that's all. You usually appreciate that when you're under stress."

"*Stress?* This is more than stress, but you're too young and foolish to know the difference! You can cheer me up by getting the hell out of my sight."

With her floral-pattern dress only half buttoned, Jade grabbed her sandals and fled. As she opened the door to the outer offices, Rahma shook his head in dismay. The sex with her was so great that at times he was blind to her faults.

He shouted for Artie.

Moments later the loyal hubot hurried in, and looked where the Chairman was pointing, at the holo-report. "Have I missed something new here?" Rahma asked. "This looks like a rehash of what we already know."

After reading it, Artie said, "You're not mistaken, Master. The investigators seem to be filling time."

"And wasting mine."

"Perhaps I should check right now and see why they even sent this?"

The Chairman could have done that himself, by sending a mental command. But he nodded wearily. "OK, check with AOE and let me know."

"Yes, sir." Artie lifted one of his artificial, realistic-looking hands. A beam of red light shot out of the palm, dissipating the red letters of the holo-signal and replacing them with an urgent message to AOE headquarters in Berkeley.

Watching Artie's face, the Chairman saw intensity in the dark blue eyes that had once belonged to Glanno Artindale and were now used by another comrade. There were similarities between Artie and Glanno in the way they behaved and the way they served the Chairman without question, but not as sycophants in either case, not in a vacuous manner. They guided him intelligently, gave him good counsel.

He missed his friend, the man who had made such important contributions to the revolution and had died heroically, the man who had briefly been Rahma's male lover. Rahma remembered the good times they'd had together, the intimate moments and the unfortunate confrontation they'd had when

Rahma refused to give up his women. After that, Glanno flung himself more into the revolution, and Rahma always wondered if it was why he died—Glanno had a devil-may-care attitude after their brief, ill-fated fling, and he became more confrontational against the police, provoking the pigs, making himself a target.

Following Glanno's death, Rahma felt guilty for a time, but eventually he succeeded in putting that out of his mind, because of the governmental challenges that needed his attention. He tried to do so again now, remembering instead what a great adviser his friend had been, and what a brilliant scientist he'd been, working tirelessly to resurrect extinct species.

"Well," Rahma said to the hubot, as he got into his underclothes. "Any response yet?"

"Just a moment, please." Artie was processing information, sorting through overlapping pages of information that floated in the air, with white tabs on them.

The Chairman slipped on a green-and-gold robe and hemp sandals, then draped a golden peace-symbol pendant around his neck. "Come on, come on. What are they saying?"

The hubot let out a whistle. "Something *is* new this time, sir, an attachment they forgot to send. The AOE just received it in the last hour. An automated soldier has been found, something the searchers didn't notice earlier. In the excitement of the attack, this one fell from an aircraft into a forest thicket."

"Give me a quick summary, Artie."

"Yes, sir. The captured robot had a self-destruct mechanism that failed to operate. Our people have completely disabled the mechanism, and they've found no evidence of Corporate involvement." He paused. "Instead, it points to the SciOs."

"What? Why do you say that?"

"The self-destruct mechanism in the first place, Your Green Eminence. You know how secretive the SciOs are, and how their sensitive machines are all fitted with destruct mechanisms if anyone tampers with them."

"That's nothing. Self-destruct mechanisms have long been used to guard sensitive information."

"There's more. The robot's programming indicates that the attackers used both human and robotic troops, and listen to this—the three aircraft had artillery pieces that were the equivalent of Janus Machine Splitter Cannons, capable of turning targets into gooey masses."

"There was no evidence of that in the aircraft wreckage or on the battlefield."

"No, sir. For some unexplained reason, they used conventional weaponry, perhaps because their Splitters were inoperable. As you know, such technology is known to require extensive maintenance by SciO technicians."

"That's true. But SciO technology? How can that be possible?"

"Hard to say. There's more here, and I'm trying to give it to you in the right order, on a priority basis. The captured robot has sketchy, coded programming that indicates it was part of a military force that came from an underground base thousands of kilometers away, in central Mexico. And they tunneled underground from there to here—bringing troops and war matériel in that tube-shaped transport vehicle."

"*Tunneled?* All that way?"

"That's not all, sir. They did it in four hours."

"*Underground?* They used supersonic subterranean transporters?"

"That must be the transporter wreckage we found. Keep in mind, this could all be bogus information, programmed into the robots to throw us off."

"I don't like the sound of this," Rahma said.

"Nor do I, Master."

Just then, an alarm sounded, three piercing beeps. The earlier message arrived after an eight-beep alarm, indicating a much higher urgency. As Rahma sent a mental command to accept the new message, he saw it appear in red, replacing the previous one and all of the additional files that Artie had accessed.

The Chairman read, shaking his head. Yet another problem. The Panasians had finally discovered that GSA operatives had taken one of their rare snow leopards and they were causing diplomatic trouble, demanding the animal's return. But they didn't seem to know how the snow leopard was taken; they didn't know about enhanced virtual reality—EVR. If Hashimoto ever learned that the Green States could put avatars in Panasia, he or his advisers would wonder how—and experts might figure out that the GSA had compromised a Panasian satellite.

Since the inception of the GSA twenty years ago there had been a series of incidents between the two nations, and several times the Panasians had threatened nuclear retaliation. There were countless issues separating the GSA and Panasian governments, and no reasonable person thought they could be resolved short of war. The only question Rahma had was when the inevitable full-scale confrontation would occur. But this time, Hashimoto's message was more complex. "My government does not want nuclear war," he wrote, "but I cannot ignore the unauthorized excursion by your operatives, and the theft of one of our valuable animals."

Rahma read the words over and over, wasn't sure how to take them. What did Hashimoto have in mind? It couldn't be anything good.

As Artie stood by, the Chairman considered all of the recent events, and wondered if there could possibly be some connection between the bellicose, argumentative government

236 • BRIAN HERBERT

of Panasia and the disturbing Bostoner attack. Some of his advisers had been theorizing it was a military test, a probe of GSA defenses, and the enemy weapons had failed to work properly.

A chill ran down his spine. If a connection existed, the terrible war between nations was about to begin.

But where did the SciOs fit into all of this?

27

All life-forms on the planet have the right to live in dignity.
—a saying of the Green Revolution

JOSS AWOKE WITH a feeling of edginess, and went about his morning toilet. He moved quickly, taking advantage of his heightened metabolism, but didn't bother to shave, even though the stubble of beard on his face was getting longer than he usually kept it. He'd never worn a full beard or mustache, and this put him in the minority of modern men, but it didn't seem to have had a limiting effect on his career. The six men in the Berkeley Eight, and other adult males who wanted to show they were green zealots, liked to cover their faces with hair, but people could still advance themselves without that, by demonstrating competence in green technologies.

In embarking on his career as a greenformer, however, Joss had not anticipated the incredible alterations that would take place in his body. Yesterday, he'd discovered an ability to generate an energy field around himself that kept flies away from him, or he could kill them with bolts of energy if he preferred. Remarkably, top-secret technology had become embedded in the cells of his body, and he was figuring out how to use it. Each day that passed, he learned more about it.

No wonder the SciOs were so interested in him, and he knew they'd be here soon, bothering him again. He'd intimated to the medical attendants that he would be more cooperative with them today than he had been the day before, when he'd felt annoyed by their constant tests, their unending probes. But he did not feel at all cooperative, and sensed that this day would not go well. He just *knew* it.

The challenge was how to handle their demands with poise instead of doing something he would regret, something that would make an already bad situation even worse. The pesky SciOs were like the annoying flies, and he strongly suspected that Dr. Mora had ordered the insects to be released in his quarters, just to see how their lab rat would react.

Joss smiled. If only . . . He caught himself. Could he possibly accomplish what he had in mind?

He ate breakfast alone, a customized cereal-and-fruit mixture from a dispenser in the kitchen alcove. Afterward he stood in the entertainment chamber and looked up at the observation cameras in the corners, the spy eyes that were watching him. "You may come in now," he said.

Moments later, Dr. Mora and a female research assistant entered. "Are you feeling better?"

"Better than what? Than yesterday? Or before the explosion?"

Dr. Mora took a step forward, smiled in a kindly way. "Is there anything we can do for you, Joss, anything to make this easier? You know we have to conduct the research, but I want to make it as comfortable as possible for you."

"Is that right? Well, then, I think I'd like some extended time off."

"I'm sorry, but that isn't possible. It is urgent that we keep moving forward."

"Your superiors told you that."

"Perhaps, but nonetheless it is true. Something extraordinary happened to you, and you hold the key to a scientific doorway that no one has ever been through before. A doorway to incredible human potential."

"*Mutated* human potential. *Freak* human potential. What do you want to do, put people into ReFac buildings and blow them up, trying to replicate what happened to me?"

"No, but your body is a gold mine of genetic possibilities. At any moment you could . . ." He paused.

"Die?"

"I was going to say, lose your powers. Death is only one way. The powers could just vanish and wouldn't be there for us to analyze. At this very moment, you might not have what you had yesterday."

"It seems to me that my genetics, whatever they are now, wouldn't just fade away. And if you're so intent on studying me, perhaps I should bill the SciO Dark Energy research division by the hour, by the minute? I have value, don't I?"

"Of course you do, but—"

Joss stared at the floor. "Maybe we should take an inventory of what I can do and set a value for each of my skills. Then you can pay me."

"Of course you deserve to be compensated, but that isn't something we should waste time on here, not until the important experiments are concluded."

"Concluded? You're leading me on, Doctor. You and I both know that I'll never be released. You SciOs will always find some reason to keep me locked up."

"That isn't true."

"Then when will I be let out? *When?*"

"That is not my job to determine."

"All right, whose job is it? Bring that person in here, along with your SciO moneyman and a couple of lawyers, and let's draw up an ironclad agreement. In exchange for X greendollars I will permit myself to be a lab rat for Y amount of time."

"You're being preposterous."

"This situation is preposterous."

They glared at each other. Then Dr. Mora whispered something to his research assistant, who left. She returned quickly, accompanied by SciO security officers carrying short-barrel tranquilizer rifles.

"We don't have time for games," the doctor said. "These sessions will continue, with or without your permission."

One of the SciOs pointed his rifle at Joss, seemed to be waiting for the doctor's command to fire.

Joss moved both hands quickly, releasing black strands of energy into the air that whirled and spiraled and wove themselves together into a crackling black net. He thought of the energy field he'd created to deflect the flies, and put more effort into this one. He added to the strands in the air, creating a tight-mesh black net that wrapped around him and took on the shape of his body.

He heard percussive noises, saw the barrels of the tranquilizer rifles flash red. Instinctively he dropped to the floor. He saw a volley of tranquilizer darts hit the netting on his side, depressing the barrier ever so slightly and then bouncing off, as did others that followed. More SciO security officers appeared, but Dr. Mora waved all of them back, to the doorway that led out into the corridor.

Joss stood up, and when he did, the protective field remained with him like an article of tight clothing, still retaining his shape. To sustain it, he didn't have to add energy by moving his hands around. He just *willed* the field to remain in place, and it did.

With considerable satisfaction, he watched the doctor and the security men trying to penetrate the shield with their hands and the butts of the rifles, pushing and pounding on it as hard as they could, without success. It didn't even flex for them, disrupted all attempts.

"I think we're finished for today," Joss said, calmly, sensing that his voice was not blocked by the field. "I'll let you know if, and when, we will resume."

He pointed a hand toward one corner of the room, mentally commanding a black wave of Splitter energy to fire and melt the surveillance camera there. Then, whirling, he did the same to three other cameras in the room, turning them into dark, dripping streaks on the walls.

The doctor and his companions left, grumbling as they stalked away.

It was a small victory for Joss, but he knew that the SciOs were likely to consider him even more strange after this, and more dangerous.

28

History speaks of this, if anyone cares to listen. Look at the American Revolution and the concept of equality for all men, or the Marxist ideal of a ruling proletariat, or the strict environmental canons of the Green States of America. No matter the laudatory ideals under which a government is formed, it always gravitates toward an oligarchy, a small ruling class that accumulates vast wealth from the system and lives in castles, palaces, chateaus, or villas, enjoying far more of the fruits of life than other people. There are no exceptions of note. Egocentric human interests invariably prevail.

—entry in one of Artie's data banks (analysis made in response to some of Kupi Landau's government criticisms)

IN HIS OFFICE on the Montana Valley Game Reserve, the Chairman watched a desk screen that received images from bodycams on the hubot Artie. He turned the screen away from morning sunlight. With so many pressing details of national defense to tend to himself, Rahma had dispatched the loyal aide on an urgent matter, to meet with the Director of Science and question him about the evidence of SciO technology found at the site of the Bostoner attack. It was early evening, and Artie had flown to Berkeley on his boss's private jet, *AOE One*. Before leaving, Artie had made arrangements to project an avatar of himself back to Montana whenever he wished, so that he could check on the Extinct Animals Laboratory, and even perform tasks there remotely if needed.

The hubot was just arriving at Ondex's mansion now, walking up the front steps . . .

Rahma heard a beep, signifying the arrival of a message. Tapping a key on the console in front of him, he created split-screen images and then viewed a communiqué from the young Eurikan Prime Minister, Grange Arthur. The man was offering to use shuttle diplomacy to resolve the ongoing GSA-Panasia tensions. Rahma scoffed at the idea, didn't see how relations between the nations or their leaders could possibly be resolved short of war. The differences were simply too great, the mutual animosity too extreme. He would order an aide to respond negatively.

He then reviewed a report from the AOE Chief of Staff on his own military preparations that were being made, the movement and positioning of war machines and troops. In view of the apparent underground attack near Bostoner, there was no telling where or when the enemy might strike next. He had no doubt of a Panasian connection, but could not prove it yet.

Just then, he heard a rapping at the door—Dori Longet's characteristic *tap-tap-tap*. Another busy morning. He took a gulp of strong coffee.

"Enter!" Rahma called out, but she was already opening the door before he said this, and entered carrying a valise. "This is under diplomatic seal," she said, "straight from Premier Hashimoto himself. It's been scanned and is not dangerous."

"And the contents?"

"Just papers."

Rahma waved a hand, and she broke the seal to open the

valise, from which she removed a sheath of papers. She placed them on his desk.

"What is it now?" Rahma asked. Opening the sheath, he spread the contents on his desk. The papers had an unusual texture, rough to the touch. As he handled them he sniffed at an odd, difficult-to-identify odor, but it dissipated quickly and he put it out of his mind.

Then he nearly gagged at the sight of a color photograph of the lifeless body of an immense polar bear lying on ice, the throat of its long neck slit and bleeding. Dressed in Arctic gear, Hashimoto stood over the body, grinning and holding a bloody knife. There was a second, even more gruesome, photograph as well, showing the Panasian leader and a companion hacking off the legs of the bear, for some macabre, unknown purpose.

A short cover letter from Hashimoto read, "Knowing what an animal lover you are, I thought you might like these pictures of one of the last polar bears on Earth."

"Damn him!" Rahma brushed his hand across the desktop, scattering the photographs and letter. That bastard was a constant irritation in his side, a burr that he could not seem to extract.

AS DORI LEFT the Chairman's office with a sheath of papers under one arm, she saw Jade Ridell sitting in the waiting area, wearing a red halter top with a peace symbol on it, and a short skirt with a fringe. The two women glowered at each other.

Despite telling her parents she wasn't concerned about Rahma's other women, it was beginning to irritate her that Jade was sleeping with Rahma more than she was now. He seemed to be shifting his relationship with Dori to one that was almost pure business—with only occasional moments of intimacy. And even when those moments occurred, she sensed that he was losing his passion for her. He might not even be conscious of it yet, but she certainly was.

Later that day, she sent a message to her parents, letting them know the bad news.

EXASPERATED, THE BEARDED Chairman looked at the desk screen, which had only one set of images on it now. Artie sat on a settee in the eighteenth-century French parlor room of Arch Ondex's home in the Berkeley hills. It had been an unannounced late-morning call, but Artie was Chairman Rahma's emissary—an extension of the Chairman himself—and Ondex was taking overly long to appear. A gesture of disrespect. It was silent in the parlor, with a servant having left more than ten minutes ago to announce the visitor. Artie held a rolled parchment on his lap.

The Chairman could switch remote views, using different bodycams on the hubot. For a moment he focused on the antique Beauvais tapestry upholstery of the couch.

Tapping buttons on the console, Rahma wrote, "Do you see the loose golden threads in the upholstery?" His words appeared on the bottom of the desk screen.

"I see them," Artie replied, looking down at the couch. More words on the screen, as the aide's AI thoughts were transmitted.

"I want you to pull at those threads."

"Pull at them? But this is a valuable antique."

"My *time* is valuable, and the longer I'm made to wait, the larger the hole I want you to make. Simultaneously, I want you to grind your heels into the antique Aubusson rug beneath your feet—it dates back to the time of Louis XV. We've been here for twelve minutes, Artie, waiting! In eight minutes, go and find Ondex yourself. This is an urgent matter."

"Yes, Master." While Rahma looked on, his hubot pushed the parchment aside and started working at the upholstery and rug.

Ondex's gaudy pink-and-white mansion was a relic of old San Francisco money, derived from the railroads, ships, and gold mines of the family's titan of industry, R. Sibbington Ondex, and passed on from generation to generation. Eventually, after the fall of the United States, the regal old home was taken apart and reassembled in the Berkeley hills, on a commanding spot that provided a fine view of the blue waters of the bay and the reservation for humans.

To move the home before the greenforming of the San Francisco peninsula, the grand old edifice had been taken apart carefully, with the pieces numbered meticulously and later put back together at the new location. The house was saved because of the contributions to the Army of the Environment made by Arch Ondex, the oldest living male descendant of the late tycoon—and because the family had been environmentally and socially conscious for more than half a century, contributing large amounts of money to national parks and endowments for the poor. As a result, they were among a privileged few who were permitted to keep their generational family holdings, and to live outside the boundaries of the reservations.

In those heady days when the Green Revolution was just starting out, Arch Ondex had been a critical source of wealth and scientific technology that fueled the great victories of the ragtag populist army against Corporate forces. Now, despite the man's aristocratic, condescending manner and other traits that the Chairman found grating, he always tried to keep in mind the earlier essential contributions.

During his administration, Rahma had also been forgiving

when other members of his original cadre acted up. Kupi Landau and her recurrent outspokenness was a prime example, because he never knew what she would say next, or who would be on the receiving end of one of her insults. So far she had avoided the cardinal sin of speaking against the Chairman himself, but at one time or another she had criticized virtually every other leader of the GSA, including Director of Science Ondex and Sigourney von Wallis, Director of Relocation, the latter of whom she had accused of taking graft—a charge that remained unproven. It didn't mean it wasn't true, only that no one could obtain solid evidence against her yet.

In one sense Rahma didn't like Kupi's unpredictability, but in another he very much appreciated her candor, because she often made him think about important issues, especially about the excesses of leading politicians and purportedly green business people, an elite that she sometimes referred to colorfully as "limousine liberals." Von Wallis, like Ondex, lived in a mansion, and so did almost all of the others.

Just before Rahma's deadline, Ondex strode into the parlor in a red smoking jacket, a long wooden pipe in his mouth. He looked quite decadent. From the remote viewing position, Rahma glowered. As the head of SciO, this was one of the people who had benefited the most from green businesses, as correctly noted by Kupi. He also had a political stronghold, making him even more entrenched.

Her criticisms of him had led to one of Ondex's tirades the year before, and an argument between him and Rahma over how best to handle her. In the end the Chairman had prevailed, saying he would handle it, and that Ondex should go and wallow in his wealth. Of course the Chairman had done nothing to punish Kupi, and he didn't think he ever would—not unless she did something a lot worse than speaking her mind.

"Sorry to keep you waiting," Ondex said. According to Artie's sensors he was smoking regular burley tobacco. The Director sat on the opposite end of the couch, placed his pipe on a holder beside him.

"You kept the Chairman waiting," the hubot said, "not me."

The Director of Science scowled, but took a tug on his pipe instead of responding. His lamb chop sideburns were not as bushy and wide as usual.

Artie rubbed his chin thoughtfully. "The Chairman has instructed me to notify you that he's been having second thoughts about allowing you to keep your family mansion, where you live so much more comfortably than the average citizen. There are other family properties in question as well."

Reddening, Ondex said, "He knows why we were allowed to keep our properties. The entire GSA Council voted for it, to reward our past service to the Earth. Your master cast one of those votes."

Shaking his head, the hubot said, "Chairman Rahma says that your family has special privileges only as long as you contribute to the welfare of the Green States of America. You must always keep that in mind."

"I have to listen to this, after everything I've done for the cause?"

"While you've been enjoying the high life, someone has been using SciO technology to develop military vehicles that burrow underground, and Splitter weapons."

The elegant man leaned forward. "What do you mean, SciO technology? There is no proof of what you say!"

With a wave of one hand, Artie opened the confidential holo-report that he'd been authorized to show. From his remote vantage, Rahma watched with interest as Ondex read it and looked at pictures taken during the Bostoner attack.

Sweat broke out on Ondex's brow and ran into his eyes.

He wiped the moisture away several times, but couldn't stop the flow. "This is not evidence. The attack aircraft did not use any Splitter weaponry."

"No, but it was aboard."

"That must be a mistake. How could the GSA operative who wrote this report know what secrets are contained in Splitter technology?"

"The information comes from a robotic soldier in the attack force, not from the GSA. The three aircraft were transported to the attack site in a military transport vehicle that burrowed thousands of kilometers underground."

"Nonsense. It's all inaccurate data and conjecture." He smiled stiffly.

Artie leaned close, spoke his own thoughts. "Do you SciOs have a secret tunneling technology like that, something to go long distances underground at high speed and then cover up the tunnels behind them?"

"No, I don't think . . ." He paused. "No, we have nothing like that."

"It sounds like very advanced technology, wouldn't you agree?"

"Absolutely, unless the attackers left behind false clues, and no technology like that exists at all."

"Well, they sneaked up on us somehow, wouldn't you say? If not by tunneling, then how did they do it?"

"I have no idea."

"Surely with all of your scientific knowledge and wizardry, you SciOs can solve it. Chairman Rahma is the spiritual head of the Green States of America, and you are in charge of science." Artie wagged a thick, humanlike forefinger. "This is not the Chairman's failing. It's a failing of your scientists to figure it out."

"Need I remind you that the Army of the Environment is under Chairman Rahma's control, not mine?"

"But you provide many of the key weapons, and the science to build them, and now we've been attacked by an unknown, dangerous enemy who may have SciO Splitter technology and the ability to transport military assets across long distances underground." He opened the rolled parchment. "Chairman Rahma has decided to formally declare a State of National Emergency, enabling him to legally demand the full contribution of the SciOs. To begin with, he wants a list of all SciO research programs."

"A State of National Emergency? This is preposterous! I've never heard of the technology that you're—" He fell silent and looked away.

Accessing his internal data banks, Artie said, "After we defeated the Corporates and the GSA Charter was drawn up, the Chairman allowed you to keep your technological secrets, in return for which you agreed to enhance our military research and development capabilities if formally called upon to do so."

Director Ondex grimaced.

"Well, he's calling on you to do that right now," Artie said, "in the State of National Emergency." He handed the parchment to him.

Ondex gave the document a cursory glance, slapped it down on a table, where it curled back up. "But a list of all of our research programs? He's not being reasonable."

"Neither are our enemies—and the Chairman is not certain how many we have, or how advanced they are."

Looking at one of the bodycams on Artie's belt, Ondex said, "I know you're eavesdropping on this meeting, Rahma Popal, and I'm going to level with you. Several years ago we had a top-secret vanishing tunnel program that was an offshoot of Janus Machine technology, but nothing came of it.

The program was a complete failure, and the entire team of inventors committed suicide."

From the Montana Valley Game Reserve, the GSA leader typed a response, which Artie received in his data banks and then passed along. "Chairman Rahma wants to know what vanishing tunnels are."

"Well, the technology never worked, at least not on the scale needed to make it practical. In theory, it was supposed to be a system in which a tunneling machine split through the crust of the planet, propelling itself forward, while an earth- and rockforming system at the rear—like greenforming— closed the tunnel off, making it look like it was before."

Hesitation, as Artie awaited another message. "My master wants to know what happened to the bodies of the suicides."

"They're in SciO crypts, beneath our Berkeley headquarters."

Hesitation, as another message came in from Montana Valley. Receiving it, Artie spoke: "You control your employees from job to grave—and the Chairman knows why. You're afraid someone will come up with a way to read human memories from cells and other genetic detritus, even after the employees are dead—and that would risk revealing SciO secrets. Hence, all of the remains are closely guarded."

Ondex nodded, grudgingly. He chewed at one side of his mouth.

"It's even rumored that living employees contain self-destruct mechanisms in their bodies to prevent anyone from gaining access to their cellular material."

No response.

"You will exhume the bodies for government inspection," Artie said. It was not a question.

"Inspection?"

Artie nodded. "The Chairman wants me to observe the exhumations and collect data."

"That's highly unusual."

"It's just the beginning. The Chairman has commanded me to stay with you until we get to the bottom of what looks like a major SciO technology leak. I am not to leave your side. Not until my master releases me."

"Is that in the National Emergency document?"

"Section Four," the hubot said. "Maybe you should read the whole thing."

29

The relationship with the government of Panasia continues to slide. They are the primary suspect in the failed Bostoner attack, and in other transgressions against the sovereignty of the Green States of America. On both sides, forces are on high alert; nuclear missiles are aimed and ready to fire. How is this different from the international tensions when Corporates were running things on the American continents? Where is the sustainable peace we were promised by Chairman Rahma?
—Berkeley Free Radio, one of the dissident stations

IT WAS PAST midnight when Arch Ondex and the hubot took a clearplex-walled elevator down to the ninth level of the mausoleum. As they passed each level of the subterranean facility, Artie saw long rows of crypts in all directions. Most were empty, because this was where the SciOs interred their dead, and the organization had only been in existence since shortly before the founding of the country. Every person who ever worked for the SciOs would be laid to rest here when they died, and in time it would become crowded with bodies—but for now it was sparsely populated.

"We never permit visitors," Ondex said, "but under the circumstances, and considering the degree of trust the Chairman has placed in you, we are making an exception."

"Thank you," Artie said, though he knew the Director had little choice—unless he decided to contest the State of

National Emergency. Artie was on his own here, without the overseeing eyes of the Chairman, due to the late hour and matters of national defense he had to deal with early the next morning. The hubot was video recording everything, though—and he would collect data for further tests.

The elevator stopped, and Ondex led the way out, then down a well-lit corridor. "The only occupied crypts are in this area. As you know, we require the interment of all employees here." He looked back over his shoulder and smiled stiffly. "After they pass away, of course."

"Naturally." Artie also knew that the bodies were sealed in the crypts shortly after death, and never cremated because that was against the SciO belief system. Ironically, Ondex led an organization of scientists who had quasi-religious beliefs and secret rites.

Artie heard voices. He and Ondex rounded a turn, and ahead they saw a group of SciO security officers waiting beside a metal gate, accompanied by a tall, officious-looking woman in a white suit-dress.

"You may commence," Ondex said, after introducing Artie to the woman, Dr. Mariah Kovacs. She was in charge of the DNA sampling that would be conducted today—information that would be passed on to Artie for further analysis. The Chairman needed to have the identities verified and then run searches for additional information through the Greenpol data system, all of which made sense. The SciOs and their paranoia about cellular memories had been overridden.

The officers opened the gate and entered an arched alcove that contained the crypts of the research team that had committed suicide over their failure. Artie had little doubt that it had actually occurred, because the SciO leadership was known to be very demanding, and unforgiving of mistakes.

Using power tools, the officers cut the seals around seven

crypts, and slid the caskets out onto the floor of the alcove. Moving in close, Artie recorded in his data banks the name on each crypt: Kee Wong, Joel Nero, Mae Pitol, Vanna Solomon, Dylan Bane, Triston Lalley, and Kent Hopkins.

Opening each casket, Dr. Kovacs took cell samples from the decaying bodies, using a compression-extraction needle. Artie noticed that she and the officers recoiled from odors in the caskets, but with his mechanical components he was able to take readings on the smells without being bothered by them. Peeking in, he saw that five of the bodies were well preserved, while two—Solomon and Lalley—were desiccated, from leaks in the seals. With each extraction, Dr. Kovacs dutifully transferred cellular and genetic data to a scanner on Artie's body.

One by one she ran through the identities, checking the bodies against identity cards for the deceased employees. "Nero, check," she said. "Pitol, check. Hopkins, check. Bane—" She paused, ran another test.

Looking at Director Ondex, she said, "Problem here, sir. This is not the body of Dylan Bane."

"Not Bane?" Ondex looked into the casket, while Artie moved closer to see better.

"Look here, sir," she said, using a scalpel to lift a flap of skin from the well-preserved though yellowing face. "See that? It's a fake skin overlay containing Bane's DNA. But going deeper and taking an internal organ sample, it's clear that this is the body of a different man, made to look like Bane, and seem to be Bane. The autopsy doctor only took a cell scraping from what he thought was the epidermis, and came up with Bane's DNA. Not suspecting anything, he didn't bother to go deeper."

"If this isn't Bane, who the hell is it?"

"We don't know yet, sir."

"Damn it," the Director said. "This means Bane is on the loose."

"With SciO technology," Artie said. "Obviously, he knows how to make the vanishing tunnel system work to transport military forces underground, over long distances."

Ondex slammed a fist on the edge of the casket, then grimaced and grabbed his hand. "I think I broke it," he said.

That's the least of your problems, Artie thought, as he watched tests being conducted on the other bodies, and received additional data through his scanner. There were no more surprises.

"You are not to notify the Chairman of this yet," Director Ondex said, as the doctor and her assistants completed their work. "I must go to him personally in order to provide him with important information beyond what you have learned here today, beyond anything that is in the cells or genetics of these bodies. For the sake of national security, it is best for Rahma to learn it all at once, and directly from me."

"What is the additional information?"

"That will be revealed when I am face to face with Chairman Rahma. Come with me now. We shall leave immediately."

Artie nodded, but he secretly transmitted a backup file to the GSA data storage facility in Montana Valley, along with an electronic tickler that would notify the Chairman of its presence tomorrow, and enable him to access it.

These SciOs could be tricky, and he didn't want to risk losing the data.

IN THE MISSOULA Reservation, a black-garbed figure cut through the cool shadows of night, moving from street to street, following the directions that his sister had given to him. He carried a small duffel bag.

Uvander Crumb was an anarchist soldier, a lieutenant in the Black Shirts, the Army's vaunted Revolutionary Guard. He had fought in the front lines of the Corporate War, had seen his comrades fall around him, had been in the cheering throngs when Chairman Rahma declared victory and established the Green States of America.

Yet tonight's assignment was not on any duty sheet, was not known to his superiors or to anyone else in the armed forces. It was known only to himself and to his older sister, Kristine Longet. She didn't even want her husband to know, or their daughter.

Now he stared up at the glass-walled apartment building she had designated. It looked like any other building in this mid-green neighborhood, and everyone inside was asleep with the lights off, following strict schedules laid out for them by the government.

Uvander understood the necessity of what he was doing. It occupied a realm beyond any moral constraints, compunctions, or laws. It was the sworn obligation of a brother to a sister, and with such an important matter there could be no discussion of nuances. It was a matter of duty. Family duty.

Using a security code he had obtained surreptitiously through his military and police contacts, he slipped through the service entrance of the building. When the door closed behind him he activated a small, powerful flashlight. Except for the beam of illumination this provided, it was pitch dark in there. He moved quickly through the corridor, glancing occasionally at a hand-held screen that provided him with a blueprint of the building.

Using additional codes, he passed through one doorway and then another, closing doors softly behind him as he proceeded. Finally he stood in a large room that had a very high ceiling and mezzanines, with metal stairways and walkways connecting the levels. Through an elaborate arrangement of chutes and bins, this was where garbage was collected from the apartments above, in a system that separated the refuse for each unit and enabled inspectors to examine it regularly, looking for eco-violations.

Uvander climbed four stairways, then hurried along a walkway until he located the bin for apartment number 2095, which he had been told was occupied by the Ridell family—enemies of his sister. He'd never seen Kristine like this before; she was extremely upset and determined to take action, telling him that she'd met the father of a young woman who was harming Dori's career, and something needed to be done to get the young woman—and her entire family—out of the way.

He unzipped the duffel bag and poured its contents into the bin—plastic bags he'd dug out of an old Corporate landfill, and washed off. A garbage inspector was due to examine these bins the following afternoon, and would not like what he discovered.

30

It became very clear to us on the revolutionary council that the Corporate-induced lifestyle of conspicuous consumption was not sustainable for our planet, that man could not keep usurping the resources of the Earth without consequences. Others had warned of this before us, but we carried the banner of environmentalism into battle.

—Chairman Rahma, in an interview
with *The Green Times*

ACCORDING TO THE wall screen it was midday, with bright, sunlit clouds on the horizon, east of the hills and tall buildings of the Berkeley Reservation for Humans. Joss stood in front of the projected image, cursing it for not being a real window view. For all he knew, it might not actually be midday; it could be nighttime. At the moment he loathed the SciOs and their technology, and felt an overwhelming desire to be free and breathe whatever gasps of outside air he could, for as long as he could.

Looking up at a surveillance cam, he said, "I'm not going to be your lab rat anymore, Dr. Mora, so I issue you fair warning. Stay out of my way and no one will be hurt."

A woman's voice came over an intercom, the synthesized one he'd heard before. "Don't try anything foolish, Mr. Stuart."

Ignoring the computerized warning, Joss rose to his feet

and strode to the thick door that led to the hallway. He wondered if he was the only human awake in the research facility this early.

He corrected himself. The only *sentient*. With the altered, darkened color of his skin, and the green, vinelike scars on it, along with the odd powers he had acquired in the explosion, he wasn't sure exactly what to call himself, other than this.

Joss felt the gathering roar in his pulse, and wove a small force field between his fingertips. Then, enlarging the field, he wove a protective net of black light around himself—leaving small openings in the energy field at his fingertips.

Through the gaps he fired controlled blasts of Dark Energy. The heavy door melted away, and he strode through it into the corridor.

Alarm klaxons sounded, and through the net he saw white-uniformed security officers running toward him. "Stop!" one of them yelled.

To demonstrate his power, Joss blasted a hole in a wall near the officers without hitting them, and walked toward them because the exit was in that direction. Looking terrified, they moved out of his way.

As he marched past an open doorway, a medical technician appeared suddenly and fired a sedative gun, a volley of red, whisper-silent projectiles. All of them bounced harmlessly off Joss's threadlike shield.

Dr. Mora emerged ahead of him and stood in the middle of the hallway, his arms outstretched in a halting gesture. Medical attendants stood behind him. "We must work together!" he shouted to Joss. "Don't do this! We'll make a new arrangement!"

Joss ignored him and continued on, with his energy field repelling them, knocking them aside. He went past them, shouting, "I'm making my own arrangement."

More people appeared, along with robots, but the energy barrier knocked them aside without the necessity of Joss taking conscious actions, or even sending mental commands. It was a repellent field, a disturbance area around his body that prevented anyone from getting too close to him. They couldn't penetrate the field to inject him, tie him up, or shoot projectiles through. The field prevented every attempt.

Defiantly, Joss marched out of the bleak gray building and onto the streets of the Berkeley Reservation for Humans. As he strode down the shaded sidewalk, he saw white-uniformed SciO security officers following him, and other people pointing, beginning to take notice of him.

Joss didn't understand what had happened to him in the explosion of the ReFac building, but his powers were obviously more than the "cute little talents" mentioned in government reports about him. He wasn't sure what to do with his paranormal skills, or what the purpose of his life was from this point on. He only knew that he would never return to SciO control again.

Then he shuddered, remembering that he had SciO technology immersed in his cells.

31

Joss Stuart was said to be an orphan, left in a bundle beneath an oak tree on a moonlit Pacific Northwest night. From low-hanging boughs above the crying infant, night birds called out, making so much racket that a man went to investigate. In a pool of moonlight, he found a child wrapped in rags and covered in leaves up to his neck, with only his head showing.

—a news report, "The Birth of Greenman"

AT AN ACCELERATED pace, Joss walked down one sidewalk and then another in the forest of high-rise buildings, following signs that led to the Old Town district of the Berkeley Reservation. He had only a vague idea of why he was going there, an instinct that this was the direction to go because it was where the green movement began in earnest, and where he thought he might find some comfort.

Behind him, a gathering crowd followed, people shouting to one another, identifying him and commenting on the strange appearance of his skin and the net of black light around him, and what he'd done to break out of the SciO facility. To keep them at bay, he maintained the web of energy for half a meter around his body, which blocked anyone from touching him and repelled those few foolish individuals who got in front of him and attempted to block his path. He just kept going, giving anyone in his way a gentle nudge, trying not to hurt anybody. In the distance to the east, the sun was peeking around buildings.

Gradually Joss walked faster, and noticed that people needed to run to keep up with him. What would happen if he actually began to run? He inhaled a deep breath, continued walking rapidly as he thought about this question. He hesitated doing that, felt a fear of what he was becoming, and just wanted to get away from people and be alone so that he could *think*. Without being watched, he needed to consider everything that was happening to his body, with no inquisitive scientists taking readings on him, monitoring his every move, and recording his every word.

In various doorways and intersections he saw men and women in SciO robes watching him, using hand-held communication devices to report on his movements. These observers didn't try to interfere, didn't join the throngs.

He reached Old Town, where the buildings were much lower, vintage brick and wood frame houses featuring white pillars, sienna tile roofs, and ivy on the walls. Some had empty flagpoles where fraternity and sorority banners once flew, before the GSA declared all such organizations illegal and disbanded them. Government caretakers occupied some of these structures now, maintaining the neighborhood for historical purposes.

Almost a century ago, in the 1960s, there had been student revolts on these streets and on the nearby University of California campus, demanding free speech, world peace, and environmental protection. In those days the police had been called "pigs" by young protestors, and there had been open warfare between the two sides—but nothing on the scale of 2041–43 and the Corporate War, when more than four million people perished.

At an intersection, SciO security officers converged around Joss, but he broke free and hurried across the busy street, moving quickly around the myriad electric transportation vehicles—taxis and various sizes of buses. Just then a large truck rounded the corner and skidded, trying to avoid him. It happened quickly, and in the press of traffic Joss wasn't able to get out of the way. One of the front fenders hit him so hard that it lifted him into the air. He landed on the street uninjured, didn't feel anything and just rolled away, protected by the energy field around his body.

As he rose to his feet he heard a woman exclaim, "Did you see that? The man hit the pavement softly, and rolled away like a tumbleweed!"

SciO and Greenpol officers ran toward him from different directions, with the two agencies probably coordinating their efforts. Joss began running, and as he reached a busy thoroughfare it surprised him how fast he could go. On a long stretch of sidewalk, he was outpacing taxicabs on the street, even as he darted around pedestrians.

Joss rounded a corner, ran up a narrow street past a pea patch, where schoolchildren stood attentively while a female teacher read to them from *The Little Green Book*. Continuing on, he scrambled up steps to the top of a hill, where a number of elegant old private residences stood, like the structures he'd seen below, and all appeared to be very well maintained. He didn't see anyone as he ran along one street and another.

Hearing the throb of a helicopter, he hurried into a yard and vaulted over a wooden fence, reaching the backyard. Here the weeds were high and the white paint was peeling off the house. Peeking through a window, he saw the interior in shambles, with kitchen appliances torn out and debris scattered on the floor—indicating that the government only cared about the appearance of the properties from the street.

Still hearing the helicopter noise but not seeing the aircraft, he tried the kitchen door handle and the door squeaked open, scraping the sill and floor. Entering, he pushed it shut behind him. The helicopter noise grew louder, then diminished until he could not hear it any longer. Minutes passed, in which he stood in a shadowy doorway where he could not be seen from the air, listening and afraid to move.

Gradually, silence permeated his awareness, and complete stillness. But as he crossed the kitchen, he couldn't help making noise when his shoes crunched on broken glass, and the old fir floor squeaked. Joss inspected every corner of the house, from the low-ceilinged basement to the tattered bedrooms on the second story, where torn and stained mattresses were scattered on the floor, beside the remnants of nightstands and leaning dressers, with their drawers out and strewn around. He saw rat or mouse droppings everywhere, but selected one mattress and wiped it with a rag, including the floor around it. Then he lay down on it, using a rolled-up old robe for a pillow.

As he lay there he noticed that he'd been perspiring from the activity, and he was warm. Gradually, as minutes passed and he cooled down, he realized it was cold in the house, but he could tolerate it, and didn't care. He just wanted to be alone and away from prying eyes.

An hour passed in which he lay there, listening, waiting, and thinking. Despite the earlier helicopter noise, he didn't think anyone had seen him. It was probably a police aircraft checking the area, maybe looking for him or just doing a routine flyover.

Joss heaved a sigh of relief, and finally fell asleep.

HE DREAMED HE was being chased across an immense industrial site that was still operating, with hundreds of stacks belching dark pollutants into the sky. He couldn't see his pursuers and didn't know who they were, but felt certain they would kill him if they caught up with him. Joss ran inside one of the large buildings, but to his amazement he found it was actually a ponderosa pine forest with streams and lakes. No machines and no people.

Knowing that this could not possibly be real, Joss tried to wake up, but found himself unable to do so. He saw himself from above, lying on the forest floor in a fetal position, sleeping. "Wake up!" he shouted to himself. "Wake up!" But his sleeping form did not move. He kept shouting, but gradually the words grew more and more distant, receding into the wilderness.

As he lay in the forest he heard a thrumming noise, an alien sound that grew louder as his own voice grew more distant. A machine noise, he decided, intruding on the beauty and solitude of the woods, threatening not only him but all other life that depended on this precious ecosystem. Moments later, he heard something accompanying the machine noise, voices and footfalls. He felt warmth on his face and sensed something drawing him toward it, lifting him.

The voices became shouts, and suddenly Joss sat straight up, squinting in bright beams of light. He blinked his eyes, and for several moments he couldn't focus. Noises clashed around him, unidentifiable in their cacophony. Something stung his arm, then his leg.

Joss realized he was on a mattress, then felt hands lifting him to his feet, and someone attempting to confine his wrists in a restraining device. SciO security officers! They filled the bedroom, some carrying powerful flashlights. It was nighttime.

He felt a little groggy, realized that the stinging had been sedative shots. Anger suffused him, and the grogginess subsided quickly. He pulled one hand free, and with it he wove a black net of energy around him that crackled in the air and pushed the intruders away. They grunted and struggled mightily against him, but ultimately the force field repelled them, leaving them cursing.

"There's no use trying to take me prisoner," Joss said. "Didn't Doctor Mora tell you what I can do?"

One officer stepped forward, a woman in a tight uniform, with two silver bars on her glistening green helmet. "Before your recent unfortunate incidents, you were known for your loyalty to Chairman Rahma's government. If that's true and you weren't trying to deceive anyone, I'd like you to put yourself in our shoes, and in the shoes of the Chairman himself. If you do that, and you're honest, you can't help but see that we can't leave you here, can't let you stay on the run like this. Here in the Green States of America, every person must be accounted for. It is the law, a just and proper law."

Joss hesitated, wished the explosion had never occurred, and that he was back in his old life with Kupi Landau, leading a Janus Machine crew and traveling around the GSA, doing good work.

"I just want my old life back," he said.

"That's not possible, not since the explosion changed you."

"I can still supervise a Janus Machine crew. Send me back to my crew and let me resume my old life. If you do that, in my spare time, when I'm not working, I'll try to be cooperative. I cooperated with Doctor Mora until I lost hope that I would ever be permitted to go free. The SciOs wanted to make me a test animal for the rest of my life, wanted to make *that* my career, in exchange for room and board in a velvet-lined prison. Well, that's not the career I want."

"Let me understand what you're proposing," she said. "If you're permitted to resume your old job with your old crew, you'll open yourself up to further SciO investigations?"

"Within reason. Look, Officer, I want to know what's happening to me too, but I won't be abused, won't permit anyone to run roughshod over me. I want you to take me straight to my J-Mac crew, wherever they are."

"I'll be right back." She left the room, returned fifteen minutes later. "We have a deal," she said. "They're sending a copter to pick you up and transfer you to a private SciO jet. Your crew is in the Northwest Mexico Territory, near the Sonora Reservation for Humans."

Joss didn't ask who gave her the permission. He only cared that an aircraft was being sent for him, and he would soon be away from this place.

Minutes later a small helicopter landed in the street, then lifted off into the night sky with lights blinking and Joss in the passenger seat. On the way to the airport outside the Berkeley Reservation, he considered possibilities, and a troubling thought flickered across his mind: they could transport him somewhere remote and try to keep him there, too far from civilization to return on his own.

They wouldn't dare, he thought. The SciOs needed his co-operation for their experiments.

32

It is said that when Chairman Rahma Popal heard of Joss Stuart's powers, he wept. Whether from sorrow, joy, or even envy, it is not known.

—"The Mutant Man," a black-market article

IT WAS A retro-style private plane that looked like a twentieth-century Learjet but larger, with a carbon-fiber fuselage and two supersonic FocuSol engines that were powerful enough to propel a much bigger, heavier aircraft. The passenger cabin continued the retro theme with wood paneling and art deco styling (reminiscent of Pan Am and TWA in the 1930s) that cleverly concealed modern creature comforts.

In the cabin, Dr. Mora had provided extensive details to Joss about the supersonic plane and the young man had listened politely, all the while looking out the window at the pastel sky of approaching dawn, trying to determine if he was being tricked and taken somewhere other than the agreed-upon place. Perhaps it was an accumulation of Kupi's cynicism about green profiteers that he'd listened to over the years, combined with his own negative experiences as a SciO prisoner, but Joss was beginning to distrust people, and even the government, something he'd never anticipated. He didn't like feeling that way, had always tried to be positive and optimistic, but reality was pushing its way in on him, changing him.

"We're going a little north to avoid storms," Mora said, as

if anticipating Joss's concerns. The two of them sat at a small round table. "Then we'll swing south toward the Sonora Reservation. Don't worry. Our pilots know what they're doing."

Joss didn't respond, just stared out the window. His vegan casserole and a glass of soy milk sat untouched before him.

At the forward bulkhead of the passenger compartment, the stewardess opened a wood-panel cockpit door to take coffee to the pilots, providing Joss with a brief view of two men wearing old-style blue-and-gold airline officers' uniforms and caps, before she returned to the passenger cabin and closed the door behind her.

Gazing out the window from this altitude, Joss was having difficulty determining where he was. He saw a vast wilderness below of pine forests, lakes, rivers, and craggy mountains, and no visible reservations for humans. It was disorienting. His stomach rumbled, burned from acid.

The plane banked, and as time passed, the landscape and colors metamorphosed, from greens and blues to the dry browns and golds of canyons and high desert plateaus. Presently he saw high buildings jutting out of the desert, gleaming like a mirage in the afternoon sunlight. It was one of the least-populated reservations, with a much smaller core of high-rise buildings than others.

"The Sonora Reservation for Humans," Dr. Mora announced.

Joss nodded, concealed a sigh of relief. It looked as if the SciOs were keeping their word to him after all, and he might not need to use any of his contingency plans to oppose these people. Even so, he would remain wary.

HE DIDN'T WANT to do anything before seeing his crew, didn't even want to wait for them to return to the hotel from their day's work. Immediately after landing, Joss boarded a solar-powered vehicle, an off-road, teardrop-shaped sedan driven by a SciO security officer. They headed northward across the dusty expanse of high desert. Since Joss's J-Mac crew would be working in the area for at least another week, Dr. Mora remained back at the reservation, saying he wanted to set up a facility to do further research work on Joss, under a schedule the two of them would arrange. It was a warm afternoon, and even though the windows were up and the sol-air-conditioning on, Joss still smelled the gritty dust that penetrated the vehicle's seals. Within an hour, they lost sight of the reservation.

On the bumpy ride to his crew's worksite, Joss identified areas that had recently been split and greenformed with native seeds, so that cacti and scrub brush grew over what had once been towns and roads—forming new patches of plants that had not yet matured as much as those around them. In this region, as elsewhere all across the Green States of America, even the smallest and most scattered blights of human civilization were being returned to nature, so that all citizens could be relocated to the reservations, and confined there for the most part.

Joss understood the need for this, and looked forward to rejoining his crew, with whom he could perform work that would take his mind off those peculiar and disturbing changes that had taken place in his body. Through it all, he hoped that he could maintain control over the destructive power. Perhaps he would receive a stroke of luck, and the intrusive energy would wane; he didn't really want any part of it.

Through the dusty windshield of the vehicle he saw the profile of a Janus Machine, and felt a rush of pleasure when he made out the familiar numerals on the side of the big truck: 129. It was his old rig, and the black cannon was firing at a site in the opposite direction, though Joss was not sure of the target.

When the car arrived and the crew saw him through an open window, they stopped work and rushed to greet him. Kupi Landau was the last to jump down onto the sand. As Joss stepped out into the warm, dry air, he saw her grinning at him. "It's about time you showed up for work!" she exclaimed.

The aging mechanic, Sabe McCarthy, tilted his owl helmet up and patted Joss on the back. "Good to see you, boy!"

"What do you mean calling me boy, you old fart?" Joss said, grinning. "Have your forgotten I'm your boss?"

The others gathered around him, and he gave each of them a hug, the longest for Kupi. It was good to see all of them with their helmets tilted up, showing their dusty, grinning faces.

As Kupi pulled away from the embrace, she touched the keloid scar that crossed Joss's forehead and ran down the side of his face like a green vine.

"I've lost some of my looks," he admitted.

"Oh, I don't think so at all. You have a much more interesting appearance now, and quite sexy."

Joss grinned. She sounded sincere. He saw a balding, black-bearded man walking toward them from the Janus Machine, carrying his helmet under one arm. Joss didn't recognize him.

"I'm Tom Ellerby," the man said, "your place mark while you were away." He leaned forward, gave Joss a strong handshake. "I operated the Seed Cannon, anyway. Kupi's been running the show."

They exchanged small talk. Then Ellerby said, "Kupi has a little more work to do, and then we can greenform. Your cannon is loaded with native hydroseeds tailored for the locale and weather, ready to go. You feel like firing it off in a few minutes?"

"I don't know," Joss said, "maybe you should finish this

site." He looked toward the area that had been split, saw a scarlike slash in the landscape, a large trench that was partially full of water. "What exactly are you doing out here?"

"Rerouting an underground spring system," Kupi said. "Repairing it, actually. Strip miners and oil-well drillers played havoc with the landscape and the aquifer, disturbing the ground and diverting the natural flow of water. Chairman Rahma wants to bring more people into the Sonora Reservation, but can't until the water supply is improved. Following instructions from the AOE Corps of Engineers, I've been using low power settings to rearrange dirt and rocks, improving this section dramatically."

She pointed at the long open trench. "See how the water level is receding? It's going exactly where it should now. The Corps just inspected the site and said we can seal up the hole." She scowled. "People say anarchists only destroy things. This proves otherwise, eh?"

Joss nodded. And looking at Ellerby, he said, "Why don't you go ahead after she's finished? I'm just here to see everyone today. We can work out the duties afterward."

"Nothing to work out," Ellerby said. "I'll take a transfer to another crew, and you can have your old job back." He was quite pleasant, but seemed ill at ease.

"All right," Joss said, "but I want you to go ahead and shoot the cannon this time. You selected the seeds and loaded them, so by rights this is your assignment."

"You two work out the details," Kupi said, walking toward the Janus Machine. "I've got a trench to fill."

While Joss watched from the safety of a blast barrier, Kupi fired the Splitter barrel repeatedly, using low power settings to move mucky soil back into the trench, after which she covered it back up and evened out the surface so that no depression could be seen in the topography.

When it was his turn, Tom Ellerby fired the Seed Cannon twice, showering hydroseeds over the disturbed, moist ground.

Moments later Joss stepped out from behind the blast barrier and greeted Kupi as she climbed down from the Janus Machine. "I was beginning to wonder if I would ever get my life back," he said.

"The experiments are finished now?" she asked. The pair strolled around to the other side of the Janus Machine, where they gazed out on the restored landscape.

"Not yet," Joss said. He explained the arrangement he had with Dr. Mora and the SciOs.

"Sounds better than before, anyway," she said.

Joss heard the sound of a vehicle behind him, and voices, but he didn't look in that direction. Instead he peered out at the worksite and said, "Ellerby missed a section."

"He's not as skilled as you," she said.

"It's quite noticeable, maybe thirty meters square." He pointed toward the foreground of the site. "See it?" He felt his heartbeat surge.

"Yeah. I'll tell him to refire the cannon."

With the acceleration of his pulse, Joss felt a peculiar sensation. He seemed to be absorbing a lot of energy from the warm sun overhead and noticed the green, vinelike scars on his arms bulging, and tiny, bright green scars on his fingers that he had not seen before.

Involuntarily he raised a hand. It grew rigid, and green light lanced out of his fingertips, bathing the flawed area in a wash of sparkling green particles, a rain of color. A chill of realization ran down his spine.

It didn't seem possible, and yet. . . .

He squinted, and on the ground in the flawed area he saw seeds now, spread evenly and ready to grow—and he knew they had not been moved from the rest of the site. Somehow he had generated them from the natural environment, and they were exactly the right mixture.

"How did you do that?" A man's voice, behind him.

Turning to look, Joss felt as if he were in a dream, unable to extract himself from it. His heartbeat slowed. Two men and a woman approached him, in matching dark green business suits.

"I'm Lucero Wiggins," the older of the men said, the one who had just spoken. He had a sparse blond beard. "Publisher of *The Green Times*. And these"—he designated the pair with him—"are my reporters. I ask you again, how did you do that . . . that trick?"

"It was not a trick, and I don't know," Joss said. "Look, I really don't want attention from the press. I've already agreed to cooperate with the SciOs for their continuing investigations."

"Can you still use the Dark Energy?" the female reporter asked. Small and prim, she had oversized glasses and her hair was secured in a tight bun. She stared at him intensely, reminding him of a SciO laboratory technician.

Joss stared at her, felt enough irritation to cause the fingers of one hand to darken and glow. He waved his hand angrily, making slender black strands appear in the air and linger. He glared at a basketball-size rock, and a black thread of energy shot at it like a whip, melting it into a gray mass.

Then, taking a deep, calming breath, Joss caused the black strands of energy to dissipate, by force of will. "I had no idea I could greenform as well as split. I don't understand what's happening to me at all."

"Marvelous!" the other reporter exclaimed. "Most interesting. How do you feel when you do these things?"

"Anxious and nervous," Joss said. "And hyped up. My metabolism becomes like a hummingbird's, making my heartbeat feel like ten times normal."

"Doesn't that frighten you?" the woman asked.

"Yes, but not so much for myself. I'm more afraid that I'll misuse the powers and hurt someone." Joss paused. "I suspect the powers will eventually wear off, or at least I hope they do. They are just an aberration, can't last." He took another deep breath, continued to calm himself. At least he had some control over his body, but the unwanted presence had a way of activating itself without his conscious intent.

The publisher and reporters asked a handful of additional questions, and Joss tried to be cooperative. Then, at his request, they departed, agreeing to contact Dr. Mora for additional information, and to seek permission to observe future experiments. As they opened doors and climbed into their overland vehicle, Joss noticed another passenger inside, sitting in the back with the reporters. Though he couldn't make out the face in the interior shadows it was a man, Joss decided, his face shaded by the brim of an outback hat. Something seemed vaguely familiar about him, but the doors closed quickly, blocking Joss's view with dark, tinted windows.

Unable to make a memory connection, he put the question out of his mind. The man's identity didn't matter, really, and he was probably a complete stranger. So many citizens resembled one another in appearance, and he encountered a lot of people. Besides, he had too many things to think about that were far more important.

33

We humans have a habit of celebrating the grotesque, the macabre, the most base and tasteless of all things. And yet, paradoxically, we claim to be the most advanced of all species.

—Glanno Artindale, personal observation
(on the eve of his death)

CHAIRMAN RAHMA POPAL had awoken with a feeling of uneasiness. It was just past dawn now, and he stood on the large balcony outside his bedroom, smoking a pipe of North African hash and gazing out on the colors of the sunrise as they opened up over the greenery of the game reserve and the snowcapped mountains beyond. The powerful marijuana infused his lungs and his consciousness, making him feel a little less anxious, but not enough.

Squinting into the light he saw something in the sky, an object that was drifting downward, dropping slowly toward the earth. He hurried to an antique spyglass on a tripod, and saw that the dark, squarish object was suspended from a barely discernible parachute, its fabric containing the mottled colors of the sky.

This should not be happening. He looked upward, for any sign of an aircraft that might have released its cargo, but saw nothing, only wispy clouds whose undersides were awash in color.

The parachute and its cargo set down in the distance, on a

patch of grazing land favored by elk. Two were nearby, and took hardly any notice of the encroachment. Rahma saw his special police rushing to their small patrol aircraft; four of them took off and headed for the site.

He watched through the spyglass, which was quite powerful despite its vintage. Then, hearing voices on his intercom system, he went to a terminal screen just inside the door. There he saw his guards scanning the cargo, transmitting images to him. Something odd and square was inside. He sent a command for them to open it.

The men did so, and removed a strange object that looked as if it had white fur all over it. To his horror, he realized that it was a stout table made of loosely fitted bones, with furry white legs and hooves for feet.

"There's a short letter with it," one of the guards said, holding a piece of paper up to the camera.

Rahma read it, felt a chill run down his spine, followed by a hot rush of anger on his face. "A little something for your office," the note read. "Don't worry, this polar bear won't bite you." It was signed by Premier Woo Hashimoto of Panasia.

A table made out of the remains of a polar bear? It was a grotesque affront against nature on so many levels, not just an attack on Rahma himself. How had this horror gotten past his national defense system? So many questions to be answered, but at the moment, his thoughts were filled with more anger than logic, and a longing to get even. It must be the same dead bear he'd received photographs of earlier, with its legs being hacked off.

"What shall we do with this?" the security man asked.

"Bury it," Rahma said, trying to calm himself.

———

DOUG RIDELL HAD seen long, dismal trains like this before, stopping in the Missoula Reservation, but he'd never expected to board one. Through bleary eyes he watched three powerful engines and a long line of tattered boxcars come to a stop in the station, the brakes squealing loudly. This train was older than most, and more run-down.

He squeezed the hand of Hana on one side of him, and little Willow on the other. Both of them were shivering and crying. Around them stood other families and individuals who were being sent away, all kept in a group by uniformed Greenpol officers in sparkling green uniforms, with shiny helmets and glistening jackboots. Some of the "deportees" looked stoic, others sad or afraid, and a few were obviously angry. Doug felt anger too, a rage that he could hardly control—and deep concern about what was going to happen to his family. But he knew it would do no good to display his emotions; he'd heard of the police killing people for less. He needed to stay alive, for the sake of his wife and daughter.

Maybe Jade would hear of this and get help to them. They had not been allowed to send her a message, or even to contact their friends. It had all happened so fast. Only hours ago, they had been whisked away from the lives they had known—he and Hana from their jobs, and Willow from her school—not allowed to take any possessions except the clothing they wore. They didn't even have jackets. No one in their apartment building would know what had happened to them, although as time passed they would figure it out.

The big question Doug had, and which he didn't want to voice to Hana, was whether they were being relocated to another reservation for humans, or if they would be turned over to the anarchists for recycling.

He looked at her, saw the fear in her tear-filled eyes, and the worry. She was wondering about this, too—and no one was giving them any information.

IN THE THREE additional weeks that had passed since Artie first flew in the pouch of the glidewolf, the creature had grown to very large proportions, a marsupial the size of a large horse, with a wingspan of almost seven meters. The growth rate had been so rapid that the robotic technicians in the lab were monitoring it daily, using electronic scanners to determine dimensions and weight. Curiously, after a period of enhanced growth that lasted for weeks and weeks, it seemed to have stopped in the last two days. No additional growth at all during that period. It was as if the creature had been desperate to reach a certain size, thinking it didn't have much time to achieve its goal.

Artie was still in Berkeley with Director Ondex, but the hubot had projected an avatar of himself back to the Montana Valley Game Reserve, to continue his work there while he waited for instructions from Ondex about their travel arrangements. Standing in enhanced virtual reality at a bank of monitors in the Extinct Animals Laboratory, Artie wondered if his own educated guesses—the missing data that he'd added to the genetic mix during the laboratory creation of the glidewolf—had anything to do with the size of the creature. The *beast*, he corrected himself. Certainly it was much larger now than the skeletal remains of the extinct animal that had been found on Lord Howe Island, between Australia and New Zealand.

It was early evening, shortly after his shift of duty ended as an assistant to the Chairman. In reality, such shifts never ended, because the hubots and humans around Rahma were always at his beck and call—and besides that, hubots didn't need to sleep, so they tended to be called upon after hours more than the humans. It was about to be that way now, he realized, because his internal sensors—linked to monitoring stations in the building—reported to him that Chairman Rahma was on the slidewalk and about to enter the laboratory.

He heard the double doors opening behind him, and the familiar soft-soled cadence of Rahma's sandals as he approached.

"I always know where to find you," the Chairman said. "Or, I should say, your avatar."

"As it should be, Master," Artie said, turning the avatar to face him.

"A few days ago, your glidewolf became agitated when a sycophantic eco-cop named Andruw Twitty tried to get to me without the proper appointment. After my guards refused entrance to Twitty, the wolf followed his car for more than seventy-five kilometers before turning back."

"Hmmm," Artie said. "Remember I told you that the glidewolf had an affection for you? Maybe she's being protective of you, sir, sensing something bad about Twitty, a danger from him. Animals often sense things that humans do not."

"She's being protective of me? How maternal. Maybe she thinks I'm her cub, then."

"Don't be too quick to scoff at what she might sense. This is largely an unknown creature, with unknown characteristics."

"Well, her sensory abilities can't be that great, because her entire species went extinct."

"On an island long ago. But this is a different place, a different time. Maybe there's a reason why she's made her appearance here and now."

"I came down here to discuss a different matter with you." He told Artie about the brutal murder and butchery of the polar bear by Premier Hashimoto, then asked, "I assume that you could create new polar bears in the lab, if they go extinct?"

The hubot's avatar nodded. "Presumably, though we might need a second laboratory to the north, where it is colder than here. Although each species presents different challenges, at least in this case the genetic material would be quite fresh. Just give me the word, sir, and it will happen."

"Not yet."

As they spoke, Artie saw the marsupial wolf glide down from a tree in the habitat, landing gently on the ground and tucking its wings. It stared directly at the Chairman through the glass barrier.

"Why is she staring at me?"

"I don't detect any hostility; quite the opposite. Thankfully, she's not focused on me, which suggests that I'm no threat to you."

"What an odd thing to say. Of course you're no threat to me. You're the revenant of Glanno Artindale, remember? My most loyal and true friend."

"Look at the size of her pouch," the hubot said. "It looks big enough to carry you, me, and a couple of other passengers. You wanna give it a try? I'd have to ride with you by EVR, of course."

"Maybe later. I'm pretty busy right now."

"All right."

The Chairman left quickly, saying he had to attend a meeting about the strange Dark Energy powers of Joss Stuart, the mutant eco-tech who was being called "Greenman."

RAHMA POPAL KNEW that *The Green Times* was not really a free press. Rather, it was a mouthpiece for his administration, a tool of propaganda used to influence the people across the tightly controlled, heavily censored GSA holo-net, to convince them of the environmental ideals and belief system of the dual-continent American government. In addition, the periodical ran human- and animal-interest features.

Only yesterday, the publisher of the news service and his reporters had gone to see Joss Stuart for a feature story, and had interviewed non-SciO citizens who came into contact with him, including the informant Andruw Twitty, who had remained inside a vehicle at the J-Mac jobsite, concealing himself behind tinted windows while the publisher interviewed Stuart.

Now at the Montana Valley Game Reserve, the Chairman was ready to hear firsthand what the publisher had learned about Stuart when they met, and what witnesses had said. . . .

"Twitty?" Rahma said, scowling after he heard the information. He sat with his visitor inside his own office, in a sitting area that looked out on the game reserve. "I know that worm. Everything he says must be taken with a grain of salt. He thinks too much of himself and advancing his career."

"That doesn't mean his information is wrong," Lucero Wiggins said. "In fact, we have corroboration from other sources of Stuart's strange powers and dangerous behavior."

The Chairman glowered, but nodded.

"Because of the unusual nature of Joss Stuart's powers," Wiggins said, "and the possible military implications, I thought I should come to you with this story before publishing anything."

Rahma leaned across his desk. "Military implications? You mean his Dark Energy power? But it has only limited range, like a Splitter handgun, from what I hear."

"Think about the defensive net he is able to cast around himself, sir. It deflects people who try to get close to him, but what if it can also deflect bullets—and what if it could be enlarged to immense proportions, encompassing our entire nation? And sir, what if the conditions of the ReFac explosion could be replicated under laboratory conditions, creating more people like Stuart? These are matters we would like to include in a story about Mr. Stuart. Subject to your permission, of course."

"You were right to come to me," Rahma said. "Don't publish anything yet. This will require further thought and discussion. In the meantime, bring me every piece of information you develop on him."

Wiggins rose to his feet. "Yes, Your Eminence. I will do that with pleasure, and I shall await your further instructions."

After the publisher left, Rahma considered the bizarre situation. Gazing out on the preserve, he saw a large grizzly sniffing around the grassy central area, looking for scraps of food. It wasn't the first time a bear had been sighted near the buildings. He always marveled at the magnificent animals, but kept his distance from them.

Refocusing, Rahma wondered what sort of genetic and cellular mutations the ReFac explosion had triggered in the body of Joss Stuart. What if an entire race of Stuarts could be produced, capable of splitting, greenforming, and casting defensive nets? How would they be bred and utilized? The thoughts startled and intrigued him: an entirely new race of human beings!

When considered with the genetic researches that his hubot, Artie, was performing, it boggled the Chairman's mind. Instead of a small number of hubots and robots involved in creating and caring for resurrected extinct animals and endangered species, there might be a much, much larger program involving Stuart's genetics, perhaps an entire new government department. Of critical interest to him, the mutant's abilities had military possibilities.

Rahma had often wished that humankind could be improved. But would a race of Stuarts make things better, or worse? Humans with splitting and greenforming powers! He found the possibility fascinating, but troubling. Humans already had both destructive and creative inclinations, and a race of people like Stuart could expand both extremes, potentially widening the gap between them. All of the humans in the new race would be armed and dangerous.

What would that mean for the Earth, and which side of human nature would ultimately prevail? Knowing what he did about people and their foolish, selfish tendencies, he assumed the worst.

But he also wondered if the opposing, Janus-like powers could be segregated, if an entire race of greenformers could be created without the conflicting, destructive side. Genetic engineering could accomplish exactly that. For lingering moments, Rahma marveled at the thought of people with incredible creative powers, all instilled with a deep moral sense about the welfare of planet Earth. Finally, an entire race of people that would not disappoint him!

It hardly seemed possible. But then again, neither did Joss Stuart.

34

Millions of years ago, prehistoric man began to use tools and weapons, and this separated him on the evolutionary chart from his simian cousins. Now, ironically, there is a potential for mankind to not need certain tools—because the seeds of destruction and resurrection could be *in* his fingertips, rather than *at* them.

—His Eminence Rahma Popal, ruminations on Joss Stuart

A CREATURE OF habit, the Chairman awoke early in the morning and sat up on the futon sleeping mat. Beside him, a woman stirred and then stretched, letting the blanket slip from her naked torso. She gave him a kiss on his bearded mouth, rose without bothering to cover herself, and walked into the bathroom.

He admired her curves and the way she moved, the graceful, sensual sashay. Descended from the Lakota (Sioux) Indians of the Great Plains, Valerie Tatanka did not look anything like his favorite, Dori Longet, or Jade Ridell, both of whom were curvaceous. In her mid-thirties, Valerie was tall and slender, with long black hair, high cheekbones, and dark, sensitive eyes. A shy personality, she didn't talk much (though she was quite scholarly), and at times that was what Rahma needed, physical affection without the conversation that sometimes led to stress and conflict. Not that he was averse to talking at depth with women, especially with the intelligent, well-read

Dori, but sometimes he liked to get away from all of that, and just succumb to his passions.

Like Dori and Jade, Valerie was smart, much more than just a pretty face and a good lover. She was the doctor in charge of the medical clinic on the game reserve, a two-story yurt where one other doctor and two nurses worked. She was overqualified for her duties and had been offered promotions to major hospitals, all of which she had declined, saying she preferred to remain here, not far from where her people used to roam the plains. On a de facto basis, she had become the Chairman's private physician, in all but title. She was also much more than that to him.

Now Valerie emerged from the bathroom and put on an embroidered dress, beads, and sky-blue Lakota moccasins. Then, with hardly a word, she kissed him again and departed, waving cheerfully to him as she went through the doorway.

Left alone, Rahma ate a large bowl of oatmeal with slivered pecans and chopped apples in it. Afterward he slipped into a formal robe and strolled out onto the grassy area in the midst of his compound of yurts. He was thinking about the busy day ahead of him, meeting with his top military officers to assess the defensive measures that were being taken on an emergency basis. In the two months since the failed Bostoner attack, there had been smaller incidents that did not suggest any usage of SciO technology, hit-and-run strikes that did not appear to be coordinated.

As usual, Dori Longet was waiting for him on the grass. Each morning that weather allowed, the two of them took a stroll together, and went over his daily schedule. The small blonde had a VR heads-up display in front of her face, with the information on it. "Director Ondex is on his way here, sir. He sounded very upset on the sat-call he made, insisted you would want to rearrange your schedule to see him."

288 • BRIAN HERBERT

As Rahma and Dori fell into step together, the Chairman asked, "What does he want this time?"

"He didn't say, only that it's extremely urgent. I confirmed this with Artie, who is still with him, then took the liberty of promising the Director we would fit him in. Artie indicates that an important discovery has been made, but he also says that Ondex insists on passing the information on to you personally, and not through the hubot."

"Most peculiar."

"Ondex seems to be pulling rank on him."

"But Artie is my direct representative, and no one outranks me." He paused. "Not technically, anyway."

"Artie indicates that he's transmitted the new information into a backup file here at Montana Valley, and you can access it today with the codes you know. However, the Director is quite insistent that he be allowed to address you first to explain the situation."

"The 'situation,' eh? Must be something serious, perhaps even incriminating. He's obviously worried. Well, when is he due to arrive?"

"Within half an hour, sir. Your first scheduled appointment was supposed to be at seven thirty, General Preda and Admiral Hansen reporting on our west coast air, land, and naval maneuvers. Shall I move them back an hour, and every other appointment afterward? You have a crowded calendar today."

Glancing at the tattoolike chrono embedded in his wrist, Rahma grunted in affirmation. It was shortly before seven. "All right. I guess I can hold off on accessing Artie's file until he and Ondex get here. But if they're late, I'm not waiting."

"Yes, sir."

The pair went over the other appointments quickly, and then Dori left to make the revised arrangements.

Chairman Rahma was about to return to his office when he heard a roar of engines and saw a VTOL plane descending, with the propellers on its wings tilted up in the position of helicopter rotors. The craft set down on the grass.

Then, with the rotors still spinning, a rear hatch flew open. Arch Ondex disembarked and hurried across the grass, approaching him. He was followed by Artie.

"Shall we go to your office?" Ondex asked, as he reached the Chairman.

"We'll meet out here," Rahma replied, noting that the Director's left hand was in a cast, which he explained was from slamming his fist on the edge of a casket when Artie was with him.

The Chairman gestured for the patrician man and Artie to accompany him, and they set off across the grass, toward a nature trail that ran beside an electronic pasture fence, invisible except for blinking red lights on top.

Keeping up with the fast pace, Ondex said, "I need to tell you more about the vanishing tunnel project. I've already told you it was a top-secret research program, an offshoot of splitting and greenforming technology, and it failed, with the entire team of inventors committing suicide."

"And the bodies of the suicide victims?" Rahma asked. He paused to stare out at a herd of antelope on the other side of the fence.

"One is missing, that of Dylan Bane, the brilliant scientist who was in charge of the program. He probably murdered the rest of his team."

The Chairman shook his head, shot a hard gaze at Ondex. "He took the vanishing tunnel technology with him, didn't he?"

"Right, seventeen years ago, and the traitor tried not to leave any records behind, though we found some clues. Without knowing he was still alive, we've had a crack team working on the technology ever since, and we've made some progress toward developing it ourselves. Our best people are working on it."

"But you're not there yet?"

"No, there's an ongoing problem with scaling the technology up to the proportions we need for military purposes. The tunneling system uses splitting and greenforming machinery at the same time, and there have been a number of promising clues as to how they work in tandem to bore through the earth. We *are* catching up."

Rahma glowered at him. "But you're not there yet."

"No, but we're confident that we will solve it." He trembled noticeably, almost stumbled into the electronic pasture fence, which would have given him a moderate shock.

"I want results, blast you! Where is that son of a Corporate whore hiding?"

"We don't know. Not yet." Director Ondex looked like a scolded dog. He hung his head, fearful of meeting the Chairman's gaze.

"Our military forces are already on full alert," Rahma said, "so there's not any more we can do. And what are we defending against? A phantom? Your rogue SciO inventor is either leading his own forces against us or he's turned the technology over to the Corporates, the Eurikans, or the Panasians—or some combination of them." He heaved a deep sigh. "Maybe there's yet another foe we don't know about yet. In any event, we have powerful enemies, potentially aligned against us in an unknown form."

"I've put our best scientists on it and our labs are working around the clock," Ondex said, scratching under the cast on his hand. "We'll either solve this or die trying."

"The effort may be too late," Rahma muttered.

Ondex didn't respond. He looked dismal, but the Chairman felt no compassion for him, only anger for his part in letting dangerous technology escape. Before this revelation, SciO security had seemed impregnable, but Rahma knew now that was not the case.

"Why hasn't Bane made another attack like he did at Bostoner?" the Chairman asked. "Why the delay?"

"I have no answer for that, sir."

As Rahma gazed out on the pristine beauty of the game reserve, he thought of all he had tried to do in forming the Green States of America, and of the ideals and efforts that were likely to go to waste if his country went to war. He felt what a deep and extraordinary loss that would be.

He also felt very much alone, because no one on Earth cared as much as he did about the welfare of the planet.

35

Many anarchists are unaccounted for. Following the Corporate War in which their violent methods proved useful to our cause, some of them discovered that they could no longer fit in, and vanished. Presumably a number of them are living in the wilderness, having gone there to avoid being arrested and recycled. Others perished there, and became food for predator animals.

—a GSA statistical analysis of population decline

THE LONG TRUCK bumped slowly over a rough desert pan, following satellite coordinates that had been laid out by the local dispatch office. It was midday and unseasonably cool for autumn, with the sun hiding behind a layer of clouds. Joss and Kupi sat in the passenger dome behind the driver's cab of Janus Machine No. 129, wearing crisp, clean uniforms with peace symbols on the lapels. A holo-map projection floated in the air in front of them, over an instrument console.

This was Joss's first greenforming gig since returning to duty, and he felt trepidation as he looked through the dusty clearplex, not knowing what awaited him. He wanted to return to his normal activities, and this job was a step in that direction. But he felt trapped by circumstances, needing to work to get his mind off his concerns, while knowing that he was only delaying the inevitable. Whatever he was becoming physically, he would become, whether he wanted to admit it or not. Despite his hopes, he had a sinking sensation that the powers would not wane.

"We're like Shiva in this machine," Kupi said, "the Hindu god of the universe's creative and destructive powers. The destroyer side wears a necklace of skulls—that's me, the Black Shirt—while the creative side is a phallic symbol. That's you, in case you're having trouble keeping up." She ran a finger over a vinelike green scar on his arm.

"An interesting line of reasoning, the way your logic invariably leads to sex. I've been wondering. Is that all we have between us, the physical relationship?"

"Of course not. I like to think we're good friends, too." She looked hurt.

"I'm sorry. I didn't mean that the way it came out. Of course we're good friends. Thank you for caring about me after my accident, for visiting my hospital room when you could. And for keeping the crew together in my absence."

"You're a better crew chief than I am, Joss."

The truck rolled over an especially bumpy area, jostling them around. "Maybe they should have brought in the heavy-lift copters and flown us to the site," Joss said.

Kupi pointed ahead of them, down a slight hill. "We're almost there," she said.

Through the dusty dome, Joss saw a sprawling complex of low-lying buildings, surrounded by a broken-down wall of adobe bricks. He checked the holo-map, said, "Villa Cabrón. *Cabrón*—that's a bad word in Spanish, isn't it?"

"Uh-huh. This was a fortified company town, run by a drug lord known as El Cabrón—'The Son of a Bitch.' He controlled every village in a hundred-mile radius—a reign of terror, from what I hear."

"Why wasn't it greenformed earlier?" Joss saw vehicles parked outside the compound wall, and people walking around, the privileged who were able to get permits to leave their reservations.

Kupi shrugged. "Just another bureaucratic detail to mop up for all I know, from someone's list. Not too much grows naturally around here, does it? Maybe that has something to do with the delay, because a few more straggly plants instead of buildings aren't going to do jack for worldwide air quality."

Out on the flatlands, Joss identified small cacti, succulents, mesquite, and varieties of scrub brush that grew in arid climates, and he thought of how hardy such plants were. In a sense, they seemed admirable to him—and considering this for a moment, he thought these plants were more admirable than flora that grew in less-demanding climates. People were that way too, it seemed to him; they were shaped by their environments.

As they neared the compound and parked just outside the front gate, people gathered around the big machine and watched while the crew set up the outriggers and inspected the various components. Kupi went out to the turret platform and stood by the railing, but Joss remained inside, having decided to wait until the last minute before going to his station at the Seed Cannon. Some of the people were looking at him in the dome and pointing.

More vehicles showed up, and more people. The crew set up a clearplex blast shield, and directed the onlookers to step behind it, then cleared stray animals with sonics. Joss saw a desert hare scurry off, and a flurry of rodents. He thought there must be five hundred observers out there with off-reservation permits, which was unheard of at remote jobsites. They had come to see Greenman, with vines on his skin; there could be no other explanation. They wanted to see a carnival sideshow.

As soon as the observers were in a safe place, Kupi tapped

keys on the instrument panel to generate splitting power. Joss heard the gathering roar, and saw her fire Black Thunder in an unusual manner, a slow-arcing, wide-spraying shot that disintegrated all of the buildings, fencing, and other structures with just one blast. It was something that most other Splitter operators could not do, a crowd-pleasing demonstration of her skills.

Most of the time she didn't bother with this technique and just blasted away repeatedly, until everything was turned into goo. She never announced in advance what she intended, which Joss found interesting. At times, she had a tendency to be creative in her work, even artistic.

When Kupi was finished, Joss adjusted his helmet's headset so that he could hear a past-century John Lennon song, "Imagine," and then climbed into the bucket seat behind the Seed Cannon. He tapped the opening sequence, causing the turret to spin around slowly, so that the glowing green barrel pointed at the work area. He fired twice, spraying seeds over every square meter of the destroyed villa.

When Joss completed his portion of the work, he climbed down onto the turret platform and removed his helmet, to talk with Kupi.

"Hey, Stuart!" a man shouted. "What do you need the Janus Machine for? Show us some of your tricks!"

Joss shook his head, turned away.

"Come on! We drove all the way out here to see you!"

"Well, drive all the way back!" Sabe McCarthy shouted. "Who invited you? We're on duty, doing the Chairman's good work."

Some people booed, while others called out, demanding to see Joss's special talents.

"This isn't a sideshow!" Kupi shouted.

"I'm sick of my 'talents,'" Joss said to Kupi as the two of

them turned and went inside the passenger dome. "I want my life back to normal."

They closed the door, shutting out the crowd noises. "I don't think you'll ever be completely normal again," she said. The two of them hadn't made love since his return, and he didn't know when—or if—they would again. He felt very tense.

THAT NIGHT, JOSS went to bed thinking about the seeds he had generated two days ago, without the use of equipment or SciO seed cartridges. Green light had lanced from the vine-like skin of one hand, bathing a flawed area on the ground, a place that Tom Ellerby had missed.

He wanted to know what had happened to him, enabling him to generate new life like that. Joss seemed to be evolving or mutating toward something, learning new powers as he changed constantly. Though curious at times, he was not really eager to discover more about his abilities, and wished they would be gone in the morning when he woke up.

Yes, that would be perfect. He tried to visualize it all gone, and even more, that it had never occurred at all. None of it, and that he'd dreamed the whole thing, an incredibly realistic dream.

Joss went over this idea in his mind, savoring possibilities, considering ramifications, looking for bits of evidence that none of it had ever really occurred. He tried to remember details that would prove this premise, evidence to remove a mountain of doubt. There must be something obvious.

As he went over events repeatedly, his mind circling, he began to drift off to sleep. But sleep within a dream? It seemed impossible, and yet it might very well be occurring anyway. . . .

In the dream (within a dream?) he again saw the Sonora

jobsite where the J-Mac crew had been cleaning up the landscape after digging trenches to repair an underground water supply. A patch of moist, ungreenformed earth had remained after Ellerby fired the Seed Cannon; the man had skill limitations, was not up to Joss's standards.

Going over that day again, Joss saw the vinelike scars on his skin bulge and glow, and he saw in a detailed, breakaway view that this was from the sun generating photosynthesis in his body. It was a frightening realization.

His dreaming gaze wandered over the dry landscape, away from the area that Kupi had hit with the Splitter cannon, and which Ellerby had greenformed so imperfectly. Joss found himself staring close-up at undisturbed soil with all of its organic, cellular, and genetic components. Moments later he realized it was raw material, because he drew upon those ingredients and greenformed without equipment, rearranging the soil and coalescing it into the varying shapes of seeds for plants that were suitable for the Sonora region—seeds that he scattered over the jobsite in a rain of sparkling green.

Joss's mind seemed to be controlling this, telepathically generating the seeds of life from waste dirt, as if he were God.

Stunned by the dream, he awoke and sat straight up in bed. His heart was racing, and perspiration drenched his clothing. He'd had odd dreams before, including the one in which he imagined powers he did not actually possess. But this one seemed different. It was as if he had been given a window into the secret workings of his own drastically altered body.

36

With all the talk of extraterrestrials in the past century, the UFOs and purported alien autopsies, it seems that we have finally found a "green man," but he's homegrown. He's an Earthling, not from Mars at all.

—underground newsletter

BACK IN SEATTLE, Andruw Twitty had begun to give up on getting another audience with the Chairman. After being turned away from the guard station of the Montana Valley Game Reserve, he had made a series of additional attempts in the past week, sending daily messages to Rahma by sat-call, courier, and holo-net, each time saying he had important, damaging information to discuss about Joss Stuart. But to no avail. He had received no response whatsoever. Just silence.

All of his former roommate's belongings had been inventoried by SciO security officers and taken to a storage facility at the Berkeley Reservation, where the SciOs had been investigating his strange and disturbing powers—powers that seemed to increase each time Twitty heard about them.

A few days ago, upon learning that Stuart was on a J-Mac crew in northwest Mexico, Twitty had applied for a permit to go there. The request had been granted by his Greenpol captain, the woman who had earlier ordered him to take time off his duties as an eco-cop and use his unique relationship with Stuart to see what he could find out about him. Twitty had gone surreptitiously to observe Stuart and had reported his findings to his superior. But then, without explanation, she'd ordered him to return to his normal duties.

After a day of routine police work, he was in the health club on the seventy-eighth floor of the government-run apartment building. Later in the week he was scheduled to receive a new roommate, but he wasn't looking forward to that, or to continuing the old routine at work. He still had not obtained everything he wanted from the Stuart connection. Maybe some angle would occur to him while he was exercising, some way of getting back on the assignment he really wanted—the one he hoped would promote his own career through his past relationship with the famous Mr. Stuart. He did some of his best thinking at the gym.

This facility had a number of features that he could only categorize as novelty items, because they didn't really need to be that way. The unique vertical swimming pool was a case in point, and always seemed to him like a waste of time and energy—something designed by techno-geeks just to show it was possible.

Throughout the reservation for humans, horizontal space was at a premium, but they could have done this in a more traditional way, instead of causing a swimming pool to run up the side of a long, three-level interior wall! Looking in at it through the viewing windows, it seemed to be an optical illusion, with the water remaining in the pool and people walking beside it like flies on a wall. But it was no illusion.

In his tight-fitting swimsuit, Twitty passed through an airlock into a small chamber, and lay down on a wooden bench in the corner, with his feet against one wall. It was humid in there. He heard clicking and sliding noises, and presently he identified the *fwwmph!* of a gravity shifter. A moment later he found himself standing on the "wall," with the bench against his back. Then, stepping through a second airlock, he entered the swimming pool chamber and dived into the water. So unnecessary, all of this technology and expense to set it up, but it did work, and was visually exciting.

He swam fifteen laps and was going to do more, but felt a twinge in one shoulder blade and paddled toward a ladder on the side. Twitty was just about to climb out when the implanted chrono in his wrist buzzed. The digital dial shifted, revealing a message there. The Chairman wanted to see him after all. Elated, he dressed and prepared to depart.

CHAIRMAN RAHMA POPAL usually had other people do things like this for him. But now, under the circumstances, he felt he needed to do it himself.

Jade Ridell stood in front of his desk, waiting for him to speak. At first she had been smiling, but now, as she saw his somber expression, she began to look worried.

"What is it, my beloved Chairman?" she finally asked. She wore a long dress with images of exotic animals on it. Her red hair was formed into a ponytail, held in place by a silver clasp he had given to her.

He looked away for a moment, at the wall sign that read ALL FOR GREEN AND GREEN FOR ALL hoping it would give him the courage for what he needed to do next.

"I really don't like having to tell you this," he said, looking across his desk at the young woman. He took a deep breath, because he had grown to care for Jade, more than most of the women he had known in his life.

She looked frightened now.

"Here it is," he said. "Your family has been arrested for a serious eco-crime, and placed on a relocation train."

Tears came instantly to her dark green eyes. "Where have they been sent?"

"I can't answer that, but because of your family's disgrace you can no longer work here." He almost choked on the words. "Jade, we can't spend time together anymore."

"My Chairman!"

"I'm sending you back to the Missoula Reservation to report to the Job Assignment Office, with orders that you are not to be penalized in any way for the actions of your family. I'm giving you a break."

She didn't look grateful. Darkness spread over her face, and she fought off tears. "You won't tell me where my parents are, or my little sister?"

"They're being processed by the system. We must have faith in the system." He waved a hand dismissively.

She shot him a hard glare, but turned and left without another word.

Afterward, in the silence of his office, Rahma thought of her, and wished it might have been otherwise between them. But he could never spend time with a daughter of eco-criminals. It would undermine his stature and authority.

THAT EVENING A uniformed, jackbooted Andruw Twitty stepped from the VTOL plane, where he was greeted by an aide who identified himself as Artie. This was undeniably the most famous hubot of all, from what Twitty had heard, with the human eyes of a dead war hero.

Unseen by the visitor, the large glidewolf soared overhead, circling the yurt compound and gazing down, watching every move he made. Though Twitty didn't know this, the creature had reached its full adult size now and was a common sight in the sky over the game reserve, so that few people or hubots on the ground took notice of her anymore.

Several times, Twitty looked upward nervously, remembering what had happened before, but in the waning light and mottled cloud cover he did not see the animal at all. But it was there nonetheless, and as Twitty and Artie entered the administration building the glidewolf settled quietly onto the rooftop.

Twitty followed the hubot to a third-floor office in one of the yurts, where Chairman Rahma sat at a large bamboo desk, studded with commemorative plaques that bore the faces of revolutionary heroes.

"You asked to see me," the Chairman said. "This had better not be a waste of my time."

"Oh, it won't be, sir." Twitty removed his helmet, looked back nervously as the door shut behind him. The hubot remained in the room and stood by a balcony door, staring at him.

"Well?" Chairman Rahma said, glaring.

"There is more to Joss Stuart than the government realizes, sir. I'm very concerned that he's being permitted to go back to work on a Janus Machine crew. That's sensitive, important work, and he should not be trusted with it."

He paused, waiting for a response—but the Chairman didn't say anything.

Letting his visitor remain uncomfortable, Rahma Popal flipped off the screen of a report he had been reading, the latest on the tensions with the Panasian government and their intractable premier, Woo Hashimoto. The fool was issuing a personal challenge to Rahma, suggesting that they meet in hand-to-hand combat and fight to the death, with the victor vanquishing the other nation. He offered an odd choice of weapons: knives or swords.

What an idiot he is, Rahma thought. *Knives or swords? I am a man of* peace, *not of violence!*

He had to admit, though, that the thought of sticking a blade into Hashimoto's gut appealed to him. Yes, it would be nice to do it personally, and watch him bleed to death, then hack him to pieces the way Hashimoto had done to the polar bear.

It occurred to him now, as it had before, that he could present himself to Hashimoto in the form of an avatar—in enhanced virtual reality form. That way he could at least frighten the man, and perhaps cause him to hurt himself.

Rahma envisioned his own bearded avatar chasing Hashimoto through his palace near Shanghai, wielding a virtual reality sword—perhaps one that was emerald in color, or some other impressive variation of green. It would be amusing to catch the Panasian leader in his underwear and force him out into the open, subjecting him to public embarrassment. Or Rahma could intervene on one of Hashimoto's numerous hunting trips, perhaps preventing him from killing an elephant or some other magnificent wild animal. The Chairman had seen images of the fool setting off on big-game expeditions, dressed in a heavy bearskin coat and carrying a large rifle, as if he thought he was an Asian Teddy Roosevelt, going after a grizzly bear.

But such thoughts were emotional, he realized, and not really rational. They just enabled him to let off steam.

Rahma heaved a deep sigh. He needed to deal with this other problem standing in front of him now, a gangrenous creature in the form of a Greenpol officer. The Chairman had never liked Twitty, whom he considered to be one of the worst opportunists he'd ever seen. Nevertheless, he had a prying, investigative mind and just might have something important to say. The problem was determining truth from embellishment.

The Chairman watched the stocky, mustached man twitch as he stood before the desk, heard his voice quaver as he finally continued. "I have information that is potentially damaging to Stuart, but out of loyalty, I thought I should confide in you before going anywhere else with it. At the hospital Stuart used Splitter power to injure and frighten me, and later he threatened to kill me if I didn't stay away from him."

"Knowing your personality, I can't say I blame him. I'm getting irritated with you myself. Now tell me something important, if you have anything."

"Stuart sabotaged the ReFac building, sir, I'm sure of it. I think he's been working with the Corporates, spying on us, obtaining information for them and concealing his strange powers as long as he could, using them to commit sabotages."

"For the Corporates, eh? And your evidence of that?"

He shifted on his feet. "W-well, it h-*has* to be the Corporates, doesn't it? The SciOs told Greenpol that they ran DNA and other identity tests on Stuart when he was held by SciO researchers, to make sure it wasn't a hubot of him that's been displaying powers, with splitting and greenforming technology built into the body. It's really Stuart all right, or more accurately it's a biological hybrid of him with no robotics whatsoever, a human fused with plant cells and Dark Energy."

"I already know this. Tell me something new, or get out."

"Stuart either sabotaged the ReFac building," Twitty said, "or it blew up accidentally while he was trying to obtain secret information from it."

"You're saying, then, that he already had strange powers before he went into the ReFac building, but if he already had secret SciO powers, what could he have possibly wanted in one of their ReFac buildings? And if he was trying to destroy the place, why would he do it in such a clumsy fashion, where it would be obvious that he was the one responsible? And if he's so powerful, why did he go into a coma? I'll tell you what really happened: Stuart didn't have any unusual powers before the explosion, but in the normal course of his duties he was injured in the blast, and fundamentally changed by it."

"That is one possible explanation," Twitty admitted.

"It's the only *plausible* explanation, unless you're a complete, bumbling idiot."

"OK, sir, let's assume you're right about one thing, that Stuart didn't have any powers before the explosion. But what if he was still a Corporate spy and a saboteur, as I said, and he was trying to find out things in the Recharge Facility, things he wasn't supposed to know? What if he did something inside that activated a SciO self-destruct mechanism, on a big scale?"

"Stuart is not an enemy agent. He's been checked thoroughly and has held two high-security jobs, first as a Greenpol cop like you, and later as a greenformer."

"But consider the fact that Stuart's lover and crew member, Kupi Landau, has made a constant stream of complaints against your government. She's known to have a rebellious nature, never fully cooperates with authorities, and only grudgingly performs her eco-tech job operating a Splitter—because it fulfills her anarchistic craving to destroy things. Maybe she and Stuart both had something to do with the explosion. Your government needs to be cautious of Landau's violent nature, sir."

Rahma hesitated because Twitty had struck a chord concerning Kupi and other anarchists who could potentially turn against the government, something he'd been concerned about himself. But he didn't reveal this, and said, "I will not hear any more accusations against two loyal citizens of the Green States of America." He narrowed his eyes dangerously. "Perhaps it is people like you we need to be wary of, Officer Twitty."

"Sir?" The Greenpol man fumbled with his helmet. His pale gaze darted around nervously.

"Yes, manipulative, self-serving weasels who will do anything to ingratiate themselves with their superiors, even at the expense of other people, even at the expense of the truth. Does that sound at all familiar to you?"

"I'm, I'm not like that, sir."

"There's a rotten stench in here," Rahma said. He rose to his feet and went onto the large balcony for a breath of fresh air, where he stared out at the greensward without saying anything. He saw a vulture circling in the foreground. A cool breeze blew against his face, and he thought it might rain soon. Behind him, he heard Twitty asking Artie if he should go out too, or if he should wait inside.

While Artie went out to ask, Twitty followed him as far as the doorway and stood there. Rahma watched the eco-cop peripherally, saw him inch out onto the balcony, just a step or two.

"My gratitude to your parents can only go so far, and you've overextended yourself," Rahma said, looking sidelong at Twitty. "You're a wormy, scheming bastard if I've ever seen one. Make no mistake about it, my eyes are on *you*, and not on Stuart or Landau." He faced the Greenpol officer directly, saw the little man's hands shaking as he held the helmet.

"With all respect, you're mistaken, sir. You don't seem to understand the gravity of the situation." He reddened in apparent frustration, and took a step forward.

Artie shouted a warning. "Back away from the Chairman!"

Surprised, Twitty jerked and lost hold of his helmet, which bounced on the deck and rolled toward the Chairman. Rahma kicked the helmet aside, while Twitty froze where he was.

Hearing a noise overhead, Rahma looked up. To his surprise, he saw the glidewolf creeping down the exterior wall of the building like a huge bat, right above them.

Looking up, Twitty saw the creature, too. He cried out, but it was too late for him.

With a sudden movement, the glidewolf swept a powerful wing downward, scooping up the Greenpol officer and hurling him off the balcony. In midair Twitty screamed, then hit the ground headfirst, making a sickening sound like a cracking melon. He didn't move. Blood pooled around him.

The glidewolf soared out from the wall, circled the fallen form of Twitty, and set down near him, where she remained, lying on all fours and looking at him without going nearer. The vulture came closer, circling overhead.

Two guards approached the body cautiously, their handguns drawn, watching the animal. "Put your weapons away!" Rahma shouted, seeing that the creature's eyes were focused on them. A tall, black-haired woman hurried to join them. It was Dr. Tatanka, in a white medical smock, wearing a bead necklace and her Lakota Indian moccasins. Just that morning, the Chairman had received a personal note from her, about the need for them to make more time for each other in their busy schedules. He hadn't responded yet, but thought he might just decide to make her his new favorite, elevating her over Dori.

The men reholstered their guns, but the glidewolf remained alert, tense.

Dr. Tatanka knelt over the body and checked the carotid artery. She looked up at the balcony, shouted, "No pulse, Mr. Chairman. He's dead."

"No loss," Rahma shouted back. He tossed the helmet to the hubot, said to him, "I guess he should have worn this, wouldn't you say?"

Artie's dark blue eyes were sad, in a manner that reminded

Rahma of their original owner, Glanno Artindale. "Thank you for the levity, sir, but it always saddens me when I see someone die."

"I know, but it was unavoidable. Twitty was not the type of person who deserved to live in my ecological utopia anyway."

"I'll take his body to the recyclers, sir. At least he'll do some good for the Earth that way."

Rahma nodded, then went downstairs with Artie and over to the body, where they spoke briefly with Valerie Tatanka and the guards.

Afterward, watching the hubot carry the body away, the Chairman had an odd feeling of pleasure. He was essentially a non-violent man, but there were exceptions, people who needed to be eliminated for one reason or another.

He wished it could be as easy to eliminate the Panasian premier.

Rahma knew he could not continue to avoid Hashimoto's provocative behavior, at the risk of appearing weak. One of the Chairman's military advisers wanted to strike against the Panasian capital city, Shanghai—blowing up the Panasian government center while lawmakers were in session. Other advisers recommended conventional strikes against Panasian military assets. The Chairman rejected such ideas, fearing they would invite nuclear retaliation.

It was his observation that Hashimoto seemed to be treating the situation as a personal game between the two leaders. Maybe the Panasian leader was not as insane as he appeared to be. Maybe he really didn't want a nuclear war, and thought he could avoid one by keeping the level of confrontation down—while not losing face in the process.

To some people, turning a beautiful animal into a table was a small thing. It might be that way to Hashimoto and his cronies, though from the depraved man's messages it was clear that he understood how much of an affront the mutilated polar bear was to the Chairman, and to the highly moral premise on which the GSA was born.

For such a crime, Rahma needed to do something to get the Premier's attention, something that revealed Panasian vulnerability. Rahma didn't want to do anything too small, or anything too large. But he intended to send a message that he—and the Green States of America—were not to be trifled with.

In recent days he had been considering the destruction of an expensive new bridge that had been built over the Yangtze River—a motor-vehicle span designed and constructed by Woo Hashimoto's brother-in-law, and which had been named in honor of the Premier. It was a matter of considerable controversy in Panasia, and thousands of brave people had gathered at the construction site to protest it, in part for the cronyism and nepotism involved with channeling so much money to a brother-in-law, but also for the sheer waste of the project itself, involving a bridge that was not needed by anyone except the Premier himself, and his wife. It just so happened that Hashimoto's palatial estate was on a hill with a view of the new bridge, and rumor held that his spoiled wife wanted the expensive structure as an easy means of getting quickly to the high-end clothing and jewelry stores on the other side.

If Rahma destroyed the bridge, he needed to do it in such a manner that the Premier and the Panasian people knew he'd done it and why, and that the structure was not destroyed by the people themselves. In that way, Rahma could embarrass the Premier while preventing him from making a nuclear response for obvious personal reasons that had nothing to do with national security. It would put him in a box, and might very well mean the end of his political career. If that proved to be the case, Rahma hoped he would be replaced by someone more reasonable and levelheaded. It was a chance he was willing to take.

Later today, Rahma would give the go-ahead for the destruction, but only in the middle of the night, so that there would be no loss of life (the bridge was not heavily traveled)—and he wanted his hackers to make a Panasian holo-net notification one hour before the demolition, a general statement that the GSA was sending a message to Premier Hashimoto and the good people of Panasia, and exactly when they would be sending it. Through this carefully choreographed action (and a follow-up explanation with more details), the GSA was likely to get considerable sympathy from the already-unhappy Panasian populace.

Chairman Rahma would like to see the look on Hashimoto's face when he heard the explosions and looked out his window. He smiled to himself. At last he had come up with something that was not a mere act of destruction, but was instead a powerful statement.

He looked over at the glidewolf, who remained where she was, lying on all fours a few meters away. Her muscles looked coiled, as if ready to strike. Cautiously, the Chairman walked toward the animal, speaking to her in a reassuring tone, as if she could understand. "You did me a service today, did the GSA a service. If you hadn't killed Twitty, I might have found another way to accomplish it."

He reached out to the creature and petted the soft, reddish brown fur on her head, looking all the while at her muzzle and into her pale yellow eyes, where he thought he saw a spark of sentience or at least of deep awareness, perhaps even what religious types might call a soul. There was much about this creature that he didn't understand, and perhaps never would. He saw her muscles relax and felt a slight vibration in her flesh, like a purr of contentment, but soundless.

"I have so many favorite females who live with me on this reserve," he said, glancing back at Dr. Tatanka as she returned to her clinic, "but you could be the best. Yes, in your own way you are the very best of all."

This seemed to please the creature, because the soft vibration intensified, and the yellow eyes looked softer, gentler—even maternal, it seemed.

"I can't have you living here without a name, though. What shall it be? Glida, perhaps, because you glide through the air? Or Soara? No." He petted her more, and a name came to him. "I shall call you Gilda from now on. Yes, I like that very much. Gilda it is."

He stepped back from the marsupial wolf, and the animal stood on its haunches, then raised its immense wings into the air, where they caught a breeze and lifted her off the ground, a graceful takeoff toward snowcapped mountains beyond the valley. For several moments she circled at low altitude, as if checking to be certain everything was all right with the Chairman, and then flew out across the greensward. Rahma had an increasing feeling of comfort about her being with him on the game reserve because of her protective nature toward him and the way she sensed things, sensed danger. At some level, perhaps in the future if Twitty had managed to finagle his way closer to the Chairman, the man might have posed a physical threat to him.

One day soon Rahma wanted to take Artie up on the offer after all, and go for a flight in the pouch of the strange creature.

Gilda.

She soared high above the trees and vanished from view.

37

There seems no limit to the number of psychotics who find their way into leadership positions around the world. I am a most notable exception.

—Chairman Rahma Popal, classroom remarks

PROBLEMS WITHOUT END.

For years there had been a variety of them on the resurrected vanishing tunnel project, with one problem leading to another, and apparent solutions leading the researchers into entirely new and more complex difficulties. The quest for the holy grail of vanishing tunnels was like working to find the solution to a complex puzzle box, only to discover more puzzles inside, and when they were solved, still more inside them.

It was driving Director Ondex crazy. He needed this technology so that the Army of the Environment could gain control over military operations on the ground. He didn't want to activate the satellite-based Janus Machine, which was a doomsday device, too powerful to ever actually be used, except as a bargaining chip. In contrast, vanishing tunnel technology had practical advantages, and he needed to get it developed. Ondex wanted the GSA (and, by association, his SciOs) to use subterranean military forces to oppose and defeat Dylan Bane's forces in the Americas.

To protect the GSA government in the event of attack, Chairman Rahma and the rest of the GSA leadership had access to subterranean bunkers at a number of locations, including beneath Ondex's own home in the Berkeley hills. As an added precaution he had built even more bunkers to accommodate his valuable SciO employees, and in the current state of heightened tensions he had ordered some personnel to sleep in those bunkers every night, and to make every attempt to remain near them during daylight hours, for quick escape. Whoever was developing the vanishing tunnel technology— Bane, presumably—might have already perfected it, and could strike in a big way at any time and place, without warning.

When the SciOs began a new research program after the apparent suicides of all vanishing tunnel team members, they'd developed small, functioning prototypes, but had not been able to scale them up to practical sizes.

Then, two years ago, they had finally been able to construct medium-size prototypes, and they had worked . . . but with limitations. The prototypes (unmanned and remote-controlled) drilled and closed underground tunnels that were around three meters in diameter, and through those openings small machines could travel up to one hundred seventy kilometers, leaving no trace of their passage—but at around that range the tunneling prototypes always shut down and were crushed by earth and rock.

His scientific teams were making progress on the research project, but it was going too slowly. Even details that might have been easy were not really that at all. As but one example, conveying liquefied dirt and rocks from the Splitter array at the front of the voleer to the rear was not a simple variation on old tunnel-boring technology, in which mud and other debris was moved out of the way. Instead, this was a problem of precise timing, of coordinating the speed of splitting atoms at the front of the machine and conveying them to the rear, where they were immediately earth- and rockformed behind the craft. To accomplish that, and to keep the machine tunneling forward at high speed, the designers damped down the front Splitter Cannons to reduce their efficiency, so that they matched the reformative speeds at the rear. This was controlled by a sophisticated computer system that enabled the two ends to communicate with each other, enabling them to coordinate important details.

So far his team of researchers had solved more than eleven hundred serious problems and tens of thousands of smaller ones, with an unknown number of each remaining. It had been a monumental struggle to get the prototypes up to three meters in diameter, and now the scientists had reached another plateau, because they could not make the diameter any larger, or extend the range.

Because of the impracticality of earlier small tunneling machines, the researchers had not performed extensive range testing for them. The current range problem was a surprising development, and a troubling one. Conceivably, a three-meter-diameter tunneling system *could* work for military applications, although highly modified war machines would need to be developed to fit inside the transporters as cargo, and it would be easier to use robotic soldiers (that could be compressed and packed tightly) instead of human fighters. But the problem of range was now the biggest one facing them; one hundred seventy kilometers was of little value. Theoretically, the machines *should* go farther, but they would not. At a certain point the machinery not only stopped, but it did so in a very bad way.

In recent months, manned test pilots had been risking their lives, cramming themselves inside the three-meter tunneling machines, taking readings, making adjustments, and dying horribly when things went wrong and the machines were crushed. . . .

From his Berkeley hills mansion, Ondex watched a wall screen with a live video feed of yet another test run involving yet another death-defying pilot—trying to push the experimental envelope and make the breakthrough discovery that would take the development team to the next level. It was late afternoon, and his vanishing tunnel research team had been working around the clock, day after day, week after week. He checked on them regularly.

This time the scientists were hoping for success with a tiny, incremental increase in boring size, so they had constructed a machine with a hull that was only a few millimeters larger than the previous prototypes. The hull and interior had thousands of built-in sensors, collecting a wide range of data and transmitting it to the researchers—information on cutting angles, hull speed, transfer ratios of splitting and earthforming, and more. There were many variables.

The new machine started to drill with its Splitter array, and then began to move, slowly at first, and then faster. Director Ondex felt his pulse quicken when the underground range reached one hundred kilometers, then one hundred ten—the craft was slowing down, but still going forward, slightly faster than earlier tests. Speed seemed to be related to range, and they'd been working on variations, combinations, on keeping the sensitive machinery going.

A webwork of illumination played around the machine where it was splitting earth and rock at the front, bright purple threads of light that sparkled and stretched to the limits of the freshly dug hole. The light beams gave the illusion of shoring up the tunnel—a tunnel that was only a little larger than the machine itself, and moved with it.

Ondex felt a surge of hope. Maybe it would be different this time.

But it wasn't. The slightly bigger machine stopped abruptly

at one hundred fifty-two kilometers and the tunnel collapsed on top of it, crushing the pilot and splattering blood on the screen, before it went dark.

The Director stared in horror and dismay, then looked away and cursed. They would have to dig the machine out, inspect it carefully, and try to figure out what went wrong. *Again*.

THAT EVENING, ONDEX could not sleep, no matter how many pills he took. His mind kept churning, filled with the endless problems that seemed to have no solution. His broken hand throbbed inside the cast.

Then a coded sat-call came in. He sat on the edge of the bed, waiting while the decryption programs ran their course. Presently he heard Soledad Oliveira on the other end of the line. She was one of his top researchers on the vanishing tunnel program.

"Sorry about the late-night call," she said, sounding breathless. "We've just made a major breakthrough. It turns out we were closer to a solution than we realized. We've been poring over the data from the tunnel collapse this afternoon. That pilot didn't die in vain. Just before the end, he saw something on the heads-up display in front of him, a seemingly minor piece of data that we didn't recognize for what it was at first. But it turned out to be the key."

She rattled off a stream of technical details that Ondex had trouble understanding. But the bottom line was that they *could* build large, long-range machines now, capable of transporting armies and military equipment. The engineers were certain of it. The solution was remarkably simple, and right in front of their faces all the time—but in the midst of so many details, it had been overlooked by both human and AI researchers.

Finally he asked, "What was the pilot's name?"

"Just a moment. Oh, here it is. Patrick Dennehy. An Irishman, one of our best test pilots."

"*The* best, Soledad. He was the very best! Now that we have the solution, I want every new tunneling machine to bear a plaque with that brave man's name on it."

"Yes, sir."

"Marshal all of our resources and focus everything on a massive construction program. I want the machines built fast, I want them built right, and I want full secrecy on the operation to protect the technology, and to contribute to our element of surprise."

"I'm on it, Mr. Director."

After that, Ondex still could not fall asleep. But this time it was for a different reason.

38

We humans spend our lives in fragile containers,
wreaking devastation and ruination all around.
—Chairman Rahma Popal, Introduction to
The Little Green Book

DYLAN BANE WAS one of those leaders who didn't require much sleep. Throughout history there had been a number of them, a small percentage of industrialists, military leaders, politicians, and other leading citizens. For them, as for Bane, there wasn't enough time in the day to accomplish everything of importance. No matter how much they achieved, no matter their fame or wealth or power, they wanted more, craved more.

Sometimes Bane compared himself to one of them, the military genius and emperor Napoleon Bonaparte. Reportedly the great man required a scant fifteen minutes of sleep a night. Bane didn't even need that much. Twelve minutes at most, and he was ready to go again. For him it was a matter of intensity of time, of quality of time. He slept as he lived, putting tremendous focus into every moment. But now he had a special problem, requiring not only time but enormous resources.

It was more than a week after the natural disaster that forced him to abort the San Diego operation and every other target for now—instead devoting all of his resources to the massive underground recovery operation that was under way beneath the central highlands of Mexico. It had been going on for three days.

His hands gripped a railing as he stood on a high platform watching the ongoing extraction and rescue work, and listened to the hum and clank of machinery and the shouts of rescuers as they removed people and called for medics. It was all makeshift and hastily dug, making space for a temporary medical center inside a new underground cavern just west of the destroyed base.

He sighed. After so much work, designing and constructing voleers to transport war machines and soldiers, his squadrons hadn't even gotten off their starting blocks. Before they could launch, two earthquakes had struck—the first one disabling electronic systems for most of the voleers, and the second inundating the entire Michoacán base. Luckily, he'd gotten one squadron out before the cave-in, so this provided him with machines to dig back into the disaster site.

Part of the work involved reburying hopelessly crushed voleers and piling the dead in mass graves. Not all of the voleers had been destroyed. His crews had removed seven of them relatively intact (along with survivors), and already four of those machines were back in operation, digging new tunnels in an attempt to rescue other stranded ships and crews. There were fourteen thousand survivors so far, half of them injured, and more than nine thousand dead. . . .

As work progressed, Bane had officers tallying up the remaining military assets and personnel and moving them to a new subterranean base beneath the frozen tundra of the North Canadian territory, where earthquakes were far less prevalent. Leaving a skeleton crew back in Michoacán to mop up operations there, he was getting close to understanding the extent of his military losses. Of the original forty-five voleers, he had seventeen still in operation, and of the original seventy-two thousand human soldiers and other personnel, there were just shy of twenty-eight thousand still alive and able to resume work, along with eleven hundred robotic fighters. Some soldiers were injured and eager to return to duty, while others recovered in their hospital beds, and perhaps a hundred more were likely to die from their wounds.

Most of his fighters were ideologically bonded to his cause to destroy the GSA, so Bane was heartened by their attitude and the way they were getting on their feet rapidly and resuming their duties. But his reconstituted assets were not nearly enough for what he had in mind. He put out feelers to his secret, powerful allies, telling them he needed additional funds to rebuild the fleet and bring in more fighters and war matériel.

39

Life is a dance of opposites,
of alternately warring and making up,
then beginning the cycle all over again.
—**Anonymous**

FOR TWO WEEKS, Joss continued to lead his Janus Machine crew on various jobsites outside the Sonora Reservation for Humans, while performing his own specialty of greenforming with the Seed Cannon. He was intent on establishing a new personal routine and doing his part for the environment, but at each site he found an increasing number of unwanted observers, more than a thousand now, according to the old mechanic who did a rough count, Sabe McCarthy.

Each day the intruders shouted questions and demands. He didn't like the carnival sideshow atmosphere, felt like a freak with his unusual appearance and the bizarre abilities they wanted to see. But he ignored all of the people and instructed his crew to do the same—except to remind the observers they were just doing their job, and that did not include dealing with the public or even with SciO, Greenpol, or various other government workers who happened to get passes and were not there on official duty.

For anyone who *could* prove they were there on official government duty, Joss took them aside and provided them with any information they needed, usually about splitting and greenforming conditions that the crew was encountering at various sites. For any other questions that happened to arise about his physical transformations and powers, Joss deferred to the bi-weekly sessions he had decided to grant to Dr. Mora and his SciO research team, and to whatever they wanted to report. In a laboratory environment they had been testing his ability to split matter, to generate greenforming seeds at will, and to shield himself with a protective net of black light.

Today there were two J-Mac jobs, and they'd already completed the first, an assignment to repair the faulty work of another crew that had failed to properly clean up and seed the site of a Corporate agribusiness farm that had been using toxic chemicals on its crops.

Now Joss's crew was on its way to a site that had been overlooked previously, a hidden ravine where old motor vehicles and other junk had been dumped and were rusting away. For a change, Joss and Kupi rode in the forward cab with the tall driver, Bim Hendrix, as the truck bumped across the desert. In the side mirrors Joss saw clouds of dust billowing behind them.

That morning he had heard about Andruw Twitty; reportedly he had died of a heart attack at the Chairman's game reserve, but that sounded suspicious, because Andruw had been young and healthy, having passed stringent police physicals that were required every year to remain on the force. As for the reason that Twitty was at the game reserve, Joss agreed with Kupi's assessment that he had probably gone there to say bad things about the two of them, lies and distortions. Even so, Joss tried to stop thinking ill of the dead man, preferring to remember good things about him.

In the back of his awareness, Joss heard Bim Hendrix telling stories, and Kupi laughing. The driver was a wellspring of humorous anecdotes.

"Okay, that's enough from me," Hendrix finally said. He'd been talking for the better part of an hour. "Now let's hear someone else's best funny stuff. Hey, Joss, how about you?"

"Anything we had to say would pale in comparison with your stories," Joss said. "Right, Kupi?" He nudged her in the side.

"Oh no," she said, "I'm just full of anarchist jokes. You wanna hear some? Did you hear the one about the Black Shirt, the Corporate president, and the eco-criminal, all deciding at the last minute that they wanted to get into heaven, no matter all the bad things they'd done in their lifetimes?"

Hendrix groaned, said he had heard the long and convoluted story before, a variation on what used to be called "shaggy dog stories" in the pre-revolution days. "Not again," he said. "Please, not again."

The three of them chuckled and then fell silent. Intermittently, Joss glanced over at the navigation holo that danced in the air beside the driver. Leaning to his left, Joss studied it and then saw the ravine ahead of the rig, just coming into view.

"Almost there," Joss said.

The driver slowed the long truck and steered it onto a wide expanse of rock. Near the edge of the ravine, he stopped and got out, looking for the best place to set up. This was one of his other duties.

"Remember I said we were like Shiva, the Hindu god, when we operate the Janus Machine?" Kupi said.

"Uh-huh." Joss watched Hendrix as he walked along the rim of the ravine. From the truck, Joss saw dented, rusted vehicles and appliances heaped down there.

"I've been thinking about it," Kupi said. "With your raw

ability to split and greenform, that gives you both Shiva powers, too—destroying and creating."

"I guess that's right. But my abilities are small-scale. I'm no god."

"Do gods even exist?" she asked.

He smiled. "Not for anarchists."

"Or Greenies," she said, "unless it looks like a tree."

40

I will tell you a little secret, my friends. Some of my fellows on the revolutionary council called me "Father Earth." They said Mother Nature was tired and overworked, and she needed help.

— Chairman Rahma Popal, his first Berkeley speech, delivered at Sather Gate on the old campus

LSD, MARIJUANA, METHAMPHETAMINES, cocaine, heroine, and more—in the form of food, injections, or pills. All in colorful packages that were arrayed neatly on a tray held by a pretty female servant, who knelt beside the Chairman where he sat cross-legged on the deck. The girl had short, curly black hair, and her skin was golden brown. He did not know her name.

It was a bright, sunny afternoon, and Rahma rode in the clearplex viewing compartment of a solar soarplane as it flew silently over the Montana Valley Game Reserve. Director Arch Ondex and two uniformed AOE officers sat with him in a small circle, also cross-legged, with animals and plants of the game reserve visible through the clear floor beneath them. The others were General Rolph Preda, the supreme air and land commander for the GSA, and Admiral Karlos Hansen, in charge of naval operations. Each of them held a copy of *The Little Green Book* on his lap, having read passages from it aloud during their meeting, looking for inspiration to face their current leadership challenges. Even Rahma, who had written the slender volume packed with ideas, liked to refresh himself by thumbing through it from time to time. He called it "going back to the basics."

"That's enough for now," Rahma said, closing his own copy. Then, while the others shut their volumes, he intoned one of the quotations, "'In Green We Trust.'"

"'One Nation Under Green,'" the others said, in unison. It was the response specified in the book, following any passage read aloud by the Master himself.

Not far behind them flew the large glidewolf, Gilda, whose protective attitude toward Rahma had become accepted by the Chairman as an everyday occurrence. According to Artie, the animal was keeping its distance from him and from everyone else, but not from Rahma, whom she monitored constantly, as if they were of the same family. She seemed to have only one goal in life, day after day—his protection. Whenever Gilda was missing from her eucalyptus forest habitat, she was usually found on the rooftop (or clinging to an exterior wall) of whichever building the Chairman happened to be in. The creature tried to conceal herself and remain in shadows, and despite her size she was pretty good at this.

The Chairman looked over the offerings on the tray held by the servant, selected a Mary Jane brownie and peeled the biodegradable cello wrapping off partway, so that he could nibble on the delicacy. This was one of the gourmet snacks kept in the well-stocked cupboards of the game reserve's communal kitchen.

He'd been feeling a little worn-out today, hoped he wasn't coming down with something. A nagging tickle in the back of his throat suggested otherwise.

Earlier, he had been thinking about Jade Ridell, missing her and feeling bad about sending her away. For a long time he had stared at one of the printed images he took of Jade in the aviary, with the little exotic bird perched in her hair and the comical expression on her face. It had been one of many good times that he and the young woman had shared. His eyes had misted over.

He knew where Jade was working in the Missoula Reservation now, waiting tables in a gentleman's club. He'd had nothing to do with her getting the job; he'd only checked on her afterward, and he would again, from time to time. Perhaps, after the passage of a few months, he would recommend that she be given a more important job, one that took advantage of her intelligence and not just her stunning beauty. But he could never be with the attractive young woman again, could never even see her again. Her parents had acted disgracefully, and in the Green States of America nothing was worse than an eco-crime.

Rahma tried to put Jade out of his mind. In his position, he could not afford to be sentimental. He'd felt close to women before, and there was always an ending point for each relationship, and a beginning point for another—with a great deal of overlapping because of the number of females involved. With a deep sigh, he told himself that he needed to get over Jade, but sometimes that did not seem possible. . . .

Through the clear floor of the soarplane, Rahma saw a simple monument in the grassland below, where the mutilated body of the polar bear had been buried. Hashimoto had turned a rare, treasured animal into a table! It was a . . . he hesitated to use a non-secular word, but it was a sacrilege. Yes, a sacrilege, indeed. An affront against the holiness of nature. He loathed that man, but at least Rahma had the satisfaction of knowing that the Premier's pet bridge had been destroyed; Rahma had gotten the good news from Artie just before boarding the soarplane, bolstered by the news that some of the Panasian people were daring to say the GSA had done a good thing, and that the boondoggle bridge should never be rebuilt.

Despite the deep-seated hatred that ran between the two leaders, Rahma was proud that he had taken steps to avoid nuclear war while doing everything possible to bolster GSA defenses, thus thwarting whatever his archenemy might have in mind, be it small or large. He didn't want innocent people to die in a nuclear exchange. A war on that scale would surely be the biggest environmental disaster in history—a legacy that he, of all people, did not want. For the sake of the planet and its living organisms, he needed to do whatever he could to avert all-out warfare, short of inviting Hashimoto to share a water pipe. He shuddered at the thought.

Chewing slowly and letting the savory brownie melt in his mouth, Rahma watched the attractive servant move to the other men, all of whom selected doses of harder drugs. The Chairman didn't mind that they did this on duty, as long as no one overdid it. After they made their selections of minimal doses, he waved the serving girl away. She went into the rear compartment, closed the door behind her.

Beneath the soarplane the Chairman saw a magnificent Arabian stallion racing across the grassland beneath them, ahead of half a dozen other horses, of varying breeds and colors. The graceful manner in which they galloped across the land, their manes and tails flowing, always gave him a rush of pleasure, and today the experience was enhanced by the brownie, which was particularly good. He felt its soothing drug taking hold of his consciousness, brightening the colors he saw and making him more lucid. The deciduous trees of the groves were in full color, the glorious gold and brown hues of fall.

For more than two hours the men had been floating on the air currents, discussing military matters over lunch and transmitting coded orders to subordinates. A week ago, Director Ondex had revealed the breakthrough in the vanishing tunnel research program, and the SciOs had performed successful tests since then. Now they were hurrying to set up a full-scale manu-facturing program to build large tunnel machines that would be capable of making surprise attacks against the enemy.

Rahma and the military officers wanted more information, but in his usual fashion Ondex was refusing to provide it. Even so, they had come to an understanding. The Army of the Envi-ronment would focus on building up conventional and nuclear forces and on beefing up defenses even more. As to where and when the foe might strike next, no one had a clue. They knew only that they had to prepare themselves defensively and offen-sively, as quickly as possible. On that much, they both agreed.

The solar soarplane, operated by one of the Chairman's hubot pilots, flew low but not too low, making hardly any noise in its smooth passage over the animals. The craft was perhaps fifty meters above the ground now, and its passengers had just finished their meal. The drugs were for dessert.

Across the circle of people on the floor, Rahma saw the dark eyes of Admiral Hansen sharpen from the small packet of cocaine he had just snorted. His features were ruddy and weathered from years spent on the sea, with deep creases around his mouth and eyes. "People are saying that Stuart is an eco-messiah," he said, "that he's appeared on Earth at this time for a reason, to fulfill a fateful purpose. What do you think, Mr. Chairman?"

"If he is a green messiah, it doesn't really matter what I say, does it?" Rahma coughed, took a sip of water to clear his throat. He'd been feeling run-down in the last few days.

"But is he that, or is he a genetic accident from the ReFac explosion?" Ondex said. "Fate or accident?"

"Accident," General Preda said. A tall officer with a flair for style, he wore a yellow silk scarf around his neck, and an an-tique medallion commemorating the 1968 riots at the Chicago Democratic Party convention.

"My scientists have been conducting additional tests on him," Ondex said, "and his powers—while interesting—seem to be rather limited. For example, he's only been able to split small objects, and his greenforming capacity is not great. The latter power was latent until recently, and we had thought he would get more proficient at it with time, but he seems to have reached a plateau. Dr. Mora thinks that Stuart doesn't want greater powers and has subdued them—either intentionally or subconsciously. We've also taken cellular samples for laboratory use, attempting to clone Stuart, but thus far there has been no success. Whenever the technicians attempt to manipulate the disembodied cells in any way, they wither and die."

"A defense mechanism?" Rahma wondered.

"Perhaps. In any event, unless we can solve that, we aren't going to be able to create more of him by any process. You know the history of problems trying to clone human beings, and in his case he's only part human, making it even more complex. But even if we could replicate him in some manner, how much power would the copies have, and of what use would they be to us? We can generate more power with machines than he possesses."

"Oh well, at least we checked it out," Admiral Hansen said.

"Maybe Stuart is a sign, though," Rahma suggested, "a sign from the spirit of the planet that only this type of human will enable us to reach the Golden Age I seek; only this kind can live in harmony with the environment."

"One who both destroys and reseeds?" Ondex said.

"Why not?" the Chairman said. "My old friend Kupi Landau sent me a message yesterday, drawing a parallel between Joss's powers and those of a Hindu god. Perhaps there are gods of the Earth—Gaia, Shiva, Mother Nature, whatever you wish to call them—and maybe Stuart is a genetic reaction to the historical excesses of human beings on this planet, a mutation that will change the course of humankind. Think of it, gentlemen! Maybe he's destined to breed and create more of his kind naturally, and with their powers, as limited as they may be, the new race might still dominate other humans and change how they treat the planet."

Although Rahma did not express reservations about such a superbreed now, he still felt them. In Stuart and in SciO machines, the power to destroy seemed more dominant than the power to create; evil seemed stronger than good, more ferocious.

"A new race? What a mesmerizing thought," Karlos Hansen said. He looked around. "Where's that cute serving girl? I'd like another snort."

"Enough for now," Rahma said. Looking at Ondex, he said, "As far as I know, you haven't done any experiments to see if Stuart can breed with an ordinary human woman. Is that correct?"

"We're looking into it." Ondex looked wary.

"Well, what's taking so long? I've been busy with other matters, or I would have asked you sooner." Rahma wanted to know if the new race would succeed; he felt a compulsion to know.

"We're discussing the possibilities, but we haven't decided how best to go about it—either mating Stuart with one or more females, or taking sperm samples and performing in vitro fertilization. Optimally we'd like to reproduce a female version of what happened to him in the ReFac explosion, for the best chance of reproducing more of the same type. There are numerous options, and we're taking it slowly and carefully, always seeking to avoid injury to Stuart himself. Fortunately, he is a healthy young man."

"I presume you've extracted sperm cells from him?"

"We have, but as far as we can tell they are normal human

cells, oddly uncontaminated. Perhaps, though, the secret of whatever he has become is buried very, very deep within them."

"Just think of it," the Chairman said. "A sustainable human race that could live in harmony with the environment. Now that would be something!" *If good triumphs over evil*, he thought.

"Greenmen and Greenwomen," General Preda said. "And little kids, whole families with vines on their skin. Maybe the new race could be grown in the ground, like ivy, or potatoes."

"Don't be ridiculous," Rahma snapped. And to Ondex, he said, "Why don't you call for female volunteers to mate with him now, and others to be put into ReFac building explosions, in an attempt to create female versions? As a third line of attack on the problem, do the in vitro fertilizations. I'm surprised you aren't exploring all of the options now."

"I can see why you feel that way," Ondex said, "but we've had our hands full with Stuart. He has not been the most cooperative subject."

"So I've heard, but you have large resources. In any event, why treat him with kid gloves? Why not take him prisoner in a show of force? Use a hundred men if you have to. His powers are limited, as we know. Use some of General Preda's armored vehicles and whatever tranquilizer weapons you need."

"We tried to tranquilize him," Ondex said, "but he spun that defensive net around himself, that force field."

"There must be a way to penetrate the field!"

"Maybe, but we don't want to hurt him, or kill him."

"I agree, but keep looking for openings, and be aggressive. There must be some way of taking control of him. With all of your SciO resources, you should be able to come up with a way. In the meantime, use the sperm samples you have in vitro."

"All right, but first I'm going to ask him for his cooperation and see how he reacts to the suggestion of mating him."

"Give him some of the women in your harem, Rahma," Preda said, "maybe that serving wench. You've got some nubile nymphs of the forest around here, from what I've seen."

Chairman Rahma shook his head. The General must have consumed extra portions of whichever drug he selected, despite Rahma's ongoing prohibition against getting high on duty. But instead of scolding him this time, Rahma continued to focus on Ondex and said: "I want you to think of every possible way of figuring out what happened to Joss Stuart in that explosion. Study his brain patterns, the way he moves, the skin conditions where splitting and greenforming beams exit, everything."

"We're doing all that," Ondex said, "and more. We have eighty lab technicians analyzing his blood, and more going over other samples and audiovisuals, and it's all very baffling. With the exception of the pigmentation and scarring of his skin, and certain chemical changes, his organs and other body functions seem to be functioning normally, giving us no indication of where his powers come from. The plant cells and other alien elements are in there with his human cellular material, in his blood, muscles, and bones—and they're all getting along just fine."

"A whole race of Joss Stuarts," Rahma said, nodding as he imagined the wondrous possibilities. "That could really be something. But I wouldn't want them as independent and defiant as he is. That part would have to be subdued, for the greater good. And as for the violent side, the Splitter side, we must find a way of dealing with that, too—just as we have subdued the anarchists and put them to good use for our cause."

"I'll see what I can do," Ondex promised.

41

Life is a keyhole for peering into the universe.
—Jamadi Sukar, one of the
pre-revolution green prophets

JOSS AND KUPI sat by a sunny mineral pool, not far from a job they had just completed, cleaning up an old, deserted town and resort site and returning it to nature. The water was warm on his bare feet and legs, heated by underground thermal activity. The pair was taking a much-deserved break late in the afternoon, after working hard for several long days. They wore no clothing, nor did the other five members of the crew who were with them, scattered around the perimeter of the pool.

A century and a half ago, this area in northern Mexico had been a popular destination for people seeking the health benefits of mineral springs. At one time there had been an elegant Spanish-style hotel on the other side of the network of pools, serviced by a passenger rail line, though all of that had long since been abandoned, leaving a falling-down ghost town, torn-up tracks, and rusting old rail cars. But the mineral springs remained much as they used to be. Some of the rocks around the pool had ornate or simple graffiti carved into them, the names of lovers who had passed this way and perhaps hoped to return one day and find where they had made their pledge of fidelity to each other.

"A Splitter rifle could clean off the graffiti," Joss said, running a finger over the rough edges, "but I kind of like the idea of leaving it like it is. Technically, we might be in violation for doing that, but I can't see where the carved hearts and poems of lovers hurt anything. These are petroglyphs, not that Chairman Rahma cares about archaeology or human history, but I'm making an on-site judgment and I say leave them."

"Well, aren't you getting decisive," Kupi said, with a smile. "And brave." She stood up and began to dress.

"I just think environmentalism can get ridiculous at times."

With a nod, she said, "Tomorrow we're supposed to clean up the rest of the rail line, including the old cars and the tracks. As an anarchist, I enjoy using the Splitter, but I agree my job can get silly sometimes. I can't see what the tracks are hurting out here in the middle of nowhere. I mean, weeds, shrubs, and trees are growing all over them, and the tracks can barely be seen."

Kupi sighed and fell silent for several moments as she put on her clothing, a black blouse and trousers. Then she made sure no one else could hear and said to Joss, "Look, there's something I just learned this morning, before going on shift. I have a SciO friend, a contact deep within the organization. He risked his life doing what he did, but he had a letter delivered to my hotel room on biode paper, the kind you open up and read and it crumbles to dust seconds afterward. He didn't sign it or use his name anywhere, but I know it was from him. It had to be."

"Who are you talking about? An anarchist? There are anarchists in SciO?"

"It doesn't matter who my friend is, and besides, I know a lot of non-anarchists. You're one. It only matters what he said, and he's giving us a heads-up that the SciOs are going to try to take you into their full custody again."

Joss glowered. "I don't think they can because of my protective net, and my other powers. I blasted away doors and walls and walked out of their facility, and they couldn't stop me or get close to me. But why would they even try to recapture me? I'm already cooperating with them a couple of times a week."

She shrugged. "Maybe they don't want to play nice with you anymore. Anyway, at your next session with Dr. Mora they're planning to rush you with a force of robots and overwhelm you, preventing you from escaping through sheer numbers, robots that keep coming at you—by the hundreds and even thousands, if necessary. They don't think you can maintain the energy required for your defensive net indefinitely, and they plan to block you from moving and then close in on you with sedatives when you weaken and your shield goes down."

Glancing at his implanted chrono, he said, "That means sixty-eight hours from now, a little under three days. If the information is right, their plan could work. My energy has to come from somewhere, and logic says it can't be infinite. Logic and the laws of physics, however they come into play in my case."

"Or are other laws at work that we don't understand?" she wondered. "Has something paranormal happened to you, unexplainable by science?"

Shaking his head, Joss said, "There must be a plausible scientific explanation, linked to the explosion."

"Well, anyway, they intend to make their move, and you need to decide what to do about it."

"What if the information is wrong?"

"Can you risk that? Do you want to risk that? Maybe you don't care, if you just want to give up your body for science or whatever, but I just thought you'd like to know."

"And I appreciate that." Joss considered the revelation as he got into his own clothing, then said, "Kupi, for some time now you've been on the fringe of acceptability with the government due to your comments, and it's only a matter of time before you go over the line and the authorities take you in. That might already be in the works, with Greenpol intending to arrest you when the SciOs get me. It could be coordinated between the two agencies, for all we know. But however it plays out, it's only a matter of time before they get both of us."

"You're probably right."

"For different reasons, neither one of us fits into the system anymore." Joss pulled on his trousers. "Look, I don't want you to make more out of what I'm about to say than you should, because I've already told you that I don't think we can continue as a couple. You must accept that, and I think you have. I still want us to be friends. Very good friends. I want the best for you, Kupi."

Her eyes misted over. "And I want the best for you. Most of all, forgetting my own welfare for a moment, I want *you* to be safe, and I'm very worried about what those SciO bastards intend for you."

He nodded, envisioned himself doped up on sedatives and confined in an impregnable facility, with white-robed lab technicians probing and picking at every part of his body, no longer needing his cooperation for their endless, intrusive experiments.

"Now I'm going to suggest something radical," Joss said. "I think both of us need to vanish from the system. Not as lovers, but as friends. As survivors."

Kupi looked at him quizzically.

"Remember we were on that eco-tourism flight over the Columbia River gorge, and you told me about renegades living in the forest, surviving off the land?"

"Sure, the forest people—anarchists, religionists, and others. I told you it sounded idyllic, a simple, happy life, but you weren't so certain." She narrowed her gaze. "You aren't think-ing of—" Her voice trailed off.

Joss chewed on his lower lip, made a face as he tried to envi-sion what it might be like to live in the wilderness, away from the comforts of the life he'd known all his life. But away from the stresses too, and the dangers. He was at an impor-tant decision point in his life, a point where he needed to re-gain control over it as much as he could.

"Can you get in touch with any renegades in the woods?" Joss asked, trying to overcome his apprehension. "Could they help us break out of the grid and disappear? We're slaves here, and we need to break free."

A moment's hesitation. Then: "I like your idea, your brav-ery, and your willingness to try something new. Yes, I'm sure I can find someone to help us, Joss."

"But what about the computer chips in our brains that the government uses to track us by satellite?"

She smiled. "There are ways to either get rid of them or dis-able them. I have friends who know how."

He took her hands, and held on tight. "All right," Joss said softly. "We're going."

42

Anarchists are the most misunderstood of people. They do not operate with the usual motivations of human beings, the customary systems of rewards. They have their own off-the-beaten-path goals and value systems. They find niches in which to survive, because ultimately that is what they do best. They survive.

—Chairman Rahma Popal

SOUPY GREEN DARKNESS surrounded them.

Joss and Kupi moved through the night like ninja fighters, wearing hooded black outfits and night-vision goggles that had been provided for them, following a shadow-shape in the green murk, made that way by light enhancers in the goggles. An anarchist from the forest had come to get them, a bearded young man who introduced himself as Acky Sommers.

It occurred to Joss that this could be a SciO trap, designed to lure them to a place where they could neutralize his powers and capture him. His senses were on full alert as he listened to every sound while peering through the goggles, watching for slight movements around the perimeter that might indicate attackers.

The darkness was a double-edged sword, he realized, concealing him to a degree but also enabling potential attackers to hide. The young anarchist had not said much, only a few whispered instructions as he met Joss and Kupi outside the Sonora hotel where they had been staying with their crew.

Wearing ordinary clothing and carrying a valise, he had passed a hand-held electronic device over their brains quickly, to disable the tracking chips in their cerebral cortexes. Then he led the way through shadowy side streets to a doorway in a high wall, where he used an electronic key to go through, emerging into the night outside the reservation for humans. There he opened the valise and distributed dark clothing and goggles.

Now the trio ran across a sandy expanse toward a rock outcropping. As they reached the rock and ran around one side, Joss saw an aircraft waiting in the murky greenness, glistening ever so faintly. It had articulated wings that drooped slightly, like the ornithopter that Joss and Kupi had taken on the eco-tourism flight over the Columbia River gorge. But this one was longer and sleeker.

They climbed inside and took up positions on a three-person power-station strip inside the bubble cockpit, with Joss at the rear. At Acky's direction, they left their goggles on.

"We won't have to work too hard," he promised, looking back from the forward station, where he also had the piloting controls. "This thing has whisper-quiet motors and enough remaining solar charge to fly us all the way, perhaps with only a small boost from us when we feel like moving around and expending a little energy. I flew it here on my own, working moderately at the controls, and only used a quarter of the available charge."

"I'm assuming we need to get there in darkness," Joss said. "It's a long way to the Pacific Northwest. Are we going to set down somewhere and conceal ourselves during daylight hours?"

"Not necessary. We'll make it all the way before dawn. I guess I forgot to mention that the wingspan becomes short when we reach two thousand meters and the solar jet assist kicks in. This is an advanced craft that my people stole from the SciOs, but it's like a lot of their stuff. It has sealed compartments that we don't dare touch. We figured out as much as we could without tampering with the internal systems, and everything seems to be well built."

"Let's hope it's good enough to get us where we want to go," Joss said, "and that it has no tracking system to report where we are."

"No problem on either count. It has anarchist-designed stealth technology that we've set with our own codes. So far no one has been able to detect the craft; when we fly, we're as invisible to outsiders as air."

"Anarchist-designed?" Joss said. "*Anarchist* technology?"

"We were front-line fighters in the Corporate War," he said, "but it's also a little-known fact that our members include scientists and other people who worked in Corporate labs, and later in SciO facilities, before opting out of the system and escaping from hit men who were sent after them."

"Geniuses who don't fit in?" Joss said.

"You could say that."

"Sounds like you've got it all figured out," Kupi said, as the plane rolled along the hard ground and soared into the air like a large butterfly. The three of them worked smoothly at the stations, providing a flow of energy to the articulated wings, reducing the need for reserve power.

Joss felt a new sense of excitement, and of hope.

AFTER FIVE AND a half hours, Acky announced, "We're here."

They had removed their night-vision goggles a few minutes ago. Dawn was just beginning to break, with the eastern horizon glowing golden over the mountains, putting them in profile.

The aircraft had flown in starlit darkness over the vast northwest greenbelt of the Green States of America, periodically

passing over reservations for humans that were only dimly illuminated in order to conserve energy.

"That's Mount St. Helens," Acky said now, pointing. "It had
a big blow eighty-three years ago." Joss and Kupi had briefly
discussed the same thing on their earlier eco-tourism flight.

The aircraft slowed, and Joss heard a smooth whir as the
wings extended farther out on either side, with flaps down.
He and his companions worked the power stations slowly,
and the craft descended.

"I'll take it from here," Acky said when they were a couple
hundred meters above the ground.

Below, Joss saw a grassy meadow in the midst of tall ever-
greens. The pilot circled the meadow several times, slowing
and going lower, then pushed the hand bar of the power station forward and landed on a surface that was only a little
bumpy.

As Joss stepped out in the gray light of dawn he saw people
running toward them from all directions, emerging from the
woods. Men and women, they were dressed in heavy coats,
bundled against the early morning chill. He was surprised to
see what looked like fur coats on some of the people, and fur
collars on other garments. Even the use of artificial fur was
verboten in GSA society, and he'd only seen pictures in history books of people wearing such grotesque products, complete with long dissertations about why it was immoral to kill
animals for any purpose. But Joss would say nothing of his
feelings; he needed to make his way in a new reality.

These looked like wild humans, with lean, dirty faces and
unkempt hair. The men's beards were long and untrimmed.
All of them wore small patches on their arms or lapels, showing the golden image of a sun cut in half by the horizon.

"I'm leaving you here," Acky said, as he got back into the
plane. "These are not my people." He looked at Kupi.

"Thanks for everything," she said.

Acky nodded. He taxied the plane around for the longest takeoff route, then gathered speed down the middle and lifted off.

"He doesn't have far to go," a white-bearded old man said. "We all share these woods." Small and wrinkled, with a mane of white hair, he introduced himself as Mord Pelley, saying he was the tribal leader of the Dawn People.

The man's name sounded familiar to Joss, but he couldn't quite place it. He heard a low but distinct buzzing sound, like a hive of bees around them, and asked about it.

"Something we got from the Black Shirts," Pelley replied, "a localized transponder system that veils heat, visual, and sound signatures, making us virtually undetectable to outsiders. But when it's dark we still use night-vision goggles instead of lights, and remain silent, just to play it safe. The system is mechanical, after all, and could fail."

The old man led the way into the forest. "These woods are full of tribes like ours, and of smaller nests of anarchists, with all of us working in networks for our mutual survival. Each group is limited in size because of the limitations of the veiling transponders, protecting no more than around two hundred and fifty persons. Each group has its own codes and signal frequency, which we share with the ten anarchists in Acky's group. There could be as many as three hundred thousand people living in the wilds of North and South America, undetected by GSA authorities."

Joss let out a whistle of surprise.

"All with veiling technology?" Kupi asked.

"Hardly," Pelley said, shaking his head. "Lots of people get captured by the authorities, but my tribe has electronic and manual systems to deal with various eventualities. Here's one of the ways we protect ourselves." He handed tiny veiling transponders to Joss and Kupi and showed them how to clip them onto their earlobes. Joss felt only a little pressure in his ears as he secured his, a sensation that soon dissipated.

"Think of the anarchists as our security forces," Pelley said, as he inspected the two transponders. "They're really quite good at it."

"In more ways than I realized," Joss said.

"We have two hundred and twenty-seven people in the tribe," Mord Pelley said. "Plus two, for as long as you wish to remain. You come highly recommended by our Black Shirt friends."

43

What are the limits of human endurance?
Sometimes I think my mission in life is to find out.
—Mord Pelley, to his tribe

PREVIOUSLY, JOSS STUART had only heard rumors about this alternative way of living, a realm he had not been certain actually existed. Just the same, he had occasionally imagined what it might be like to be in the wilderness all the time, how different it would be from the confines and strict rules of the reservations for humans, and from his life on a J-Mac crew. But in the end he always came back to the same conclusion, that it wasn't suitable to him.

Now, faced with the reality of the alternative domain, he would have a chance to find out for sure. He didn't seem to have any better choices.

"This is the real green life," Mord Pelley said. "Unlike anything you've experienced before."

"I can see that," Joss said, as he and Kupi followed the elderly man through a compound of simple lean-to structures and tree houses that were accessible by primitive stairs, rope ladders, and rope baskets. There were even rough-hewn rock stairways leading down to underground habitats, storage chambers, and worship rooms, with covered entrances topside. It looked as if everyone in the settlement had come out to see the newcomers, young and old alike. He noted a handful of children playing games, and dogs that walked the perimeter of the compound, as if on guard duty.

After racking his brain, Joss suddenly remembered where he'd heard the name Mord Pelley. The man was a notorious eco-criminal, a wanted fugitive who had disappeared nine or ten years ago. Joss caught his breath. In his earlier career as an eco-cop, he had busted people like him for violating the morals and sacred-Earth principles of the GSA. This man had been a trusted contributor to the Green Revolution, before running afoul of the Chairman.

Pelley led the way to a pair of open-air structures, lean-tos made of tied-together branches and cedar-bough roofs, with pine-needle floors. "We built these for you when we heard you were coming. It will be your obligation to contribute to the work of constructing future habitats, and to perform other tasks that are necessary for the continued existence of our community. Later, if you prefer to live underground you can, but most people like it topside, especially when they first arrive."

Joss and Kupi nodded. Then she said, "As I told you in my message, my companion has special talents."

"Yes," Pelley said, looking at Joss. "I had already received some information on you from other sources. It is most interesting to meet you in the flesh."

"And you," Joss said, without revealing what he knew about the fugitive. He noticed people coming in for a closer look. For a moment he caught the gaze of an exceptionally attractive young brunette as she pushed her way past other tribal members.

"Joss's ability to greenform without equipment could be used for gardens," Kupi suggested, "or for other plants you might need around here." She looked at Joss. "Could you create vegetable gardens?"

"Maybe," Joss said. "I haven't tried yet."

"It's too late in the season," Pelley said.

"I forgot about that," Kupi said.

The old man looked at the sky, turning his dark eyes heavenward. "The weather is turning colder at night, though the days are still warm. We're expecting a storm system soon, and lots of rain." He pointed at men digging a drainage ditch around the settlement. "In addition to the old standby of holding our fingers up to the wind, we have developed alternative methods of predicting weather, based on patterns of plant growth as well as animal and bird behavior."

"Is the electronic veil your most advanced use of technology?" Joss asked. He still heard the buzzing of the veiling transponders, but was getting used to it, beginning to tune it out of his consciousness.

"Maybe," Pelley said, "and maybe not. We have a few gadgets for this and that, depending on our needs and priorities."

Kneeling to look into his own lean-to, Joss estimated it was around four by two meters, and saw that it had a floor of evergreen needles. The enclosure was barely large enough for him to sleep in, and had no amenities. It didn't even have a mat. Despite the primitive living conditions he felt an odd sense of relief, and very little of the apprehension he had experienced when he and Kupi decided to flee into the wilderness.

"Not very fancy, is it?" Joss turned at the sound of a woman's voice. It was the attractive brunette. Perhaps twenty-five years of age, she had shoulder-length hair and hazel eyes. She wore a dark blue parka open at the front, revealing a heavy shirt that curved over her smallish bosom, with the tails tucked into her trousers. Her clothing was typical of her companions, warm and practical.

"It will do," Joss said.

"I'm Evana Popal," she said, with a smile. "Everyone already knows who you are."

He frowned. "Popal?"

"I'm one of the Chairman's daughters," she said, with a shrug. "It's really not a big deal. He has hundreds of children; some say there are more than a thousand of us."

"I see." Joss noticed that Kupi was looking on, her face a mixture of sadness and acceptance.

"Did you grow up on the Montana Valley Game Reserve?" Kupi asked.

Evana shook her head. "No, I'm one of the others, scattered around the Green States. I think I was born in Baltimore, before it became a human reservation and a GSA military base. But I've never been sure. My mother was always sky-high on dope. It was a friend of hers who told me who I was." She nodded toward Mord Pelley. "Later, this man adopted me as his daughter."

Looking at the tribal leader, Joss said, "Mr. Pelley, I recognize your name because I used to be an eco-cop."

"I was a bad person," he said with a hard smile, "advocating individual property rights, trying to protect my land against green Communists who wanted to take it away from me and use it for their own purposes. What a nerve I had, trying to keep them from trampling over what I'd worked for all my life."

"And they got your property anyway."

He nodded somberly. "I had three thousand acres in West Texas near Palo Duro Canyon, the prettiest ranchland you ever saw, right on a fork of the Red River. I worked hard for that spread, as my father and grandfather did before me. I hoped to pass it on to my son, Barret, but the commies brainwashed him, turned him against me. Then they rezoned my land for green manufacturing, and under an aggressive GSA law of eminent domain they offered to pay me a pittance for it. I shot and killed three government agents when they served a notice on me, and I've been a fugitive ever since."

"You're the one who came up with the word 'greenatics,' aren't you?" Joss said.

"My term for rabid environmentalists," Mord said, nodding. "Like Kupi here, I have been noted for my government criticisms, such as my observation that the government is a spoils system for revolutionaries who are either not qualified for their high-level jobs or are profiting unfairly, at the expense of others."

"You're also known for hunting deer, elk, bear, and other animals, leaving their carcasses where the authorities will find them," Joss said.

"Yes, for that too," he said. "I was a businessman when the GSA took over. I had a corporation, but I was not a bad 'Corporate' at all. I gave my ranch hands stock ownership plans, medical and retirement benefits, generous perks. Hell, they even swam in my pool. But the GSA lumped my company and others like it in with the onerous, greedy corporations and Wall Street manipulators, sweeping us aside so that they could replace us with their own green industries, their own cronies and payoff systems. You've said similar things yourself, Kupi." He patted her on the shoulder.

"But I don't leave animal carcasses around."

The old man smiled ruefully.

"It seems that we all have interesting pasts," Kupi said.

"And all of us opted out of the system," Mord said. "There are many people like us living in these forests and other remote places, people who don't care for GSA politics, the Berkeley Eight, the Chairman, or any of it. We just want to lead simple lives, away from all the pressures, the injustices, the bureaucratic intrusions." He waved an arm, indicating the forest around them. "My American dream used to be a ranch. Now it's this."

"Sounds like exactly what I need," Joss said, "as long as I'm not asked to perform any tricks."

44

The revolutionary environmentalists twist science to get what they want, saying they're using the "best available science" to determine public policy, when in fact these are code words for cherry picking from a repertoire of biased scientific studies. Arguing with the Greenies' faulty science is like shouting into the wind, because they will disregard or minimize evidence that disputes any position they are trying to assert. Your points will be ignored, and you will be demonized.
  —J. Harrison Cunard, one of the Corporate presidents who was tracked down at the end of the war and executed

THAT EVENING, JOSS and Kupi were given a welcoming supper of forest greens and spicy wild rabbit, a communal meal that was held in a large underground shelter where the people sat at long tables and benches sculpted from the stone floor of the cavern. At the event, Mord Pelley regaled the guests with his self-reliant philosophy of life and with stories of the glory days when he owned a big ranch in West Texas.

Soft yellow lights provided dim illumination in the cavern. Even though the tribe had veiling technology to prevent satellites, heat sensors, and other forms of detection from perceiving their whereabouts, they liked to play it safe and not use lights on the surface unless absolutely necessary. Hence, solar-cell fixtures were left out in the daytime in order to gather a charge and were then taken underground each evening—and not used in the lean-tos and other abodes on the surface, where most of the people preferred to sleep. For those areas, the settlement had a limited number of night-vision goggles, supplemented by the ones Joss and Kupi had brought with them.

After the meal, Joss, Kupi, and others who lived on the surface went to their lean-tos, using the goggles to see their way in the darkness. One of the young men showed them how to use the sleeping foils provided for them by the tribe. The foils, utilizing stored energy from solar panels and treetop wind generators, had dials to control the interior warmth. Using a rolled-up coat for a pillow, Joss fell asleep quickly, cushioned only slightly from the hard ground by the pine needles.

Hearing voices in the morning, he awoke to find that Kupi had already arisen, and was nowhere that he could see. It was only dawn, but in a clearing by the sleeping quarters he saw many men and women doing their stretches and morning exercises, including Evana Popal, who wore shorts, a T-shirt, and no shoes. Noticing him as he peered out, the pretty brunette smiled and waved, a cheerful gesture.

He washed quickly in the icy water of a nearby stream, then joined the others in the clearing, taking care to find a place away from the young woman. He'd never been outgoing with strangers, but admitted to himself that he found her attractive. While beginning his own exercise routine, however, he couldn't help sneaking glances at her as she went through an energetic series of deep knee bends, crunches, jumping jacks, and full push-ups. She and the others wore the familiar half-sun emblem on their shirts or shorts.

Dawn People, Joss mused. Now he understood why they called themselves that, because they arose so early.

For years he had suffered from tight hamstrings and quads caused by jogging, so he had his own routine of leg lifts and stretches, which he performed while the others went through their individual sets, without any central coordination. Evana was doing pull-ups now from a tree branch. Obviously, she was in exceptionally good shape.

Joss did his own sets of push-ups and crunches, wearing gray shorts and a sleeveless T-shirt, so that his muscular physique and the strange vinelike scars on his skin were quite visible. As he finished his routine, he looked around for Kupi. Still no sign of her.

Coming over to him, Evana put her hands on her hips and asked, "You got anything left?"

"Sure. I was just loosening up."

"A few of us are going on a run through the woods," she said. "Not too far. Six or seven kilometers. You interested in joining us?"

"I don't know if I have the right shoes, but I'll give it a try."

She looked at his shoes, which were actually lightweight hiking boots, for use on lower elevations. He'd selected them because they were comfortable and waterproof. "Those might work." She lifted a bare foot, showing a thick callus on the sole. "I won't wear any."

He smiled, and nodded.

She introduced him to two other men who were going with them, Zeke Ambrose and Theo Garcia. Ambrose was middle-aged and wiry, while the olive-skinned Garcia appeared to be around thirty like Joss, but a little heavier.

Following her lead, they jogged several times around the meadow where Joss and Kupi's plane had landed, then went up a steep, rocky streambed. Evana scampered ahead, but Joss (not wanting to amp up his own metabolism too much) slowed intentionally and fell in with the other men behind her, talking as they climbed, grabbing hold of tree roots and avoiding loose stones.

Though he'd never worked with the SciOs, Garcia had an

avid interest in science and technology. He was one of the people in the tribe who invented or constructed practical things that they needed for survival in the wilderness—catch basins, game traps, fishing lures, wind turbines, solar collectors, and the like. Ambrose was less talkative, only made occasional comments about flora that he could identify, or about interesting birds he saw or heard in the forest.

Ahead of the men on the slope, Evana ran barefoot, moving swiftly and smoothly, not using any handholds.

"Pretty amazing, isn't she?" Ambrose said, as the trio took a short break to watch her.

"Quite a specimen," Joss said.

"She has her eye on you, by the way," Garcia said. "All the men in the village would like to be on the receiving end of half the smiles she's already given to you."

Joss reddened. "I didn't notice."

He continued effortlessly up the hill ahead of the other two men, then onto a game trail where he'd seen her go. As he made his way, he couldn't help thinking about her. He didn't want to do anything impulsive or foolish, though. In the past he'd had relationships with attractive women that he came to wish had not occurred. For a time he'd thought that he and Kupi might be a couple despite their age difference. Now that he knew it wouldn't work between them, he was back on "the market," so to speak. Evana was perhaps six years younger than he was, with an outgoing personality, and she had undeniable physical attributes. But maybe she was *too* outgoing, *too* friendly. If she was that way with him, she was undoubtedly that way with other men, and he didn't like that. Was she manipulative? He couldn't tell yet, but suspected that might be the case.

She waited on the trail ahead, her hands on her hips as she

looked back at him. "It's about time you got here!" she exclaimed.

"Yeah," Joss said, making a decision to behave coolly toward her. He stood beside her, looking back down the steep incline for their two companions, who were out of view.

Evana made a couple of attempts at conversation with him, but he didn't bite. "You're not even breathing hard," she finally said, "so I know you're not too out of breath to talk. Are you the shy type?"

"Maybe I'm not a type at all. Maybe I'm just me."

"Intriguing comment. I guess you don't like me, then." He looked at her steadily, measuring, judging. She smiled sweetly but not vacuously. He saw intelligence in her hazel eyes, and playfulness.

"I didn't say that," he said.

"Good, because I'm beginning to like you."

"Scars and all?" He lifted his right forearm, showing her the vinelike green scar on it.

She nodded. "Scars and all."

From below, Joss heard one of the men call out. "We're going back down, Evana! You liar, this is more than seven kilometers! And it's straight up! Can you hear me?"

"I hear you, Theo!" she shouted. "See you back in the village!" Looking at Joss, she said, "That's what we call the collection of hovels we live in—the village." She turned to continue up the game trail, on a section that headed away from the streambed and widened, so that they were able to walk side by side.

"I don't think I should go much farther myself," he said, stopping on the trail after a while. "I should get back and let Kupi know where I am. She'll be worrying."

"Is she your girlfriend?"

"A friend."

"More than that?"

He smiled tentatively. "A good friend."

"She's more than that," Evana said, moving past him and down the trail, heading back. "A woman can always tell."

"We were a couple once, that's true. But that part of our relationship is over."

"Why?"

"Well, aren't we getting personal? Maybe I've already told you too much."

"What will we talk about on the walk back, then?"

"Nothing, I guess. How about *your* life story?"

"I have an unusual father, but his eccentricities have not been passed on to me."

"You think the Chairman is eccentric, eh? Well, I suppose he is, but he has a good heart, and the best of intentions for this planet. I say that despite the problems I've had fitting into his utopia."

"Mmmm, a good heart. Yes, I suppose that might be true, but his methods? I have a great deal to say about that."

"I'm sure everyone in the village does."

The two of them turned around and walked silently down the trail for several minutes, with her taking the lead when the way narrowed.

Then she said with a glance back at him, "I used to play in the woods near my home as a child, making forts and secret passageways through the underbrush. It was my own magical world, my special private place. Until the revolution took it all away." She kept talking, though he made no response. "How ironic that Chairman Rahma took away our freedom to go into natural places—at least without off-reservation permits. It seems counterintuitive to me."

She paused to wait for him, and gave him a sweet smile that seemed genuine to him.

"This forest reminds me of my own first memories," Joss finally said, as they continued on. "Someone abandoned me in the woods when I was a newborn, left me under a tree, with leaves piled on top of me."

"That's horrible!" She stopped and turned to face him, blocking his way. "Are you making that up?"

"I wish I were. No, it's true. I was a foundling, taken in by a family."

"You were covered with leaves? That's atrocious. Your mother did that, or your father? Was somebody trying to bury you or keep you warm with the leaves?"

Joss shrugged. "Who knows? My first memory is of crying, and then of a man finding me and lifting me up into his arms. He was a big, burly man, Trig Stuart. I took his surname after he and his wife adopted me, but I've always called them my uncle and aunt."

"Mmmm. You're from the woods, and you have unusual powers, including an ability to generate seeds for plants. What are you, some kind of a weird forest creature?" She touched the vinelike scar on his forehead.

"No, just coincidence. As you've undoubtedly heard, I was in an explosion a few months ago, and transformed by it. There's a logical explanation for my powers, and it's nothing supernatural." He grinned. "I'm weird, yes, but not *that* weird."

"I see."

He looked at her intently, saw kindness in her eyes and said, "Evana, I'm sorry if I've been unfriendly toward you."

"Oh, I understand perfectly! I tend to be too outgoing when I like someone, and that can frighten people off. Are you scared of me?"

"Of course not." But he admitted to himself that he was fearful of her, a little. Joss was having feelings of affection for this young woman, and they were coming on too quickly for his comfort. He needed to slow things down. But not too much. He liked what he was feeling, and what it portended for the future.

They continued down an even narrower section of trail, with him behind her. "What was your family like?" she asked.

"Uncle Trig and Aunt Gertie were great in every way. My childhood couldn't have been better. They raised me in a loving home, let me participate in sports, and gave me a good education that enabled me to do well in the Green States of America. I have no complaints about them." His eyes misted over. "She's gone now, but Uncle Trig is still doing OK."

"I get the feeling they weren't hippies, that they were a good old-fashioned American family, with apple pie on the counter and Sunday dinner at Grandma's."

"Pretty close, though all that changed in the revolution, when Uncle Trig joined the Army of the Environment and was forced to give up the Protestant religion he'd practiced all his life. He won medals for heroism, but didn't want to make the military a career. He and Aunt Gertie were always sad about not being able to adhere to their faith, but they went along with the new system."

Joss held on to tree roots or low branches whenever he could to keep from falling, made his way down the trail carefully. In contrast, Evana was sure-footed in her bare feet, sometimes waiting momentarily for him before continuing to make her way along the trail.

"You're still close to your uncle?" she asked.

"We stay in touch, but I don't see him much anymore. I'm an agnostic, but after my aunt died, I got ahold of a black-market Bible and gave it to him."

"Good for you. That was a brave thing to do."

"Maybe, but I needed to do it."

"My mother was a flower child," Evana said. "She lived with Rahma Popal, a few years before he was involved with the Berkeley Eight and the Corporate War. He's had relations with a lot of women, and fathered an uncounted number of children."

"So I've heard. I doubt if there are very many children like you, though. You're one of a kind."

"We're individuals, both of us, not types!"

"That's right!"

"With all of my brothers and sisters, cousins, aunts and uncles, can you imagine what my family reunion would look like? It would be complete pandemonium."

"Sounds like it."

"Do you believe in love at first sight?" she asked. The trail was so steep downward that even she had to slow considerably to keep her footing. She helped him down a difficult, slippery section of small, loose rocks.

"I don't think so," he said. "People are superficial, concealing what they're really like. It takes time to figure them out."

"Well, I don't know if I believe in love at first sight, either. But I think I could fall in love with you."

"Don't be silly. You don't even know me." He felt a chill of pleasure run down his spine, and thought he might be blushing. She looked back at him, but if she noticed, she didn't say so.

"Maybe you're right. Oh well, I only said I *could* fall in love with you. I didn't say that I already have."

Joss fell silent as they made their way back down the hill to the meadow, and into the forest settlement. With Evana's bold declaration, he wasn't sure how to handle the situation. He wished he had met her under more normal circumstances.

Normal, he thought bitterly. He didn't know what that meant any longer. He longed for the way things used to be, before the ReFac explosion, even before Chairman Rahma and his zealots took over the Americas.

As they entered the village, Joss saw Kupi speaking with the white-bearded tribal leader, Mord Pelley, standing with a number of villagers.

"There they are!" someone shouted.

"What's the matter?" Evana asked.

Kupi glared at Evana, didn't say anything. Then she looked at Joss disapprovingly. Joss moved away from Evana, stood nearer to Kupi.

"Terrible," Mord said. "Theo Garcia has been murdered."

"What?" Evana said. "We were just with him and Zeke, until they got tired and went back."

"Zeke stabbed him to death."

"How could that be?" Evana asked.

"Fifteen minutes ago we found Garcia in the meadow, bleeding from a knife wound to the stomach. He said Zeke Ambrose did it. Then, gasping, he said, 'Zeke is not what he—' and then he died."

"What did he mean by that?"

"We don't know. But it could be that Ambrose is not what he appears to be, that he's an operative of some sort, planted by the GSA or the Corporates."

While Joss and Evana tried to comprehend what had just occurred, Mord Pelley spoke with the anarchist Acky Sommers and other men who were coordinating an effort to find the fugitive, tracking his localized transponder. The men departed quickly.

Then the old man gazed at the villagers who were gathering around him as the awful news spread. "I'm afraid our tribe has been compromised," he said.

45

We suspect that Dylan Bane is using the vanishing tunnel technology to carry out highly lucrative robberies and burglaries in Eurika and Panasia. Police reports from overseas indicate that witnesses have seen small tunneling machines pop up out of the ground, with one or two armed men aboard each craft who carry out a quick crime caper and then escape like gophers. Somehow Bane is getting the mini-craft overseas and using them for criminal moneymaking activities—in areas he considers easier pickings than the GSA police state. This suggests that he might have important overseas allies.

—a confidential Greenpol report

"I HAVE FAIRLY good news for you," Director Ondex said.

"That's an odd way of putting it," Rahma said.

At midday, the gray-bearded Chairman and the tall, patrician Director walked through the immense aviary and greenhouse complex, atmospherically controlled zones that were filled with endangered birds and plants from all over the world. Exotic birds swooped low overhead and called out to one another, a loud, screeching cacophony.

"Our first vanishing tunnel machines are close to readiness."

"How close?" The Chairman coughed, had been feeling increasingly run-down in the past few days. He had resisted efforts by Dr. Tatanka to treat him, hoping to beat whatever it was on his own. He had always considered himself a specimen of health, and rarely got sick. But he thought he had the flu now. According to the doctor, it was probably an Asian variety that was going around, and she worried whether he could beat it without her help.

Continuing to cough, Rahma wondered how such a virus could have found its way across the seas, considering the terrible state of relations between the GSA and the Panasians. Maybe it was a new weapon, a way of infecting the populace. Whatever it was made him thirsty, and he was drinking a lot of fluids.

Suddenly he remembered the sealed diplomatic valise containing a letter and offensive photographs that he'd received from Hashimoto. *Sealed* valise, with an odd odor inside that dissipated quickly. He cursed, and clenched his teeth. Had the outrageous leader found a way of transmitting the illness to him through contact with those papers? Too late to do anything about that now, except to call Valerie Tatanka and let her treat him. But what if it was something really insidious, something incurable that Panasian scientists had discovered?

"We'll be ready in a few weeks," Ondex said, finally answering the vanishing tunnel question. "Perhaps five or six at the most, and we'll be loading the machines with military personnel and hardware."

"We don't exactly know where to hit the enemy, though, do we? And we aren't sure if Bane is acting on his own, or if he is allied with another force: the Corporates, the Panasians, the Eurikans, or a combination thereof. Maybe one we don't even know about."

"I strongly suspect it's the Panasians," Ondex said. "In order to obtain raw materials and other necessary components for our technology, we have extensive operations—and our own SciO operatives—overseas. We have developed new circumstantial evidence—*strong* circumstantial evidence—that

Bane has been relying on the Panasians for financial support, and perhaps for more than that."

"Any Corporate involvement?"

"We suspect so, coming from elements that relocated overseas after we drove them out of the Americas. But the new evidence points most directly at the Panasian government. We're providing this information to the AOE chiefs of staff right now."

"What about the crime capers Bane has been carrying out overseas, including in Panasia? Their government lets him do that?"

"Sure, to throw us off. The Panasians have to be his chief benefactor."

"I thought so, I thought so! That Hashimoto needs to be exterminated, but how to do it . . ."

"I have something more that will interest you, Mr. Chairman," he interjected. "Perhaps I might have told you about it earlier, but there is no harm done. In fact, I think you will be pleased."

"Very little I hear from you ever pleases me, but very well. Let's hear it." Rahma paused to look closely at an intensely red African orchid that looked too large for the slender stem supporting it.

"Our researchers have been busy. Last year we developed a powerful new splitting and greenforming machine that can be fired from a satellite. We call it the SJM, for Satellite Janus Machine."

The Chairman arched his eyebrows as he looked at the aristocratic man. "How powerful?"

"With one satellite-launched weapon, we could spread Black Thunder all across Asia and the Pacific, destroying the entire Panasian nation before they could make a nuclear response, and greenforming over the land afterward. Or, we could do the same to Eurika—but as I said, the Panasians are our more likely foe."

Rahma sucked in his breath. "When can you make it available to us?"

"It is theoretically functional as we speak, but hasn't been fully tested."

"How on Earth do you test something like that?"

"Well, we've run through all of the laboratory projections, and every time the thing causes huge theoretical devastation, and then seeds the entire disturbed area—millions of square kilometers. For obvious reasons we can't perform real tests, but we're still certain it will work. Keep in mind that these important new developments—the vanishing tunnels and satellite weapons—are derivations of Janus Machine technology. Think of tributaries from a great river of technology, or branches from a tree. We keep finding new applications, new possibilities that stem from the core of knowledge."

The Chairman nodded.

Continuing, Ondex said, "We've had the satellite in geostationary orbit over our northern continent for six months, having slipped it seamlessly into the place of a GSA communications satellite and then putting the comm-system back online with hardly a moment of down time, only a few seconds that didn't alarm anyone on the ground. And our orbiter has a bonus feature."

"You SciOs and your damned secrets."

"Don't get excited. We're on the same side."

"Sometimes I wonder. You were supposed to have notified me of the new technology before putting it online."

"I know, but there are good reasons why that didn't happen. Reasons I can't go into."

Rahma muttered an expletive, and broke into a fit of coughing before finally stopping.

Waiting for his discomfort to subside, Ondex said, "As is customary, we SciOs will keep the secret of the orbital weaponry technology, but we are turning over the operation of the machine to the GSA government."

"You have perverted the proper lines of authority, Arch." Rahma's eyes burned from the sickness, were red and watery.

"My SciOs have a monopoly on the technology. You signed the GSA Charter guaranteeing that."

"I wish I hadn't." Rahma thought about how these Science Overseers were a two-edged sword. Up to now they had been helpful to the GSA, but what if they ever turned against him, and the greenocracy he had established? He realized that he could not worry about that now. There were too many pressures on him, and he had a limited number of choices.

"Think of the SJM as a big brother of the smaller J-Macs," Ondex said. "It will be one more technological advantage for the GSA, enabling you to attain the ecological utopia that you so urgently desire."

"Is a pre-emptive strike against the Panasians possible now?" Rahma asked. "Theoretically, I mean?"

"This has been developed as a defensive weapon, not an offensive one. With that in mind, its operation will be turned over to the NDS, our Nonhuman Defense System. They will make any decision to use the weapon, or not use it." He paused. "The robotic NDS technology is, of course, something my SciOs developed at your urging, because you were afraid that humans might make emotional, illogical attacks—resulting in a massive retaliation that would destroy the good work you have done."

"Yes, yes, that is correct. I could still override their decision, though, if I wish to do so?"

Hesitation. "You could, pursuant to the requirements of the GSA Charter. You would need to have extraordinary justification, though, beyond any personal animosity you might have toward Hashimoto."

"Yes, yes, you are right."

Director Ondex looked at the Chairman intensely. "Am I making the right decision here, Rahma? You won't abuse this power, will you?"

Rahma put on his most indignant expression. "I'm not crazy, Arch!" At the moment, he felt considerable affection toward his old revolutionary ally, and thought he shouldn't have criticized the man so much for his highbrow manners and lavish lifestyle. The production of this incredible new technology suggested that there were good reasons to tolerate such behavior, and perhaps even to encourage it. By their very nature, humans naturally wanted perks for themselves, rewards for their work. He didn't like it, but he had to accept it.

"You've done an excellent job as Director of Science, my friend," Rahma said. "I'm sorry that I haven't praised you more."

The two men clasped hands in the strongest handshake they'd shared in years.

"I'll turn the weapon over to the NDS in the morning," Ondex said.

"Right. I'll expect my package of operating data as well, so that I can get my own staff up to speed on contingencies."

"Of course."

The men said their goodbyes and even shared a water pipe of juana, as if it were a peace pipe between them. Ondex left soon afterward.

Alone now, the Chairman fingered the golden peace-symbol pendant around his neck. With all the weapons at his disposal and the tens of millions of people he'd put to death, some of his critics said it was disingenuous for him to wear this adornment—his vociferous enemies overseas said that, and the whispering citizens who were afraid to face him. Maybe they were right, because at this moment Rahma felt like firing on the entire Panasian nation and wiping it off the face of the Earth.

He sighed, knew he didn't really want to do anything like that. Rahma would continue to make every effort to maintain the peace, trying to downplay the personal animosity he felt toward Hashimoto. That could help to defuse things. In addition, the SciOs just might get their own vanishing tunnel technology up and running in time, enough to discourage Bane and his allies, preventing them from making a larger attack. . . .

THAT EVENING, ARTIE hurried into the communal dining yurt and caught up with Rahma before he sat down for his evening meal. A number of the Chairman's favorite women were taking seats around the large table, along with a handful of government workers who had done well enough to merit a supper with the GSA leader.

"Sir," the hubot said, "perhaps we should speak privately . . . with your permission."

Rahma nodded, and led the way to an alcove.

"We just received a strong lead on the whereabouts of the fugitive Joss Stuart. He and Kupi Landau have taken up residence in a forest southeast of the Seattle Reservation, with people who have managed to use electronic devices to avoid detection. Among them is one of your children, a young woman named Evana."

The Chairman nodded. He had so many offspring that he could not keep track of them. The name meant nothing to him, and he wasn't sure if he'd ever met her.

"This particular tribe is a gold mine of fugitives, sir. It's led by the notorious eco-criminal Mord Pelley."

"I know that name," Rahma said. The ex–ranch owner had long been one of the most wanted criminals in the GSA.

"A member decided to turn against the group and report it to Greenpol," the hubot said. "The man is telling everything he knows about a tribe of people living in the wilderness, a group that uses veiling technology we haven't been able to penetrate. Greenpol is tracking them in a new way, with robots that can actually pick up fresh scents. As you know, it's illegal to use dogs for that."

"Yes, yes." Rahma scowled. It was an animal rights issue that he had not been able to reach agreement on with powerful special-interest groups, something he had been intending to deal with when he got more time. The new robots would make that unnecessary.

"Stuart hasn't been captured yet?" he asked.

Artie hesitated as he accessed internal information. "No, the police robots are leaving right about now, and they'll get him. They've captured other fugitives in the wilderness. Greenpol has tripled the force, because of Stuart's powers."

"Keep me advised. This is important."

The hubot saluted with the sign of the sacred tree, then hurried off.

46

A thing imagined can take on its own reality.
—Rahma Popal, two years before his fame

THE DAWN PEOPLE didn't know for certain if Zeke Ambrose would reveal their location, but they had to assume he would. He'd been behaving erratically recently, and villagers had seen him arguing with his friend Theo Garcia, though no one knew what it had been about.

Only hours after the death of Garcia and the disappearance of his presumed killer, trackers had found Ambrose's transponder discarded in the woods. Out of an abundance of caution, Mord Pelley had immediately ordered the tribe to pack up and leave the village site they had occupied for nearly three years. This was not without hardship, but the downside was dire, if what they feared came to pass. Acky Sommers and his small group of anarchists would accompany them.

So, more than two hundred people set off into the deep forest behind an old woodsman named Willem Mantle, a man who knew his way around in those parts better than anyone else. Evana (wearing boots now) and Mord Pelley hiked near the front, as did Joss and Kupi. Going uphill for the most part, they traveled single-file on game trails, or spread out to bushwhack their way across rough areas of devil's club and other thick underbrush, climbing until finally reaching a network of old forest-service logging roads that had not yet been green-formed.

The younger men and women carried backpacks filled with essential items, including small hand tools, shovels, and picks. The tribe and anarchists also took their security system with them, preventing outsiders from detecting their presence. Everyone, including Joss and Kupi, wore the transponders that linked them to the veiling network, generating an electronic blanket over the entire group. The anarchists were all heavily armed, as were many of Mord Pelley's men. Joss counted four children on the trek with them, two boys of around eight or nine years old and a couple of girls who appeared to be almost teens.

The hikers passed the fallen-down, vine-covered remnants of a ghost town in the midst of second-growth fir trees, an area that was going back to nature naturally, without the intervention of J-Mac crews. With trees and underbrush grown in, they could barely make out the structures at all, just broken, vine-strangled remains of what they had once been. On the other side of town they found an abandoned mine entrance, and a game trail that ran alongside a creek for a ways and then climbed, in the direction that the woodsman wanted to go. On the trail, they stopped while Mantle examined a section of hillside that had slid in the recent past, and had very little plant growth on it.

Ahead of them, the game trail narrowed and continued across a slide area, but if anyone lost their footing there, they would fall onto the dry creek bed hundreds of meters below. He tested the trail, made it to the other side, and proclaimed it safe. Then he motioned for the others to follow.

"Take it slowly," he said. "One step at a time and you'll be fine."

Perhaps twenty people made it across, including the anarchists. Joss and Evana then set out; she was a few steps ahead of him, wearing her boots. Suddenly she lost her footing and slid below the trail, slowing her fall by grabbing hold of a sapling, but it looked as if it would give way at any moment and she would go over the edge.

Then she fell.

With only one chance to save her, Joss quickened his pulse and reached out with his right hand, shooting the black threads of a force field toward her and wrapping them around her. Cradled by the net, she stopped falling, and he brought her back up to the trail, then helped her to the other side, while onlookers cheered.

"I didn't think we needed to rope up for that," Willem Mantle said, looking guilty for not taking the proper precautions. He brought out a long rope, which he secured to a small cedar tree on one end of the slide area, and then took back to the other side.

"Watch yourselves where she fell," he said to the ones who had not yet crossed. "There's some loose soil there for a couple of meters."

To play it safe, Joss went partway out and prepared to extend his safety net again, should the need arise. With his help, and the rope, everyone made it across.

After Joss helped the last person (an elderly black woman named Nanette), Evana ran to him and threw her arms around him. The pretty young woman felt warm against his body, with her soft contours pressing against him. She trembled in his arms.

"I was afraid for you," she said softly, "when you were out there in the middle, helping others across."

As he looked into her hazel eyes, Joss had a peculiar feeling, unlike anything he'd ever experienced. "Afraid for me? You're the one who almost fell."

"I only did that to see if you really cared about me!"

"That wasn't intentional! You're kidding, aren't you?"

She nodded. "I guess I'm not as sure-footed in these shoes as in my bare feet, where I can feel the ground and rocks better. If we have to cross anything like that again, I'm doing it barefoot."

Joss had felt a sense of panic when she was falling off the trail, in the terrible moments when he thought he would lose her. This told him something important, that he cared deeply for her, and perhaps even loved her. He pulled her toward him and held her tightly. For the first time in years, since losing Onaka Hito in his youth, he believed love might be possible again.

Over Evana's shoulder, Joss saw Kupi looking on dejectedly. He pulled free and went to her.

"Kupi," he said to her, "please don't make me feel guilty for my feelings."

"I don't deserve you anyway," she said, her face a mask of sorrow and regret. "You deserve better."

He shook his head in disagreement while the others waited, looking on but not intruding.

"Go to her," Kupi said. Then with a reassuring smile, she added, "Don't worry about me. I'm resilient. I'll find somebody." She looked over at Mord Pelley, added, "Maybe him. He's old, but he's been making eyes at me."

Joss stepped back from his former lover and went to Evana, shaking his head sadly.

"How do you feel about me?" the young woman asked, her voice little more than a whisper in his ear.

He smiled softly. "I'm still trying to figure that out."

JUST BEFORE DARK, the villagers and anarchists reached a broad expanse of grassy, sparsely treed land alongside a wide river. "A hundred years ago, a town stood on this site," Willem Mantle said, "so it seems fitting for us to make a go of it here. I have fished this river many times for Chinook salmon, steelhead, and kokanee. We'll always have fresh seafood for our table."

"Or for a wedding feast," Joss said. He put an arm around Evana's waist and drew her to him.

She didn't resist. Looking up at him she said, "Are you asking me? I thought you didn't like to rush into anything. Aren't you the one who doesn't believe in love at first sight?"

"I've known you for four days now," he said. "Out here, with the experiences we've shared, that's long enough for me. Besides, we don't know how long we have together; we're fugitives from justice."

"Fugitives from justice?" Mord Pelley said, overhearing their conversation. "On the contrary, we brought justice with us!"

"And found love," Evana said, beaming prettily at Joss.

Pelley put his hands on his hips and studied his adoptive daughter, as if searching for any doubt on her part. Apparently seeing none, he said, "A wedding it will be, then, and I shall perform the ceremony!"

Kupi moved to the white-haired old man's side, smiled ruefully in Joss's direction.

"But how will we accomplish it out here?" the elderly black woman asked. Joss thought Nanette had an interesting face, careworn and creased with the wisdom of years and experiences.

The tribal leader smiled and looked up at the sky. "Why, we will visualize it all, of course, with help from the Lord. And for music, we shall have the voices of angels. I already hear them singing for us, heavenly notes wafting on the wind."

"Yes, I can hear the angels, too!" a man shouted.

"So do I!" a woman said. And others piped in: "I hear them, too!" . . . "I hear the angels!"

Joss imagined hearing the angelic sounds himself, and he could tell from Evana's serene, happy expression that she was imagining this as well.

"Now visualize this," Pelley said. "The bride and groom are dressed entirely in white, with flower leis around their necks, and after they exchange vows we'll drink wine until the wee hours of the night."

Looking over at Kupi, Joss caught his former lover's gaze. As she stood by Mord Pelley, tears welled in her eyes, but she smiled courageously, letting him know everything would be all right. He nodded to her in appreciation, felt a little better about the situation. His feelings were bittersweet. He really did not want to hurt Kupi, not after they had been through so much together. He would talk with her again and try to forge a continuing friendship with her, a way for them to go forward.

Around them, tribal members were still visualizing the gala wedding festivities. The air really was filled with laughter and happy voices, another form of music, Joss thought. He kissed Evana for the first time, and it was sweeter on his lips than any wine.

"In all seriousness," Pelley said, "Evana and Joss will have the wedding they deserve as soon as we get settled here and have time to set it all up."

People moved in to congratulate the couple on their engagement, and even Kupi joined in, seeming to accept what was happening. She and Mord Pelley chatted, while Joss and Evana speculated on when the wedding might take place, from a few days to a few weeks.

As Joss looked at the young woman and saw the depth and freshness of the love they shared, the lack of a formal ceremony mattered less to him than this very special moment. In his heart, it was as if they were already married.

JOSS HAD NOT expected to find the woman he loved in such a remote region, under these circumstances. Yet the connection of their souls had occurred quickly and unexpectedly, and Joss could not deny it.

Evana seemed to have recognized the special nature of their relationship before he did, or at least she had been more willing to admit it. Somewhat belatedly he had accepted that they were meant for each other too, and now he wanted to treasure every moment they had together. Neither of them could be certain how long they would have.

That night, they lay together in a sleeping foil on the perimeter of the camp area, but did not make love. Joss wanted to, but had the sense that it was more honorable to wait until they got to know each other better, beyond the obvious emotional and physical attraction they shared. He'd already had physical relationships with Kupi and with other women before her, and he wanted more than that. A great deal more. To honor this once-in-a-lifetime relationship, there should be an actual wedding.

For a while they giggled and tickled each other in the warmth of the foil, peering through night-vision goggles and making funny faces in the weird illumination. When she realized he wasn't going to attempt anything more, he saw disappointment on her face.

They removed their goggles, and snuggled in the darkness. "We have the rest of our lives together," she said, kissing him gently. Evana barely laid her head down on his rolled-up jacket when she fell asleep. It had been a long day.

Joss tucked the foil around her to keep away the chill of

night. Through an opening on the side of the shelter he saw that it was a clear, starlit evening. He heard an owl hooting not far away, and the urgent song of a night bird. For the better part of an hour he lay beside Evana, wondering if he could keep her safe.

He had no higher priority now.

47

Some of the details about the end of the world will not matter. In the mindless waves of destruction there will be no records or memories left. The calamity will take place with startling speed and violence. Survival? Given the circumstances, that is an incomprehensible concept.

—entry in Artie's data banks

IT WAS MIDAFTERNOON of the following day at the settlement, sunny but cold. Joss sat alone on the riverbank, watching Will Mantle as he taught Acky Sommers and other men how to fish from the shore, using stick poles and drop lines. They were on a rocky point that jutted out into the slow-moving water, practicing techniques for a more serious fishing session that would take place the next morning.

A few minutes ago, Joss had been with Evana, but she had gone back to the settlement for tea. Glancing back, he saw her with some of the tribe at a communal eating area that had been set up on the far side of the grassy land where Mantle said the main part of the old town once stood, before a forest fire wiped out the wood-frame houses, even destroying their foundations, because they were made of cedar logs. Very few signs of the town remained, a few artifacts here and there— twisted chunks of metal, a stone wall section, and part of a river-rock chimney. Mantle had heard that the people reached safety, but they'd decided to rebuild elsewhere.

Sitting with Mord and Kupi near the base of a large cedar tree, Evana wore her dark blue parka, which was filled with the soft down of duck feathers. For this trek, the tribe and the anarchists had rounded up the lightest clothing they could find. Only a few people wore heavier garments, and two of the bigger men wore bearskin jackets, from hunting in the woods.

She waved to him, and he did the same in return. He liked this riverside location, hoped it would be a good place for them to settle. Willem Mantle certainly thought it would be, and it did look promising.

Casually, Joss watched small black-and-white ducks skimming along the river, periodically diving underwater for fish and then resurfacing.

On impulse, he pointed a forefinger at the ground by his feet. A slender green thread darted from his fingertip, made a little flash on the ground, and left a small flower there. Just a tiny purple wildflower that no one would even notice.

Before he had a chance to absorb the new ability, an alarm sounded, a pulsing siren. Leaping to his feet, Joss saw villagers running in all directions on the grassy area where they had set up camp. In the confusion he could no longer see Evana.

He hurried toward the last place he'd seen her, by the cedar, but she was no longer there. Had she gone back to the riverbank looking for him? Frantically, his heart racing, Joss ran back the other way. He heard loud noises in the woods, trampling underbrush and breaking branches, getting louder and closer. Still no sign of Evana, but he found Mord Pelley organizing the anarchists and other armed defenders, ordering them into positions with their weapons. Kupi was with them, loading an energy clip into an automatic rifle.

As the defenders were running to their positions, Joss saw police robots burst from the nearest stand of trees, their metal bodies shiny green, their eyes glowing bright silver. Extending weapons built into their arms, they fired into the crowd, causing panic and screaming. To his horror, Joss saw people fall, bleeding and seriously wounded. How had the robots found this place? Wasn't the electronic security system supposed to veil everyone?

"The damned machines followed our scents!" someone shouted. "They can't see us but they followed our scents!"

·Scents? Joss took a deep breath, felt his pulse surge.

Black threads emerged from his body, spun in the air, and stretched a fine mesh around him, then extended out and over as many people as possible—maybe twenty or twenty-five. He didn't have time to count, but tried to protect as many of the living as he could and especially the four children—the boys and the pre-teen girls. He stretched the shield as much as he could with his willpower, and hoped this did not weaken the protection. The force field, while black, occasionally flashed little spots of color around the edges—blues, reds, greens, and yellows.

Mostly he worried about Evana, didn't want to think of any harm coming to her. Where was she? Joss cursed under his breath, focused all of his energy on trying to protect as many people as he could to start with, which seemed more important than using his Splitter power as a weapon. He wasn't sure if he could do both at once. Was the stretched mesh of the force field strong enough? He hoped so.

The villagers inside the protected area huddled together and spoke in low, awed tones. They reached out to touch the mesh but were unable to penetrate it, or even flex it. In the days that Joss had been with them, they had heard of strange things he'd done previously, but he had steadfastly refused to show them anything, except during the emergency on the trail. He saw Willem Mantle in their midst, talking to them, trying to keep people calm.

Peering through the mesh, Joss saw more robots emerging from the woods, firing weapons in a cacophony of noise and bright flashes of light. Now the armed villagers and anarchists were firing back, hitting robots, dropping them, sending them careening away. But more kept coming, firing relentlessly.

The robots followed scents? Could that be correct? If so, Joss wished he'd been told about the possibility before, because he might have split and greenformed behind them on the trek to this place, sweeping away all evidence of where they'd walked. Now it was too late for that.

Some of the robotic shots bounced off his force field. It sickened him to see people lying in macabre death poses outside his safety net, including five women of the tribe, all dead from grievous wounds. No sign of Evana. Where was she?

AIDED BY AN infusion of money and resources, including thousands of additional soldiers, Dylan Bane was ready to launch a series of guerrilla attacks against the Green States of America, hitting one enemy military installation after another. Adding to the voleers that had survived the earthquakes several weeks ago, he'd rushed the production of more vessels, so that he had twenty-seven in all at his North Canadian base, a facility that brimmed with military equipment, as well as thirty-five thousand soldiers and fourteen hundred robotic fighters. He planned to dispatch them against five initial targets—Seattle, Berkeley, Baltimore, Panama City, and Rio de Janeiro—and more afterward, coming out of nowhere and then vanishing.

His force, while not nearly what he'd amassed before the earthquakes, would have to be enough. He needed to strike before the enemy found a way to thwart him by moving military resources, or before they developed their own vanishing tunnel technology. With good fortune he hoped to destroy forty percent of the key military installations in the Green States of America in less than a day. The voleers would surface and disgorge military vehicles and aircraft that were fitted with powerful Splitter cannons, and they would inflict a lot of damage.

In the aftermath, Bane and his allies would assume power over North and South America. While preparing for that, he had learned a great deal from the SciOs about the layers of authority in the GSA government, the unseen networks, the hidden currents of power and influence. In his new ruling structure over the fallen GSA, he would monopolize certain secret and essential technologies, forming the underpinnings of his authority. He had worked out the details with Grange Arthur, the Eurikan prime minister—Dylan Bane's secret overseas ally, who would send in military forces and share power with him. He had other sources of support as well, but the Eurikans were by far the most significant.

Back when most of Bane's forces were destroyed in the second earthquake, he'd sent an emergency message to the Eurikans for the funding and resources he needed to rebuild. They'd cooperated but only grudgingly, criticizing him for putting all of his eggs in one basket at the Michoacán base, for not keeping his forces dispersed. Bane had taken the comments and lied to them in response, saying he agreed. Then he worked feverishly to set up another large base, but this time he selected the location with even more care than before, making certain it did not have geologic uncertainties.

Now Bane needed to move quickly to drastically reduce the military capability of the Greenies and confuse them. Devastated, demoralized, and unable to find any targets to shoot at, they would surely give up. . . .

WITH HIS VISION blurred by the shimmering force field, Joss saw Evana run past with an automatic rifle and kneel by a very old and gnarled oak tree. Somehow she'd gotten ahold of the weapon, which she fired at the Greenpol robots. To his horror, the automaton police force fired a return volley that knocked her down. She fell on her back by a raised tree root and lay motionless, bleeding from her head.

Joss felt numb. He wanted to rush to her aid, but she didn't look alive, and he needed to concern himself with the ones inside his protective field. Raw rage infused him, and he felt his heart pounding against the inside of his chest, throbbing in his ears as blood crashed through his veins.

He watched as some of the robots paused, their sensors focused on the black-mesh force field as they tried to figure out what it was. Their AI brains absorbed and processed data, developing probabilities—while other machines kept firing.

Almost ready, Joss thought, feeling a connection with his body that he had experienced previously, before discovering that he could fire Splitter energy from his body.

How many people were dead outside his protective net? Evana, too? Terrible questions inundated him.

"Get down on the ground!" Joss shouted to everyone inside the enclosure, gesturing with his palms down. The people dropped quickly, including the children.

Even though the police machines might not identify Joss visually, their data banks included information on his escape and his ability to split and greenform without J-Mac equipment, and to create defensive nets, though smaller than the one before them. Previously he'd displayed only limited destructive powers (such as punching holes in walls and liquefying rock), and Joss had not done much more under SciO laboratory conditions, so the robots would not suspect what he was about to attempt now.

Some of the robots continued firing weapons at the defensive field, but again their shots bounced off harmlessly. He suspected that in a matter of moments more of the aggressive machines would open up with coordinated blasts, and their combined firepower might be enough to break through.

Extending his arms forward, Joss saw his hands darken and glisten. Then lances of blackness fired from his fingertips, passing through small openings in the mesh and over the fallen villagers, hitting half a dozen robots, melting them into silvery-green puddles on the ground. At the same time, the armed defenders continued to fire, dropping more robots into twitching, sparking heaps. In a great thunder of noise, Joss fired his internal Splitters again, hitting more targets, while the armed villagers and anarchists fired their weapons too, some having picked up the guns of their fallen comrades. But the attackers kept emerging from the woods.

The camp lit up with weapons fire, countered by the eerie blackness of energy in Joss's protective force field, which remained intact. He kept firing, melting robots into harmless piles of gunk. He did this until there were no more attackers coming, and no more standing.

Joss saw people outside the force-field shelter rising to their feet, some bleeding and groaning, others looking shaken. Many more lay on the ground, motionless like Evana.

To protect those who were with him inside the enclosure, Joss hesitated and looked in all directions through the fine mesh enclosing them. Warily, he lowered the shield and ran to Evana.

Kneeling over her, he saw to his relief that she was still breathing, but shallowly and intermittently. Her eyes were closed, and blood ran down the side of her head. He gripped her hand and called her name. "Evana! Evana!" But she didn't respond, didn't grip back.

Willem Mantle knelt by her, felt her pulse. "Her breathing is irregular," he said. He motioned for Nanette, who appeared to only have scratches on her face and arms. "See what you can do for her," he said to her.

"She used to be a nurse," Mantle said to Joss as they watched the old woman tend to Evana, cleaning and disinfecting the wound on the side of her head as much as possible, then bandaging it and customizing a small air pillow for her head to lie upon. The injured young woman's eyes remained closed, but every few seconds her eyelids twitched.

Nanette passed smelling salts under her nose. Getting no response, she said, "I'm afraid she's in a coma. She needs a hospital."

Joss knew that was impossible. The nearest facility was at least a hundred and fifty kilometers away, and they had no way to get her there. He shook his head sadly.

"Others need my help now," Nanette said, "but I'll come back to her."

She moved away to perform triage. All over the bloody field, people were tending to the wounded. Joss learned that Mord Pelley had been killed, along with more than half of the tribe and every anarchist except Acky Sommers and Kupi Landau— both of whom he saw nearby, looking stunned but uninjured. Seeing her, he felt relief.

Counts were made. Out of two hundred and thirty-nine people who originally set out on the trek, there were only seventy-four survivors—and of those, nine had serious or critical injuries, preventing them from moving around. Other than Nanette, only two other survivors had any medical knowledge: Mantle from his experiences in the woods, and a younger man named Fareed who had once worked at a sports-medicine clinic.

Joss sat cross-legged beside Evana, talking to her without

getting any response, holding her hand, wanting to caress her but afraid to touch her face. Presently, Kupi came over and said, "I saw her grab the rifle of a fallen anarchist and fire it over and over before they brought her down. Your young lady is very brave, quite a warrior. She destroyed at least four robots on her own."

Overwhelmed by emotion, Joss said, "I've barely gotten to know how special she is, and now she's . . ." He choked on the words, remembering how they had planned to marry. Desperately, he wished he could use his greenforming power to bring her back to health. Lying there in a coma, she looked so fragile, so near death. He felt completely helpless.

Kupi shook her head sadly and said, "I'm really sorry." She touched him gently on the shoulder, then walked away to speak with Acky Sommers, who had been rounding up the weapons and ammunition, seeing what they could still use.

SINCE EARLY MORNING Gilda had been in a state of agitation, flying around the administration compound, alighting on yurts and peering in windows, obviously searching for Rahma. Unable to locate him, the glidewolf had gone back into her subterranean habitat, escaping from it into the outer office and then attempting to burst through the double doors to the slidewalk that led to the underground bunker control room, where the Chairman actually was. But these doors held, even against multiple onslaughts by the powerful creature. Finally, the robotic lab workers managed to sedate her, drag her back inside the habitat, and lay her on a bed of eucalyptus leaves.

As Artie watched this, something far more important came up. High-security data began flowing into his computer mind, electronic information from the robots of the Nonhuman Defense System. Quickly, Artie hurried out to the slidewalk and rode it to the underground bunker control room beneath the administration building. On the way, he considered the new information, and added it to what he already knew.

For some time the nuclear weapons of Panasia and the Green States of America had been aimed at each other, and the hate-filled rhetoric had never subsided. Having absorbed a critical inflow of new data, the hubot calculated the disastrous probabilities. SciO and GSA operatives had compiled circumstantial, but persuasive, evidence that an imminent threat to the Green States of America came from their arch-enemies, the Panasians. The evidence was contained in detailed intelligence reports, submitted from all over the world, and subjected to probing analyses by humans and computer systems, including the robots in the Nonhuman Defense System.

Artie scanned more details, evidence that the Panasians had dramatically increased the number of nuclear warheads in their arsenal in the past year, and were close to perfecting a new defensive umbrella around their nation, designed to shoot down incoming missiles. Such technology had been attempted repeatedly since the late twentieth century (and the GSA had their own missile umbrella), but all known systems had flaws that made them porous, in varying degrees. Maybe the Panasian version would be defective as well, or maybe not. The hubot knew that, under normal circumstances, a perfect Panasian defensive shield would present serious problems for the GSA.

But these were not normal circumstances, because the GSA had a Sword of Damocles waiting to annihilate its Panasian enemies, a secret weapon orbiting high over the planet. Ready to fire, the immensely powerful Satellite Janus Machine changed the doomsday equation in a big way. It was certain to penetrate any defense system the enemy might have, and didn't have the downside from an environmental standpoint of a nuclear exchange. After wiping out the enemy with the satellite weapon, Chairman Rahma could simply greenform over them, thus returning their lands to the Earth.

Now the Chairman was in an adjacent office with the door closed, being tended to by Dr. Tatanka for a suspected case of the Panasian Flu that was hitting him hard. Rahma had been away for only a few minutes, and in a weak voice he'd said, just before departing, that he might be a little while. In recent days the hubot had been noticing the increasing sickness in his master's voice, and was alarmed by the sallowness of his skin and his bloodshot hazel eyes. The illness seemed to be draining the great leader of fluids; he was always thirsty.

Artie was very worried about Rahma's health, and shared his superior's suspicion that it was a virus that Premier Hashimoto's scientists had transmitted through infected documents sent to the Chairman—though no one had been able to prove this so far, because the papers contained no toxic residue.

Since yesterday, Dr. Tatanka had been using a regimen of experimental drugs for treatment—with no noticeable success. Rahma had been feeling poorly since he got up this morning, with deep muscle fatigue, intestinal problems, and severe headaches. Maybe this had something to do with the glidewolf's agitation. There seemed no way to tell, but the creature did sense things, and was very protective toward the Chairman.

Just then, Artie received another transmission across his circuits from the NDS, an announcement that he'd been dreading: A huge number of missiles had been launched by the Panasians, from land sites and nuclear submarines! NDS's automated weaponry had already responded within fifteen seconds by activating the GSA's defensive and offensive systems, taking measures to intercept the incoming missiles and launch additional nuclear GSA missiles against priority enemy targets.

Artie shouted for the Chairman, but got no response. The

heavy door to the adjacent office was closed. He ran to it and pounded on it.

Still nothing.

The hubot pushed open the door, risking the wrath of his superior. To his dismay, he found no one in the room. He saw a door open on the other side, leading to a corridor.

For a moment Artie accessed an internal mapscreen of the world—his electronic viewing platform—showing that some of the enemy's front-running sub-launched missiles had already been intercepted and shot down. Less than two minutes had passed since he'd been notified by the NDS, and he was desperate to find his superior.

The hubot hurried through the door into the corridor, calling loudly for the Chairman. No answer came, nor did he see any sign of him. Where had he gone with the physician? Someone should have thought to maintain an electronic connection between them at all times.

I should have thought of it.

With the continuing stream of data, the NDS robots declared that all incoming missiles could not be intercepted, because the GSA's own umbrella defense system could not handle the surprising volume of missiles. Artie paused in the corridor to analyze the options, in coordination with the NDS. In a matter of moments the computer network determined that firing the Satellite Janus Machine would throw enough energy to confuse the guidance systems of the fast-approaching missiles and cause them to fall into the Pacific Ocean. The NDS robots were pressing for permission from the Chairman to act within another two minutes, to avert certain disaster. If he didn't provide countermanding orders in that time, then under the GSA Charter they would respond on their own.

In the Chairman's absence there were backup provisions, and Artie was responsible for the first line of them. With his unquestioned fidelity and skills, he was the one that Rahma trusted the most, not quite a sentient being but as close to it as a hubot could be—and he had been given important responsibilities. Artie only hoped he was up to the task. Many times he'd heard of the legendary exploits of the man whose eyes were implanted in his machine body, the organs of the heroic anti-Corporate warrior Glanno Artindale.

With only moments to answer the NDS, Artie shouted again for the Chairman. Still, he received no response. Rahma had not looked good at all today, and perhaps he required more medical attention, maybe even transportation to a hospital.

Precious seconds ticked by in which the hubot remained entirely calm, as he was programmed to do. Aided by the NDS, he evaluated every possibility, every danger, at hyperspeed—and saw only one option that made sense, one that would have huge consequences. With all of the data assembled and analyzed, he decided to fire the Splitter barrel of the orbiting SJM, along with the Seed Cannon moments afterward.

On his internal viewing platform the hubot opened the control panel and confirmed that the weapon was armed. He told the NDS robots to take careful aim, targeting the incoming missiles over the Pacific Ocean, as well as the Panasian continents of Australia and Asia beyond.

They did so, and fired.

48

On the left and right, zealots live in echo chambers,
seeking only to converse with people who believe as they do.
—Mord Pelley, political dialogues

JOSS SAT ON the grass beneath the old oak tree, holding Evana's hand tightly, speaking to her in low, soothing tones.

The bandage on her head was bloody, and he worried about a grievous brain injury. Although her eyelids twitched every once in a while, she had not opened her eyes since falling in the battle.

A few meters away, Willem Mantle was talking to a group of survivors who had minimal injuries. "There's no time to bury the dead," he said. "We need to move on as soon as the injured are tended to, and carry them with us."

"What's the use?" a woman asked. "More robots will be sent to track us."

"Maybe that won't matter." Mantle looked over at Joss, said to him, "You've got more talents than we've seen so far, don't you?"

"You're thinking I could split and greenform behind us to get rid of our scents, aren't you?"

The old woodsman nodded, a grim expression on his face.

"I was thinking the same thing," Joss said.

"We need to leave quickly," Mantle said. "Let's get the wounded ready."

Despite the urgency, Joss protested, "It's not right to leave the dead lying around for animals and carrion birds to tear apart. Out of respect for these people, we need to bury them."

"He's right," a man said.

"We won't be able to live with ourselves if we don't bury them," Nanette said, walking past the group and standing by Joss. The elderly woman looked tired from all she had done to tend to the injuries of the wounded, with only minimal medical supplies.

"How's the young lady doing?" Nanette asked Joss, her wrinkled face filled with sadness and concern. Maybe she was thinking the same thing he was, that it could be dangerous to move Evana—but they had no choice.

Before he could answer, Evana gasped. Her eyelids fluttered open and she stared straight ahead. To his horror she slumped over, and in his grip her hand went limp.

Nanette moved in quickly, turned the stricken woman onto her back, and with Joss's assistance administered cardiopulmonary resuscitation, trying to get her breathing and her heartbeat to resume.

"Breathe!" Joss shouted to Evana, after he held his mouth over hers to force oxygen into her lungs. "Breathe!"

They worked desperately without success, and Joss wanted to keep going. But finally Nanette stopped and said, "It's no use. I'm sorry, but she's gone."

"No!" Joss exclaimed. For several minutes more he administered CPR by himself, pumping her chest and breathing air into her mouth. Finally he fell to his knees beside her, sobbing uncontrollably. He couldn't believe this terrible thing had happened; it was horribly unjust for Evana to have her life snuffed out at such a young age, with so much ahead of her. He had lost the most special person he'd ever met, or ever hoped to meet. Their dreams of marriage and a life together were shattered.

Around him people moved away silently, leaving him a few final moments of privacy with Evana. He knew what had to be done now but couldn't bear the thought of it: her burial. In his grief he lifted her and carried her a short distance to the big oak tree, where he sat with his back against the trunk, her lifeless head on his lap. Tenderly, he caressed her face and whispered that he loved her. And he wondered if, at some waning level of consciousness, she could still hear him.

Some of the men had noticed an expanse of soft forest duff inside the woods, and they'd been digging graves there with small shovels and picks. Joss didn't participate. He remained with Evana, cradling her head on his lap and speaking to her soothingly, lovingly.

Wishing it could have all been different, he leaned back against the tree and closed his eyes, hardly able to fathom the tragedy. The devastation he felt was worse than he'd been through when Onaka left him—much, much worse. At least Onaka had been alive and could find a life without him. For Evana, it was so horribly final, and so unfair.

Little by little he began to feel an odd, impossible sensation that the trunk of the ancient oak was softening and he was sinking back into it, immersing himself in it. Thinking he must be falling asleep, he tried to awaken and pull himself out of the trunk but couldn't, and kept sinking backward until his entire body and head were inside, and Evana was with him.

He panicked, felt like a drowning man, unable to breathe.

But moments passed, long moments in which he remained inside the tree. And he was still alive. Slowly he opened his eyes and saw a mist before him, a gray-green fog that impaired his vision but was clearing moment by moment, revealing something beyond, something he couldn't quite make out. At first it reminded him of looking through night-vision goggles, but with each passing moment the greenness sharpened and grew lighter.

In this alternate realm Evana was back with him, reanimated, uninjured, and sitting at his side. She spoke his name, her voice like a beautiful bell in his ears. The two of them were inside the tree, or seemed to be, and the interior space was substantially bigger than it had looked from the outside, the size of a large room in an apartment. It was their own special domain from which they looked outside to a world they didn't ever want to live in again, a world of violence and pain. In his joy he felt the cells of the tree seeping into his body, becoming one with him, green with him.

Were he and Evana becoming the tree, merging into its cellular structure? It was so absurd that he nearly laughed at the folly of the thought, at the way his grieving mind was playing cruel tricks on him. And yet something peculiar had happened to him in the explosion of the ReFac building, something that combined his human cells with plant genetics and something even more alien. Was this an offshoot of that experience, a natural progression?

He caught himself. Nothing was natural about any of the things that had been happening to him.

"Where are we?" Evana asked. Sitting beside him in the enclosure, she no longer had a wound on her head, and the bandage had vanished.

He didn't answer, because he wasn't sure. This had to be a weird dream. It just *had* to be.

DOWN THE CORRIDOR, a tall, black-haired woman emerged from an anteroom and motioned to Artie, beckoning him. It was Dr. Tatanka, who had been giving the Chairman fusion-antibiotics and other medical treatments. The hubot heard Rahma calling out from the room, his voice saturated with sickness. "Artie! Artie, I need you!"

It was too late to stop what had already been set in motion, so Artie delayed responding. His internal viewing platform showed a burst of Black Thunder spewing out of the large black barrel of the orbital Janus Machine, spreading a swath of destructive energy across the Pacific Ocean, traveling at more than nine times the speed of sound. The water surged and churned, but whales, sharks, porpoises, and other sea life dived deep, and their populations would not be harmed to the catastrophic extent of land animals. On Panasia's Pacific islands and on their Australian continent, villages and cities were flattened, and people died.

In Artie's data systems and mapscreens he saw that there was some friendly-fire damage to GSA islands off the western shore of the mainland, behind the target area—but most of the energy surged westward, an enormous swath of destruction over the ocean, wiping out everything and causing all incoming missiles to fall short of hitting the mainland of the Green States of America. In the distance more enemy missiles were being launched, but the powerful approaching energy field was already shutting down their guidance systems and causing them to veer off course, fizzling into the sea even before the swath of primal violence went over it.

He stared, transfixed, absorbing data from the NDS robots. The blast from the satellite was far more powerful than the overconfident SciOs had projected. Black, devastating energy was crossing the Pacific Ocean and hurtling toward Australia and the Panasian mainland, with no loss of destructive energy or speed. In fact, he realized with a sinking sensation, it was actually *increasing* speed.

In the background of his awareness Artie heard the Chairman's voice, increasingly urgent and demanding.

Feeling a humanlike reluctance, the hubot made his way to the anteroom and entered. The Chairman lay on a couch, his head on a pillow, with the doctor holding a glass of water to his lips while he drank. An open copy of *The Little Green Book* lay on a table by him, facedown. Artie wondered if he had been reading his own sayings and poems, perhaps searching for something that would help now. Maybe Dr. Tatanka had been reading the volume, because she was known to greatly admire the Chairman, calling him one of the intellectual giants of all time.

"Where have you been?" Rahma asked, sitting up. He looked weak. "I've been calling for you." He reached for the book, said in a raspy voice, "I want to read you a poem I wrote years ago, something that should never be forgotten."

"But sir, I must tell you that there is great—"

"Whatever it is can wait. The thing you must understand is that this book of quotations covers matters that are of utmost importance to me, and matters that are critical to this planet."

"Sir, with respect to the planet, I must tell you—"

"Silence!" Rahma roared. He thumbed through the pages. "This book is, in fact, *me*. I wrote it in a burst of inspiration that continued without stopping for three days." His eyes were bloodshot, but brightened with excitement when he found what he was looking for. He cleared his throat, said, "I call this little poem 'The Wisdom of Plants.'"

Just then, even though he had been programmed to never argue with his superior, Artie summoned a combination of simulated human feelings—anger, frustration, and urgency—and with them he overrode the prohibitive programming. Speaking in a very loud voice and refusing to be silent despite the objections of the Chairman, the hubot got him to listen to a quick summary of the crisis, and then said, "I couldn't find you, Master, and needed to make quick decisions when you were not available."

Rahma's face reddened and his lips moved, but no sound came out for several moments. He looked shocked. Finally he set the book aside and said, "You idiot! I was right here all the time. You should have found me!"

"Everything happened so fast, Master, and much of it was automated. I used the Satellite Janus Machine only when the NDS reported that the missiles fired in response were not enough, and our country was about to be destroyed in a nuclear attack."

"Oh my God!"

The deity reference surprised Artie, but he didn't comment on it. Instead, he said, "It was unavoidable, Master, and soon Panasia will be no more because Black Thunder is going more than fourteen thousand kilometers an hour, and has actually gained speed."

"Jesus!"

It was another inexplicable religious reference from a man who had always professed to be intensely secular. Artie absorbed more data. Linked to him, the NDS computer system processed data faster and faster, assimilating it. He was transfixed by the flow of information and AI analyses, and told the Chairman the crisis was so huge that no one could have any further input. The wave of destruction was stretching out to encompass all latitudes between the northern and southern poles, and still gaining speed. It would sweep across the entire globe, not just one nation—and nothing could stop it.

"This is terrible!" the Chairman exclaimed. He pushed the doctor away and stumbled to his feet, coughing. "Are you sure there's nothing we can do?"

"Nothing! I don't know if we'll survive, though we are in a heavily fortified bunker."

"And no possible mistake?" He had to hold on to the back of a chair to keep from falling. Dr. Tatanka tried to help him, but Rahma pushed her away.

"No mistake, but probabilities point to a SciO design error, causing the SJM to be much more powerful than they said. That may be exacerbated by a perfect storm of weather conditions, solar flares, tidal forces, and other factors, causing chain reactions of destruction on the surface of the planet. And SJM is no longer operable, so a countering blast cannot be fired."

Chairman Rahma muttered an expletive, slumped to the floor coughing, then gasped and went silent. The doctor leaned over him and attached a CPR unit to his face and chest, but in a few minutes the machine reported it was no use, and shut off automatically. "He's dead," she said, her face a mask of pain and grief. She wiped away tears, quoted from his famous book of quotations, "'Ashes to ashes, green to green.'"

Out of respect, Artie repeated the words, a soft murmur.

"Rahma was a good man," she said, "a *great* man."

The hubot agreed, and felt his own simulated grief, while on his internal viewing platform he continued to receive data from the NDS. The wave of blackness was sweeping onto the Panasian mainland, wiping out cities, farms, factories, everything. Soon it would do the same to the European and African continents under Eurika's control, and then it would cross the Atlantic Ocean toward the northern and southern continents of the Green States of America.

All projections indicated that Black Thunder was rolling across the entire planet.

Behind him, he heard something breaking, smashing, an increasing noise. At first he thought it must be the megastorm, but he realized it couldn't be; it was too early. Even so, he wouldn't have long to wait for that, maybe an hour and a half, or two at the most. . . .

MOMENTS PASSED, AND from the green-illuminated realm Joss saw Kupi, Willem, and Acky outside, staring at him with incredulity, their mouths agape. Other people were gathered behind them, pointing and whispering among themselves.

Joss felt himself sliding back out of the oak tree, emerging from it and bringing Evana with him, into the clear brightness of day. And again he sat with his back against the trunk, but this time she was sitting beside him, her hazel eyes filled with surprise and wonder.

"Did that . . . Did that actually happen?" she asked, looking around. Evana had no bandages and no apparent wounds, not even the scratches on her arms that he had noticed before.

"She's alive!" a woman shouted. "They were inside the tree, and now she's alive!"

Some of the onlookers moved closer, including the children, but others backed away in fear, as if they thought it was witchcraft. On his feet with Evana now, Joss turned and looked back at the gnarled old tree, where he saw the bark shifting, seeming to float on the surface for several seconds before solidifying and returning to normal.

The villagers gasped and whispered among themselves.

Joss could hardly believe that Evana was standing next to him. He looked at her: she seemed to be in complete shock and disbelief. But she smiled stiffly and said, "I'm alive? I'm really alive?"

"You are," Joss said. He pointed a finger into the air, causing a green thread to shoot upward, and a flash of light. A bunch of wildflowers appeared just above him, purple, red, and yellow blossoms with their stems wrapped in black thread.

Reaching up, he grabbed the bouquet and handed it to her. "Welcome back, my love," he said.

"How did you do that?" She sniffed the flowers, smiled quizzically.

"I don't know."

"These flowers are real!" she said.

"So are you!" He kissed her tenderly, and they embraced.

Willem Mantle and Kupi carried the body of Mord Pelley and laid it on the ground in front of Joss. "Try it with him," Kupi urged. "See if you can bring him back to life, too." She seemed to genuinely care about the old man.

Reverently, Joss leaned over and lifted the body, then backed up with it against the oak tree. Again he felt the hard surface of the trunk give way, and once more he found himself immersed in the pale green illumination of the tree trunk's expansive interior, this time with the dead Mord Pelley in his grasp. Moments later, Joss felt the body jerk slightly, and twitch back to life. Mord tried to speak, but had difficulty forming intelligible words.

Presently, Joss stood beside the white-haired man outside the tree. The tribal leader was very much alive, and his wounds were entirely healed.

Working quickly, Joss used a variety of trees to repeat the process, pulling as many as two people at a time into the larger trees and then bringing them back out, alive. In a remarkably short time, he used the paranormal realm to restore everyone who had been killed, and then followed the same procedure for all of the injured, taking away their wounds and pains as if he were a miracle worker. Soon he found himself surrounded by the entire tribe, and all of the anarchists as well. They all chattered excitedly, praised him and thanked him.

The procedure was stunning to everyone except Joss. For him, somehow, it felt right and strangely familiar, as if a part of his subconscious had known all along that he could accomplish such incredible things.

"We don't need to run from the robots anymore," Mord Pelley said, in the midst of the celebratory atmosphere. "Not if Joss can bring everyone back to life."

"But what if *he* dies?" old Nanette asked. "Joss, how would you bring yourself back to life?"

Joss didn't have an answer for that. What were the limits of his abilities? There had to be limits of some kind, and he didn't think he was immortal, didn't feel like he was. But each time he entered one of the trees and reemerged, he felt more and more invigorated, and stronger.

What was he becoming? Joss didn't know, but he felt robust, and even more so with Evana standing beside him, still holding the wildflowers. She gripped his hand tightly.

Finally, she was gripping back.

49

We are life rafts for one another in a dangerous, unpredictable universe.

—Joss Stuart, one of his post-mutation thoughts

THE NONHUMAN DEFENSE System went offline quite suddenly, leaving Artie without an important contact to the outside world. His AI mind remained alert, searching for options. He could still attempt satellite calls to other government agencies, but he didn't know what good it would do. Perhaps he was better off not knowing any more details.

The hubot considered shutting off his sensory programs, so that he would not feel any simulated pain when the end came. But a humanlike emotion surfaced, reminding him that Glanno Artindale had been a man of courage and a hero of the revolution, so he changed his mind.

Turning toward the increasing noise behind him, Artie thought the bunker was being split apart by the ferocious black storm, arriving earlier than expected. Instead, he was surprised to see that the powerful glidewolf was making all the commotion. Finally breaking through, she burst into the room, ripping the door off the hinges and slamming it into a wall. Gilda's pale yellow eyes were wild, her jaws open and razor-sharp teeth glistening.

Standing on her haunches, the creature used her forepaws to hold the sides of Rahma's body between them, and she slid him into her pouch. Then, for a long moment, she gazed at Artie, her eyes questing, as if looking for something. Suddenly she lunged at him, but he didn't move. She stopped just short of the hubot and raised high on her haunches, towering over him.

He still didn't move.

The wolf then gripped him firmly with her forepaws and tucked him inside her pouch too, beside the body of the dead man. Artie felt the pouch tighten snugly around his body from the shoulders down, keeping his head out so that he could see.

Rahma's doctor and lover, Valerie Tatanka, stood nearby, watching silently, somberly. She held a copy of *The Little Green Book*. The glidewolf walked up to her and sniffed. Then, seemingly satisfied, the animal widened the pouch and slid Dr. Tatanka into it as well (without any protest from her), making everything snug again, with Rahma's body between the doctor and Artie.

Afterward the animal just sat there, not doing much of anything. Looking up from the pouch, Artie saw the long snout of the creature sniffing vigorously, as if smelling some sort of a scent. The animal looked this way and that with its feral eyes. Artie felt tenseness in the body, and a low, agitated pulse throbbing through the skin. He exchanged uneasy glances with Dr. Tatanka.

Artie listened carefully, aided by his electronic linkage to the bunker's security and surveillance system, and he detected no unusual noises in the structure or the outside tunnels. Everything seemed to have paused, the proverbial calm before the storm. Outside, he knew the sky would darken at any moment, and the mega-blast would scour the landscape. The NDS was still offline, but they were based to the west of him in Berkeley, so they might not have been hit yet.

He felt certain that the stygian storm would break through

the heavy techplex roof over the extinct animal habitats, but this bunker control room had layers of protection that just might keep it safe.

The hubot didn't think he would have to wait long to find out.

SEVEN HUNDRED KILOMETERS to the west. . . .

Joss looked up at the cloudless blue sky beyond the trees, but had an odd sensation of uneasiness, a powerful, ineffable feeling that something was very, *very* wrong.

On impulse, he summoned the people of the tribe to gather around him. When they were all assembled he wove black protective threads around every one of them, and found that he could extend the force field even farther than before, encompassing an entire section of forest. Now he left the shield shimmering in place, and working quickly, he found that he could merge each person into a different tree and leave them inside—utilizing cedars, firs, alders, cottonwoods, and elms, but avoiding the oak for the time being. In each case, he entered the tree with them, then slipped back out alone, leaving them inside, with their faces and breathing bodies showing in hazy, pulsing definition on the trunks—like an eerie, living form of bas relief.

Some were afraid, but Joss assured them that he was taking a necessary action. "I can't explain why, or how I know this, but something terrible is about to happen, and this is what we all need to do." At the very end of the process, he slipped Evana into the oak tree, then went back outside himself. From there, he stood sentry, gazing around at the sentient trees that were now his tribe, and up at the cerulean blue sky, visible through the mesh of the force field. Everything was eerily calm, with not even a breath of wind blowing.

AFTER RECOVERING FROM the deadly Michoacán earthquake, General Bane had regrouped his forces, to the point where he was ready to launch his attack against the GSA, in coordination with his Eurikan allies, who were scheduled to begin moving military assets toward the GSA in a matter of hours—to solidify Bane's victory. He had planned for every eventuality that he, his war-room advisers, and his allies could think of. But even the best of plans faced unknowns, things that could not possibly be taken into account.

His subterranean base was five hundred meters beneath the frozen tundra of the North Canadian Territory, in an out-of-the-way region. Earlier in the day he had performed last-minute military exercises underground, by digging and restoring vanishing tunnels over a large area, like an army of high-tech moles. During the maneuvers, he'd surfaced twice with the electronically veiled assault vehicles to carry out simulated attacks against mock-GSA facilities—destroying rock formations that had stood for millions of years.

It all went satisfactorily, and he'd gone back underground afterward, closing up both tunnels behind him. Or so he thought. Unknown to him, a technical problem had caused one of the tunnel doors to remain ajar—just a little, and no one was monitoring the security system, so he was not made aware of the problem. The lapse could not have come at a worse possible time for this man who'd been having so much trouble getting his attack force online. . . .

Shortly before the military exercises, he had been in his underground office monitoring strange radio reports of a monstrous weather system crossing the Atlantic Ocean at a very high velocity. One newscast he'd been listening to had broken off when the reporter was in midsentence. He'd tried to find another satellite station, but unknown to him, he was running out of time. . . .

Now he was back at the radio, searching for more information on the weather, but all he got was static—no news reports of any kind. Perplexed, Bane switched off the radio and leaned back in his chair to think. Then he heard something, a dull roar at first that became louder and louder, and he felt a vibration in the floor and walls that knocked him off his chair. The radio, his personal weapons, and other objects in the office tumbled on top of him or slid toward him, and he tried to protect himself by crawling under the desk. But it was moving, too.

When the Splitter blast came, it chewed up dirt and rocks around the partially open tunnel entrance and ripped the heavy door off completely, sucking it into a whirlwind that melted it into its basic elements. Within seconds, the storm surged down into the tunnel and cut through the voleer machines in the subterranean base, disintegrating and transforming them into primal goo, then surging full force into the other tunnel door, blasting that one away, too.

Bane's office, though, was accessed via a side tunnel, and he had closed a series of thick alloy doors behind him to get there. Miraculously, those doors held, and he survived. But when he emerged and saw the destruction, he wished he'd been killed in the blast.

SOUTH OF BANE'S base, the powerful Splitter blast approached the Rocky Mountain Territory. . . .

In the Missoula Reservation, Jade Ridell left a medical clinic, deep in thought as she walked in the direction of her apartment building. The doctor had confirmed a suspicion she'd been having that she was pregnant, and he'd asked her if she wanted to report to a family guidance center to have the baby aborted. No, she'd told him, her voice filled with emotion. It was Chairman Rahma's baby, and she intended to keep it. At least she would have that part of the man she cared about so much.

She rounded a corner, felt a brisk wind, and tightened the collar of her coat. Her apartment building was in view now, a glass-walled tower. Since leaving the game reserve she'd worked in a gentleman's club, wearing skimpy outfits and waiting on tables. A lot of men showed interest in her, but she didn't give them any encouragement. She had not recovered from the severe shock of being sent away by the Chairman, and of losing her entire family. There had been no word from her parents, and she was terribly worried, especially missing her little sister, Willow. The two of them used to sit and talk for hours, sharing special times. Now Jade didn't know if she would ever see her again, or their parents.

Hearing a roar, more than the normal street noise, she looked around, but saw nothing. The sound increased, and the sky darkened ominously. . . .

FOR SEVERAL SECONDS Artie heard the blast chewing through techplex, alloy, and everything else, getting louder and louder. Presently the noise level dropped off completely, and again it was quiet, but for only a few minutes before he heard another roar, like that of a great wind. The roar increased and then passed quickly, leaving stillness behind.

Now the glidewolf climbed over debris and made it out into the corridor, bringing her passengers along. Walls were partially caved in, and the slidewalk lay in ruins, but the animal climbed nimbly over more debris piles and found enough airspace to soar out toward the extinct animal habitats.

There were no longer double doors separating this area from the corridor, and where numerous resurrected animal species had once lived, only a deep, storm-scoured hole remained in the dirt, with a faint green cast to the surface where it had been reseeded. To Artie's simulated senses, the air smelled musty, and humid.

Moving her wings only slightly and perhaps catching a draft of air that Artie did not notice, the animal soared up and out of the hole. The sky was a peculiar shade of gray-blue, darker to the west where Artie assumed that splitting and greenforming blasts were continuing their course across the American continents. Though it should still be daylight now, he saw no sign of the sun and the illumination was low, as if the valley didn't know whether it was day or night.

The glidewolf circled over the strange green-seeded landscape, which had been scoured of all plants, along with the administration, medical, and other yurts, the greenhouses and aviaries, the shrine, the soarplane field, and all roads leading in and out of the game reserve. Artie thought a few animals might have survived; animals sensed things, and some would have attempted to find cover wherever they could before the cataclysm—inside caves or burrows, or in low, sheltered spots of terrain. He could only hope. Everywhere he looked the ground was barren and faintly green, and the seeds would germinate quickly, so that in a matter of weeks the entire area would look much as it might have millions and millions of years ago. He thought of birds, and worried about them. Where could they have hidden? He saw none flying, and nothing moving on the ground, either.

As the glidewolf flew across the valley, Artie looked down

where the ruins of a small, remote town had once been, having been emptied by the Green Revolution but not yet visited by a Janus Machine crew. Now none of that was necessary, because the site was gelatinous, completely smoothed over. Soon it would all be covered with vegetation, as if man had never made any mark there.

Standing inside the pouch of the glidewolf with her head out, Valerie Tatanka stared ahead, her black hair blowing in the cool air. She had tucked Rahma's body down into the pouch, forming a lump that was visible now, between her and the hubot. She still had a copy of the Chairman's great book with her; Artie had seen it moments ago.

On his internal sensors, he noted that the marsupial wolf was setting course in a westerly direction, following the track of the twin storms, somehow staying aloft on currents of wind, without the necessity of climbing trees and relaunching herself. There were no trees on the blasted landscape below—only a sea of green seeds. He didn't know where the wolf was going, or how long it would take to get there. Artie's internal programs told him nothing; he found himself unable to calculate any probabilities.

Clinging to the edge of the pouch under the soaring creature, the hubot wished he could communicate better with her, that he could understand her better. Previously their connection had been on a fundamental level, as lab manager to lab animal, with him creating her in the first place, and then providing her with the basic necessities for her survival.

But all of that was in the past, and she seemed to have evolved in front of his eyes, changing in incomprehensible ways. Without a doubt, the creature was extremely intelligent, possessing mental and sensory skills that he could hardly imagine.

It was as Rahma had always told him: animals were not

lower life-forms, and were in fact superior to humans. "Count the ways," the bearded guru used to say.

Now the Chairman was limp and dead between the hubot and the doctor, and the glidewolf who had taken it upon herself to protect Rahma was transporting his body someplace far away. To recycle it, presumably, as the illustrious environmentalist would have wanted. But why had she included Artie and Valerie, and where were they going?

DEEP BENEATH HIS mansion in the Berkeley hills, Arch Ondex stood by himself in a bunker, watching monitors and listening to the electronic chatter of robots around him as they performed their duties at workstations, coordinating with robots in other SciO and GSA bunkers around the country. The NDS had gone offline some time ago, and no one knew why. His own operation was relying on other communication links that continued to function.

In the past hour, the huge black and green clouds had passed over the east coast and the Midwest, breaching three of the GSA fortifications and one SciO bunker—or at least that was the assumption, because all communications had been cut off with those facilities. Thirty-four other SciO bunkers had weathered the storm, and even more GSA bunkers. After several minutes of communication delay, those stations were all operational again, reporting that everything on the surface of the ground above them had been completely erased.

There had been no word at all from the Montana Valley Game Reserve, so Ondex wondered what had happened there, and if he would ever see the Chairman again, a man he considered to be his friend despite their differences. A feeling of great sadness enveloped him. So much was being lost.

As the SciO leader waited, he knew there were very few options left for him, and none of them was appealing. . . .

AN OMINOUS BLACK cloud approached Joss and his companions, beginning to darken the sky like volcanic ash. From his sentinel position in front of the gnarled old oak tree, he heard an eerie, horrendous sound—violence on an immense, unprecedented scale.

He lifted his hands in the air, holding the force field in place to protect the people around him, extending outward for thousands of meters into the forest. He saw the hazy faces and forms of Evana, Kupi, and the others on the trunks of the trees in their fused state, saw the barely perceptible pulsing of the bark on the trunks as the hybrids breathed in unison with him and with one another, as if all of them were a single, linked organism.

With the energy net woven around them to form a sheltered cocoon, Joss looked through the mesh and watched a massive black cloud streak over the land at ground level, destroying everything outside his sheltered area but passing over him with hardly any effect, just a little buffeting of the force field.

The sky became dusty blue afterward. Joss waited for several long minutes, then held position while an immense green cloud swept over the ground, going around the protective cocoon like a great tinted wind, raining sparkles of green and making musical sounds that were not unpleasant to the ears. Again, Joss's shelter survived, and he saw the hybrid trees still breathing. They remained linked to him.

The entire event had been like splitting and greenforming, but on an unprecedented scale. What had happened?

An hour passed in which he waited and wondered. Inside the protected zone he heard a few forest animals and birds moving about tentatively, not knowing or understanding what had occurred. He could only imagine how still and lifeless it must be beyond . . . or were seeds already germinating out there? He released the protective force field, watched the strands dissipate.

In the distance he thought he saw something flying, but it was only a momentary, flickering vision, and when he stared hard in that direction he saw nothing, nothing at all. It must be a trick of light, he decided, or his hopeful mind contriving something that was not there, like a mirage in the air. The dreadful truth weighed heavily on him.

Not many have survived this, he thought. *We are among the few.*

Though he knew there had been widespread death, Joss Stuart felt an odd sense of peace and acceptance, that this marked a new beginning for life on Earth.

By himself, he entered the largest cedar in the rescued forest, a magnificent and stately tree that towered over the others. It was centuries old, with wide, spreading boughs that arched upward, and deep green needles. Sliding through the sleek, pale greenness of the trunk's interior to the topmost portion, he gazed out in all directions over a faint green, blasted landscape, extending far, far beyond the small area of trees and inhabitants he had saved.

Tenderly he gazed down at the oak that sheltered his cherished Evana, with her face and form on the trunk, and he saw the branches of her tree sway gracefully, in recognition of his attention. She was his mortal human love, which he retained as an important link to what he used to be, a much less complex version of what he had become today, and what he was evolving toward. On this momentous journey he would lead Evana and the others, and they would learn from one another how best to care for one another, and for the new world that had been bestowed upon them.

He felt the great cedar speaking to him wordlessly, with thoughts drifting through his consciousness from a more intelligent sentience than he'd ever encountered before or even imagined, linked to all living things on the planet.

Joss received a flow of information so quickly that he found it difficult to absorb everything. But it was a learning experience for him, and as moments passed, he was able to bring himself into synchronization with the wordless data being sent to him in a way that his human mind could never have absorbed previously, nor could any computer.

Gradually he understood, and realized that the immense catastrophe had a purpose, a reason for occurring. The plants and animals of Earth would regenerate—not all of them, but a substantial number. He learned that higher-state humans of the future would need links to trees in order to live, would have to regularly recharge themselves inside trees, a symbiosis of plants and humans. There would be a new way of traveling for humankind, using green, earth-rooted life-forms along the way, renewing strength inside them and communicating with them as brethren. It was all part of the process of enhanced evolution for mankind, the only path left open to them for their survival.

People cannot live without trees, he thought. Humans had only an inkling of this in the past, never realizing the form this relationship would need to take.

These were the great cedar's thoughts, and now they were his own as well.